it Takes 3

it Takes 3

THERESA M. KING

TATE PUBLISHING
AND ENTERPRISES, LLC

It Takes 3
Copyright © 2014 by Theresa M. King. All rights reserved.

No part of this publication may be reproduced, stored in a retrieval system or transmitted in any way by any means, electronic, mechanical, photocopy, recording or otherwise without the prior permission of the author except as provided by USA copyright law.

The opinions expressed by the author are not necessarily those of Tate Publishing, LLC.

Published by Tate Publishing & Enterprises, LLC
127 E. Trade Center Terrace | Mustang, Oklahoma 73064 USA
1.888.361.9473 | www.tatepublishing.com

Tate Publishing is committed to excellence in the publishing industry. The company reflects the philosophy established by the founders, based on Psalm 68:11,
"The Lord gave the word and great was the company of those who published it."

Book design copyright © 2014 by Tate Publishing, LLC. All rights reserved.
Cover design by Junriel Boquecosa
Interior design by Jomel Pepito

Published in the United States of America

ISBN: 978-1-62854-083-3
1. Fiction / Family Life
2. Fiction / General
14.04.07

Dedication

I dedicate this novel to a very *special* young lady…
A successful egg donor and my daughter.

Kristina
Your dream became my inspiration!

"*Special*" describes people who act from the heart;
it's a word used to describe something or
someone that is admired and precious.
"*Special*" is the word that describes you!

I also dedicate this book to those battling infertility, the doctors, nurses and donors willing to help and the beautiful children conceived because assisted reproduction exist.

Acknowledgment

Grateful Appreciation must be given to:

Kristina, your experience as an egg donor, your dreams and thoughts are what gave me the building blocks for this story. It is because of your love and encouragement that "It takes 3" became my 1st novel.

John, my wonderful husband whose love, support and encouragement gives me the courage to try new things.

My Mother Gladys Morgan and My Mother in law Jean Stone for all the love and support you give me everyday.

My friends: Pam, Beckie, Pat, Ed, Theresia, Laurel, Joyce, Jill, Jennifer, Joann, and Lisa, for your encouragement and support.

The Country Harvest Crew, Debbie, Manuel, Meghan, Breann, Lorita, Sabrina, Carla, Claudia, Julio, Angelica, Maria, Trinsa, Helen and everyone that kept asking, "how's the book going" you kept me working and on task.

Theresa M. King

Other egg donors, intended parents and families that shared their experience, feelings and friendship with me via Facebook and through my website (www.Ittakes3.me) you helped to make the stories real.

Amy Demma Esq for your myth list (www.eggdonationtoday.com) about donors who donate eggs and sperm it's very informative, thanks for allowing me to use it.

Kateri Alexander PhD, for your wisdom, knowledge and experience as an author, teacher and friend.

Dr. Libbe Hale PhD, for all your intuitive advice and ongoing support.

The staff, friends and fellow classmates from schools I have attended though-out my life, Burt and Herman Elementary Schools, Redford High School, Lackland AFB boot camp, Med school at Sheppard AFB and most recently The Conejo Valley Adult School.

Mr. Segal, Mrs. Baranski, Mr. Roznowski and Mr. Goxem, four very influential teachers in my life, because of your encouragement, I found joy in writing.

My Air Force recruiter Sargent Larry Gardepy, who made me believe I could do anything, be anything and accomplish everything if I only tried.

My extended family, friends, neighbors and acquaintances that wanted to know more, each of you gave me the encouragement to keep going.

It Takes 3

Tate publishing, for the chance to get my story published and for the help and support I needed as a first time author, this has been a great experience, I look forward to doing it again.

1

It was on a long-ago September day, when two young mothers met during kindergarten orientation; both had five-year-olds ready to begin their school careers. Orientation was day for the parents to be in the classroom where their kids would spend so much of their time. It was a day that had been proven to help alleviate some of the anxieties parents feel as they begin the process of letting go of the babies they had cared for.

These two moms arrived earlier than most; they entered the school's gates with all of the necessary paperwork completed and in hand. The kindergarten rooms were separated from the rest of the school; it had its own gates and its own playground. The gates were still locked when they arrived, so they had to wait.

As they waited outside the gates, the mothers avoided eye contact while quietly thinking about their babies, who often insisted that they were not babies anymore. The moms were overwhelmed as they thought of the babies they used to hold in their arms; it all seemed like just yesterday. They noticed big changes in their five-year-olds over this past summer, their babies were becoming youngsters with strong wills and even stronger opinions about everything—from which backpack to buy, to what clothes they liked.

Theresa M. King

Anything Mom and Dad liked, they didn't. They were no longer babies completely dependent on the parents, who protected them from the big scary world, from strangers, and bad people.

Here they were, about to leave those same babies in the hands of strangers. They were about to allow their precious babies out into the big, scary world. The tiny hands they had held so tightly, the little hands they held for so long were about to pull away into the world of independence.

Letting go is hard for any parent, leaving their kids in someone else's care five days a week was going to be harder than they had ever imagined. The anxiety had grown day by day and today it was insurmountable as they tried to be happy and upbeat for their kids sake.

Pam was Matt's mother; Matt was her firstborn, he was the first to walk, to talk and now he was her first to start school, to take those first steps to independence. Pam didn't do very well with the unknown; new places, and new people made her insecure, this was going to be difficult. Matt and Pam did everything together; she didn't know how he would handle being without her. Pam remembered her own school days and how much she loved it, how independent and self-sufficient she felt worried that Matt would be just like her. School was where she excelled, where she felt independent and on her own, free from the control of her own parents. Now she had to let her little boy go, to allow him to become independent, to soar to new heights and to find his own road to happiness. But she couldn't help but worry about the what ifs.

Pam knew that she wanted Matt to become a strong independent, young man, she wanted him to love school and excell. She wasn't sure what was going on in Matt's little five year old mind, but she knew this was going to be very difficult for her. As parents, we all know that this day will come, our child's first day of school. Within Pam's mind different scenarios played out, one in which of Matt clung to her with tears streaming down his

It Takes 3

face saying *"No, Mommy please don't leave, please mommy, I wanna stay with you"* This was her selfish thinking and certinly not the best for him. Then there was her vision of him waving goodbye with a big smile on his face as he entered into a huge building that seemed to swallow his tiny body, so happy to be a big boy. When she talked to her husband about her feelings and thoughts, he made it a point to lecture her about how Matt needed to be happy and excited about his first day of school and she needed to be careful not to put her insecurities into his head. He was right, she knew that.

Pam decided to take the happiness and sense of adventure her son had into her heart, she knew that his confidence was because of the way he had been raised. Because of the love and security they gave him, Matt was secure enough to go into that building with a smile and a wave, secure enough to move on without them, without her. But Pam knew that no matter how sensible it all sounded, no matter how hard she tried, Matt's first day of school was going to be one of the hardest days of her life. Pam wanted her husband to be with her, but that wasn't possible, he would be out of town and there was no way out of it. He was the bread winner for the family, he had to do what he had to do. Matt was their oldest and his father treated him as such, they had a baby daughter who had just turned two. Her husband told her to look forward to spending some time alone with the baby. But Matt was her baby boy, her little buddy, her little entertainer, her helper. He kept the little one laughing throughout the day. He got her to eat her peas, made her smile each and every day; she knew he would be missed.

Megan was Summer's mom. Summer was her only child, once Summer was in school, there wouldn't to be anyone else for Megan to play with, to teach or even to scold. She wondered what she would do with herself all day while her daughter was in school. School hadn't even started yet both moms were already feeling the emptiness that would be left in their homes and hearts.

2

On orientation day, there were about thirty-two parents waiting for the teacher. Most were Moms, and a couple of dads what looked completely out of place thrown in.

When the teacher opened the classroom, she invited the parents in to find their child's name; "You will find each child's name at the seat I have assigned to them, when you find it, please have a seat and I will be with you in a moment" the parents filed into the room that was neat, organized and decorated in bright happy colors. As the parents walked around the room looking for their child's seat, Pam and Megan found Matt and Summers name right next to each other. As they sat the women chatted nervously about the size of the furniture, the toys, and the brightly colored walls.

Pam leaned into Megan and whispered, "Have you ever done this before?" "No this is my first time" Megan replied. Megan then confided that she was really nervous and seemed relieved to hear Pam was too, "I can't believe my daughter is starting kindergarten already." Megan told Pam.

"Me either, it's seems like yesterday Matt was just a toddler," Pam said.

They continued sharing their fears and anxiety about the days and years to come. The teacher interrupted their conversation

It Takes 3

with an announcement, "Welcome, parents of the class of 2000. My name is Katherine Stone, I ask that your children call me Mrs. Stone, I will be your children's teacher, this is Miss. Carla Cleary, our room assistant, she likes to be called Miss Carla"

The teacher walked around the room explaining each area and what it would be used for. The reading rug was where the children would sit while she read to them, there was a computer table, a craft area and a play area. Each looked clean and ready for a new school year, a new class, new children, and the new parents. Today was a special day for parents only, the school district had designated this specific time for the parents to see the childrens classroom, to meet the staff and to make acquaintance with other parents. It was a time for them to become educated about what to expect from their child's all-important first year.

After Mrs. Stone explained each area, she stood at the front of the room and gave the parents her required speech about school policies and expectations, everything from acceptable behavior to acedemic progress. "Parents, this is the beginning of your children's formal education. Everyone here at Herman Elementary School welcomes you, we hope that your time spent here is both academically and personally rewarding. Please know that we will be here for both your children and you." She went on about who and where to go with concerns, what to do if a child needed to stay home, she talked about the school nurse as well." With all the mandatory stuff out of the way, she talked about herself. "I want to thank each of you personally for taking time out of your busy schedules to be here today. I know this is a big step for your children but it's a big step for you as well. Carla and I, as well as the entire staff are here to help you and your children, through the coming years, so please feel free to ask any question or share any concerns at anytime with us throughout the year."

Mrs. Stone was young and very enthusiastic, by the end of the orientation, each parent was excited and ready for the year to begin, even Pam and Megan were excited, this was going to be a

15

Theresa M. King

fun year. Before ending the day Mrs. Stone walked over to a big white sheet that covered something, as she rasied the fabric she exposed the biggest, cutest, fluffiest stuffed bear you'd ever seen. "This is Ralph" Mrs. Stone said as her hand moved like Vanna White turning a letter. "Ralph is our class mascot, he is a very special bear. At the end of each day, Miss Cleary and I choose a student that had an exceptional day, that student gets to sit on Ralph during story time." By the end of the orientation, Pam and Megan were becoming friends; they sat together, toured the room together, chatted easily and enjoyed each other. Mrs. Stone thought they were friends, but they explained that they had just met. "It's always nice to have friendly parents, but even nicer to see parents beginning new friendships, just like the kids."

At the end of the orientation Pam and Megan walked around the room again this time they stopped to look at the cubbies in the corner. Mrs. Stone had explained that the cubbies would be used to hold the children's important papers, notes, and other items. Each child would check their cubbie twice a day, once when they arrived and again at the end of the day. The children will be shown their cubbie on the first day of school, on this day they would find a special apron inside with their name on it, the aprons had become a tradition; a little something special from her to them.

Mrs. Stone explained; "I have found that each child feels just a little special when they receive their apron, I also think that it helps alleviate a little bit of the stress and anxiety they feel in their new atmosphere" She had been doing this since her first year of teaching. She explained "I was so nervous that first summer before my first class, I needed to occupy my thoughts and hands. I saw these aprons at the craft store so I decided to make some to keep the kid's clothes neat and clean, I'd seen what a mess they could be as an assistant teacher."

"I love to see the kid's faces, when they realize that their names are on the apron."

The sound of the bell stopped each child in their tracks, it was a new sound to them, it was loud, and it startled them, leaving the playground suddenly quiet. Mrs. Stone took the opportunity to give instructions to the children.

"Good Morning children, welcome to Herman Elementary School and welcome to your first day of class, is everyone excited?" The kids shook their heads, some yelled, yea and some clapped! "Well, my name is Mrs. Stone, and I am your teacher. This is Miss Cleary, she is our classroom assistant, and will be here through the year to help us." As she spoke a louder bell sounded. Mrs. Stone pointed up as she spoke, "That bell tells us it's time to stop whatever we're doing, to listen and line up because It is time for school." Mrs. Stone explained that for the first few days, she would call each child's name and show them where to line up. "So when you hear your name, line up and stand quietly and patiently keeping our hands and feet to ourselves, OK?. Once everyone is in line and quiet, we will go into our classroom.. Is everyone ready?"

The kids all said yes in unison this time. The teachers were clear and concise about what they wanted the children to do. Once all the kids were lined up, Mrs. Stone asked, "So, how many of you know how to spell your name?"

Nearly every child raised their hand.

"Wow, very good. When we go into the classroom, I want each of you to look for your name on the tables, when you find it sit quietly in the chair in front of it, OK?."

The kids were beginning to get antsy standing in line listerning. "One more thing: If for some reason you can't find your name, ask one of our class helpers to help you." She pointed to the big kids standing at the building.

Watching the kids getting ready to begin their first day was amazing; the kids stood tall, proud and quiet just as the teacher told them to. Pam and Megan were standing next to each other,

It Takes 3

Finally, other childen began to arrive, and another little girl jumped on the swing next to Summer, "Hi, I'm Jennifer, what's your name?" "Hi," Summer said shyly.

"What's your name?" this little girl asked again, she was a little spit fire, a little red head that was ready to take on the world. Summer finally answered her in a tiny little voice "Summer, my name's Summer" "That's a funny name" Jennifer didn't think about anything she said, she just blurted out whatever she thought.

Within minutes, all the kids seemed happy, talking amoungst themselves, and making fast friends. The moms all watched from outside the kindergarten fence, as no parents were allowed on the playground. More parents began to congregate, Pam and Megan met Amber, Jennifer's mom, and they all watched their children from a distance.

As the kids played, the parents were either talking to each other or lost in their own thoughts, until everyone was startled by a loud bell; the sound could be heard for blocks. Many of the parents brought their kids and just left, while others including Megan and Pam stood outside the fence, watching and waiting. This day was nothing like Pam or Megan remembered about their own kindergarten days; back then, parents actually walked their children into the classroom. But these were different days; most of the parents dropped their kids off, just like they did at day care or preschool. These days it seemed that children were almost expected to begin this day alone. But not every child was comfortable with this, if a child didn't go to day care or had a hard time, the parents were allowed to stay. A parent staying with a child was rare these days, but it did happen on occasion, but most children did as the other kids did. The teacher had explained all of this to the parents at orientation, it was preferred that the parents allow the child to call the shots. These days, the first day of school was a bigger deal to the parents more because this was real school, and their little kids were becoming big kids.

3

The kids enjoyed meeting each other at the park the weekend before school began; they played on the swings and slid down the slide, Summer even enjoyed playing with Matt's little sister.

On that first day, Matt and Summer were surprised and happy to see each other as they ran for the playground and jumped on the swings. Matt and Summer both loved to swing; "I can swing higher than you," Matt said in his taunting little-boy voice.

"No, you can't, anything boy's can do, girls can do better" Summer said as she pumped her legs faster and faster, trying to get higher than him.

Both kids went higher and higher, laughing as they continued to tease each other. The ease at which they played made Pam and Megan smile; the kids were getting along so well, they were having fun, until other boys began to arrive. As soon as Matt saw the boys, he jumped off his swing and joined them, leaving Summer on the swings all alone.

Summer looked sad as she watched her new friend laughing and climbing the monkey bars, with the boys. Pam looked at Megan, in a soft voice she said "sorry" but Summer continued to swing all alone, no teasing, no laughing, no friend. She looked sad; all the fun and joy she had was gone, Matt was gone.

It Takes 3

"Those first parents liked the idea so much they wanted to help keep it going for my future students, so every year the parents pitch in to help with both the cost and labor. About two years ago, one of the families who owns a print shop offered to make the aprons for me, it was their way of saying thankyou. What a gift that was, my aprons are now much nicer because of their generosity."

Pam smiled. "They are really cute. What a great idea, I know Matt will love them." As the women looked at them, Pam elbowed Megan and pointed to the cubbies "Look, our kids are right next to each other again."

Megan laughed. "They sit next to each other, their cubbies are next to each other they line up one behind the other I think these two are destined to be together."

Pam answered, "Well, you never know what the future holds. Anything's possible?"

Pam and Megan both laughed; they felt a connection to each other from the moment they met. They returned to their children's miniature seats, exchanged phone numbers and scheduled a play date at the park before school actually started so the kids would have a little friend on that first day. Everything is always easier with a friend next to you.

looking proud yet sad as they watched their children; there was no crying or carrying on in any way, at least not from the kids.

As Megan watched her little girl be the obedient child she raised her to be, following all the rules just like mommy taught her, she had tears in her eyes, tears of pride, tears of sadness, tears of joy, and as hard as she tried to stop them, they continued to run down her cheek. She felt silly, she certainly didn't want Summer to see her tears, all she could do was to wipe them away as discreetly as possible, but they were impossible to stop. Megan kept a smile on her face as Summer waved to her, and she waved back. Megan wished she could be closer to her daughter when the kids began to line up, but now she was glad there was some distance between them. Summer could see her mom under the tree, but she couldn't see the tears running down her face. Megan had shared with Pam that she was very nervous about how she was going to handle this day; she shared her fears as well as her sadness. She knew she couldn't let Summer know how she felt; she couldn't let her see any of her tears.

On the other hand, Pam seemed so together, so ready for this day she talked about how she and her husband believed that this was all just part of the growing-up process. She told Megan that they were ready and very excited for Matt to start school. Pam's strength and resolve impressed Megan, she wished she could feel some of that strength, some of that resolve.

Megan was embarrassed by her tears and her lack of control, until she looked over at Pam; Pam stood just a foot away from Megan with one hand over her eyes as if the sun were in them, but there was no sun. It took just a moment for Megan to realize that Pam wasn't shielding her eyes from the sun, she was crying. Just like Megan, Pam was crying; this tough altogether mom was shedding tears. Megan wanted to say something, but she felt bad for her new friend. Without a word, she moved toward Pam and softly put her arm around her shoulder and whispered, "Pam, wave to Matt." At that moment, Megan realized that no matter how ready you think you are to see your kids grow up, you're never really ready; it's still hard.

Pam couldn't even look at Megan or her son, the tears were a complete shock; she felt embarrassed by the words she had spoken just days before, embarrassed by her own reaction.

Pam didn't want Matt to see that she was crying, she waved, and Matt waved back;, he had no idea she was crying. All of the parents waved to the children as the teachers escorted them into their classroom. After everyone was inside and the door was closed, the parents outside began to leave.

Pam and Megan stood outside watching the door for a bit longer, after just a few momnets Megan invited Pam to her house for a cup of tea, but Pam had to get home to her daughter; she had a friend staying with her. Pam offered an invitation for Megan to join her if she didn't mind having a two-year-old under foot; they could talk until it was time to get the kids. Megan graciously accepted, and the women spent the next few hours together.

Kindergarten was only a half day, so the moms had just a couple of hours before they needed to head back to the school. The morning went fast, but after spending those few hours together, they felt that this was just the beginning of their friendship. As fast as that first day went, so did the first week, the first months. All of a sudden, kindergarten was over.

It all went by so fast; in the blink of an eye, their kids were wearing those little paper caps and gowns and receiving little fake diplomas; announced first graders at a little assembly. No longer would the kids be in a separate area of the school, safe from the big kids, no more half days; first grade was a full day, complete with a real recess and time with the other big kids. The kids were excited, summer was too long for them and way too short for their parents.

September brought new challenges for all of them. For the moms, it meant more time without the kids. Pam found that she really enjoyed spending time alone with her little girl. Megan, on the other hand, found that all this time alone was more than she wanted, more than she could handle. Megan decided that instead of feeling sorry for herself, she would go back to work, she had been trained as a nurse in the military, and it was time to put her training back to work.

Over the next few years, the women grew apart; one was at home with a little one and the other had a full-time job doing something she really enjoyed. They caught up with each other at school functions or class parties, but things had changed, life had changed.

Year after year, the kids became more involved in school and after-school activities. Year after year, they had more and more home work. Year after year, the moms saw less and less of each other.

Pam's youngest had started school and kept her very busy. With both of her children in school full-time, Pam took a part-time position at her husband's company, helping out in the office and sometimes working from home.

As the years moved forward, Matt and Summer rarely had classes together, their parents rarely saw each other; each child was finding their own niche. Matt and Summer had their own friends. Matt hung out with his sports buddies, and Summer with her dance group; they had completely separate school lives.

4

Middle School was huge compared to Elementary School, this was a place where six Elementary Schools came together and many childhood friends were lost amongst new friends. The kids were busy with new friends, new classes and more sports. Girls were growing up, boys too, Summer was into her studies and dancing, she wasn't intrested in the mall or boys. Except for her crush on that little boy she met in kindergarten. By the end of middle school, Summer was still dressing like a kid, like a tomboy. She wore jeans and a T-shirt most every day. Although she was now an eighth grader, makeup was still at least a year away for her, most of her friends were wearing it, but she wasn't., she had no real desire, until she decided to try out for cheer in High School.

Between Eighth and Ninth grade her entire summer was spent going to workshops, cheer camp, and practicing at home. During cheer camp she would spot Matt, each time she spotted him, she felt giddy and found it hard to concentrate on what she was doing. He was a handsome young man, the object of many girls affections, including her's.

Summer practiced and practiced, she got better and better, week after week her confidence grew by leaps and bounds. She practiced every spare moment; even her mom learned a few cheers, not by choice, but because Summer performed them

It Takes 3

incessantly. By the end of summer, she went into the gym fully prepared for tryouts.

When everyone was done, the girls were all asked back into the gym, they were told that those that made the squad would be contacted by phone in a few days.

A few days? What did that mean? Summer was impatient. She wanted to hear if she got on the squad or not. As day 1 went by, then day 2, 3 and 4, she tried to forget about it, thinking that she probably didn't make it, or she would have heard by now. Right?

At school, none of the girls who tried out had heard anything; every day after school, Summer would walk across the football field where she got to see Matt working out, she found herself wanting to make the squad so that she could see him more, be near him, hoping he would notice her. She still had that crush.

The following week Matt asked a group of girls that Summer was standing with, if they had heard anything. "No, nothing, I can't believe its taking so long" Summer answered. Matt placed a hand on Summer's shoulder. With a big smile and a wink, he told her, "Well, don't give up. It's not over till the telephone rings, right?"

Summer looked confused. "Do you know something?"

Matt pulled her aside. "Well, let's just say. I overheard some of the varsity cheerleaders talking about your performance, they were all impressed. Matt continued to share, everything he heard, he was certain that she made the team. Matt told her about a tradition the football players and cheerleaders had. "Just be ready because one night you may be kidnapped by the team. Summer didn't believe him, but just in case, over the next few nights, after her shower she picked out a pair of really cute pajamas, and had her hair neat in a pony tail. That Friday actually it was Saturday morning, she was awakened by giggling, laughing and hushing outside her bedroom door. The girls were so loud they woke her up. Summer watched the doornob twist and the door opened. Quickly she laid back down and pretended to be asleep. The girls jumped on her bed, clapping and singing their school's fight song. There were about six varsity cheer girls, pulling her up and out of bed, congratulating her as she pretended to be half asleep. Sitting on the edge of the bed they put her new cheer jacket over her shoulders and led her out of her room.

Summer's Mom was right there with camera in hand and a big smile on her face, tears streaming down her face as she watched her little girl's dream come true. Megan had received the call days ago, was sworn to secreacy as the coach told her what to expect and when. This was a hard secreat to keep so tonight was a big relief.

The girls walked Summer to a car where the cheer coach had been waiting. Once all the new team members were picked up, they all met at the local twenty-four-hour Denny's; there were carloads of excited girls as well as the few parents that tagged along in their own cars. Everyone ordered breakfast and talked about the plans for the upcoming year. Every girl proudly wore their new cheer jackets that had been awarded to them in this ceremonial kidnapping. The jackets had to be ordered, which was the reason for the delay in the calls. Each girl's jacket had their name and graduation year embroidered on it.

Summer was so happy; it was official, she was a cheerleader. During breakfast, the coach called out the names of the girls on each squad—first, the freshman team; then junior varsity, then varsity. The Varsity squad was made up of girls who had cheered JV or freshman the previous year. As the varsity captain announced the freshman squad, Summer's name wasn't called, which meant that she was one of the four incoming freshmen who would fill the open positions on the JV squad. Summer was also announced as a co-captain. She was ecstatic and couldn't wait to tell everyone, she wanted to find Matt. It was because of him that she looked cute and not a mess this morning, like some of the girls.

Matt made the JV football team, which meant that Summer would be seeing a lot of him. Matt had the talent and the

It Takes 3

experience to be on the Varsity team, but their school district had a rule that freshman could not participate in varsity sports.

During the year, Summer found herself watching Matt closer and closer, that little girl crush was still there. Anytime Matt was hit hard, her heart skipped a beat, she wanted to run to him, but she couldn't. As the season went on, she found herself thinking about him more and more. Her crush was becoming more, but she kept her feelings to herself. Matt was always nice and cordial to Summer, but he never showed any interest in her as anything more than a friend. They were both athletes, he was a player and she cheered for him so they were kind of like team members, but nothing more.

Freshman year went by fast. By sophmere year, Summer and Matt were both on the varsity teams, and although still cordial and friendly Matt still had no idea Summer had a crush on him.

Summer was still the skinny tomboyish girl Matt had always known, except when she was in her cheer outfit. Matt noticed her. She was a naturally a cute girl, but no one ever thought of Summer as that hot girl in school, she was reserved, and a bit on the shy side. She was the girl who owned one-piece bathing suits and had yet to kiss a boy. Summer never flaunted or flirted with the boys, she was everyone's buddy. She wasn't interested in parties or being the most popular girl in school, her studies and her activities were important to her. She wasn't intrested in boyfriends or dating (except maybe Matt), she wanted to have good friends and good times without the constraint of a relationship (unless it was with Matt). Her goal in life was to become an educated, happy adult with a family of her own.

Toward the end of sophomore year, Summer gave up on any hope of Matt seeing her as anything more than a friend. She wanted more but it obviously wasn't going to happen. Junior year was very busy. Both had their sports, classes, SATs and college entrance exams to worry about. They had letters to write and packages to put together for College. They did a lot of community service with their teams as well as on their own, they were friends, nothing more. It wasn't as if they had other boyfriends or girlfriends. They were just very focused on their futures, their college plans, and their extracurricular activities.

At the end of junior year, Summer decided to ask Matt to their Sadie Hawkins dance. For some reason, this year she felt brave enough to ask him. She thought they could go as friends. When she finally caught up with him and asked, he declined; someone else had just asked him.

Summer was embarrassed, her face turned red as her mouth turned from a smile to a frown, Matt saw her face, he felt bad, because he really wanted to say yes. He wanted to go with her, but he already committed to another friend. Summer didn't stay around to hear what Matt had to say. "Summer if I could, I would " Matt tried to talk to her, but she walked quickly and ducked into the girls locker room; she was dissappointed and embarrassed. It had taken her so long to get up the courage to ask, she didn't want another year to go by without at least trying to persue this. She was so embarrassed that she completely avoided Matt for days. Even on the field, she avoided his glances and gestures. Despite his attempts to talk to her, she avoided him at all cost. Junior year ended with Matt and Summer at odds.

5

That summer between Junior and Senior year had been a long productive one for Summer. Both Matt and Summer were excited to get the year started, to get through and move on to bigger and better things. Matt hung out with his buddies on the front steps checking out the girls, these were the boys all the girls wanted to date, the good looking guys, the jocks with the buff bods. Matt was the one with the cool head and not really into the popularity thing, but he enjoyed the attention he received from being a jock. As the guys hung out looking cool, their eyes suddenly noticed a beautiful blond in the distance. This girl was gorgeous, everyone was whispering and looking her way, every boy had his eyes on her, and most of the girls had a few choice words for her. Who was she? was she a new student? This girl walked with her head held high, back straight, and had a confidence that could only come with maturity and self confidence. Who was she? Where did she come from? As she got closer Matt thought she looked familiar, but no one knew just who she was.

As she reached the steps, Matt noticed that this girl looked a lot like his friend Summer. He wondered, *Could it be Summer?* If it was, she sure did grow up over the summer. If this was Summer, everything about her was different, and it was all good. Matt remembered Summer, she had always been more of a tomboy, with a straight up-and-down figure, hair in a ponytail, and little or no makeup. But this girl was a knockout, with a rockin' body, perfect makeup, and hair that framed her face perfectly. There was no way this could be the same girl he saw leaving the school last year Matt looked closer as the girl walked toward him, "Hi, Matt." She said. His mouth dropped, as he tried to get a hello out, he was shocked. This girl was indeed Summer, he couldn't believe his eyes.

Summer had gotten a summer job at a high-end spa, and she loved it, she loved the work, the atlosmosphere, everything. The owner enjoyed Summer's enthusiasm, her work ethics and her willingness to learn anything and everything. The owner loved teaching Summer everything and hoped this young lady would make cosmotology a career. Summer found that she loved learning all that the salon had to offer, hair, makeup, skincare, everything, she was also learning a lot about herself. She was enjoying the process of reinventing herself over the summer, and now she had dreams and plans for her future and she would'nt let anyone stand in her way.

Summer walked to class amid stares and a lot of whispers; as Matt caught up with her, matching her step for step, he began to make small talk. Summer knew she had caught his attention as soon as she walked through the front gates, and she felt pretty darn good about it. She still had a crush on him and she hoped this year would be different for them. All her disappointment from years past melted away as soon as she saw his face; she could feel the heat in her cheeks and the beat of her heart. As they walked step by step, Matt asked her about her summer, if she would be cheering for him again this year and if she had any special plans for the year. Summer told him yes, she would be cheering and she told him that she had been chosen as the varsity cheer captain and was looking forward to everything the year had to offer. Matt told her that he would be playing football again this year and he too had been chosen captain. He went on to tell her about the new car he bought over the summer and asked if she wanted to go for a ride; as he spoke, he felt flushed. Matt felt as if he was tripping over his words, he found it hard not to stare at her. He found himself very attracted to her, this was an odd feeling, he had never felt this way before, not about anyone, not her or anyone else. He was working hard at keeping his thoughts on school and practice; she had him. She congratulated him on his car and told him that she would still be walking for a while she was saving for a car of her own, but she had a new love of clothes, shoes and accessories, so her paychecks disappeared quickly. That was obvious; he could tell she had a new flair for fashion, hair, nails, and makeup too.

"Well, it's money well spent. You look absolutely beautiful." Matt told her.

Summer told him about her job at the day spa in town, she explained that everything she had been learning and doing made her feel like a girl, and obviously it was all working to her benefit; after all, Matt was all a flutter. Matt offered her a ride anytime she needed it, from practice, to work or home; if he was available, he would be glad to help her out. He hoped she would take him up on the ride he offered her that afternoon after practice, because he wanted to spend more time with her.

Summer declined his offer, so Matt took a new approach. He knew all the guys had their eyes on her, so he took the opportunity to ask her to the upcoming homecoming dance. Again Summer turned him down, she explained that her family already had plans, and she couldn't change them. Matt's head dropped, and this time he walked away disappointed. As he walked away, Summer knew he was hurt, she wanted to chase after him, to explain, but she had a class to get to and couldn't be late. She really wanted to go to homecoming with him, but her family commitment came first; it wasn't something she could get out of, nor did she want to. Matt was so disappointed and so taken by Summer that he went home and told his parents about her.

Matt's mom was not surprised. Summer had always been a little beauty. Pam had seen Summer through the years and thought she was always adorable. Her parents kept her a little girl as long as they could, and Pam was impressed. Even in high school, Summer was much more conservative than most of the other girls and hearing that her son had a crush on her made Pam smile.

All through dinner that evening, Summer was all Matt could talk about. Matt's parents felt this was more than just a crush. As he talked about this first day of school, his Mom's mind went back to another first day of school, his first day of kindergarten. As she remembered that day she smiled, so many years had passed, but that day was forever in her mind. As she listerned to her son talk, the days were so similar in so many ways. On his first day of kindergarten, he and Summer played on the swings, they talked and laughed together, they giggled and shared those first few minutes, enjoying each other. On this day, it sounded as if the the kids had experienced another special moment together.

After dinner, Matt went to his room and Pam couldn't help herself she picked up the phone and dialed an old number. As she dialed she hoped the number was still good, the phone rang, finally a voice came across the line, "Hello?"

The voice didn't sound familiar, but it was a females voice, so she asked, "Is this Megan?"

"Yes, it is." As soon as Megan heard the voice on the other end of the line, she knew exactly who it was. "Oh my goodness, Pam?" They were both so excited to talk to one another they couldn't stop asking questions, the women laughed and caught up quickly. Although Megan and Pam had seen each other in passing from time to time, they hadn't actually spent any time together in years. After they caught up, they talked about Summer and Matt and how much they'd changed, they taked about the crush the kids had on each other on and off over the years. Megan procedded to

It Takes 3

tell Pam about the conversation she had that evening with Matt about Summer. "Well, whatever this is it is much more than just a crush."

6

While this old friendship was developing into a new love, across town a young couple was struggling with their own future. Beckie and Scott were a couple that had everything going their way, until Beckie told Scott that she wanted a baby.

"A baby?" these words hit Scott right in the belly.

"Yes, a baby. I want to have a baby. I think it's time, don't you? Think about it, we couldn't be in a better position. It's perfect. What do you think?" she sounded excited.

Scott thought about it.

"Wow, a baby! A baby? Really?" Scott didn't know if he was ready for that, but he knew that he needed to choose his approach wisely; he needed to really think about it.

"Well," he continued, "we would need to change one of the rooms into a nursery, but which one, which room would we change? Your sewing room, my office, or the guest room?"

Beckie looked at him in wonder, pleased that he was considering it. "I don't know; I guess we could combine the sewing room and the office. We, can make it work?"

Scott didn't want to combine his office. "What if we combine the guest room and your sewing room? The guest room isn't really used anyway."

It Takes 3

She saw his face, he was looking a little scared, she sat on his lap, and cuddled with him. "I know we haven't talked much about children, but we both want them, right? And I'm not getting any younger and neither are you."

"Thanks," Scott said, "I guess a family is the next logical step."

Beckie had taken Scott by complete surprise. Heck, Beckie took herself by surprise. Her thoughts just came out of her mouth without thinking. For just a split second, she stopped and thought about just what a big step this was. Beckie knew that Scott needed time, she didn't push him because she needed time too.

But that night, babies were all Beckie could think of. Scott tried to think about babies and kids, but all he could think of was Beckie. He loved her, he loved their life together, and he knew a baby would change everything for them. Beckie's mind was full of baby thoughts. As she seduced Scott that night, Beckie had baby making on her mind, but all Scott could think of was making love to his wife.

Tonight she was the aggressor, and he was enjoying it; this was a rare occurrence, and he loved it. With each passing moment that they made love, Beckie found herself wanting a baby more and more. She loved Scott, and he loved her; a baby would be an extension of their love for each other. Finally after they were both absolutely exhausted, Beckie looked at this man she loved more than life itself and laid her head on his chest, listening to his heartbeat.

Feeling the warmth of his embrace, Beckie felt loved like never before as they both fell into a deep comfortable sleep. It wasn't long until Beckie entered into a dream world. At first, her dream was about their happy life together, their past, their accomplishments through the years. In her dream, she saw her body as it intertwined with Scott's; she watched as they made love, she could actually see herself become pregnant as her fallopian tubes released her egg, and Scott's sperm met it and penetrated it. It was as if she was watching a documentary on pregnancy.

She saw the cells split and multiply, she saw an embryo turn into a baby, and it was all happening in her own body.

In her dream, she could feel her nerves when she took the pregnancy test, and she felt their overwhelming joy at the positive result. Beckie felt Scott's arms around her as he kissed her and called her mommy; she loved the feeling of their overwhelming happiness. Throughout the night, as she lay in her bed dreaming, she felt her body growing; she felt her flat tummy beginning to swell with the love that was growing inside her. In her dream, she felt a joy she had never felt before. Beckie slept deeply and comfortably dreaming of their future.

As morning broke, the alarm clock startled Beckie out of her deep dream state. The alarm clock was extremely loud and annoying. Beckie usually woke before it rang, but this morning, she was enjoying her dream, but as soon as that thing began to buzz, she bolted straight up to a sitting position as if she had been shot. Once her eyes and body caught up with her and without thinking, she placed her hand on her belly and was surprised to find it to be flat as flat as it could be; she didn't expect that. She was still living in her dream world; reality hadn't quite set in yet.

As she woke up, she realized that everything she had experienced, everything she had felt, had been a dream, just a dream.

Beckie noticed Scott's look of concern, and she quickly opened up and told him about her dream. She tried to include every detail of it, and she wished he could feel it like she did. She tried to explain just how real the whole thing felt to her, explaining in detail how she could actually feel her body growing and the baby inside her.

Scott looked unconvinced. "How can you feel something you have never experienced?" he asked.

"I don't know, but I'm telling you it was amazing."

Scott listened to her intently, he saw the reality of it all, and he saw her love for a child that hadn't even been conceived yet. He also saw how real her disappointment was when she first woke up and realized it was all just a dream. Beckie's dream and her reaction to it all made Scott nervous. But as he listened to her talk about all the details, he quickly found himself wanting it all as well; he found an unknown desire for a child, their child. As he listened to his wife's experience throughout her dream, as he felt her disappointment, he too became disappointed that it had all been just a dream. After they finished talking in bed, they both got up and got ready for their day, at breakfast, they continued to discuss the possibility of having a baby. After all the talk about babies, he was surprised at the feelings he had about becoming parents. Suddenly Scott couldn't wait to see his wife pregnant with their baby, to feel and see a life growing inside her. They were in agreement: they were ready to take the biggest step of their entire life.

With all the excitement, Scott and Beckie returned to their bedroom to make love again; this time they both had baby making on their minds. Beckie was still on birth control, so it wasn't going to happen today, but they enjoyed their time together. As they made love, Scott's mind wandered a bit, and he found himself thinking about being a father, about all the responsibility that included, and he found himself suddenly very nervous. Scott was always so self-assured, and this feeling was unsettling to him. He was nervous if it happened, but even more nervous if it didn't. Then he thought about some friends he had at work that couldn't get pregnant. He thought, *Wow, what if we couldn't get pregnant?*

7

After a lovely morning making love, they decided that they were done with the birth control pills. Beckie and Scott stood at the toilet, with the last of her birthcontrol pills. Beckie had finished the actual hormone pills, this was just a ceremonial gesture of releasing the thing that kept them from getting pregnant all these years, it marked the beginning of a new journey.

This ceremonial dumping of the placebo pills was fun for them, and they laughed as they each dumped pill after pill into the toilet, and together they flushed them away.

Beckie was surprised at her relief, she had been taking those things for so long, and finally she was free of their hold on her. Now it was all about time. Beckie had heard that it could take a long time to get pregnant after being on the pill for so long; she heard that the longer you took them, the longer it could take to get pregnant. Beckie had been on the pill for twelve years already; she was afraid that it could take awhile for the hormones to leave the body. It had been suggested that a women should avoid getting pregnant for about three months at least after stopping the pill.

She'd been getting her information from her friends who had already had children, not from a doctor, but she trusted them, so for the next three months, Scott was back to the old days of using a condom if he wanted to make love to his wife, he hated

It Takes 3

condoms, but they wanted to be safe. Both Beckie and Scott knew many women who got pregnant right away after stopping the pill, and everything was fine, but they didn't want to take any chances. So for three months, they were careful, and Beckie's cycle seemed pretty much the same as it had been on the pill.

On the fourth month, Scott took Beckie out for to a very romantic dinner, complete with flowers and a special gift just for her. Scott had become very excited about their future, and tonight was the night they wanted to begin their journey to parenthood, so he bought her a charm bracelet with a heart on it, her first charm.

Through the day they shared some teasing via text and a few sexy phone conversations, so they were ready for a romantic evening by the time he picked her up.

Beckie looked lovely and smelled amazing, a new perfume Scott noticed. As they drove to the restaurant, Beckie continued teasing Scott; he told her if she didn't stop it, he would turn the car around and go home, Beckie stopped, much to Scott's disappointment.

He had made reservations at her favorite restaurant, and she was hungry; she laughed and told Scott that she needed to eat for strength. She was hungry, but not just for food. Scott was hungry too. They hadn't made love in a nearly a week. It wasn't that they didn't want to, they heard that if they wanted to get pregnant, they should abstain for a few days to give Scott's sperm a boost so it would be strong and numerous. Tonight was the night, and they were both ready and very anxious. Dinner was lovely and very romantic. It was a weeknight, so the restaurant was pretty quiet. As she sat across the booth, she would rub her foot up and down Scott's leg. Just so she could tease him under the table.

Beckie would do this whenever she wanted to act sexy or when she wanted to share herself with him in the most intimate way. It was subtle, but he loved when she did it. No words were ever needed between them when it came to their desires, they were very well matched in the bedroom, there was never a need for a lot of talking or leading of the other. Scott knew what Beckie liked, and she knew what Scott enjoyed. By the time they arrived home, they couldn't keep their hands off each other; they barely made it into their house. It had been awhile, and they were both very anxious. They made love in their living room; it all happened so quickly that it was a bit disappointing for both of them. They decided to relax with a drink and some appetizers; they even took some time to relax in their spa. This evening, their time in the spa was followed by a relaxing massage; it was something that Scott loved doing for Beckie and Beckie loved it. As Scott began his massage, Beckie melted into the mattress. Scott warmed the massage oil in his hand before softly rubbing it into her skin. This was just the beginning. Scott gave Beckie a full-body massage, spending time on both her feet and hands. As she relaxed, she began to massage Scott's shoulders until they got lost in each other. Scott and Beckie made love easily; their time making love was combined with more massaging. This night of lovemaking was soft and long, each taking time to just enjoy the caressing. After a very long evening, they fell asleep in each other's arms. Scott joked that these long massage nights would probably be a thing of the past when they had a baby, but Beckie assured him they wouldn't. She wanted to make it a priority to find time for each other; their relationship needed to remain a priority, especially with a baby.

When her next monthly cycle was as normal as ever, Beckie was disappointed; she knew it was too much to hope that it would happen so soon. As the next month came, Beckie and Scott were certain that this was the month, their anticipation was high. But all the anticipation and hope came crashing down on them, when her cramps started, and there it was, her monthly visitor right on time, again. They both knew it was a long shot that they would get pregnant within the first couple of months, but neither of them could stop the disappointment they were feeling. Both wanted this, and they wanted it as quickly as possible, but they also knew that stress could have an affect on them.

They both agreed that although they were impatient, they needed to take life as it came, relaxing and enjoying their lives, so they agreed that they would give it at least six months, probably a little longer even.

With the following month came more anticipation and stress; despite themselves and their decision to not worry, here they were worried and hoping that Beckie would not get that visitor, but sure enough, that little visitor had the nerve to show up. Scott could tell by her face. She had a face that showed everything: happiness, sadness, disappointment, concern and elation. It told on her no matter how hard she tried to hide it.

Scott just walked up and hugged her, he didn't say anything, and they went about their day, both living in a cloud of grey. Scott found himself disappointed as well, but he didn't tell Beckie, he didn't want to upset her any more than she already was.

As that first month became three months, then four months turned to five, then six months passed, and still nothing, they decided to be patient and to give it a year; if after a year of actual trying and nothing happened, it was time to consult a doctor. But after a full nine months of trying and still nothing happening, it was beginning to take a toll on them.

8

Nine months and nothing, Beckie had another one of her dreams—no, Beckie had a nightmare, a horrible, awful nightmare. In this nightmare, there were voices and demons yelling at her, telling her this would never happen. In her nightmare, she and Scott were fighting even considering divorce; it was horrible. In the end, she grew old and was left all alone. The nightmare was not very long, she woke up crying, and she had yelled out in her sleep and woke Scott.

Once she was awake, Scott tried to console her, but all she could do was cry. She told Scott about the demons flying and screaming, "Never, never ever will you have what you want." The entire nightmare reminded her of some of the old nursery rhymes like Rumpelstiltskin. Not only were there demons and characters, but there were also memories of when she was a teenager.

Suddenly she was reliving those years—the severe cramps she had experienced, the headaches, and the extremely irregular periods. She remembered her mom and dad being dismissive about what she was going through; they always felt she was overreacting. Beckie was a pretty dramatic kid and had a tendency to overdramatize things. But not without compassion, her mom gave her a heating pad and some over-the-counter medication and told her that she needed to keep a calendar of her symptoms and dates; but Beckie never did it. If she was as inconsistent as she said, it was important that she keep track of it. A calendar would give them much-needed information to take to a doctor if needed; besides, every girl should keep a calendar.

Beckie would go months without a period, but she was an athlete, and she was young. It was the months that she had cramps so bad that she had to stay home from school that concerned her mom. Her dad wasn't sympathetic, partly because he just didn't know or understand any of this. In his mind, Beckie just needed to get over it, she needed to suck it up and get over herself, this was normal; after all, she was a girl. He felt she needed to pick herself up and get on with life. Sitting at home with a heating pad and some kind of medication was just ridiculous in his mind. Night after night, the same memories haunted her, until one night the memories changed. She had nightmares about a baby being placed in her arms and then just disappearing. Nightmares about being pregnant for nine months, and then suddenly she wasn't. Strange nightmares rocking a crying baby, only to see it was just a doll. Every night Beckie grew more and more fretful about falling asleep, she tried to think happy thoughts, but the nightmares continued. Until one night, her dreams went back to her younger days again. Suddenly she was remembering herself and her mom sitting in a doctor's waiting room. Mom seemed worried about her; then there was a conversation with the doctor regarding Beckie's symptoms, some test that had been done, and more talking. Beckie remembered something about cyst or something, but when she was older and went to see a different doctor, there didn't seem to be anything to worry about. This was the doctor who put her on birth control pills to regulate her periods.

The dreams continued until Beckie woke up in tears again. This time her dream woke her in the middle of the night, she tried to be quiet, but Scott woke up after he heard her.

As he reached for her and held her, he asked, "What is it, babe? What was this one about?"

Beckie just looked at him and cried, her tears and disappointment tore at him, seeing his wife so upset from a dream or nightmare or whatever it was she saw in her sleep was more than he could take. He knew that there was nothing he could do to change it, but it all made him very nervous. What if these dreams were some kind of omen? What if they never got pregnant like in her dream? What would this do to her, to them? Would he find her one day rocking a doll? It scared him, he saw the pain that Beckie was feeling and how difficult this all was for her, and he wanted to make it better.

Time went by, and the nightmares seemed to be better, but the dreams were still there, and they still hadn't conceived. They knew they needed answers, and they needed them now, so they began to list questions for the doctor. According to her symptoms and the research they had done, if their suspicions were correct, it was possible that they could need some medical intervention in their effort to get pregnant. Their research led them to many different sites about the symptoms that Beckie had and their unsuccessful attempts to conceive over these many months. Just stopping their birth control and having sex wasn't working, after months and months; despite the fact that they were both ready, emotionally, financially, and every other way, they came to realized that there may be other things to consider, It was time to see Dr. Lipton, Beckie's OB/GYN.

9

Beckie made an appointment and Scott agreed to go with her. They both needed answers; her dreams and nightmares brought on more questions than anything else. Remembering all the talk about cyst or fibroids or whatever else the doctor was concerned about back then brought a sense of dread to Beckie. Now that these memories had come into her mind, she couldn't help but wonder if the things they read on the Internet were true. Both she and Scott read about how fibroids had the potential to cause infertility, they read about the ovarian cyst, they read horror stories about other women who were unable to get pregnant; it was overwhelming, they knew they shouldn't be self-diagnosing, but they couldn't stop reading either. They both knew they shouldn't be reading into any of what they found on the Internet, but how could they not? It had been nearly a year since they had begun their journey to get pregnant, and nothing.

Beckie even wondered, *Maybe this isn't meant to be for us?*

They talked about the information they found, they talked about the possibility that the symptoms she had been experiencing could in some way be a problem for them. At her doctor's office, Beckie was given some tests right away. The first of which was a physical exam, followed by a bunch of blood work. After the doctor completed Beckie's physical exam, she was sent to the outpatient lab for her blood work, an ultra sound, and transvaginal ultrasound, which is known as an internal ultrasound. The blood test was just like any blood test; they just took what felt like a pint of blood. The first ultrasound was easy, except that Beckie always thought her first ultrasound would be to see their baby, but this one was to see why they didn't have a baby. The nurse squeezed a little jelly on her belly and waved a cold metal wand against her skin; there on the screen was Beckie's insides.

Next was the transvaginal ultrasound. It sounded scary—transvaginal? What the hell was that? Beckie had never heard of this, and she didn't like the sound of it. Thankfully she had a really nice technician who explained it completely; before she did anything, she held up a large wand thing she called the probe. She explained that the probe would be inserted into Beckie's vagina.

"Are you allergic to latex?"

"No," Beckie said as she eyed the wand. "Why?" The technician explained" a condom is placed on the wand before I insert it. "Before doing what?" Beckie looked shocked. "You're going to put that thing where?" The probe looked huge.

The technician assured her, "I will be very gentle, I promise. If you feel any discomfort, we'll stop immediately."

Beckie was scared. "That thing is huge."

The technician explained, "We choose the appropriate probe size based off of your body size. It's not too big, I assure you. It's not a one size fits all, you'll be fine, try to relax." The technician lead Beckie through some relaxation breathing, trying to get her to relax; she talked to her building up a trust. Beckie needed to be as relaxed as possible. The technician held the probe up so that Beckie could witness her opening a new wand and a new condom; the condom was placed over the wand for extraprotection and comfort. The technician put K-Y jelly on the probe as a lubricant before inserting it into Beckie's vagina. It was a bit uncomfortable but not painful.

It Takes 3

The technician talked Beckie through the insertion, and once in place, it just felt odd, not painful. This ultrasound would give them the information they needed. If there were in fact problems with her ovaries, fallopian tubes, or uterus; this test would show it.

Beckie asked about what the technician saw. "Oh, I don't interpret the results. I just perform the test."

Beckie knew this girl had to know something. You don't do something like this without knowing what you're looking at. "Do you see anything wrong?" Beckie was trying to get a sense of what she saw.

But the tech stayed stoic. "Your doctor will go over everything with you."

It was obvious that Beckie wasn't going to get anywhere, so she decided to stop trying. Beckie and Scott had their follow-up visit scheduled for Thursday. At this appointment the doctor would go over all the test results with them. Thursday was two days away. Two days seemed like forever, they waited on pins and needles as the hours slowly passed. At the appointment, Beckie's doctor talked to both of them in length about a diagnosis she had been given years ago.

"What, diagnosis?" Beckie asked. She didn't remember any diagnosis ever being given to her, but according to her old medical records, Beckie had been told that they believed she had polycystic ovarian syndrome (PCOS).

Beckie was in her late teens, she was the right age and had all the symptoms: abnormal as well as irregular periods, extremely bad cramps as well as a terrible case of acne. She complained about having body hair that was darker and thicker than her friends or her sisters, and the doctor noticed that she had more body hair than what was considered normal for a girl her age. According to her records, tests were ordered but had never been done, there were no results to refer to.

Her doctor had noted it as a suspected diagnosis, pending further testing. As Beckie listened, she began to remember that visit; she remembered her doctor telling her something about this being a cause of infertility, but it was a blur. All of this happened so many years ago, she was so young, so certain that the doctor was overreacting, wanting more tests for more money. Going through the testing would take time and money, and Beckie had neither. Beckie now wondered if she had done what was needed back then, would be different today, but back then, it was all too much for her to understand, in fact, she ignored the entire experience.

And now here she was, years later, dealing with something that she had pushed from her mind years and years ago. Even through all of their disappointment, she never thought of what the doctor told her years ago, but she was thinking about it now. The doctor explained that the birth control pills seemed to have kept her periods regular, which, according to the records, was why they were prescribed in the beginning, but they also masked other symptoms. As the doctor talked and went over the information in her chart.

Things had improved so much that, she hadn't been to a doctor for anything more than the flu. Beckie had put all of this to the back of her mind, all but forgetting about it all, until now. After she started the pill, her cycles were like clockwork, she no longer experienced the horrible cramping or headaches, and she had always felt positive and excited about her future. Scott was a great boyfriend and an even better husband. As they discussed Beckies past, he remembered back when they first began dating, remembering that there had been some months she would have cramps so bad that she didn't get out of bed; he remembered the terrible headaches. Scott had been so wonderful to her on those days; he took care of her, got her heat packs, cold packs whatever she needed. He had no problem going to the store for her to buy her Midol, tampons, pads, whatever she needed. Buying feminine products was not a problem for him; after all, he had a mom and a sister, he knew all about those things.

It Takes 3

He more concerned for her health and well-being than she ever was, she needed him, and this was proof. After trying for months and months and not getting pregnant, here they were with a possibility that a medical condition could be the problem, a medical condition that Beckie had ignored and was still trying to ignore.

10

After this appointment and the research, Scott's concern went beyond the possible infertility they might be facing. His concern, unlike hers, was for her health, both physically and mentally. He knew if for some reason they couldn't get pregnant it would take a terrible toll on his wife, and he couldn't bear to see her hurt in any way. This was all a bit overwhelming: the doctor talked about the testing, the possible surgery, the medication—all of it could be risky. Every surgery was a risk, and the medications held their own risk and side effects. In his opinion, nothing was worth risking his wife's life for, and many of the side effects sounded more risky than he was comfortable with.

Yes, they both wanted to be parents, but Scott's first concern was for his wife and their life together. He would be fine if their little family remained just the two of them, he was also fine with checking out the possibility of adoption, it didn't matter if their baby was of their DNA or not. If having a baby the traditional way would be dangerous for Beckie, then they would find another option.

Scott and Beckie talked in length about adoption, it was always something they thought of. Through the Internet, they read about other options as well. Carrying a baby was Beckie's dream; she wanted to have her own child first. This is what she

It Takes 3

wanted, and she wasn't ready to give up on her dream, not just yet. A baby was on her list, and she wanted it to happen; if there was any way to make it happen, she wanted to pursue every possibility, and Scott agreed. He would do anything he could to help make her dream a possibility. Both were well educated individuals, and they understood the possible obstacles that lay ahead of them. They talked for hours about all the possibilities, all the testing, all the medication.

In the end, if everything failed, they knew there were options; if they found they were actually unable to conceive on their own or with help, then they would pursue these other options, but not now.

First things first, they decided that they wanted to give the old-fashioned way another few months, if the doctor agreed of course. But if it came down to it, if they needed to, they felt that they would be fine exploring the options, but for now, it wasn't something they were ready to do. They had a lot to think about, a lot to consider, but first, they needed to go to their second appointment; they needed to discuss the test results. They needed to discuss their plans with the doctor; they needed to discuss their future.

11

Beckie's doctor was happy to see that Beckie had actually completed all of the tests and actually showed up for her second appointment; he was afraid she wouldn't. At the last appointment, they hadn't gotten into her past and the fact that she didn't follow her doctor's orders, the last time she just seemed to disappear. But today she was back, and they discussed everything, especially her past. He asked Beckie why she hadn't followed through with the test that had been ordered or why she hadn't gone in for checkups.

Beckie explained, "I don't know what to say. I was eighteen, and I was going off to school, I was busy, and to be honest, I just never really thought there was anything to it." She tried to get the doctor to understand that she was busy, she had school, a job, and then Scott came into her life. "After I started the pill, things were better. I figured that was all I needed. Everything seemed normal, a little bit of cramping, some headaches, but nothing severe. I took my pills every day. I was good about that." Beckie explained that life just moved forward; she graduated, got married, and settled into her job. Life went on.

"Honestly I didn't even think about it; it didn't seem to be a problem any longer. I'm sure it probably started out as a bit of denial, but things seemed better. I honestly thought that whatever it was went away. I have a full happy life that could only be better if we had a family," Beckie told him.

She explained that she had been on birth control until about thirteen months ago when they decided to seriously try for a family, they were ready to move forward, and here they were stuck back in time, facing a supposed diagnosis of PCOS. In her mind, this was all new to her. What was PCOS?

The doctor explained, "*PCOS* is the acronym for 'polycystic ovarian syndrome,' a disorder of the endocrine system, which is a group of glands that produce and regulate our hormones. This disorder causes an imbalance of the hormones, and it affects about 10 percent of all females. So it's not extremely rare, and it's a pretty common cause of infertility." The doctor went on to explain that a diagnosis of PCOS didn't mean that they couldn't get pregnant, but it would be an obstacle. He went on, "In this day and age, with medical technology and existing medications, there are ways to help."

After all the test results were in, the doctor decided to go with a medication that was known to be successful. Beckie had her diagnosis, he had confirmed the suspicions, so before they went any further, he gave them all the information with regard to his choice of medication.

After a week, Beckie and Scott returned to begin the regimen of meds. The doctor went over everything again and told them to give the medication a minimum of three months; after that, they would need to return to his office.

"Now, I am going to plan on a six-month program, and if after that we are not successful, then we will look at other options, okay?"

Beckie and Scott were optimistic with the medication in hand. Beckie read, "Metformin."

The doctor explained that metformin was the generic equivalent of Glucophage, which was a medication used to lower insulin. He explained that insulin resistance is an underlying cause of PCOS. Glucophage or metformin was used to help stabilize hormones as well as insulin. The doctor educated them about the possible side effects of the medication, she explained that there were some common side effects that hit one out of every three patients, but they were pretty mild. They were nausea, gas, bloating, diarrhea, loss of appetite, and some vomiting. He also warned them about possible severe side effects. "The chances of you experiencing any of these serious side effects are pretty rare; about one in thirty thousand patients experience these. I also need to warn you that out of these serious side effects, statistics showed that about 50 percent were fatal."

Beckie and Scott listened, and despite any possible side effects, they were willing to take the risk. They felt the odds were in their favor, and the side effects seemed minimal; it was worth a try.

They went home and went about their lives, which included Beckie taking her medication. She took them exactly as prescribed, but with each passing month, their frustration grew; two months became three, and by the end of the third month, they still had no signs of pregnancy. Beckie was getting frustrated and having terrible nightmares again, nightmares were about never getting pregnant, never being a mom. They went through the entire three months, then returned to the doctor's office as instructed. The medication had been a long shot, but the doctor decided to use it because they had seen good results with it. The doctor suggested a six-month regimen, so maybe they just needed more time; after all, this wasn't a magic pill. But Beckie was extremely anxious and frustrated, so they talked about other options, there was no sign of pregnancy, and the meds hadn't worked, at least not yet. The doctor decided to test Scott, just to make sure there was nothing going on with him. Scott was so uncomfortable the first time he went to the lab. He just couldn't do it; being in a tiny rest room with the lab technicians just feet away, made it impossible. When he went home, he was so cranky and so frustrated with himself.

It Takes 3

Beckie thought he was so cute talking about the process of trying to produce this fresh sperm sample. He told her that the girl in the lab offered him magazines.

"Magazines? Really, with everyone just feet away? There was no way this was going to happen, and I told her so. That's when she told me I could do this at home? Why didn't she say that to begin with?"

Scott felt better. "I couldn't believe that she was referring to masturbation as a procedure." "Babe, this girl was like nineteen years old. I wasn't comfortable with the entire conversation and then she handed me a fresh cup and a brown paper bag."

Becky smiled as she grabbed his hand and led him to their bedroom. "Well, let's get this done and ship you back to the lab." The thought of his sample in a lunch bag made them laugh. "Good thing you're not taking your lunch to work."

Beckie was loving and sweet as she helped Scott retrieve the sample and offered to drop it off at the lab for him. Scott was grateful and accepted her offer immediately. Beckie returned the sample to the lab for him, and he stayed home; he wasn't worried about the results. The doctor had ordered the results STAT, and within hours his confidence was confirmed: his sperm was strong and numerous, pretty much perfect results. The doctor wanted to do some more tests on Beckie; he wanted to see if there were any changes after being on the medication. In the meantime, he ordered them to continue the meds and to have sex, lots of sex. Scott was actually excited to get these orders; he was feeling pretty good about himself and was ready to get busy, to follow doctor's orders. The stress of not knowing what they were dealing with and not getting pregnant, had taken a huge toll on them; it all slowed the intimacy part of their lives to a near stop. Scott wanted their intimacy back, they had always had an active sex life, and they really enjoyed each other in the bedroom. Now they were under doctor's orders, and he wanted to do as he was told.

12

It's been well over a year now since Beckie and Scott stopped taking the pill, and now five months had passed since they started seeing the doctor, they had been on the metformin for months and still not one sign of being pregnant. Beckie and Scott were becoming so frustrated that Beckie was referred to a specialist, things weren't happening like they all hoped they would, so it was time for a specialist.

The doctor wanted to be sure there was nothing else physiologically stopping Beckie's body from going forward with their plans. Her doctor spoke to them about the possibility of a surgical therapy. Beckie was sent to the best, Dr. Stan Werman, who was known as one of the top infertility specialist in the field. Beckie and Scott called his office immediately when they got home, but he was completely booked for months. This was not acceptable to either Beckie or Scott. They called Dr. Liptons office back and explained that the specialist was booked for months, and they couldn't and wouldn't wait.

"Is there someone else you could refer us to?" The receptionist put her on hold and spoke to the doctor, who made a call while Beckie and Scott were on hold.

It Takes 3

Dr. Werman and Dr. Lipton were friends. They had gone through their internship together. Dr. Lipton shared Beckie and Scott's story and was able to get them in the office that week. Finally something was going their way. It felt as if this was the first thing to go right since they began this journey. At their first appointment, Dr. Werman went over both of their files. In his opinion, things didn't seem to be as bleak as everyone thought. In his opinion, the first step should be a different cycle of medications.

"I know it's another few months, but I think it's worth a try. I wanna put you on a combination of drugs. We have used this combination with very satisfactory results."

Becky was upset that they were doing another round of drugs, but the doctor sounded optimistic as he shared the statistics. "The statistics show that only about 7 percent of women using metformin alone are successful. That percentage rises to about 15 percent using the combination of the two drugs I'm recommending."

Beckie certainly wasn't one of the 7 percent. She had not conceived using metformin alone, so she and Scott agreed it was worth trying the combination therapy. The doctor was careful not make any promises. "I need the both of you to keep an open mind, to try to keep your stress to a minimum. We still need to stay open to other options just in case." Beckie and Scott went home that day with a renewed hope, a renewed optimism about their future.

When they got home, Beckie began to take her prescriptions exactly as the doctor prescribed. Dr. Werman had prescribed a combination of Provera, Clomid, and Glucophage. Beckie was instructed to take the Provera for ten days, then the Clomid for five days, Glucophage was taken every day. She would repeat the process for three months. The Provera would bring on her period, and then the Clomid and Glucophage would allow her to ovulate. The doctor was hopeful this would help Beckie conceive.

They all held a lot of hope that within three months, Beckie and Scott would be successful.

But nothing happened during their first three month cycle, so a second round was ordered, after six months of medication still nothing. Beckie and Scott were beginning to think they might have to look into those other options. They had become pretty isolated over the past year, not seeing much of anyone, especially their families because they didn't want to talk about what they were going through. They knew they needed to talk to them; they needed to tell them what they had been dealing with. So before they made any more commitments to more treatment or other options, they decided to take a break. They needed a break from all of it—the stress, the medications, and the doctors.

Beckie and Scott decided to take some time for a minivacation. It was a time for them to be together and have some fun. They went to a friend's mountain cabin, they walked in the snow, ate at some nice restaurants. Beckie enjoyed all her favorites: prime rib, potatoes, and deserts—lots of deserts. They sat in the hot tub that was nestled among the snow-covered ground with a view of the mountains; it was a dream come true for Beckie.

When they returned, they decided it was time to move forward with their plans, but first, they would talk to their families. They wanted them to know what they were dealing with over the past months—the tests, the doctors, all of it. Both Beckie and Scott had pretty much avoided family events, if they attended, they were pretty standoffish. Over the past couple of years, at every event, their families and friends drove them crazy with questions: "When are you two going to have kids?" "What are you waiting for?" They couldn't take the questions over and over again, so they avoided them instead. Beckie and Scott wanted and needed to explain their situation. They needed these questions to stop, at least for now.

They both knew their families meant well, they loved them, and they wanted to share their desire as well as their frustration with them, all of them. They invited both families to their home the following evening, and of course both families agreed, thinking they were going to get some long awaited news. Scott and Beckie had ordered Chinese food for the evening, everyone liked it, and it was easy to share. Beckie and Scott told their family that they had been trying to have a baby. Scott's Mom let out a "yea", she assumed they were pregnant.

"No, Mom, we are not pregnant. That's what we want to talk about."

"But your trying?" she asked with enthusiasm.

"Yes, we have been trying, but we have had some difficulties. Truth is we've had months and months of difficulties. Everyone listened to what Scott and Beckie had been through. It was hard to watch Scott tear up and Beckie cry, but they listened quietly. After everything was out, Beckie and Scott felt better; now everyone knew what they were dealing with.

The family shared stories of friends they knew that went through similar struggles, with positive results. They also shared stories they heard in the news, stories about the stress of trying to have a baby or going through infertility treatments; it always sounded overwhelming the way the news reported on it.

But here in front of them were Beckie and Scott, two people they loved living it, the stress, the disappointment, they thought if they talked about it, they would know they were not alone.

Scott's sister Stephanie shared a story of some friends of hers that had gone through all of the IVF stuff, only to give up after months and months. This couple finally adopted a beautiful little boy; two months later, they found out they were pregnant. Stephanie's friend had a five-month-old and was three months pregnant.

"The doctor was telling us that things like that happen because of stress," Beckie explained. "Well, we are not at the adoption point yet, but it may be an option, later down the road, and if that did happen, we'd be fine."

Scott looked surprised. "We would?"

Beckie assured him that they could handle it, and if that was God's plan, they could do it. Beckie and Scott shared their test results as well as the doctor's plans; They'd been through a lot, and they both looked and sounded exasperated. Everyone listened intently as Beckie and Scott talked about all their possible options, medications, surgery, adoption; they discussed the possibility of in vitro fertilization (IVF), even the possibility of using a surrogate or egg donor. The family felt they should think seriously about adoption, the other options sounded risky, but Scott and Beckie were adamant.

Although there were other avenues, they were willing to try whatever they needed to get a child of their own, risky or not. The family listened to them, and no matter what choice they made, everyone would support them and do anything they could to help their dream become reality.

13

The evening with their families was long. They went over all the months they had been trying to conceive, the pain and the toll it had taken on them. Everyone could see and hear what the stress had done. They were glad they choose to share, to spend time with their families having their families support meant the world to them. Since their teen years, Scott and his sister Stephanie's relationship had been difficult. She was three years younger than him, and since high school, he thought of her as a pain in the ass. He loved her when she was little, but when she got older, and wanted to do everything he did. She got him in trouble, and acted like an angel whenever the parents got involved. He was a jock and well liked when she became a cheerleader, and bugged him at every event; she was annoying.

To him, she was still a pain. She was close to their parents, still lived at home, went out, and shared it all over social media. Scott felt that their parents babied her and gave her everything. In his opinion, she got everything she ever wanted and was spoiled rotten; it made him mad. But tonight he saw a different Stephanie; she didn't seem like the self-centered, spoiled brat he remembered. Tonight he saw a caring, loving person; she listened intently as he and Beckie talked about their lives.

Stephanie's heart went out to them, she hugged them, and she asked "How can I help? Really, I know that people always offer, but I really want to help you guys. What can I do?"

Stephanie meant it, and both he and Beckie could tell, but what could she or anyone else really do to help them? This evening Scott saw Stephanie's heart, she wasn't that same little brat he remembered, she had grown up, and so had he.

They talked about life throughout the evening. As he listened to her, he thought to himself, *She's amazing, so why is she still single?* Scott thought about Stephanie's past, he knew she wanted a family, always had, so why was she single?

Stephanie knew that Scott thought she was someone that she wasn't, she tried to talk to him over the years, but he wouldn't talk to her. Stephanie wanted a relationship with her brother, but without Scott wanting it, nothing happened. Scott held on to his thoughts and feelings about days long gone, and he never wanted to talk about those days or the feelings that went with them. When Scott decided to marry Beckie, Stephanie thought things would change; she thought that all the old garbage could finally be put away. With Scott having a wife, a woman in his daily life, maybe then he would see life differently; maybe he would see that family was important. She hoped that somehow she would become important to him.

Beckie and Scott wanted kids, Stephanie loved kids and hoped she would be a part of their lives, she wanted to be the best aunt. When she saw everyone at their house, she had high hopes that this was going to be a happy evening, but it wasn't. The news of their difficulties hit her hard; she felt for them and wanted to help make it better. As most young girls do, she had dreams that someday she would have a beautiful wedding, a wonderful loving marriage, and children. It was all part of her master plan; she had her life all planned out, just like her brother and his wife. They had a plan, but as she listened to their reality; she came to realize that life doesn't necessarily happen as we plan.

It Takes 3

The planning thing certainly wasn't working for them, at least when it came to babies. Beckie told them about her dreams, the one about the baby, how real it all felt, and how excited she was; it was part of the reason they started trying, and now here they were, still no baby. She was feeling devastated and pretty much defeated. Stephanie heard Beckie, and she felt her pain. She was learning that no matter how we plan our lives, God's plan for your life could be different, plans completely different than the ones we make for ourselves.

Scott and Beckie had high hopes and wonderful plans and their disappointment and pain hit Stephanie hard. She hurt for them, and she hurt for herself because she had plans and dreams of her own that didn't work out. Stephanie knew how deep the desire for children could be, children were her life's desire as well, she knew that someday it would happen, but tonight, listening to her brother and sister-in-law's reality hit her hard. A few years ago, she had been hit with a huge curve ball in her own life, and tonight she wondered if her own dream would ever become reality; she wonder if kids would ever happen for her. She wasn't in any position to have children right now, but Scott and Beckie were; they were in the perfect position. They had everything—the house, jobs, and plenty of room in their lives and hearts—yet this one thing seemed out of their reach, out of their hands. Stephanie's heart ached for them. As she listened, she found herself wanting more and more to do something to help. She loved them and would do anything to take away their sadness, to take away their pain.

14

Stephanie had a plan for her life since she was a teenager, her plan was to marry young, have two children by the age of twenty-five, and live happily ever after.

At twenty, her plan and her dreams were becoming her reality—her life was wonderful. Stephanie met a young man and fell in love. He was everything she wanted; within months, they were planning their wedding. It all happened very quickly, and she was happy. Her husband wanted everything she wanted, but he just wasn't in any hurry to have children. They agreed on a five-year plan, and although she wouldn't have two children by twenty-five, she hoped that she would at least be pregnant; she was reasonable and willing to compromise. She changed her plans, two children by thirty would be good, a slight change in plans was all, but she still had a plan.

As the years went by, she was happy, she loved her husband, they saved their money, and they began to look for a home to call their own. When they found a place they loved, they decided to make an offer, and they did. Their offer was countered, and during this process, her life took an unexpected turn.

In the realtor's office ready to sign the counteroffer, her husband suddenly backed out. "I can't do this. I need to think about all this."

It Takes 3

They had been married just over five years, and they were on the right road, ready to settle down and move forward. That day he hit her with his revelation. "I've been thinking about this. I don't think I'm ready for all of this. I want to travel, I don't want to settle down, and I don't want to have kids."

Stephanie was shocked. "You mean right now?"

"No, not ever, I don't want to be someone's father. I want to be able to just take off whenever I want." His dream was to travel the world. He didn't want to be tied down to a house, kids, or animals even—not now, not ever. He still wanted her; after all, she was hot. They argued, and he dismissed her and everything they had talked about over the years.

Stephanie was hurt; he seemed to be unfeeling and uncaring about all the promises they made to each other. Stephanie cried and yelled and even threw a few things his way, things he had given her. He had broken her, and she was devastated. She wanted him to come to his senses, she really loved him and wanted to spend the rest of her life with him, and she wanted to settle down and have a family, with him. Stephanie was devastated when he walked out, within a week she moved out of her parents home where she and Greg had been living. She needed space, she needed time alone without the peering eyes of her parents or their concern. She had her job and she had her friends, she didn't need her parents constant concern. She was depressed and within a month, she wanted to disappear, she felt worthless and broken. She tried hard to act and look strong the day her husband served her with divorce papers; he was serious: she was devastated but she took the papers, signed them and handed them back to him. If he wanted out, he was out.

Stephanie tried to move on, but it became more than she could handle alone. She disappeared from her friends, her family and she was missing more and more work. She finally called her parents. Something was terribly wrong. Stephanie denied there was anything wrong, she agreed to come over for dinner. She arrived at the house looking sad, she had lost weight, she looked tired and frail. Her Mom could tell that Stephanie had been crying, tears were still in her eyes, she was in a downward spiral.

When her mom hugged her, she nearly collapsed talking about what a failure she was and how sorry she was. They got her to the sofa and got her to talk. As her parents listened to her, they became very worried. The words she chose as she talked scared them. She kept going back to being a failure and how she couldn't do this anymore.

She kept saying, "I'm done, I can't do this anymore, I'm so sorry."

Her parents tried talking to her, but she didn't hear anything they said. She went on about her plans, her dreams and how she didn't think she would ever be a mom. "I'm going to be twenty-five, and what do I have? *Nothing*, that's what I have—absolutely nothing. I'm a nobody with nothing." She went on and on, she talked about slamming her car into a tree or a wall, driving it over some cliff or swimming in the ocean until she couldn't swim anymore. It was frightening for her parents to listen to, and they were very concerned. Her Dad sat with her while her Mom called the local hospital for some advice they suggested that she call the police department, they had officers specially trained for situations like this. The officers would come to the house and evaluate their daughter.

Within minutes there were two uniformed officers at the door, they were very nice and very comforting to Stephanie, and they spent a little more than an hour with her. They spoke to her parents and told them that it was their opinion that she was indeed in trouble, she needed help, and if she wasn't willing to get it on her own, they would need to put on what they called a 5150 (that's an involuntary psychiatric hold) for her own safety.

But Stephanie was very cooperative, her parents were allowed to take her to the hospital, she went voluntarily and was placed on a seventy-two-hour hold, still a 5150, but this was voluntary, and after seventy-two hours, they couldn't legally hold her. She ended up staying at the hospital for six weeks, she'd been diagnosed as having suffered a nervous breakdown due to the dissolution of her marriage, the feeling of loss and failure had taken a terrible toll on her.

Her parents were very proud of her for taking the necessary steps she needed to take to keep herself safe while she healed. And now here she was, listening to her brother and sister-in-law's sadness, hearing their words echoing back at her, devastated, failure, plans, loss, and many other negatives that she herself had used, but that word *failure* kept echoing in her head. That was the word she felt so much pain with; she knew this kind of thing could be life changing for him and his wife. They had no control over the end result, just like she had no control over her husband's decision. She had gone through her own devastating life-altering experience, something she had no control over but she had enough wisdom to get the help she needed. She wanted to help them do the same thing. As she listened to their pain, it brought so much of her own pain back, and she needed to do something positive, for them and for herself.

15

Stephanie felt herself getting lost in their pain, in her own pain, and she pulled back; she couldn't let herself go there, she was here for her brother, and she knew that this wasn't the place or time for her to go into her own pain. As she returned to the conversation, she listened to her brother and sister-in-law talking about giving up. Giving up? They couldn't give up. There were options, but after all this time, they wondered if they had the strength to try anything else. Could their marriage survive more failure? Despair was a black hole, and Stephanie knew it, she had fallen into that black hole, and she would do anything to keep them from falling.

As she sat there and listened, her mind was lost in finding a way, any way that she could help. Her mind raced as she thought about being their surrogate, maybe that would work, she couldn't remember why, but she thought that because they were blood brother and sister, there might be a problem.

Stephanie wanted to talk to her brother, but by this time, he was just plain tired of talking. He wanted to go home and spend some quiet time with his wife.

Beckie's sisters felt for them and offered their support in whatever road they choose to take. But Stephanie was the one who had offered to help them anyway she could.

It Takes 3

After everyone left the house, Stephanie shared her desire to help with her parents; she wanted them to help her find a way. When she left, her dad shared some concern about this desire to help her bother. He was afraid she would be hurt again.

That night was a sleepless one for Stephanie, couldn't sleep. All she kept seeing was her brother and sister-in-law's disappointment, she saw a deep dark hole with them in it. She needed to find a way to help, so she got her laptop and began searching the Internet, finally falling asleep while reading. But her mind kept racing all night long, wondering what she could do to help them achieve their dream. It was all she could think about, all she could dream about.

In her dreams, she was their angel, she helped them have a baby, she didn't know how she did it, but when she handed them a little bundle, it made her smile in her sleep and woke her up. She felt so amazing, and her brother and sister-in-law were so happy as they held the bundle, kissed her, and took photos. The light from the flash kept going off as she woke up and saw the lamppost outside her window going on and off. Back to reality and nothing had changed. She was still in her room, and her brother and sister-in-law were still without a child.

It was Saturday morning, and as soon as she woke, she grabbed her laptop, opened it up and began to research anything and everything about infertility and everything that encompassed the problem; she was committed to educating herself. This was a girl on a quest, a quest to help someone she loved, and she was committed.

But her research was not giving her anything positive when it came to a sister helping a brother. She found it was possible for sister to donate to a sister, daughter to mother, even mother to daughter. The use of family in the egg donation or sperm donation field is what the medical community calls interfamilial gametes, and although in some cases it is considered acceptable, in the case of a generic sister donating an egg or being a surrogate for a genetic brother (blood related), was prohibited. From the information she found, the medical community still considers this incest, and the facts were there: there are just too many risk of severe abnormalities to a child. Even with all the medical advances, it was prohibited.

Stephanie continued her research, even calling clinics to ask them about the possibilities. But with every call, she came up empty. Stephanie had come to the end of the line. No matter what she read or who she called, there was no way for her to help her brother. She called to tell him, but he wasn't picking up the phone. She left messages, but no return call. She wanted to talk to him. In her mind, she had made him a promise and she wanted him to know that she tried. But he wasn't getting back to her. All her hopes of them reconnecting were quickly fading away. She tried a few more times to no avail, so for her own sanity, she needed to go on with her own life.

She chalked up her brother's seemingly lack of concern for her to his stress and what he was going through, but it hurt her regardless. She didn't want to give up completely, so when she had a chance, she would check just to be sure she didn't miss anything. As time went by, she would call her brother wondering what was happening for them, but still nothing. Scott had received all of Stephanie's calls, but Beckie didn't want him to talk to her. She didn't like his sister and was very much against her helping them. In her mind, she felt his sister's offer came from some selfish place and didn't want Scott to encourage her. Stephanie seemed like a know-it-all on her messages. She used words Beckie didn't understand. Nothing Stephanie could say or do could change Beckie's mind, and Scott knew it, but he felt the same way as his wife. Instead of being upfront and talking to Stephanie, he chose to ignore her.

16

Beckie and Scott made the decision to give it a rest, at least for now. They stopped talking about babies altogether. Scott knew he should call his sister, but he didn't want to talk about any of it. He didn't want to hear what she had found out. He didn't want to hear her voice, so he continued to ignore her. He figured she would get aggravated at some point and just stop calling.

The whole thing had just become too painful, and he hated to see Beckie upset. He knew that in time they would feel better, they were both still hopeful that this would somehow just happen for them. Although they were feeling so far away from their dream, they knew deep within their hearts, they would get through this.

Time continued to pass, and neither of them brought up the baby topic, the greatest disappointment they ever had to face. They were finally finding solace in each other, they were sharing their thoughts about everything. Their love life had rekindled. They were making love again, no longer were they just having sex to make a baby. They found their love making helped them to relax and feel connected again.

Scott and Beckie had come full circle and were finally able to talk about babies again, but instead of being all consumed, their conversations were now much lighter and more about if it happened and not about making it happen. They were able to joke about being told to go home and have sex. Scott loved that prescription so much that he framed it and put it on Beckie's nightstand, and it was still there.

Beckie hated it. It was like a big sign next that spelled *failure* to her. Scott took the framed prescription and put it in a drawer; they should have done that sooner. But tonight it was all light, and they actually laughed about that a prescription because on the back, the doctor and written down the "steps" they were to follow in their effort to conceive.

> Step 1: Beckie and Scott were to avoid lubricants, as they can damage the sperm. Even saliva can slow the sperm down, so no oral sex. A water-based lubricant was prescribed if needed.
>
> Step 2: Beckie needed to learn what days she ovulates. These were usually the days about around halfway between her periods. She could also chart her temperature as well, or she could get an over-the-counter ovulation kit. Once she finds out her dates, they would move to step 3.
>
> Step 3: Beginning three days before ovulation, she and Scott should have sex, but not every day. The doctor suggested every other day.

He explained to them that fresh sperm will survive in a woman's reproductive tract for five to six days, so every other day would be more than sufficient. Every other day was good, and this should also help keep sex from becoming a chore, as well as keep Scott's sperm recharged and strong.

> Step 4: The doctor suggested that they take their time to be romantic, to work at the foreplay, have romantic dinners, and when they did make love, they should slow down and really enjoy each other.
>
> Step 5: This step could potentially help promote conception. After Scott and Beckie had intercourse, he wanted Beckie

It Takes 3

to place a pillow under her hips and lay still for about twenty minutes.

It all sounded so romantic and doable in the very beginning, and it was. They followed the doctor's instruction, and their love making was intense and passionate back then. They both felt like newlyweds all over again, and neither of them could get enough of each other.

But with daily life, work, and disappointment after disappointment, they just couldn't keep the pace. They had come to that place where this whole thing seemed more like a chore. The days of long passionate love making sessions had become another chore they needed to get done. It was overwhelming. They had always enjoyed each other in the bedroom or any other room for that matter. Neither of them wanted to lose the desire they had for each other, but they did. This had become really hard for them. Month after month disappointment after disappointment brought them to the conclusion that they needed to consider those other options. They spent an entire evening discussing the possibility that their own plans and desires for a family may need to take a different course, a different road. But they were not giving up. They were just taking a new path. Beckie just couldn't let go. She didn't like talking about options and alternatives.

Beckie had been so good through all of this, she had taken her medication on schedule exactly as prescribed, and still nothing happened. They had given up for their own sanity, but they still had hope. For now, they decided to work on their relationship, on the time they spent together, and reconnecting on a higher level. They weren't scraping the whole baby thing, but they were putting it on the back burner, for now.

Scott needed Beckie to talk to him, and finally with a lot of coaxing she did. She cried at what she saw as a failure. They held each other and talked throughout the night. Somewhere late that night, they fell into each other's arms, exhausted. Beckie gave in to her pain and sobbed into Scott's shoulder. He held her tight and caressed her hair softly. He told her how much he loved her and that their children would come. Somehow, someway, he knew it. He looked her in the eyes as he said, "Beck, my life is complete. It has been since the day you married me. I don't need anything else. Sure, kids would be nice, but as long as I have you, I have everything."

Beckie kissed Scott, as they made love, softly, slowly, and without any expectations. It was the first time in months that they made love without any thought of getting pregnant. Tonight it was just about them and their love for each other.

17

Beckie slept soundly after she and Scott made love, no dreams, no nightmares. She was completely at peace. The next morning she woke up with a smile on her face, a smile that Scott had missed. From this day on, they lived each day with each other and for each other. There wasn't a bunch of talk about babies or pregnancy. They were content with their lives, things were going well for them, and they were happy. It had taken them awhile to get to this place, but they were here. It had been some time since they had seen their families, so Beckie and Scott decided to attend a family BBQ. They knew everyone had been concerned for them, and although they talked on the phone once in a while, they hadn't seen them.

Beckie looked forward to the day, she always enjoyed a glass of wine with Scott's dad it had become a kind of tradition between the two of them. There was food everywhere. The smell of all the different food cooking in the house and the BBQ smell mixed with all the flowers blooming in the yard hit Beckie hard. Her tummy was already a bit upset, and the smells made it worse, so she passed on the wine; she just couldn't do it. Beckie passing on her father-in-law's wine was not normal, and everyone noticed, but no one said anything, at least not to Beckie. The family thought that maybe she was just sick, she had been very quiet, and she seemed to spend a lot of time in the restroom.

When Beckie was back outside with some of the family, Scott had gone in to get her some water, and his sister Stephanie followed him in. She was a little angry at the calls that he never answered, but for now, she was worried about Beckie. She didn't look well, so she asked him if she was all right.

Scott hadn't noticed what Stephanie had noticed. He knew she had a bit of an upset tummy and a headache. She wanted to take some aspirin, so he was getting her some water, but he didn't notice the trips to the bathroom, nor did he notice that Beckie wasn't drinking the wine. Stephanie's concern took him by surprise, but her next question really got him.

"*So?* Are you guys pregnant?"

Scott looked shocked at the question. "No, I wish. Why? Why would you ask that?"

"Well, Beckie always enjoys Dad's wine, but she hasn't even touched it, and she's been in the bathroom like every fifteen minutes, and she's not drinking anything. She's nauseous and has a headache, and the smell of the BBQ is bothering her. Those are all symptoms of pregnancy. I know you've been trying, so?"

Scott interrupted her and was a bit annoyed. In his mind, here she was again, Ms. Know-It-All, sticking her nose where it didn't belong. He took offense to everything she said.

"No," Scott said, "there have been no changes since last time we saw you, so please just drop it." Stephanie wasn't buying it, and she didn't drop it. "Well, something's going on with her, she doesn't look sick, and we all noticed. Are you sure she's not pregnant?"

Again Scott cut her off. This time he was angry. "Yes, I'm sure. Maybe she's just sick. Did you ever think of that?" Scott was mad, and he didn't want to talk to her any more. He stormed off and took the water out to Beckie. Scott returned feeling like an ass for going off on Stephanie; he wanted to apologize. But Stephanie told him that she was serious, she

It Takes 3

really wanted to help, but through her research, she didn't find anyway she could. She told him that she had been reading a lot about egg donation and surrogacy, that she had been spending a lot of her spare time researching ways to help them make their dreams a reality. But despite her strong desire, from all of her research, there didn't seem to be any way for her to be their helper. Scott was her blood brother, so she was not a candidate to donate eggs to them, nor could she be a surrogate. She was really heartbroken about her inability to help. She felt as if she had failed them, and it made her sad. She told him that she had found some adoption sites and some agency names in their area if they were interested. This was a very difficult conversation for Stephanie to have with her brother because they didn't really have a relationship no matter how much she wanted it. She hoped this would be her chance to change their relationship to the kind that she desired. She really wanted to be the one to help them, she wanted to be the one with some of their answers, she wanted to be their angel here on earth.

Stephanie was always willing to give others her all, she knew her brother didn't know that about her, and it hurt. She wanted their relationship to be as important to him as it was to her, she needed him to know her, and she was willing to try anything. If Beckie were her sister instead and if Scott were her brother in law, she could have been the one to help them. She could have donated her eggs to them, she could have even been a surrogate if they needed a surrogate. If only this were the case, she could have been their answer. But the facts were he was her bother, and there was no way she could be the one to help. She was afraid her relationship with Scott would never change. It would never be what she wanted and needed. She missed the relationship they had as children. They were close back then. They played together, had water fights, rode bikes, and played games. She tried to remember when that came to a stop. She tried to remember when he decided to stop being her brother. Not only did he stop acting like a brother, but it also seemed that he completely stopped caring about her at all. When did this all happen? Why did this happen?

18

Beckie didn't drink at all during the entire family BBQ, it wasn't that she couldn't, but her stomach was upset, and she didn't want to make it worse. She felt everyone looking at her; she felt the stares and heard the whispers. She knew everyone was talking about her, probably wondering if they were going to announce they were pregnant or something, just because she wasn't drinking and didn't feel well. The thought that they had the nerve to talk about her made her mad, and she wanted to leave. Everything was making her sicker. She needed to get away from the stares, the whispers, the wondering. She had cramps and had to pee consistently. Maybe she had a urinary tract infection, she felt hot, maybe she was getting the flu, or maybe she ate something bad. She had been in the bathroom every fifteen to twenty minutes it was irritating her, but she couldn't stay out, she tried, but she had to go.

Scott had disappeared, and she couldn't find him. He had left her alone, and she was angry. Finally, she found him and told him that she really didn't feel well. She wanted to go home. Scott offered her a soda water, but she just wanted to leave, so they made their excuses and left for home.

Theresa M. King

Beckie sat in the passenger seat facing the window and quietly cried. When Scott asked her what was wrong, she broke like a dam.

"Everyone was staring at me. They were all talking about us, whispering about me. I just couldn't take it any longer. I know they were talking about me being pregnant, just because I didn't feel good and didn't want to drink." Beckie was getting herself all worked up. She was so emotional that Scott pulled off the road to console her.

"Honey, no one said anything like that to me. What do you meant they were talking about you? Did you hear them?"

"No, but I heard them whispering, I could tell what they were saying, I saw them looking at me, watching me. It was awful." Beckie was not at all herself. She was so emotional. He had never seen her like this. Scott tried to reason with her, but the more he made sense, the worse she got. Scott was getting nowhere with her so he continued to drive home. All the way home, Beckie was quiet, wiping tears form her face. Scott tried to talk to her, but she wouldn't say anything for the rest of the ride home.

When they got home, Scott recommended that she try to relax. He offered to draw her a bath. He told her he would make dinner for them, but instead of being grateful, she got angry and stormed off. She nearly ran to their bedroom, slamming the door behind her. Scott stood in the hall shocked. This was not like her, Beckie didn't have temper tantrums, she was the talker in the family, and she had never stormed away from him like this, not even during an actual argument. Scott figured the stress had just gotten to her, the months and months of medications, the disappointment, and now she thought everyone was whispering behind her back. Maybe it had all just come to a head, and she needed time to calm down. She had been pretty moody lately, and that was out of character for her. She had been complaining of some other aches and pains as well. So maybe she was getting sick. Scott felt guilty for the way they had left his parents home,

It Takes 3

so he called his mom to apologize for their abrupt departure and for Beckie's moodiness.

His mom was great, she was understanding, but she was concerned about Beckie. Everyone was.

As they talked, he opened up to her about Beckie, something he rarely did with her or anyone, but he was confused and becoming exasperated at all this extreme behavior she was displaying. As much as he tried to ignore it, it wasn't getting any better, and he was concerned.

Matt thought Beckie might be sick, but he couldn't get her to go to the doctor. She told him that she was sick of doctors, sick of tests, sick of it all.

His mom's voice was low and full of concern. "Son, are you guys sure she couldn't be pregnant?" she asked innocently and out of concern for them.

As soon as he heard the word *pregnant*, Scott interrupted her, and he blew up. "Really, Mom? Really? That's exactly why we left, so Beckie was right. You guys were talking about her. She said people were whispering about her being pregnant. Really? I stuck up for you, and she was right. Don't any of you understand how hard this is for her, for us? Your looks, your whispers, those were more than she could take. It's more than I can take. Let's put all this to rest right now. *No*, we are not pregnant. I wish we were, she wishes we were, so please, everyone needs to just let it alone. Stop asking, stop assuming! I, we can't take it anymore." And with that, he hung up the phone. He was so angry, and he didn't really know why. He paced the room, grabbed a beer, and went outside to sit; he needed to sit. He needed to sit with his anger, he was angry—oh boy, was he angry. He was angry at his mom, angry at Beckie. Hell, he was angry at the world, and he was really angry at *God*. But how dare his mom? Beckie was right all along. Or was she?

19

Days went by, and Beckie was still angry, Scott was still angry, but he knew he needed to put a stop to all of this. He needed to talk to Beckie. He needed his wife, he needed to talk about his conversation with his mother, he needed to make this better, somehow, whatever this was. But when he brought up the conversation with his mom, Beckie lashed out at him again, yelling at him about being disloyal to her about stabbing her in the back. Scott wasn't understanding why she was saying those things, he was confused, he had never seen her like this. It was as if she were a completely different person, as if someone else had taken over her body. This person was not his wife. He wanted to erase all of the past months, he wanted their lives back, he wanted this crazy person to go away, he wanted his wife back, he needed to get back to normal. Their lives had been thrown into an uncontrollable spin, and he needed to make an effort to somehow put their world back on its axis. So far nothing was working. He tried talking to Beckie, but she just shut him out. He tried flowers, and he found them in the trash. What could he do?

So the next evening, he had decided to try and apologize to her, for himself, for his mom, for his family, for everything. He knew that at some point, she would have to talk to him. He gave her time to think, thinking made him angry and confused, all he

It Takes 3

wanted to do was share his feelings with her, he needed her, and he wanted her to need him. After a full day of her locking herself in their room, she finally came out, looking frail and tired. It was as if she had worn herself down. She was calm, so he asked her to go out to dinner with him, and she agreed. He figured that if he took her to dinner, she couldn't yell or run from him. In a public place, she had to listen to him. He wanted to talk to her about her moods, her outbursts, her nausea, the frequent bathroom visits, and the family BBQ. He wanted to talk about all of it. Scott was very careful not to use that P- word. He wanted her to hear him, hear the pain he was in because of her moods, anger and depression. He never used the P-word, but as he tried to get Beckie to understand and he heard his mom's words respoken, he realized that he had indeed overreacted to her just as Beckie had overreacted to him. As he spoke, he realized that all his mom did was share her concern for her daughter-in-law. During dinner, he knew he wanted to call her as soon as possible; he needed to apologize. It had taken him some time, but he finally realized that his mom's feelings were not out of line. His mom had every right to feel the way she did. Beckie had all the symptoms that would make anyone think she was pregnant.

Throughout dinner, Beckie and Scott had a comfortable conversation. They enjoyed the evening together and came to realize that the past days had been hard for both of them, and she gave him her word that she wouldn't shut him out again. It was a good night.

When they got home, Matt called his mom and apologized for his outburst. He had been very rude to her and if she were mad, he deserved it. But she wasn't. As a matter of fact, she was nothing but loving to him. She assured him that she understood, they were stressed, and she understood it. They had been going through a horribly stressful time, but she was there for them.

Scott had really opened up to her. He asked his mom for advice, if there was something he could do to try to lessen Beckie's stress.

This was the first time that Scott just talked to her. He talked about his life, his feelings. He just talked and talked and talked.

While Scott let go and just rambled, she told him to be patient with Beckie. She asked him if they were seeing her doctor anytime soon.

Scott explained that they had not seen the doctor in a while. They had put the whole baby thing on hold, but with her symptoms, he thought they should. As concerned as she was for her daughter-in-law, she was enjoying this time with her son; the open communication was like a gift. Although the conversation was pretty one sided, it made her smile. She knew this time was priceless, and she hoped it was a sign of things to come. She sat in a comfortable chair and enjoyed their conversation.

20

About a week after the BBQ, Beckie to began to wonder what was going on with her. She wondered if her mother-in-law could be right. She didn't have the flu. Something was going on with her, and she felt nauseous, irritable and bloated. She was eating odd combinations of food. Even her coworkers were questioning her odd lunches. Beckie had a turkey sandwich with pickles and horseradish on it for lunch. She didn't think much about it, she had made the sandwich at home and put a pickle on it, she wanted some mayo on it, but there wasn't any. There was, however, a packet of horseradish on the counter, so she put some on her sandwich, sparingly at first, but it was so good she put more on.

As she was squeezing the horseradish on, a coworker walked through the door, looked at the packet, and said, "You know that's horseradish, right?"

Beckie looked up, "Yea, it's good. Here, want a bite?"

"Yuck, no way. Are you pregnant or something?"

That was the moment that Beckie stopped and thought about the possibility. Deep down she had begun to wonder, but it seemed so impossible that she dismissed it as soon as it entered her mind. She didn't even mentioned it to Scott, but she wondered. It was a long day, and she was tired, but she didn't sleep well.

As she thought about it, she admitted that she was nauseous nearly every day, just a bit and mostly in the morning. By day's end, she was exhausted, and now that she thought about it, she couldn't remember the last time she had her period. She was pretty regular even after stopping all the medication, but as it seemed like a long time since her last period. She thought about everything, and became more and more suspicious about the possibility.

Beckie thought she was being silly, she was nervous to even consider this a possibility. Beckie went to work feeling pretty crappy, and she had talked to a friend at work, a woman who had been through two pregnancies. Beckie talked to her about her symptoms, and her friend told her that she had many of the same symptoms early in her pregnancies.

"Just take one of those home test, they're cheap, and what have you got to lose?"

Beckie took her advice. If the test was positive, her crazy behavior over the past weeks would make sense. With her friend's encouragement, she decided to do it. If that was positive, then she would tell Scott. If it was negative, she would keep it to herself—no harm, no foul. Just the thought that she had symptoms of pregnancy made Beckie giddy, but she tried not to get excited. It had been a long time since she stopped all the medications, her chances were pretty slim, but she had nothing to lose by taking a home test. She didn't want to stop at the store close to home; she didn't want anyone seeing her buying a pregnancy test. She felt a little silly when she took the test to the register, she felt a little like a teenager sneaking to buy the test, but she bought it, figuring she had nothing to lose. She had tried to convince herself that she had a touch of the flu or something; it had been going around the office. She paid for the test and took it home reluctantly. A home pregnancy test seemed so silly to her. She opened the box and read all the instructions, carefully. She didn't want to make any mistakes. Then she went into the bathroom with her little stick,

It Takes 3

armed and ready. As she sat down, she actually smiled, feeling a little silly. If she hadn't gotten pregnant on the medications, how could she possibly even consider that she could be pregnant now when they weren't even trying? She didn't expect anything to happen. Five minutes was all it took. As she waited, she began to wonder, *Could this be possible?* She thought about all the symptoms she had. Yes, this could be possible, highly unlikely, but possible.

The minutes ticked away ever so slowly as she waited to check the results. Finally the timer chimed, and the five minutes were up; she walked back into the bathroom filled with apprehension. As she reached the counter, her stomach flipped, and her heart pounded. Her brain knew that when she looked at that stick, it would be *negative*, but her heart was racing and hopeful as she approached the stick. Before she looked, she took a deep breath. She looked and saw a *positive* sign. She stared at the stick waiting for the result to change, she knew that couldn't be right, and that wasn't possible. She stood directly over the stick, she stood there staring at it, she couldn't stop looking it. The stick showed a very bright plus sign. In complete and utter disbelief, Beckie pulled the directions out of the trash and reread them. Maybe she had done something wrong. But the instructions were very clear and very simple: a plus sign meant she was pregnant. The front of the box showed a stick with the same sign and the words "99 percent accurate" right there in big, bold letters.

Beckie thought, *This couldn't be*. But here she was looking at a positive sign. How could this happen? After being on a combination of medications for months, after all the tests, the months of trying everything they could and still nothing had happened then, this seemed unlikely. They had completely stopped trying altogether months ago, and now she's standing in front of a positive sign on a home pregnancy test? Was this really possible?

Then she thought maybe this was just another one of her dreams, but no, that's not possible because there she was in the mirror—yep, that was her. Right there in the mirror, that was her reflection, this was real. Despite the box saying their test was 99 percent accurate, she still she didn't believe it. She thought maybe she had a defective test, so she returned to the store to buy another test. She wanted to do it again before Scott got home. Beckie read that the best time to perform the test was first thing in the morning, she had done this one in the late afternoon, so maybe the results weren't right.

At the store she actually bought two more tests, one for when she got home. She wanted to double-check the results she had already gotten, but then she wanted another test for the next morning so she could use her first morning sample. She read that a morning urine sample was the best and most accurate to use; it gave her the best chance of getting an accurate result. Beckie wanted so badly to call Scott, but she didn't want to say anything to him until she was sure, but she wanted to share this with him. Then again she didn't want to get him all excited if this was just a false alarm. When Beckie got back home with her two new pregnancy tests, she opened the box, read the instructions again. She was so unsure about that first test that she figured reading the direction again couldn't hurt. Maybe she had missed something.

As she was reading the instructions, she noticed how much her hands were shaking. She followed the directions exactly as they were written, again waiting the five long minutes but this time she stood over the test stick and watched as the white paper began to turn pink; soon the little bit of pink turned into a nice, dark *positive* sign. Beckie was in shock, she was shaking, but she still didn't let herself completely trust the results. She needed to do it in the morning using her first morning urine just as the directions said; they would be the most accurate. She thought that maybe that test would be different so she held her excitement and kept it to herself, until she was sure.

As she sat alone waiting for Scott to come home, she felt her insides well up with hopefulness, her eyes welled with tears, until she heard Scott's car pull in. Beckie ran to the kitchen where she had started dinner, and she began to chop an onion. That was her cover for the tears. She wasn't ready to tell him about her afternoon—not just yet. As she sat quietly, she realized just how excited she was about the possibility. As much as she tried to contain it, she was already completely invested in the possibility of actually being pregnant.

When Scott arrived home, she told him to get comfortable as she finished making dinner for them. After they ate they spent the evening in front of the fire watching some of their favorite television shows, it took everything she had not to say anything to him. She had decided that even if the morning results showed a positive sign, she still wouldn't say anything until her doctor confirmed the results. Beckie wanted and needed to go to bed early; she wanted to go to sleep so that the morning would come faster and so that she wouldn't be tempted any more than she was to tell Scott.

It was a night full of sleeplessness; she even read a book during the middle of the night. Sleeping was hard; she was so hyped up about what could be. The next morning couldn't come fast enough, reading made her tired, but as hard as she tried, she never really did sleep. She had a few little catnaps as she anxiously waited for morning to come. She tried to sleep as Scott showered and got ready for work. Scott woke her up not knowing that she had called in sick. Beckie usually left the house after Scott, so her being in bed when he left wasn't out of the ordinary. As she waited for Scott to leave, she grew more and more anxious.

21

As soon as she heard the garage door close, she jumped out of bed like a small child on Christmas. She had needed to pee for a while, but she held it. As soon as the coast was clear, she grabbed her third HPT (home pregnancy test), unwrapped it, sat on the toilet, and peed on it. She knew the procedure by now, and she waited five minutes; even before the five minutes were up, there it was—that same bright-pink positive symbol. This time she allowed herself to be excited as she did her happy dance, a happy scream escaped her throat, but she quickly calmed herself down and tried to hold her excitement in check. If she didn't, she would pick up the phone and call Scott. She was in utter disbelief, but she needed confirmation. She needed to call her doctor, but it was still too early, so she showered and went to the kitchen for a bite to eat. She was famished.

At 9:00 a.m., she picked up the phone and dialed her doctor's office, she asked for the nurse, she didn't want to tell the receptionist. When the nurse answered, Beckie told her everything. She was so excited that she talked really fast. The nurse could tell that she was excited and that she needed to have confirmation. Beckie told her all about the drugstore test, that she had done three of them, and all three were positive no matter what time of day she did them. She explained that she wasn't sure how accurate these HPTs were.

The nurse explained that when done properly, an HPT is pretty accurate, but because of Beckie's history, they needed to be sure. The office set her up with a lab appointment early that same afternoon. The nurse told her that they will be doing a urine and a blood test to check her hCG levels. *hCG* is an abbreviation for "human chorionic gonadotropin, the hormone that appears naturally during pregnancy. The presence of hCG helps the doctor confirm pregnancy and the age of a developing fetus. The excitement that Beckie felt was nearly more than she could stand; it was all more than she could let herself believe.

Beckie tried to keep her voice calm as she agreed to a romantic dinner with her husband. He could tell that she was feeling better when she answered the phone. It was the first time he heard her happy voice in a while, and he told her so.

"You sound good, babe?"

"I feel good, finally, after feeling so crummy this morning. I finally feel like that black cloud has lifted."

Beckie sounded great, so Scott asked, "So, you wanna go out to dinner then?"

"Yes, I would love to go out to dinner with my handsome husband. I'm going to go into the office for a little bit this afternoon, but I should be home by the time you get here." Beckie's appointment was at three so she figured she would beat Scott home by at least an hour.

Beckie sounded great, and it made Scott smile. For the first time in months, she sounded like her old self. Scott called her back a little later to see if she had a preference in restaurants, but she didn't answer her phone. He didn't know it, but she was on her way to her doctor's office. She had turned her phone off. She knew she couldn't talk to him, not without telling him about the test. Beckie had decided to tell him everything at dinner tonight, no matter what happened at the doctor's office, whether this was all real or just a false alarm. Beckie felt bad that she was keeping this from him and that she had lied to him twice today already, once about being sick this morning and then again about going in to work for a bit this afternoon. She knew that he would forgive her, she needed the time to go to this appointment, and she needed to do this alone. Beckie had been doing this for twenty-four hours now, and still Scott didn't know anything about it; she felt bad, but she felt this was the right thing to do.

When she walked into her doctor's office, she was glowing. Everyone knew why she was there, and they were all very excited and hopeful for her. The nurse gave her a cup for a urine specimen first. Beckie knew how to obtain the perfect urine specimen. When she came out and handed the nurse her specimen, it would be a little while for the results. In the meantime, the nurse weighed her and put her into a room. She took a vial of blood from Beckie and told her that the doctor would be in to see her. If this was all true, it was a moment she wanted to share with her patient.

In the room, Beckie waited impatiently for the doctor and to hear the results; it seemed like a lifetime before the doctor entered the room. Beckie could tell immediately from the look on her face that the test was positive, she wanted to jump off of the exam table, she wanted to hug the doctor, she wanted to hug everyone.

The doctor shared Beckie's joy, she was happy for them, she knew how badly they wanted this. With Beckie's history, the doctor wanted to do one more test; she wanted to do a pelvic exam on Beckie. When Beckie heard more test, she was concerned and asked her why. Why a pelvic exam? She understood the blood test, she knew that was a marker of how far along she was, but the pelvic?

The doctor explained that although the urine test was very accurate, she just wanted to confirm it. The pelvic exam would confirm her pregnancy as well. During the pelvic exam, she was looking for any uterine enlargement and softening as well as a slight-bluish color to her cervix. The bluish color of the cervix would indeed confirm a pregnancy.

Of course Beckie agreed to the test; anything to confirm the results. The doctor gave her a gown to change into. Beckie changed quickly and lay on the exam table. The doctor reentered the room and put on her gloves and warmed the speculum as she checked Beckie. Without saying a word, the doctor completed her exam quickly, removed her gloves, and wrote in Beckie's chart. "Everything looks great. By all indications, you are definitely pregnant, I would say you're about six to eight weeks along, but we'll know more when we get the beta HCG results." The doctor was thrilled for her as was the entire office staff.

As Beckie checked out, she made her next appointment. It was amazing that after trying so hard only to give up, here she was pregnant. Beckie was so excited she could hardly stand it. Her next appointment was in a week, at this next appointment they would be taking another blood test, and she would have her first ultrasound for her pregnancy. They would be taking some measurements of the fetus with the ultrasound.

Beckie couldn't wait. She finally let herself be excited. As she touched her belly, she had a tear in her eye and thought she could feel just the tiniest signs of a baby bump, but her tummy was still pretty flat, but soon there would be a baby bump. Today's appointment took a lot longer than Beckie had expected, and she was late getting home. Scott had tried to call her, but her phone was still turned off. She was so excited she didn't even think about it. As she drove home, she pictured Scott waiting for her. When she turned into their drive, she was disappointed that he wasn't standing there. Beckie had thoughts of stopping the car and running into his arms. That wasn't going to happen.

Scott was sitting in the house waiting for Beckie, and he was just beginning to get worried, he didn't expect her to be late, but he knew that sometimes she got caught up at work so he hadn't called her office yet, but he was thinking about it.

Finally he heard her car pull in the drive, and he went to meet her. He thought she would call; he was curious to hear about her day. By the time she got out of the car, he was already at her side. He took the briefcase from her and asked, "What's up? What took you so long? I was beginning to get worried. Were you stuck in a meeting or something?"

"Well," Beckie said, "let's go inside."

He could see on her face that whatever was going on in her day, it was good; she was beaming. For the first time in months, she looked truly happy. He had almost forgotten how beautiful she was when she was happy.

Scott had to tell her, "By the way, babe, you look absolutely beautiful today."

As they entered the house, Beckie couldn't wait any longer. "I have something to tell you."

"You do? What is it?" Scott was curious.

"Yes, I sure do," Beckie said. "You see this face?" Beckie said as she circled her face with her index finger. "Well, this is the face of a very happy girl."

"Yes, I can see that. You're actually beaming."

Beckie was smiling from ear to ear. She hadn't stopped smiling since she left the doctor's office. All Beckie could do was grab Matt's hand and lead him into the living room; she placed him in front of the sofa, put her hands on his shoulders, kissed his lips, and gently pushed him down. Beckie still hadn't shared her news; all she could do was smile at him. Scott was becoming anxious. He wanted to know what she was beaming about.

"What's going on?" he asked. "What are you up to?"

"Me?" Finally a word came out. "Well…" That was all she said, and she disappeared into the hallway.

It Takes 3

Scott watched her with wonder. *What is she up to?* When she returned, she had something in her hand, a piece of paper.

Scott smiled as she straddled him. He hoped she was going to seduce him right there in their living room, and he was ready. Who needed to eat? Beckie still had a smile on her face, but this smile was different; it was bigger. If that were possible, it was brighter too, as if something had her beaming from the inside out, and he wanted in on it. She kissed him again, he started caressing her, he thought she was coming on to him, but she stopped him and handed him the paper.

He didn't want the paper in his hands, he wanted her in his hands, but she wasn't letting him do anything else, so he took the paper and unfolded it. He saw the logo from a lab on the top of the paper. With some trepidation, he began to read what was on it.

"What is this?" he asked. All she could do was point, so he looked closer and saw that the paper was some kind of test results from the lab that they had frequented, the lab that her OB-GYN's office used. "You went to the Doctor? Today?" It was a question full of concern.

"Look," is all Beckie could say as she pointed to the results area of the paper this time.

"What is this for? Why were you at the doctor's?" He knew it couldn't be for anything bad; she was smiling much too much for it to be bad.

"Just look," she said. As Scott looked at the paper, he saw two different tests listed, a folic something or other and a beta HCG. He knew the beta HCG was a test they had done before. It had something to do with her hormones, but why was she having these tests? On the paper, he saw a bunch of numbers in columns, but he had no idea what he was looking at. "What is all of this? I have no idea what I'm looking at. What are these for?"

Beckie pointed to the numbers and finally words, "See that? See those numbers? Those numbers right there?" She was pointing at the HCG test. "Those are the most awesome numbers ever." Beckie was nearly dancing in his lap, Scott started to say something, but she interrupted him. "Why is that you ask? Well, let me tell you, sir."

Scott interrupted her, "Yes, I see the numbers, now stop messing around, what is this, why did you have tests done? And why didn't you tell me you had a doctor's appointment? Are you all right?" Scott was beginning to get frustrated. Why was she doing this to him?

"Well," Beckie finally said, "those numbers mean you and me, us, the two of us, we are going to be parents." Scott heard her words, he saw her excitement, but he suddenly looked lost. Beckie shook his shoulders. "Scott, you're going to be a daddy, finally. We're going to be parents. Can you believe it?" Scott's mind couldn't grasp the meaning of her words, he heard them, but they weren't processing in his mind; he couldn't believe what he thought he was hearing.

"What? What are you saying?"

Beckie stood up. "Scott, we're having a baby!"

That word hit him. "Really? You're pregnant? We're pregnant? Really?"

"Yes, I am, and I went to the doctor to confirm it."

Suddenly Scott looked serious. "You did this without me? Why, what made you?"

Beckie stopped for a moment; she had to be honest with him. "Well, I actually just found out for sure."

"What, you mean for sure?" Scott was confused.

"Well, I'm late because I was at the doctor's office, but yesterday I took a home pregnancy test, and it was positive. I didn't believe it, so I didn't say anything to you. I'm sorry, forgive me? I wanted to be sure before I said anything, and actually I took three pregnancy tests before I went to the doctor, two yesterday and one this morning, and they were all positive."

"You knew yesterday?" Scott looked confused.

It Takes 3

"Wait, let me finish, even after the third positive test, I still didn't believe it. I just didn't trust the home test, so I called the doctor. She saw me just a little while ago; that's why I'm late. I'm sorry I didn't tell you, but I needed to be sure, and it was totally worth it. She confirmed it. We are in fact pregnant, probably about eight weeks, according to these results and the exam she did on me. She says we could be a little more or a little less, but we'll know more next week. We get to have an ultrasound next week. Can you believe it? We'll actually get to see the baby, our baby." Beckie was so excited she didn't even breathe. "Oh, can you be there next week? It's Thursday at three? Oh, Scott, can you believe all this? Can you believe we're pregnant? Here we thought I had some kind of stomach bug." Beckie laughed as she remembered thinking she had the flu or something. "I guess you could say it was a bug, a little bug that's growing inside me." Beckie stood up. "Scott, we're having a baby, finally!" Beckie started to do her famous happy dance.

Scott held her by the shoulders. "Stop that," he said. "You'll hurt yourself or the baby." Beckie smiled, she knew it wouldn't hurt the baby, but she stopped, just for Scott. That evening they decided that they would order dinner in and stay home; they wanted to enjoy their news privately. They called for pizza delivery so they didn't have to leave the house. They were both so excited and relieved, as well as very grateful; neither of them could believe this was actually happening to them. That night they searched the Internet to learn what they could about the first months of pregnancy, they made a promise to each other not to tell anyone until at least after their first trimester; that was only a couple more weeks. If she was already eight weeks or so, they only needed to wait a couple more. By then they would also have the ultrasound picture, their first photo of their little one. They could share it when they told their families. They were both so excited; they knew it was going to be hard to keep this to themselves. After all, they had been through. They needed and wanted to tell someone, but who? After a lot of discussion, they decided they had to tell their parents, the grandparents-to-be; they had been through so much with them that they thought this would be some much needed happiness for all of them.

22

After a couple of days, Scott called each of their parents and set up an evening dinner date. Scott called both of their parents because Beckie didn't trust herself not to spill the beans; she knew if she heard her mom's voice, she will would cry, and she would share the news.

Easter was coming, so they told them that they wanted to do dinner to celebrate. They told them that they would be unable to attend the family Easter celebration this year because they had other plans with some of their friends. They invited both sets of parents, and although a bit unusual, it wasn't completely out of the ordinary. They had all gotten together in the past for other celebrations, so no one would suspect anything. But during Scott's conversation with his mom, she became suspicious, she was already suspicious, but the reasons he gave her for the dinner made her even more suspicious. She asked him if everything was all right. She asked Scott if something was up, but he denied there being any ulterior motive, but he was lying to her, and she saw the red flags. Scott felt bad about lying to her, especially after their last conversation. She had been right all along, but he couldn't tell her that, not yet at least. When she hung up, she told her husband about her suspicions; she told him that she had a strong feeling that Scott and Beckie might be announcing they were pregnant at dinner. Her husband thought that she was jumping to unnecessary conclusions, and he didn't want her to be disappointed if she was wrong. He thought that she was living in her own little world when it came to Scott and her hopes of being a grandma. He really didn't think things would ever change between them, even if he did have a child; he didn't think Scott would ever include his mom much in any pregnancy or even in the baby's life. Everyone knew they had been trying to get pregnant for some time now, so even if they were to announce it at the dinner, it wasn't that big of a surprise to him. He had no idea that Scott and Beckie had actually stopped trying, that they had put the whole thing on the back burner, he had no idea what a toll all of this had taken on them.

Scott's dad was very old-fashioned when it came to such things. Scott's mom felt so strongly about what was to come; she was filled with nearly uncontrollable joy and excitement. Her excitement was so overwhelming that she needed something to keep her busy for the next few days. She decided to get busy with her trusty little crochet hook, she loved to crochet, and after so many years of making things for friends and family, she couldn't wait to get started making cute baby stuff for her own grandchildren. So she quickly got busy choosing patterns and yarns. She wanted to choose something that didn't involve any specific colors or gender. After choosing a cute teddy bear pattern, she decided she wanted to make two instead, one in pink and one in blue, the variegated yarn she thought she would use was just too neutral for her grandbaby's first gift from Grandma. If they did make the announcement she was anticipating, she would be ready with a pink and a blue teddy bear. She would give both of them to the kids, since they wouldn't know the baby's sex yet. That way, either way they would have the baby's first handmade gift from her.

The day before the dinner, she had finished both of the bears and began to have second thoughts about taking them to the

It Takes 3

dinner. She wondered if the bears were a good idea, she didn't want to make either of the kids mad, and Beckie could be pretty hard on her, if she felt that she crossed some kind of invisible line of right and wrong. But after much consideration, Pam decided to take them anyway. She had taken the time to make them and although she was afraid that Beckie might take offense or think Scott had told her something, it didn't matter. Scott was her son, and even after all these years, she could still read him pretty well even over the phone lines.

The evening of the dinner was upon them. Before leaving the house, she tucked the two little bears into an oversized handbag so no one could see them. If things went the way she thought, when the time was right, she would give them to the kids, if she decided to. Scott's parents were the first to arrive at the restaurant, and Beckie's parents arrived soon after; the parents chatted comfortably among one another before the kids arrived about twenty minutes later. This was nearly a half hour after the time they set, they were usually a little late, it was expected, but tonight they were later than usual.

When they entered the restaurant, Beckie was carrying two small Easter baskets. She set one in front of each set of the parents. The baskets were wrapped in colored cellophane, and she told the moms to go ahead and open them. In each basket, there was a bit of Easter candy, a photo frame, and a small pair of shoes, baby shoes. The frame said "Grandparents" on it, and there was a little boy shoe and a little girl shoe in each basket. As Scott's Mom opened the cellophane, she saw the baby shoes and the frame immediately, and she knew what it meant, and she was very excited, so excited that she was ready to burst. She didn't even need to look any further, but she acted as if she were still looking through the basket, but right there in front of her, that frame said it all. As Scott's mom sat on pins and needles, Beckie's mom took each item out of the basket and looked at it. Nothing seemed to be registering with her, she wasn't getting it, she didn't seem to understand what the kids were trying to say, but everyone gave her time to get it. Scott's mom wanted to shout, "They're pregnant!" But this was Beckie's mom, and she thought it proper to wait for her to realize what the kids were saying, but she was taking so much time.

Before she could react, Beckie and Scott burst out, "We're pregnant."

Then her mom reacted! "Oh, now I get it. These are baby things."

It was indeed a very exciting night for all of them, everyone was thrilled, and they enjoyed the evening, toasting with water glasses in honor of Beckie's pregnancy—no wine or champagne. At the end of the evening, Beckie and Scott swore each of them to secrecy, they explained that it was still very early in the pregnancy, and they just weren't ready to share the news with the world yet. Beckie needed them to know that after all they had been through, they had to tell someone and who better to tell than the grandparents-to-be.

23

Stephanie's brother and sister-in-law were pregnant, but Stephanie had no idea; she wanted to help them but couldn't, and now they didn't need any help. After a lot of soul-searching and much consideration, Stephanie had finally come to the conclusion that although she couldn't help her brother and sister-in-law, she could in fact help another couple in a similar situation. She had spent a lot of time researching and soul-searching. She had taken everything into consideration before making her decision. She ran many different scenarios and thoughts through her head and considered each of them in great depth. She researched both egg donation and surrogacy, and once she made her decision, she felt a peace and a calm about it deep within herself. After reading all the facts and all the statistics, she decided that the surrogacy thing was not for her, but the idea of being an egg donor was something she felt she could do and feel good about. She held a gift within herself, so instead of letting her eggs flow down the drain month after month, she could donate them. She could help a couple who couldn't have children without the help of a third person, without an egg donor.

Stephanie wasn't ready for children of her own, but she was willing to help someone else, someone who was ready. Stephanie had a dream in her own heart, and someday her dream would come true, but for now, she wanted to help someone else achieve theirs. After watching her brother and sister-in-law struggle with infertility for months and months, she made her decision, and she was excited about it, but before she went any further, before she filled out any interest forms or anything, she wanted to discuss her decision with her parents. She wanted their thoughts and opinions regarding her decision, and she hoped they would support her. She had talked to them about egg donation as well as surrogacy when she was researching it for her brother, but she hadn't kept them up to date.

As she talked to them about her research, they listened to her about the journey she had been on. So far, they saw the joy it brought her; the thought that she could offer such a gift to another couple brought joy to her, and it was obvious. She had her parents' blessings, so she met with her brother and his wife as well; after all, this all started because of them, for them. She explained everything she had learned about egg donation. She shared some of the stories of people who became parents using donor eggs. Stephanie had talked to her brother before, back when she was researching ways to help them, but she never really talked to Beckie about any of it.

"I'm sorry I couldn't do this for you guys," she said as she shared her disappointment that she was unable to help them.

Beckie seemed surprised that Stephanie had even considered helping them. Beckie thanked her for wanting to help. Scott and Beckie were both impressed that she had taken so much time to learn all she could and was willing to do such a wonderful thing for someone else. Both of them were on board with her decision; after all, it was her decision, her reasons impressed them, and they were behind her 100 percent. Stephanie wanted and needed everyone's support; being an egg donor involved her family as well as herself. Although she didn't consider children conceived using her eggs as her children in any way, they would share DNA with her family. Genetically all of them would all be connected to any children born using her donated eggs, and she needed their support. It was important to her, everyone was on board, and she was ready to move forward.

Scott wanted to tell Stephanie their news, he thought she deserved to know, but Beckie had siblings too, and she didn't think it was fair to tell one and not the others, and she wasn't ready to tell everyone. Scott felt that because Stephanie was the only one who offered to help them, because she was willing to give them a part of herself in order for their dreams to come true, she deserved to know. Beckie, on the other hand, held firm in her decision. She felt that just because Stephanie offered, she didn't think it was a reason to tell; it was too soon to share their news. Although Scott didn't completely agree, it was Beckie's body and her choice; he had no say in the matter, so he went along with it.

Stephanie had her family's support, so she completed her research and began to take the necessary steps, to be one of the donors in the donor registration bank. She continued her research and read as much as she could about the entire procedure, from registration to retrieval; she learned the time frame and read any stories she could find regarding egg donation. Stephanie learned everything she could about what being a donor actually entailed, she read blogs on infertility, about egg donors, and about recipient parents as well. She checked out many different infertility clinic websites and read anything and everything she could. Stephanie followed her heart and followed through on her decision. She made phone calls to clinics with any questions she had, and she contacted women who had been donors from blogs. Stephanie got all of her questions and concerns answered before filling out the necessary interest forms online. Every clinic site had a contact information form for women interested in more information, and she filled out a few different forms online. While doing all of this, she had moments of doubts. She wondered about her feelings in the future. Would she still feel the same way she did today? Stephanie didn't want to ever regret her decision; she knew that any decisions she made would be with her forever. Her childhood dream of marriage and kids had come and gone. The years and plans she had for her life were gone. She still had time for those things, and she knew that, but with each passing month, her own eggs went unused, eggs that could in fact make someone else's dream come true. Life was so different from what she had imagined or hoped for, so different from what she had planned, she knew she couldn't change the past, but she could make her future better; she could also make someone else's future better.

So instead of allowing herself to fall into a depression about all her lost dreams, she decided to do something positive with her life. Filling out the interest forms was the first step. This was the beginning of a new life that no longer revolved around her. Stephanie was tired of feeling sorry for herself whenever things didn't go her way. She had plenty of disappointments in her life, divorced by twenty-five, dating men with commitment issues. Stephanie gave and gave, she trusted others with her heart, and they broke it, so here she was, still single, no family of her own, no kids, yet she felt stronger than she had in a very long time.

As much as she knew, she wanted all these things herself, she was confident with her decision, and she considered everything in great depth. It took her a long time to consider if being a donor was the right thing for her, and the conclusion was that it was indeed the right thing for her. She knew it in her head, and she felt it deep within her heart.

25

Stephanie felt confident that she was able to give this gift, a gift that could lead to a new little life in our world. This was something she could do, and she could do it with honor and pride in herself. This was her opportunity to do something really good with her life, and she was ready to do it. In her heart, she knew and completely understood that if her donated eggs resulted in a pregnancy and a birth for a family who wanted it so badly, then she would be happy. And there was no way she would consider the baby hers. Yes, the baby would share some DNA, but the recipient would carry the baby, her body would provide the life-sustaining forces needed to produce a baby, the receipient mom would be the baby's mom.

Stephanie considered her eggs a gift; she believed that when a gift is given, you expect nothing in return. A gift is or should be given from the heart, with no expectations to receive anything in exchange. Stephanie knew that her gift of egg donation would only give a family a chance and only if everything went well, would a family receive the gift of life, and that made her happy, just to think that she could provide something like that, that she could possibly be the one to help someone achieve their greatest desire in life. Whenever she thought about it, Stephanie could see a couple the moment they found out that after years of trying, and years of failure, they're finally pregnant. It all happens because of her decision to be an egg donor. Stephanie thought about the moment when the recipient parents would get to hold their little miracle in their arms, a life that would not have been possible without the gift of her donated eggs. Thinking about moments like this left her feeling happy and content and ready to help. Stephanie hoped that she would be successful in providing some hope to a couple. As she thought about the possibility of this happening, it brought a smile to her face and a warmth to her heart; this was something Stephanie was becoming more and more excited about. She thought about possible ramifications that could possibly come up, and despite any of them, she was ready, but before moving on, she thought about it all again, considering everything for a second time. She took her time; after spending all the time she did on the research and all the soul-searching she did, she filled out the application.

The Internet had become her new obsession; whenever she found new information, it led her into an entirely new direction. She read medical journals, blogs, websites, anything she could; she had never read so much in her life, and she liked it. Stephanie continued to talk to family and friends about her findings, her decision, and her conclusion that she was doing this. So many people referred to the child as hers, or as her biological child or genetic child, something like that. She tried to explain that if a recipient couple was successful, the baby was theirs; it wasn't hers at all. She got into some pretty heated debates. She knew she needed some way to explain how she felt about it without using the word *baby*; as soon as the *baby* word came up, it always brought with it questions or statements that the baby was in some way her child, and it wasn't, not in her mind.

Stephanie felt that if a baby, which was the desired result, was born using her egg donation, in her mind and heart, she had only provided one of the ingredients used to make that baby possible. If a child resulted with all the proper ingredients coming together,

It Takes 3

that child belonged to its parents—the two individuals who worked hard to make the baby happen. She tried to make it clear that a baby could not exist without the recipient father's sperm, the recipient mother's uterus as well as her egg, but her egg was only one of the ingredients. If any one of these ingredients were missing, there was no child, which was why she was donating; the eggs were missing. Stephanie wanted everyone to know that she was just providing one of the necessary ingredients; she tried to explain that she believed that her contribution was much like a cup of sugar or an egg to complete a cake. She needed a simple way to explain it all, a way for other people to understand how she felt about donating her eggs, and this is what she came up with. "If my neighbor came to my door needing an egg to make a cake, if I had one, I would give it to her. I wouldn't think about it. Without the egg, they couldn't make a cake—no egg, no cake. Just because I gave them an egg, I don't expect to get the cake. It's for them, probably for some celebration or something; it's not mine. I wouldn't even expect a piece of the cake; it's theirs. I wouldn't expect them to return an egg to me either, but someday I may need to borrow an egg, and I hope one of my neighbors will give one to me."

Whenever she would use this analogy, people seemed to get it. With this one statement, people understood, they got it, and Stephanie usually did not have to defend herself or her decision. With these words, they understood exactly what she meant and how she felt—no egg, no cake. It was as simple as that. This one statement stopped a lot of controversial conversations, which made Stephanie happy. Her decision was made, and now the process begins. Stephanie had filled out her first application; all that was left was to wait for someone to contact her.

26

A mother's intuition is an amazing thing; two children who first met in kindergarten, who grew up, grew apart and then found each other again. These two kids had known each other for many years, but this year, they were different somehow.

Matt felt drawn toward Summer, a draw he couldn't explain. He found himself making every effort he could to see her as often as he could, before classes, between and after classes. He told a friend that he felt like a stalker. Summer noticed that she saw him more often. Every time she met his glance, she blushed. The glances became smiles and then a quick "hello," "how you doin'?" and then finely short conversations.

One Friday afternoon, Matt asked her to the next school dance. Summer was thrilled, and accepted right away; she was afraid if she didn't, he would ask someone else. What she didn't know was that Matt was just as excited and had no intentions of asking anyone else out. He knew how the other guys were talking about her since they had returned from summer vacation, and he wasn't taking any chances. Summer was so excited that when she got home, she told her mom, who was excited for her daughter. Summer had never really been interested in boys. She was focused on her studies and her cheerleading. Summer wasn't one of those boy-crazy girls, and she didn't seem interested in

It Takes 3

dating, until now. All of a sudden she was talking about a boy nonstop. The boy's name was Matt, and her mom wondered if he was the same Matt they had known since kindergarten.

Summer and her mom went shopping for a dress to wear to the dance. It was an informal dance, but Summer wanted to look her best. Her mom was excited to share this experience with her daughter; after all, a first date only happens once. After a long day of shopping, Summer found the perfect dress and the perfect shoes. The following Friday after school, Summer had an appointment for her first set of acrylic nails and her first pedicure. This wasn't just an exciting time for Matt and Summer; it was exciting for their parents as well. Matt was in fact the boy from kindergarten so Summer's parents knew who he was. Over the years, they had heard his name from time to time. Summer talked about him, his reputation, his accomplishments, and his popularity. He was a football player, and he was a really good one; he was often in the local paper, so they knew who he was. But recently they noticed that their little girl had been bringing up his name more and more; she had a crush on Matt on and off ever since kindergarten, but it seemed as if their little girl's crush was becoming more.

The following week, Matt joined Summer for lunch as often as he could. He loved looking at her from across the table and was very excited about their upcoming evening together. The morning of the dance, Summer woke up excited to get through the day; although she knew she would see Matt at school, she couldn't wait till she saw him in the evening. The dance began at 7:30 p.m., so Matt told her that he would pick her up at 6:00 p.m.

He wanted to make a good impression on her parents. He wanted to be relaxed and have time to sit and talk to them a bit. He asked his dad for advice on what to do, and he took his dad's words to heart. Matt didn't want to rush anything about the night, beginning with picking her up. There would be snack-type food at the dance, so they both decided to eat dinner with their families beforehand.

Matt was excited to see Summer all dressed up, he knew she would be beautiful, and she was excited to see him as well. Matt was nervous when he rang the doorbell as he stood and waited for it to open; he could feel his heart race when he heard the doorknob turn. There on the other side of the door was a familiar face; it was Summer's mom. Matt remembered her through the years, and she hugged him and escorted him to the living room where Summer's father stood and extended his hand to Matt.

Matt felt the nerves again as he met this man for the first time. After years in the same school, Matt had never met Summer's dad. Matt and Summer's Dad talked about school, college, and sports. Summer's mom went upstairs to get Summer and make sure that everything was perfect. Summer was sitting on her bed all dressed and ready to go. She wanted to answer the door, but her mom told her that made her look too anxious. Her mom was still old-fashioned, and she wanted her to make an entrance. She came to tell Summer that it was time.

Mom went downstairs to get her camera. She told Summer to give her a minute or two before coming down the stairs. This entrance thing was pretty silly, but she did it. After all, this was important to her parents. Summer watched from upstairs as her mom returned to the living room, and Summer began to descend down the stairs slowly—head up, hand on rail. Matt knew Summer would be beautiful, but when he saw her floating down the stairs, his jaw fell to the floor. She had told him she would be wearing a light-pastel coral dress so he could coordinate with her if he waned to.

Matt did, and he coordinated perfectly, so did the flowers he got for her. Matt put his ensemble together with the skill of Tim Gunn, the fashion guru. Matt's parents took a few snapshots before he left the house, but they wanted to take more. They asked him if he could bring his date back for more photos; he

It Takes 3

never answered them. As soon as he got to Summer's house, her mom was snapping photos like the paparazzi; it made Matt smile. The night had started out really well. Before he left his house, his dad offered "his baby" to Matt. "His baby" was his dad's beloved Lexus. This was the car that Matt had only driven once, and that was with his father. Letting Matt take the car for the night was a surprise, but allowing him to drive it all alone made Matt feel pretty darn grown up.

Summer's dad sat and talked to Matt about everything from curfew to speeding to drinking and driving, most things parents talk to kids about before a first date. Matt promised that he would obey all the laws, the rules, and the curfew. After all the photos and all the talking were done, Matt escorted Summer to the car where he had placed her corsage on the seat next to him, he wanted to take it into the house, but he forgot it. He opened Summer's door and felt like a man; he had a feeling that he was opening the door to his future. Summer saw the flowers on the seat as Matt reached into the car and got the box and handed it to her. "Open it."

Summer opened the box, and Matt took the flower out and proceeded to pin it to her dress. Matt was gentle, afraid of sticking her with the pin, but he got it on. Neither Matt nor Summer realized that Summer's mom and dad were on the porch taking photos of the moment with their zoom lens. When Matt leaned and kissed Summer on the cheek, they heard a quiet "awwww" sound coming from the house. When they turned, the embarrassed parents just waved and blew kisses. Summer was embarrassed as she tried to sit in the car like a lady. Matt closed the door gently after making sure Summer and her dress were completely in the car.

Matt walked around the front as he waved back at her parents still standing on the porch. Summer was embarrassed by her parents spying, but she soon forgot about it as she was lost in Matt's kindness and the way he smiled at her as he walked to his side of the car and jumped behind the wheel. Summer felt herself begin to relax as they pulled away, on their way to the dance and out of her parents' watchful eyes. Summer tried to apologize for her parents, but Matt thought they were cute, and she told him that the stairwell entrance was her mom's idea. But at least her Dad didn't answer the door polishing a gun, maybe it was good he didn't own one. Her dad thought it was better to be in the living room waiting for "the boy" as he called Matt.

Matt listened to Summer talk about her parents. He thought they were cute, and then he asked if she would mind stopping back at his house. His mom had asked if they could come by and take a few photos. He told her that he was afraid to ask. He was going to call his parents and tell them they wouldn't make it. But the evening had been so perfect. He didn't want to disappoint his mom. Summer was fine with the idea. It warmed her heart to hear him so loving to his parents, to put his parents' wishes ahead of his own.

When Matt and Summer arrived at the house, his parents were very welcoming. They enjoyed talking to the kids and taking photos. Matt's dad wanted a photo of himself with the lovely Summer, as he called her. So many pictures were taken between the two houses, and they hadn't even gotten to the dance yet. Each of their parents gave them money to have portraits taken at the dance, as a memory of the night. This dating thing was new to all of them, and who knew what might happen? This was a huge milestone, the kids thought their parents were being a bit over the top, but first only comes once in a lifetime. No matter what the future holds for these two, this night would be frozen forever in photos.

When Matt and Summer got to the dance they saw some friends, found their table, and took a minute to relax, kind of. Their school put on an amazing dance, with an old Hollywood theme complete with red carpet. The night was fun for both of them; being there together made them the talk of the evening.

It Takes 3

It was at this dance that they shared their first slow dance. They nervously took each other's hands. Matt put his arm around her waist and pulled her close to him as they swayed to the music.

Summer moved her arms around Matt's neck. Matt's arms wrapped farther around her waist. Summer loved the feeling of his arms around her. She buried her face into his neck, breathing in the smell of his cologne. Matt rested his cheek on her head, taking in the scent of her herbal essence shampoo. Both enjoyed being in each other's arms as they danced.

During the last dance of the evening, Matt held Summer again as he told her how much he enjoyed being with her. As the last song came to an end, Matt looked deep into her eyes and said, "I so wanna kiss you right now."

Summer smiled and whispered, "The chaperones will see."

Matt leaned in and softly kissed her lips. Summer felt a shock of electricity throughout her entire body and didn't want to stop, but they were at a school dance and public displays of affection (PDA) were frowned upon, so they had to play it cool. When the evening officially ended, they walked back to Matt's car and stood at the door. As Matt reached for the handle, Summer leaned in for another kiss, but just a quick one before getting into the car. Matt walked to his side and scooted behind the wheel, but before starting the car, he turned to her with a big smile. "Thank you for such a wonderful evening, Summer. I had a great time. So, can we do this again?"

Summer leaned in for a hug, and they kissed again. This time there were no eyes watching them, no parents, no teachers, no one; it was just the two of them. That kiss led to another, and soon they found themselves entwined with each other. Not wanting to stop, they were lost in the passion for each other. Neither of them wanted the evening to end, but they promised to be home by midnight. They met some friends at the local Denny's for a snack at 11:00 pm It was now 11:30 pm, time was getting away from them. After some quick conversations, it was time to say good-bye. They had just enough time to make it home before curfew. Matt drove Summer home and walked her to the door. It was 11:50 pm They were on time and noticed the curtains in the living room part as they walked up the sidewalk. Both of them smiled knowing that her parents were checking on them and probably watching them. It was funny for some reason their spying didn't make either of them mad; they actually thought it was cute.

 Matt kissed Summer good night despite the spying eyes. This kiss was a sweet one, not the same passionate kiss they shared on the dance floor or the ones they shared in the car. This was a kiss for the parents. Matt hugged her and whispered, "Your parents are watching, us." Summer smiled and Matt asked, "Meet me in the quad early tomorrow?"

27

Summer met Matt in the quad, and from then on they were a couple. They became a steady and very committed couple. By the time the yearbook went to press, they were the couple of the year. They were named "most likely to get married" by their classmates. The love they had for each other was apparent to everyone, including their parents. This was no high school crush. They were excellent students, enjoyed being active as well as the work they did in their community.

Both of them were accepted to their first choice colleges. Unfortunately, the schools were states away from each other. Their love for each other continued to grow through the years; they talked about their future, being so far from each other. It was going to be hard, and they were honest about just how hard it would be. They had talked that it would only be four years, but suddenly four years sounded like an eternity. After a wonderful summer, it was time to say good-bye, time to move forward without each other. It was heart wrenching for both of them. Matt was headed to the East Coast. Summer would be going to a school in the Midwest. They promised to talk every day. They could Skype or Face time too. At school, each of them settled in to their new routines. They continued to talk every day and every night. Summer missed her home, her parents, and her friends, but most of all, she missed Matt. She missed his hugs, she missed his strong arms holding her, and she missed his kiss. The days moved on, and they were both doing well. They had friends, enjoyed their studies and classes, but they missed each other desperately. They were planning their future despite their long-distance relationship, they wanted to be with each other, but school took priority for now. They saw each other as often as possible on school breaks, long weekends, and vacations. Time together was rare, and it became even more precious to them. Each separation became harder and harder as they grew closer and closer.

Summer had fought depression since her move, and with every good-bye, the time she spent in a state of depression became longer and harder. The long-distance relationship was taking a bigger toll on her than anyone ever thought it would. The first year felt like an eternity, and she couldn't stand being so far from Matt. By the end of the year, she knew it was just too much, so she decided to change her career path. She had been going to school to get her finance degree, but that needed to change. Being so far from the one she loved had just been much too difficult for her. During their first summer vacation, Matt and Summer talked about the previous year. Summer told Matt that she didn't want to return to college the following September; she had made a decision and was standing by it.

Summer's decision concerned Matt, but before any final plans were made, they took advantage of summer vacation. Together they took a road trip to spend some time together with no distractions. During their vacation, they talked about their future, and they talked about school. Summer was unhappy not only with the distance between them, but she found that college life wasn't for her. Summer wanted to go to cosmetology school, she loved the time she had spent at the spa, and college seemed like a long road when studying something she wasn't really interested in.

It Takes 3

"There's a great cosmetology school near your school," she told Matt. Matt missed Summer just as much, and he wanted her closer to him as well.

"I would love to be closer to you. What are you thinking?" Matt was curious.

"Well, you know that I loved the whole spa experience. I think I'd like to go to cosmetology school, become a hairdresser, there's good money in it, and it's something I can always do. Someday when we have kids, I can work around their schedules. It gives me a lot of flexibility."

"You've been thinking about this, haven't you?" Summer had everything figured out, and Matt wasn't surprised. Summer was always planning ahead. Although she would be quitting college, she had applied to a Cosmetology School near Matt. Matt was ecstatic with her decision and couldn't wait to have her with him. It was his idea that they get an apartment together, they could combine their small incomes, and have a place of their own.

Matt and Summer had it all planned out, but they still needed to talk to their parents, especially Summer's. It would be hard, but they had to do it. The parents all listened to them, and although they thought a transfer would be good, Summer dropping out didn't go over well. Summer explained her plans, she had a good plan, and her reasons made sense. Summer decided to also get a bachelors degree in business. A business degree would help her after she completed cosmetology school and worked for herself. Her parents were impressed with her plans, but not about their choice to live together. They were afraid that Matt and Summer's shacking up, as they called it, would interfere with their studies and keep them distracted. Matt's parents were afraid Matt would lose focus and drop out, and what if Summer got pregnant? What then? Matt and Summer understood how their parents felt, although it was an obstacle, they could work around it. Neither of them thought they would get their full blessing but hoped for their understanding. They had agreed that regardless how the parents reacted, they were still willing to do what was best for them.

Excited about being together and getting their first apartment together, they looked until they found the perfect one, good price, good space, and close to both of their schools. Matt and Summer were ready to begin a new chapter of their lives together.

As each year passed, they both enjoyed school and life. Matt worked part-time at the local hospital, and Summer found work at the local salon. Their jobs were close and easy to get to, their schedules were flexible, and their bosses were understanding. Matt loved his work at the hospital; his patients were important to him, especially the children. He often went into work a little early or stayed a little late just to visit with the kids; whenever he could, he tried to make a child's hospital stay a bit brighter by brining them a special book or toy. Matt loved to see a smile on a sick child's face. They brightened his day as much as he did theirs. No matter how sick the kids were, they always had a smile for him. Caring for others was a characteristic they both shared, and they spent some of their spare time together sharing their love with others.

Matt and Summer had everything going for them, even their parents finally got on board and supported them. They still didn't agree with their decision, but they supported them in it. Moving in together had proved to be a good thing for both of them. They both excelled in their studies and were getting closer to graduation. Matt's graduation was first. It would be just two days before Summer's. Both of their parents would be staying in town to attend each graduation.

28

Ever since high school, the kids had talked about their future, their careers, and marriage; they talked about everything. After nearly six years together, their love had grown more and more every year. Matt knew this woman was his life. She was the one he wanted to spend every day with, have children with, grow old with. She was the love of his life.

Summer felt the same about Matt, he was the only man she wanted, he was strong and safe, and he made her happy. Matt wanted to do something special for Sumer for graduation; after all, she was graduating from college with a BA in business as well as completing her cosmetology license. He wanted to do something really special. Surprising Summer was always a tough thing to do, but he was working on it. He had been working on it for months now and couldn't wait for graduation.

Matt and Summer enjoyed spending time with their families. They shared their favorite restaurants, sights, and friends with them. During one of their dinners, Summer's mom took the opportunity to bring up their future. After three years of living together, there wasn't a ring on her daughter's finger. She knew they lived as if they were married. Although she liked Matt, she was still not comfortable with the living arrangements.

Theresa M. King

Matt's graduation was perfect, from the weather to the speeches; it was a great day. Matt's parents, Summer, and her parents were all there as he received his degree. Matt graduated with honors and was recognized for his achievements during his football career. Matt had been scouted but was never drafted, which was fine with him. He was ready to begin his work with special-needs children. The evening ended, and everyone made plans for Summer's graduation the following day. As everyone arrived at Summer's school, taking photos, Matt's dad remembered and talked about that first night, the night of their first dance back so many years ago. He talked about the photo he had his wife take of him with the kids. He talked about how even back then he knew that Summer was a special young lady he just didn't realize how special. Matt's dad had a feeling from the very beginning that this new relationship between his son and this young lady was special, that this girl was special. Summer was good to him, she always let him talk about things that interested him, and she listened to him as if she cared.

After spending some time with her guests and taking photos, it was time for her to join her class in the gathering area for their processional. It was finally time for her to take that long-awaited walk across the stage, to receive a well-deserved diploma. As each graduate's name was called, friends and family yelled, catcalled, and applauded.

Finally they called Summer's name. As she began to take her first step, she looked up and noticed Matt standing on stage next to the school's chancellor. The sight of him confused her, but she continued to walk and receive her diploma. Their parents were taking photos near the stage. Not one of them were in the seats she had left them in. Seeing them made her smile, they had done this at Matt's graduation as well, but why was Matt on stage? Confused, she looked forward, and Matt was still there. As she turned from looking at the parents, she saw Matt dropping to one knee. When she reached him, he extended his hand to her. The

It Takes 3

stadium was alive with cheers. Summer stood in front of Matt and the chancellor with a look of shock as he opened a box and held it out toward her.

The chancellor put the microphone near him as he spoke the words, "Summer, you have been on a journey that has come to an end, a journey that has brought you to this day. Summer, I am here on my knee to ask if you would take the first step in a brand-new journey, one that will take us a lifetime to complete. Summer, I am asking, will you marry me?" Summer heard each of Matt's words as she stared at a box that held the most amazing ring she had ever seen. The ring was perfect; it sparkled brilliantly under all the stage lights. Summer thought of all the planning that Matt must have done to make this moment happen. Matt's words were well thought out and so well planned. How long had he been planning this? When did he find the time to buy the ring? Where did he get the money? He must have been saving every penny he could for a long time, because it was incredible. So many thoughts, so many feelings going through her all at once. She was surprised, happy, excited, and overjoyed. She was smiling, laughing, and crying. She had so much to say, yet she couldn't speak.

Summer was shaking all over as she offered Matt her hand. Matt smiled at the sight of Summer being overwhelmed and speechless. He had never seen her like this, and it made him smile. Watching her unable to get a word out made him love her even more. Summer tried to speak again, and still no sound came out, so she just shook her head vigorously in an up-and-down motion. The entire stadium burst into a roar. Summer continued moving her lips, trying to say yes, until finally, "Yes yes, yes" came out of her as she smiled and laughed through the tears. Matt stood as she grabbed him into her arms, hugging and kissing him with no regard to the crowd watching them. When they parted, the chancellor smiled, congratulated them, and handed her, diploma.

Matt and Summer continued across the stage arm in arm. As they reached the stairs, Matt raised their clasped hands into the air, signifying victory. He had done it, and he was happy. The crowd reciprocated with cheers, whistles, and applause.

Both sets of parents were waiting for them at the other end of the stage. Each of them was crying. This had been a surprise for them as well.

Matt's dad hugged Summer and said, "What took him so long? I knew you were the one from the beginning. Us old guys know the good ones, you know." Summer's dad shook Matt's hand and hugged him. "Good job, son, you did good. It's about time."

This day took a lot of work on his part. He had to get the school's permission first, and then he had to get the chancellor to approve it. Matt had talked to his parents about his decision. He met with Summer's parents to ask both of them for their daughter's hand in marriage, but he didn't tell them when or how he was planning to ask her.

As the family got a good look at the ring, they all approved. It was beautiful and a perfect choice for Summer. Unknown to any of them, Matt had some of his fellow students in the film department catch it all on film. He wanted to surprise everyone with the edited version. He planned to play the video at their wedding as long as she said yes.

After the newly engaged couple worked their way through the crowds, they received congratulations and well-wishes. After everything was done, they were on their way to a luncheon that had been planned. After all the nerves and excitement of the day, they were all really hungry and ate well, enjoying the meal with a nice wine as they all toasted to their future. Everyone chatted about future plans. Since no one knew, the parents wanted to throw them an engagement party. Matt and Summer didn't really want all that. They felt that things like that were for self-centered people and really silly if they were going to have a large wedding. But their parents wanted to do it. Summer was an only child, and this seemed really important to them. So they decided to allow the parents to do it. Matt and Summer knew their moms loved this kind of thing, so it would be perfect. Matt and Summer still needed to pick a wedding date before any further plans could be made. They wanted to have save-the-date cards printed and ready for the party. The engagement party needed to take place, before everyone found out in other ways. These days news got around fast with today's social networking, things like Facebook, Twitter, and other social media.

Matt and Summer had discussed wedding dates before, so they didn't think that would take long. They promised that as soon as they agreed on a date, they would call the moms so they could get the cards ordered.

29

Matt and Summer chose a wedding date eighteen months in the future, which gave them a year and a half, plenty of time to settle into their postgraduation lives as well as plenty of time to plan this day without a lot of stress and time constraints. They both wanted to have plenty of time to share every step, every detail, and to enjoy the whole process. They were both looking forward to planning their wedding, a day to share with all of their family and friends. They wanted everyone they loved to be there. Both moms got everything in order, and the engagement party was planned and set. The engagement party was for immediate family and very close friends only.

Matt's mom and dad had set up their home for a lovely night of appetizers, champagne toast, and a nice sit-down dinner served by Matt and Summer's favorite restaurant. For dessert, they had a fun engagement cake made, complete with a photo of Matt and Summer from the proposal. The night was fun and light, full of toasts and stories about everyone, from Matt and Summer, their parents, and their grandparents. It was all in all a lovely evening, spent with very special people who loved them and wished them well.

Both Matt and Summer received a lot of advices on this night, everything from things to do for the wedding, to how to pace themselves on their honeymoon. The evening flew by, and at the end of the night, Matt and Summer were exhausted. As they sat at home, they realized that this was the beginning of the next eighteen months of their lives, and they knew it would go by fast. Relaxing and thinking about the months to come, Summer pulled out a note pad and pen and started with one of her famous lists of things to do.

While Summer made her list, Matt wrote things on a list of his own, a list of things that he wanted to be sure he didn't forget. First thing on Summer's wedding list was to book the venue they both wanted. They wanted to marry in a quaint club house that they both loved, it was on a lake, and it was beautiful. They both hoped it would be available on their chosen date.

The next day, Matt made the call and crossed off the venue. It was first thing done, deposit made, date set up.

The next thing on Summer's list was shopping for her dress. She was very excited about this. Shopping for a wedding dress had been something that she had dreamed about for many years, and finally she was going to do it. She asked both of the moms to go with her, she had decided not to have anyone else come with them, she wanted this to be a special day for the three of them. Summer's mom was fine with it, she had never seen this as a day for just her and her daughter, and she always assumed that Summer would have her wedding party as well.

Having just the moms with her was special. The three women had lunch plans, and then it was off to the many dress shops. Summer still didn't know who her maid of honor would be, she really wanted it to be her mom, but she knew that wouldn't really be fair; as the mother of the bride, she had enough to do already. Summer needed to put some thought into who she wanted to stand next to her, someone who would provide the assistance she might need, someone who was in a position to do all of this.

Summer didn't want to go into the specialty stores in LA, they were expensive, and she had a budget. She didn't want to spend too much money on a dress she would only be wearing a few hours. Her dad told her to just worry about finding her dream dress first. Then they would figure out the money. Summer wasn't into the big designers. She didn't even know any of them by name or design. She heard names like Vera Wang, Maggie Sottero, Kenneth Pool, or Lazaro. But she had no idea why they were so popular or why they were worth the prices. But she was about to find out. Summer began to search the Internet to get an idea of what she liked. As a child, she dreamed of being a princess at her wedding, but as she looked at the different styles, she found that she actually liked many different styles. Looking at all the styles available was getting confusing, so Summer printed out some of her favorites, and it was off to the boutiques.

Summer wanted to show the consultant what she liked, what she had printed out. The first store she choose to start with was a little local boutique. Her first dress was a big princess ball gown, with sleeves and a high neck. It resembled her mom's, the one that she played dress up in years ago, but it was too matronly. Summer wouldn't even walk out of the dressing room in it; it wasn't her dress.

The next dress was chosen by the consultant for her, and it was her mom's favorite pick so far. This dress hugged her body perfectly in all the right places, not too tight, not too loose. It was perfect with its beautiful lace and well-placed rhinestones. Summer felt beautiful, she looked beautiful, everyone thought so. Even other brides in the shop commented on how beautiful she looked.

As Summer stood in front of the mirror, the consultant placed the perfect veil on her head. The veil made the dress even more beautiful. It finished it to perfection. The lace trim around the veil lay perfectly around her face as well as the hem of the dress. Tears came to both mothers' eyes as well as Summer's. She was a vision, and it was perfect. This was the first place they had looked, but there was no need to look any further. Summer didn't need to try

It Takes 3

on anything else, she knew this was her dress, and it was perfect. Not only did it look perfect, but it was also within her budget even with the veil and other accessories so they bought it, right there. The dress was hers, and it was ordered.

Summer's mom wasn't sure if they should purchase it. She was concerned that it may be too soon. What if she found something else? Summer assured her mom that she was done, this was her dress, and the consultant explained like a husband, when you find the right one, you stop looking."

With all the fittings involved and the shipping of a dress, this was a good time frame. If anything were to go wrong, they had plenty of time to get it right. Dresses had to be shipped from the design houses, leaving a possible problem with it getting lost or damaged—you just never know—so having this kind of time would keep everyone's anxiety level to a minimum.

The dress shopping went so well that the ladies went to a really nice place for lunch and talked about other wedding plans. They also talked about Summer and Matt's future regarding family and careers, but mostly family, kids to be exact. How many and how soon would they start trying? After all, they had been together for years, and they weren't getting any younger. They shared laughter and secrets only women can share. It was a nice day for all of them. Summer made Matt's mom feel like the other mother of the bride, not just the groom's mother. Summer had fun with both of the moms. As she listened to them talk, she sat back and wondered about her own life, the one that was yet to come.

Both of the moms were nearing sixty, and she wondered if she would be as young looking if she were their age. She thought that her mom seemed younger now than fifteen to twenty years ago. It was odd. Was it her mom who had changed so much, or was it she herself? Summer's mom carried herself with so much confidence, and she seemed more outgoing than back when Summer was a teenager; it was weird.

Theresa M. King

When Summer was younger, she wanted to be the hip and cool mom when she had kids of her own, the one who understood everything her kids were going through. She wanted to let her kids do all the things that her parents wouldn't let her do, go to parties, stay out past 10:00 pm, drive wherever they wanted. She thought that was what she would have wanted.

But now in her late twenties, she had different thoughts. Now she wanted to be more like her parents, the whole strict-parent thing seemed to work for her and for Matt. His parents were even more strict with him than hers were with her. She wanted her kids to grow up just like she and Matt had, grateful for the things they had, grateful for the people in their lives, respectful of others with a caring and giving spirit. They were brought up to not want everything they saw, they were hardworking and responsible even as teenagers, and that's what she wanted for her own kids.

Although when she was young she envied the kids whose parents let them have and do any and everything they wanted, paying for everything for them, she had seen the end result of the kids brought up like that, and most of them had become adults that felt entitled. Some of them were lost in the world of drug and alcohol abuse, and others had lost their lives from drug overdoses or alcohol-related accidents. Not all of the kids were the spoiled ones, but too many for her to count. She was grateful to her parents for how they raised her, they were strict, but she knew that they loved her, and she now understood where their strictness came from.

She was now at a point in her life that she could hear their stories and the trials they went through. She could listen to their history about drugs in the '70s and the friends they lost. She could hear about family who had died and the stories about heart disease, diabetes, cancer, and those who died of accidents or even suicide. As she listened to the stories of how they became the adults they were, she saw each of them in a whole different light. Her parents had become more like friends to her over the

It Takes 3

past few years, and she loved this new depth to their relationship. During the next few months, some days seemed to fly right by, while other days seemed to drag on like time were standing still; it was all very exhausting.

Both Summer and Matt were enjoying the whole planning process. Matt was especially enjoying the food tasting that they were able to enjoy while they picked a caterer. They enjoyed a few full meals provided by caterers that were trying to impress them with their choices. Summer and Matt made these "business" meetings into minidates; they knew that the decisions they were making were special for them as well as for their family and friends. They wanted to enjoy the meal being served, but more importantly, they wanted their guests to enjoy it as well. They didn't want to have some superfancy menu full of food that no one could pronounce let alone enjoy; they were happy with a simple home-cooked kind of menu, which brought them back to the little local restaurant that they loved so much.

This was just a small family restaurant that was close to their home, and this was the place that they frequented. Okay, they were there nearly every day. They knew the owner and all of the staff. They had planned on inviting the owner and some of the staff to the wedding, they didn't want them to work it, but so far, all the caterers were too foo foo for them and ridiculously expensive.

So they called Debbie, the owner of Country Harvest, and asked her about meeting with her to talk about the wedding. Debbie was very excited to cater Matt and Summer's wedding. She knew just what to offer them. Although they knew her menu by heart, she scheduled a tasting of some other items she did for events. She looked forward to sharing this time with them. Matt and Summer laughed at her scheduling an actual tasting, because they knew her entire menu so well, but she didn't tell them she had a surprise for them. Debbie made an amazing presentation for Matt, Summer, and their parents. She went out of her way to make their choices tasty and a little different from what she served in the restaurant.

Matt and Summer chose a meat, chicken, and pasta dish that was out of this world. Debbie also gave them a vegetarian dish to offer their guests. No one could compare with what Debbie had offered, neither by food or cost. She was amazing, and the couple booked her. So now the food was taken care of, and it was perfect.

Next would be their cake and flowers. After just a few short months, they were already about half-done with the major items. That made both Matt and Summer happy. Big stuff was the easiest. They knew it would be the little details that would give them the most headaches. After all, they still hadn't even chosen their wedding party.

Matt had his best man, and that was it. Eighteen months seemed like so long to get everything done, but the months were flying by, and they needed to make a decision on a wedding party, the wedding colors, music, favors, and what to do about the alcohol? Still, so many details. Matt had been going to the church since childhood, and Summer joined back in high school. It was a place they both enjoyed, and the pastor knew them well. He was the person they wanted to officiate at their union. When they asked him, he was more than happy to perform the service for them. These were two very special people. He had watched them grow and looked forward to their future.

Since returning to the area, buying their first house and settling down they had been very involved in the church again. After their engagement and return home, they helped to begin a young married couples' group, and it had grown every month. They were very proud of it.

Summer and Matt were both held in high esteem among their peers as well as the elders at the church. Their love for the Lord was evident in their lives and their love. The days went by all too quickly as they tried to enjoy each and every step toward their new lives as husband and wife.

30

Eighteen months had seemed like such a long time when they choose their wedding date, but here they were, the morning of the wedding. After all the planning, all the anxiety for everything to be perfect, today was the day; today was Matt and Summer's wedding day.

Summer and Cathy, her maid of honor and her bridesmaid Amber arrived at the church early to meet with her friend Cindy from the salon. Cindy was an amazing hairdresser as well as a makeup artist. She had offered her services as a gift to Summer, who accepted graciously. Summer had arranged for two other friends to come to style the moms as well as her wedding party. Summer had some quiet time with Cindy before the others arrived. Soon the room was filled with girls, dresses, makeup, perfume, and hairspray. They had a good time as they each ohhed and ahhed at one another.

Once the girls were dressed and ready, both Summer and Matt's mom helped Summer get into her dress. Summer made sure that Matt's mom was a big part of everything that day; after all, Summer was her daughter too. She had been for some time now. Summer was beautiful as her maid of honor placed the veil on Summer's head; everyone teared up.

Summer looked around the room. Every woman in the room held a very special place in Summer's heart and in her life, and she was honored they would be standing beside her as she promised her life to Matt.

Matt had also arrived at the church early, he had grown up in this church, and he wanted to spend time with the pastor and both of the dads. This was the day that Matt would become someone's husband, it was something he took very seriously, and he wanted some time with the three men he considered his mentors. They talked about Matt and Summer's future, about family, kids, and religion; the men talked about everything that mattered. The morning was light as the guys put on the final touches and checked one another's attire.

Brian, Matt's best man and best friend, as well as Jeff, his groomsmen arrived. Everything was in place, everything was ready, there was nothing left for Matt to think about, he felt relaxed and ready. As time got closer, guests began to arrive, the flowers arrived, and Brian went to the girls' room to tell them. Both of the moms came out to check and make sure everything was ready. Pam took Matt's boutonniere out of the box; she had tears in her eye as she carefully pinned the flower to Matt's lapel and stood for yet more photos. The photographers took photos of Matt and his dad, Pam watched as she knew everything was ready, and her men looked handsome. Pam stepped in and held her son's face in her hands, she kissed his forehead, just as she had done so many times before. "You are very handsome, sweetheart. I am so proud of you." The photographers were there, capturing this moment for future memories.

With tears in her eyes, she kissed him again, this time on the cheek. The men were ready, guests were arriving, it was time to go see how the girls were doing. The entire day was being video taped by the same guys who had filmed the proposal. The guys had spent hours at the church and at the venue the night before getting everything set up. The church was perfect, they set up all the proper lighting and sound equipment to make sure they captured every emotion, every word for their friends. They had photographers and videographers everywhere. A crew was with Summer and the girls since early morning, as well as with Matt and the guys; there was a crew set up outside, inside, and one set up at the alter. Everything was checked and double-checked; everything was ready. The church was set up like a movie set. There wouldn't be a single word or moment lost, not if these guys had their way.

As the guests arrived, the guys outside snapped photos and began to film. The guys made certain that they would capture everything from beginning to end. This would be a very special gift for two people they thought so highly of.

The church's worship band would be playing for Matt and Summer. A friend would be singing a special song chosen for them as well. Every detail had special meaning; everyone in attendance had a special place in the couple's heart.

Once Matt's parents were settled in their seat, the processional began. As the maid of honor entered and walked down this aisle, Matt felt his heart swell with happiness. In just a few moments, the love of his life would enter and begin her walk toward him. Matt was smiling his nervous, happy smile. Until all of a sudden, his smile turned into a full-faced beam. There in front of him, straight back, down past the white runner stood a vision, an *angel*. There was a glow, the sun rays were radiant behind her from the sunlight that came through the window in the vestibule, Summer looked like an angel from heaven. All Matt saw was Summer. It took him a moment to notice her parents standing next to her, one on each side. The music reached a crescendo. Summer's parents kissed their daughter and then took each other's arms and walked down the aisle, alone. Matt hadn't expected this. As they walked directly to him, Summer's mom kissed him on his cheek, and her dad shook Matt's hand and brought him close and whispered something to him. Matt smiled as he looked at his bride standing in the glow.

Finally, she began to walk, or as Matt saw it, she floated toward the front of the church. She was indeed a vision—his vision, his angel. Summer decided that she wanted her mom and dad to walk down the aisle together without her. They married young and had never had a wedding. To Summer, this day signified family and love not just their own but also for those who came before them and for those who would come after them. Everyone had walked down the aisle, and all that was left was Summer, this moment belonged to them. This day was also about giving respect to their parents and the marriages they had.

It was a beautiful wedding with a lot of intimate personal touches showing their love for each other as well as their families and friends. Their guests laughed, they cried, and everyone felt Matt and Summer's deep sense of love and respect not just for each other but also for everyone that they loved.

The pastor knew this couple, and he knew them well. It was very obvious in the ceremony, the way he spoke to them and the memories he shared. He shared everything from the young people they were to the adults they had become, from the teasing to the crush, to the love that he watched grow. He shared their walk with the Lord, their growth in their faith, and the love they had for helping; it was special. Matt and Summer were very attentive to every little detail, she wore the perfect dress, and she carried beautiful flowers. Each little joke, each little memory, along with the little details of their relationship made the ceremony even more special. The day was not yet over as the ceremony ended with Matt and Summer declared husband and wife among cheers and applause. It was perfect. The sight of two people in love pledging their faith and love forever and each guest feeling like this was truly one of those forever loves.

As the bride and groom went through the traditional reception line, guests began to leave for the reception, and so far everything was perfect. The reception hall was beautiful yet not over the top, you could tell that their focus was on the wedding, the reception was a celebration of the same. This was not a wedding that was all about looking like a Hollywood production; everything was tasteful and elegant. Even their wedding favors were simple, a net of dove candy pieces and a photo of them at the local pier with waves behind them; a place they both loved was placed on a magnet for each guest to take home.

Everyone had a wonderful day full of fun, laughter, and great memories. Summer and Matt were exhausted by the end, but they were happy and in love. After the wedding, they stayed at the hotel where they had their reception. They had their home, but the thought of staying in the hotel with room service sounded like fun. They thought they could take the two days to just be together. They would be in Hawaii after that, and they wanted to enjoy the islands.

Matt and Summer enjoyed the honeymoon of their dreams, which was made possible by a group of friends. Not only did they make the honeymoon possible, but they also made it even more special with champagne and appetizers delivered each evening. With each surprise was a different note. Some of the notes were funny, while others were serious and poignant, but each note was special and with a great touch. They used the money they received from the engagement party to book fun touristy things. They did everything from snorkeling and swimming and watching dolphins, to helicopter rides and dinner cruises. They were so busy seeing and doing everything they could, they didn't have much time to just relax, so after the ten days of nonstop activities, they decided to extend their honeymoon five more days, not to stay in Hawaii, but to spend it at home, alone, no phones, no television, and no socializing. No one knew they were coming home, their family was only told they were extending the honeymoon.

When they arrived home, the entire house had been cleaned, organized, and decorated. They loved it and wanted to call everyone, but they wanted the next five days alone even more. The past few weeks had taken more out of them then they thought it would, and they were exhausted.

Matt and Summer bought the house before the wedding. It was a lovely home in a family-oriented community, close to good schools and close to family and friends. It was move in day that they met Jeff and Amber. The two couples had much in common and became very close friends quickly.

31

Matt and Summer enjoyed married life as they celebrated their first anniversary. Matt had the evening catered by their favorite restaurant. He wasn't much of a cook, so he didn't even try. They had been married for a full year, and he loved her more today than he ever had. She was his life, his love, his everything. Matt had set up a small, romantic table in front of the fireplace in their bedroom. This was their favorite place in the entire house. He set the table with a beautiful tablecloth, their wedding china, crystal, and silver. He had placed flowers all over the room, and a special large bouquet of Summer's favorite flowers next to their bed. The bouquet was complete with roses, peonies, and baby's breath. He ordered her favorite dish from their favorite restaurant, which had been delivered. He looked around, and everything was perfect.

Matt took the time to spread red rose petals from the romantic table for two, down the hall into the living room where he would be waiting for her. He lit candles, which gave off a romantic glow throughout the house.

Matt bought himself some sexy, silk pajamas and a nice short, silky robe; he also bought himself an ascot and a handsome pipe, just for looks. Hugh Hefner would have nothing on Matt on this night. Matt put the ensemble together because he knew it would make Summer smile. Okay, she would laugh hysterically, but he loved to make her laugh, and that was why he was doing it.

He laid a beautiful negligee on the foot of their bed. It was sexy but not trashy, he spotted it when he was out shopping for himself and couldn't resist. He had a very romantic first anniversary evening planned for them, and it had all come together. They talked about their first anniversary throughout the year. It was the night they planned to begin to work on starting their family.

Yes, they planned to have sex tonight, and if all went as planned, this could actually be the beginning, but regardless, it was going to be a memorable evening for them.

Summer arrived right on time. She had been at a spa the entire afternoon. It was a gift Matt had given her. Matt had told her he couldn't get the day off, but he'd get home as soon as he could. He didn't have to work. He lied to her and he felt bad, but he needed her out of the house. When Summer arrived, she was surprised to see Matt's car in the driveway. She was happy that he must have come home earlier than expected..

The house had a lovely glow in the windows; it was obvious that he had candles lit and she felt a warmth of love through her body, "how sweet" she thought. As she entered the front door, she saw Matt sitting in his silk pajamas, complete with an ascot, silk robe, pipe hanging from his lips.

"Welcome home, darling," he said with some kind of an Irish, British accent. Summer broke into a full laugh, snorting and all. "What?" Matt said innocently as he stood up. "You don't like my new look?"

"Oh no," she said, "you look adorable." She tried to get the words past her laughter. He did look pretty cute. As Summer laughed, she walked up to him, removed the pipe as she held his face in her hands, she laid a big smooch on his lips. As she did kiss, Matt pulled her down into the chair and on his lap. As they kissed, they caressed each other, working themselves into a deep desire for each other. Matt held her as he stood up, placing her

It Takes 3

feet on the ground, he said "Take my hand, and close your eyes." "Where are we going?" Summer said with some trepidation. "Trust me" Matt said as he led her into their bedroom. Summer could tell where they were headed as she smiled and smelled the scent of roses in the air. When they reached the entry to their room, Matt stopped. "Ok, Open your eyes."

Summer opened her eyes to flowers and rose petals everywhere. She looked back down the hall and saw a line of rose petals that led all the way to their bed and to the table in front of the fireplace, so many flowers. It was lovely and smelled like a flower shop. The table in front of the fireplace was the most beautiful table, all set up; it was just like a table you'd see in a romantic movie. Sitting on one of the plates was a beautiful box, wrapped in beautiful paper, and the fire was lit. Summer turned to Matt, but he was gone.

A few seconds later, he arrived carrying two Styrofoam boxes. Summer knew he had gotten her favorite salad from the restaurant. As he served his lovely wife, she took the serving tongs from him. "Let's just eat out of the boxes."

Matt smiled. That sounded good to him, no dishes. Matt handed her the box. "Open it."

As she slowly opened it, she hummed the stripper song by David Rose. She was trying to open it in a provocative manner. Summer was working on turning Matt on again, and it was working. Summer took her time, and Matt couldn't take the teasing another minute. He was getting all worked up. He tried to kiss her as she finished unwrapping it.

Summer held him off when she saw the beautiful, blue felt box. "Hold on, there's plenty of time for that. Patience, my darling." Summer opened the box, and inside was a beautiful heart necklace. Matt explained that he had the necklace made especially for her, it had both of their birthstones in the center. Matt's stone was a little larger than hers. It also held ten diamond marques surrounding the heart. As he placed the chain around her neck, he told her "each of the diamonds will be replaced someday with our kid's, birthstones."

Summer counted the diamonds. "Ten?, we're not having ten kids? Are we? she asked.

Summer's favorite movie had always been *Cheaper by the Dozen*. She had the original and every remake. Matt knew that when she was young, she wanted ten children. But as she got older, they knew that would never happen, but she always had fun teasing Matt. So Matt turned the tables on her.

Summer excused herself; she walked down the hall into the foyer to get the gift she had for Matt. It was a mantel clock, a very unusual mantel clock. It was actually a large bottle with a clock inside. Matt collected clocks, and this one had a message stuffed in the neck of the bottle.

Matt laughed, "A message in a bottle?" The note was actually the sheet mucic to Jim Croce's "Time in a Bottle" It was their song. Throughout the years, its words had grown in meaning. It was a sweet gift, and he loved it.

Summer also gave him a beautiful watch, this was her way to give him a daily reminder of those words After the gifts were opened, they settled into their meal and gazed into each other's eyes. They toasted to everything—their love, their life. The evening was perfect, their lives were perfect.

After dinner, Matt moved the table away so they could lie on the floor in front of the fire. They talked and within minutes, they began to make love. Summer whispered, "This evening is amazing, so romantic. Are we in a movie?" She remembered their engagement, then the wedding. She asked with a wonder in her voice "Are you filming this?"

Matt smiled. "Oh, that's a great idea, I should have thought of that, hold on, let me call the guys."

Matt laughed as Summer lightly and lovingly hit him on his forearm. "That would never happen, so don't even think about it."

It Takes 3

Matt held Summer in his arms as they made love again there on the floor. This time Summer got up and stood in the room taking in everything Matt had done. Their room looked beautiful filled with flowers and candle light, he had made the bed and even put all his clothes away. It was all so beautiful, then she noticed a beautiful negligee in her favorite color lying neatly at the foot of their bed. Matt walked behind her and held her in his arms, "Matt this is all so amazing, you are amazing." All she wanted, all she could think of was feeling Matt's naked body next to hers. She kissed his neck, then his shoulder,, her presence alone could excite Matt, but tonight she was more passionate than ever. They were in love, and after the evening they enjoyed, all he could think about was making love to her again. Summer always enjoyed their intimate time together, they were a perfect match. Matt always took his time, with her, he enjoyed pleasing her, and she knew just how to please him. They got so much pleasure from pleasing each other. Matt and Summer's love making was never about themselves, it was always about pleasing each other. It had been a long, long night of making love. Throughout the night, they took breaks, got a snack, then made love again and again. Summer couldn't believe their stamina, this was unusual even for them,.

As they made love, they talked about getting pregnant, about twins, even triplets. Finally completely exhausted, with sweat pouring from both of them, they fell into a deep, deep sleep.

The next day was Saturday, neither of them had to work, so Summer got out of bed, showered and put the negligee on, then she woke Matt up in a way that pleased him as well as got him aroused. Summer began kissing him and caressing his entire body. Matt laid there enjoying her softness, before opening his eyes. "Am I in heaven? Are you my Angel?" In his half-asleep voice, he asked, "Is it a sin to make love to an angel?" They laughed and fell into each other's arms, making love one more time.

Finally, reality crept into their fantasy in the form of hunger. Both of their stomachs had been growling, they both tried to ignore it, but it finally got the better of them. After they got up, they showered together, and then drove to the local marina for a lovely yet late lunch at the water's edge. They talked about their lives, they had it all—well, almost all. The evening had been so wonderful and so passionate that they both talked about how they hoped their evening would result in a pregnancy. But fot now they enjoyed each other. It would be weeks before they could know.

Weeks passed, and nothing changed, that evening was the beginning of their journey to have a baby.

32

Matt and Summer had made the decision to have children and they worked on it night after night. Yet month after month, her period showed on time, just like clockwork. A month passed and still nothing so Matt and Summer began to read books, they read books about getting pregnant, ovulation, timing: anything they could read they read. They even scheduled sex, they tried different positions, different food, anything they read now became part of their sexual experience. Soon it began to feel more like a job than making love. Through all of this, they both tried hard to keep things light, they had read about the stress, and didn't want their joy to be taken away from making love, but it was.

As they celebrated their second wedding anniversary, they tried to make it just as romantic as the first. They tried to renew the lust, and the desire, they had for each other, but they couldn't get over their concern, and as hard as they tried, it had begun to feel forced.

Getting pregnant was heavy on her mind, and she began to wonder why they weren't pregnant yet. It certainly wasn't for lack of trying. After their second anniversary, they both began to wonder if something could be wrong although they had only been married for two years, so it was still a bit soon to really worry.. They both rationalized the situation, but deep down, they were beginning to get concerned. They read that stress could have an impact on success,and no matter how hard they tried, they knew they were stressed.

Together they decided to stop trying to force this baby thing, they agreed that when the time was right, it would happen, no more temperature taking, no more weird positions, no more reading. But after their third wedding anniversary and still nothing, they decided to find out what if anything was going on.

Matt and Summer needed answers. They had a nice home and good jobs, they had savings, they had great insurance, they had each other and were very much in love, they had been married over 3 years, they had everything—well, they had everything they needed, all the things they had worked hard for, but there was this one thing they wanted, and it was eluding them.

So why wasn't she pregnant?. It was time for both Matt and Summer to see the doctor. It was time for checkups, and they needed to know if there was something wrong. Was it possible that there was something physically stopping them from getting pregnant, from realizing their dream of having a child? Summer made appointments for both of them for the following month. Since it wasn't an emergency, there was no hurry. A month later was the first opening the doctor had for a physical.

Summer and Matt were able to get their blood tests and some other tests done before their appointments. Summer had the first appointment, and she went without Matt. To her surprise, the doctor voiced some concerns about Summer's ability to get pregnant. He told her that he wasn't sure getting pregnant would even be possible. Summer's blood test held some odd findings. Summers hormones showed an unusual decrease in estrogen, her testosterone levels were also lower than normal she would need more tests in order to pinpoint the reason for this. Summer was too young to see results like this. Summer was shocked at what she heard. How could her hormones be so low and she not know it? The doctor asked her a list of questions, did she experience

It Takes 3

hot flashes?"Only when I think of Matt," she laughed. The doctor didn't seem to appreciate her joke as he went on asking questions, lack of sex drive? are you irritable? Moody? Have your periods changed? Shorter, longer? Missed? Heavier or lighter? Vagina dryness? He went on and on. Summer could answer yes to some of these, but there was a reason for some of it. They had been trying so hard so of course she could be irritable, depressed or have a lack of desire. But her doctor seemed concerned and ordered more tests, so there were no answers for her yet. Matt's appointment was the next day, and Summer went with him. The doctor explained that all of Matt's tests were normal, but because of their situation, she wanted him to do a fresh sperm count, it would only take a few moments, but the specimen had to be fresh, she was afraid that the last sample may have sat too long. So off to produce a new sample, returning with a fresh specimen, the doctor ran the necessary test and everything with Matt was good. This was good news, but it made Summer sad, this meant that the problem was her.

At Summer's next appointment, Matt was with her when the doctor came in and explained that her hormone levels are much lower than they should be, he had them rechecked but included a test to test her estradiol levels and it was well below 30 which was a sign of menopause. "Menopause, Im not old enough for menopause." Summer was surprised. "Yes, that is true to a point but menopause can happen early." "What?" Sunner interrupted, but the doctor continued. "We also ran a test that measures your follicle stimulating hormone, known as FSH. This is the hormone that causes your ovaries to produce estrogen, we know your estrogen is low. So we are concerned and sure enough your FSH is high, much higher than it should be, anything over 40 indicates menopause. I'm sorry to say that you are in fact menopausal. But before we close the book on this, let's get a few more tests."

Summer cried as Matt held her, this was shocking news and completely unexpected. "let's do some checking to see if everything else is alright, OK?

Matt tried to stay strong as Summer collapsed in disbelief; at that moment, their world was crushed, they had always wanted children, they wanted at least two, and now they were being told that it would be impossible. The doctor kept talking, she talked and talked, but all Summer heard was "blah, blah, blah." Matt tried to understand what the doctor was saying.

"Listen, this isn't the end. There are options for you. There is a bit of a silver lining. I know it's not what you want, but don't take kids off the table just yet." The doctor went on to explain that although Summer could not conceive, this condition does not affect a woman's uterus, so they had options.

"So what does all of this mean then?" Matt asked.

"Summer cannot produce eggs, hasn't ever, she cannot become pregnant in the 'normal fashion,' but the good news is that it's not impossible for her to carry a pregnancy. It's something to think about."

Summer heard her when she said not to take kids off the table, but what did she mean? "So what are you saying? Is there a way that we can have kids?"

The doctor went on, "Well, we know there's a reason why you were not getting pregnant. We know what it is and why it is."

The doctor explained, "Summer, this is nothing that you could have prevented. It wasn't something you even knew about. She went on to explain that Summer wanted to experience pregnancy, and using an egg donor would mean she could. "Summer, for you to actually get pregnant, it is going to take three: Matt will need to provide the sperm, a donor would provide the egg for you, and you will provide the uterus, a safe life sustaining womb."

"Wow, three people to make one baby, what a world we live in." Matt said as he hugged his wife. "This is good news, right?"

It Takes 3

They all knew how much Summer wanted to have a baby, and an egg donor would give her that opportunity; it was an option, probably the best option.

Being unable to produce the eggs needed to conceive, she and Matt needed a third person to make their dream a possibility.

When they left the doctor's office, Summer was pretty depressed; after asking all her questions and hearing all the answers, there seemed to be no way for them to have a baby that was theirs—genetically, that is.

Summer thought out loud, "If we use an egg donor, the baby would genetically be yours and the donor's. It won't be mine, it won't be ours." Summer sounded so sad thinking about all this.

Matt listened to the pain in his wife's voice. "Babe, it will be ours. The donor is just giving us a small yet important piece, but you will be the one carrying the baby, our baby for those nine months. You will be the one that will actually give our baby life.. Without you there is no baby."

Summer loved what Matt said, she would love any child just as if it were genetically theirs; they had talked about adoption so the baby being genetically conncted to them wasn't the end of their desire Egg donation was something they never thought they would need to consider. It was something that they had barely heard of for that matter.

Summer had been researching her diagnoses on the internet, she read about other women getting pregnant despite their diagnoses, some with the help of IVF, maybe she could be one of those women?

"Oh, the Internet," the doctor said, "self-diagnoses, what a wonderful thing." But the doctor explained that her numbers were both too high and too low, she wasn't a canidate, the likelihood of success was slim to none. Egg donation in her opnion was the only option for Summer to experience the joy of pregnancy and birth. The doctor had Summer's full attention now as she explained that although the baby would not be 100 percent connected to them genetically, it would have Matt's DNA. She explained that every patient she had that chose egg-donation, felt the same love and connection to their baby as any other mom. She explained that soon after implantation, these moms never even consider their baby's genetic makeup.

The doctor felt that using an egg donor was the best scenario for them, it was a lot to take in, she gave them a bunch of literature to take home and referred them to an excellent fertility clinic in her building. She went on to explain that a lot of tests would be repeated by the clinic. She explained that they would be going through counseling and some education before they moved forward. By the end of the appointment, Summer was still pretty upset, but she felt better than she did when she first walked in. The idea that she should be able to carry a baby as well as give birth was at the very least a ray of sunshine within all the darkness they had experienced It was so much to take in, but Matt was like a sponge, learning and listening to every detail, as his mind soaked it all in.

As they drove home, they were exhausted, but hungry too, it had been a long day. Summer didn't want to eat at their regular place. She was too upset to face anyone that they knew. Anyone looking at her would be able to tell that something was wrong, they'd ask questions, and she wasn't ready to share anything with anyone.

Matt drove to a dark, cozy restaurant he spotted on the way home. Here, they were safe, no one knew them. They both needed time to digest everything from the diagnoses to the possibility of using an egg donor, it was a lot and Summer needed to be alone with her husband.

33

Matt and Summer met with the fertility clinic. They had questions. After meeting the doctors and the staff, they made the decision to go forward with the egg-donation process. The clinic was comfortable, well organized, and very clean. The staff made them feel comfortable and welcomed. They really liked the doctor as well. He was very down to earth and had a great bedside manner. He was also very confident that he could help them in their endeavor. Summer and Matt didn't sign anything at the consultation, and the clinic told them to go home and consider everything they had been told, to take time, to look over all the information they had been given. They were given information regarding the clinic's egg-donation process, info about the donation as well as the recipient procedures. They were also given a proposed contract to look over. They were encouraged to have an attorney look it over as well. They both went over all the information with a fine-tooth comb. They had a lawyer friend of theirs look over the proposed contract.

After some time, Matt and Summer called the clinic and scheduled their first appointment. It took them about two weeks of consideration before making the decision that this was what they wanted to pursue. For two weeks, Matt and Summer talked about different forms of IVF. They talked about adoption and where all of this would fit into their lives, but after all their consideration, egg donation was the procedure they wanted to pursue. During their first appointment, the doctor sat with both Matt and Summer to spend time with them.

He explained, "Fertility treatment can be a long, strenuous procedure, so I like to get to know as much as I can about my patients." This was the time he explained the entire process of egg donation with them, and he explained the clinic's entire procedure. Everything was exactly what their doctor told her. As the doctor talked about the procedure, Summer understood what the doctor was talking about. She had read everything and done some research on it after their appointment.

Summer and Matt were scheduled for all the necessary tests needed to move forward; some of the tests were being performed for a second time, and still others were being done for a third or fourth time. The doctor explained that the clinic had pretty strict procedures they had to adhere to, and each must be followed as laid out, and this was just one of those procedures, and once the testing was completed, they would move on. He explained that he had seen her test and the deformity. He told them that he was confident that they would find success, and in time, they would have their hearts' desire.

Summer and Matt met the office coordinator and was told that the entire staff was there to assist them in getting the results they all hoped for. The cost of the procedure included all of the testing, and if they found something to be wrong, then they would discuss the need for further treatment, but usually by the time a patient entered the clinic doors, they had already done all major tests or treatments. Once at the clinic, each patient received testing based on their personal diagnoses and their personal journey. All of Matt's tests came back normal, and although it was a relief, no one expected anything different. Summer's results were also the same as each of the other times; these test only confirmed her diagnoses of the fact that she did indeed have a severe deformity, and they confirmed

It Takes 3

that she was unable to conceive a child the old-fashioned way. He agreed that surgery was much too risky, and this was indeed her best option. After all the ultrasounds, x-rays, and blood tests that had been preformed, the doctors were certain that she would be able to carry a baby to term. She explained that given the success of the clinic's egg-donation program and retrieval rate with their donors and the successful procedure they used for fertilization and implantation, they were confident that Summer and Matt would find success with them.

Summer and Matt felt pretty confident with their choice of clinics, and they were done discussing all of this; they were ready to get started. With all the testing complete, Summer and Matt were scheduled to meet with the donor coordinator to view donor profiles. This was the appointment when they would be able to see photos and read about their background, medical history, educational level, and family history that were included in their profile packets. This was very exciting, especially after being told that she definitely couldn't get pregnant, after hearing that she thought her desire to have children was gone, but here she was with her husband, getting ready to choose a donor. She and Matt would choose the woman who would help make their dreams come true. If today's search was successful, if they found a donor, a young woman willing to help them, they were on their way. Knowing that Summer was able to carry a baby and the news that she could give birth to their baby herself made looking for a donor a very serious event; the dream of having a baby, of giving birth could really happen. Her dream of having a baby had changed a bit, she wouldn't be getting pregnant the old-fashioned way, but the fact that she could was a blessing, and at this point giving birth was her ultimate goal. After everything they had been through, they finally felt hopeful. They felt happy and excited for the first time in about a year.

Before their appointment, Summer and Matt talked about what they both wanted in their donor. They agreed that they wanted their donor to resemble Summer in every way possible. Since Matt would be providing his own sperm, they wanted a girl who looked like Summer and liked the things Summer liked. Despite the fact that the baby wouldn't share any genetic DNA with Summer, she wanted to give the baby a chance to look as much like them as possible. Summer knew that after carrying the baby, her the connection with their baby would be just as strong as Matt's genetic connection; after all, she would carry the baby for nine months, and she would bond, feeling the life grow and move inside her. She was glad that Matt would have that genetic bond. Summer wasn't really worried about the baby looking like her or Matt, she knew that babies born to couples naturally looked very different than their parents, but since she got to choose, she hoped to find a donor with as many characteristics like her as she could. After all, since she and Matt would never have a child that was a genetic combination of them, finding a donor who resembled her gave her the only chance to see what their child might look like, sort of.

Matt and Summer were escorted to a room that held the profiles, books of all donors; they were both surprised by the extensive library the clinic had to choose from. They were surprised to see that there were so many girls willing to donate such a personal piece of herself. There were so many to choose from, they were pretty confident that they would find at least one possibility. Looking at all the faces and reading all the bio's, Summer still was unsure that she would be able to make a choce. This wasn't like going to the store and picking out a dress or something, she was choosing the woman who would provide them with something very special, something that would change their lives. This women would be providing something that she lacked. It amazed her that there were so many women willing to donate, her heart went out to each of them. In her heart she thanked each and everyone of them.. It was an odd feeling that they would get to choose a donor, their donor, the women that would be an integral part in providing their child's genetic traits, the eyes, the nose, the ears, the mouth, and the smile. They focused on the women that resembled Summer, a girl that had a smile like Summer's, Matt wanted their child to have that smile, and it was that smile that captured his heart.

Matt really wanted a young lady that had Summer's skin tone too, not too light but not dark either. They were amazed that they could choose a donor based of all the things that were important to them. Summer was a beautiful, blond-haired, blue-eyed, medium-built woman, with a complexion that was absolutely perfect; they really didn't think it would be too hard to find a girl like that in California. But they really wanted a girl that was loving, family oriented and creative.

Summer and Matt were both California natives, and they decided to choose a California girl to be their donor as well as to keep their cost down. Using a girl from another state could mean travel, and travel meant more cost. The clinic they chose was near their home, but they had donors from all over the United States; although it sounded good to have a donor miles away, they didn't want to incur any more expenses than necessary.

34

As they sat with all the books, full of these amazing women, Matt and Summer took a moment, "It's been a long road, are your ready for this?" Matt asked as he kissed Summer. They talked about everything they had been through, everything that had brought them to this place. Summer wondered if they would find their perfect donor today or if it would take them more time; she wondered if the perfect girl was in any of the books.

She wondered, *What if she isn't? What then?*

Summer and Matt looked at many of the books and nothing, but there were still more to go through. The doctor told them that they didn't need to do it all in one day, they could take their time, but Summer wanted to continue, but she needed a break; they both needed a break and some lunch, so they went to the cafeteria in the building. While they enjoyed lunch, they talked about the books, the girls, and returning to the office to continue their search, as they chatted, the waitress couldn't help but overhear them. Matt could tell that she had heard them, and when she came back to the table, he told her that they were clients of the fertility clinic upstairs and that they were in the process of choosing a "mom" for their child. It sounded odd, even to him, but that was what they were doing, and he needed to lighten it up, he needed to laugh, and at the sound of his own

It Takes 3

words, he found himself chuckling. The waitress knew the clinic and its staff well, and many of them ate in the cafeteria often. She smiled, and he said, "Yeah, we need a mom to make our baby egg-s-tra-special"

The waitress smiled and told them that the clinic was nice, she told them that she had worked with them, she had been an egg donor years ago, and that was actually how she found her job. As soon as the waitress said she was a donor, Summer perked up; she asked the waitress if she minded sharing her story.

"No, not at all."

Summer went on to ask her how she felt about the entire experience and if she knew what had happened to the couple she donated her eggs to. The waitress explained that when she did it, the donors were never informed about the outcome. Summer listened as she told them about her experience. "I don't know why they call it donating though. I know the procedure's very costly to the parents. I was paid to do it, but seriously I would have done it for free. I couldn't imagine not having kids."

Matt asked, "You have kids?"

"Yes, I have two, but I didn't have any then. When I donated, I didn't even have a boyfriend, didn't have any luck in that area. Boy, can things change. It's been just over three years since I donated. Within three years, I met a great guy, got married, and had two children."

"Wow, that's amazing." Summer was surprised. "After you had your kids, did you regret donating?"

"No, not at all. After I had my kids, it made me feel even better. I was able to give someone the gift of life, and that feels awesome. After I had my first child, I realized just what a gift they are. It made me feel really good to know that I was able to give someone the chance to feel what I felt. You'll see that feeling when you have the first moment you get to hold your little one, it'll work out for you, I know it will. Good luck."

Summer smiled. "Thank you, from your lips to God's ears." Summer was grateful that she shared her feelings and her experience; she told her that she was an angel for doing what she did and thanked her for being a donor. Summer thanked her for herself and for the couple that she helped years ago. Summer found herself hoping that somewhere there was a child running around, about four years old, who was loved so much—thanks to this young lady. Summer talked to the waitress "Do you have any idea how amazing you are? Thank you for talking to us about your experiemce. We really appreciate your honesty." Summer wanted to know more about the medical experience, about what the donor went through medically. She knew about the procedure on paper, but to get a firsthand account was something that couldn't come from the doctor or the internet. The doctor had told her about it, but hearing a donor's perspective was priceless. She wanted to know if it was painful and how long was the entire process. The information the waitress shared gave Summer and Matt a deeper understanding of the kind of person it took to be a donor and to give such a gift to a stranger. They were glad she shared her experience with them, they appreciated it,. They told her a little about their own experience and explained how grateful they were for her. "I know that the couple that received your donation is very grateful," Summer talked to her and told her that regardless if a women got pregnant or not, no matter what, women like her are the ones that give them a chance and hope. "Without you we have neither, so I thank you for every infertile women out there, thank you.." Summer explained that she had lost all hope, until now.

Matt and Summer took her words and her feelings to heart, and they thanked her for her help and her insight. They left her a surprisingly large tip, just their way of saying thank you not only for her service, the conversation, and the information she shared, but it was also a thank you for being an egg donor. This young lady spent her break time talking to them. After she returned to work, Matt and Summer took their time, finished their meal, and relaxed a little before heading back to the clinic to resume their search.

The clinic was quiet when they returned, so they took advantage of the quietness to talk to some of the office girls. Matt and Summer could tell that each of them loved their jobs, and they all shared the same caring spirit. Even when things didn't go well, they still provided real solutions for people who had all but given up on having a family. Now they were one of their couples, they too had all but given up, and now here at this clinic, they found hope, and they found understanding and caring. They found a rainbow full of hope, and they hoped they would find the pot of gold at the end. To them the clinic had come to symbolize a bright, beautiful rainbow, you know the kind, the ones seen only after a really severe storm.

Matt and Summer had arrived at the clinic full of excitement and anticipation, full of new hopes and new dreams. The questions today were, Would they find a donor? Would they find the right donor, and would they find her today?

Matt and Summer returned to the room, there were still so many books to go through, so many profiles to look at, and every one of those books was full of donors. The donors were already prescreened and background checked by the clinic. There were also a couple of books that had profiles of what the clinic called "proven" donors. These were donors whose donations had been proven with a pregnancy and/or births. These were the women whom many couples went to first, but Matt and Summer were saving them for last.

The coordinator assigned to Matt and Summer explained that some of the women in the "proven" book had already been booked and wouldn't be available for months. Matt and Summer were not necessarily looking for a proven donor. They were looking for a look, certain characteristics, and they needed to stay focused on that. As they looked at profile after profile, it warmed their hearts to see so many women ready to provide others, people they didn't know, such a vital ingredient needed to fulfill their dream of having a child. Summer and Matt had been overwhelmed when they first entered the room this morning, but now they were much more comfortable as they read a few of the biographies, the reasons these girls were doing this. It was heart warming. As they read, some girls were doing it because they were adopted and wanted to help other couples wanting a family. Some had decided to do this because they knew someone who had used egg donation to have their children, and others had family members that were infertile and wanted to help them but couldn't for different reasons. None of the girls mentioned the financial aspect although she was sure that at least for some, it was the motive, at least in the beginning, and those ads promising big money sounded good. Summer was certain that after hearing about all that is involved in donating, it weeded out the girls in it just for the money. It took a lot for a woman to go through the entire process, and money, although nice, wouldn't be worth it, at least to most. Summer and Matt tried to pick out girls who were probably money motivated. They laughed and made some silly jokes about it as they went through page after page of girls. They were prepared to go through every single book in the office, and decided that every face was worth consideration.

Looking at all the profiles was overwhelming. There were so many different types of women to choose from. Every ethnicity and combination of ethnicities, little girls, bigger girls—they had everything to choose from, every combination of characteristics as well, but they were focused. There were blondes, brunettes, redheads, and everything in between. There were fair-skinned, olive-skinned, and freckled-skin girls, and girls with blue eyes, brown eyes, gray eyes, and green eyes. There were short girls, tall girls, and girls that were considered average. Some of the girls were thin, and then others were what would be considered full size, all the girls were healthy, and they were all beautiful.

It Takes 3

As Matt and Summer looked and talked about how and who to choose, the nurse coordinator, came in to talk to them about what they wanted in a donor. She knew they were looking for a girl that resembled Summer, but she wanted them to understand that just because a girl had the right outer characteristics, it didn't guarantee that a child conceived using her donated egg would have the same characteristics. She explained that although the child would carry her genes, they would not be exactly same; after all, our genetic makeup reaches back to past generations, not just our mothers and fathers. Each of us is made up of every generation that came before us. Also once her egg is inseminated, Matt's family history comes in to play, so it wasn't a given that the child would resemble a fully genetic child of theirs; she wanted them to understand that. Summer and Matt understood, but they felt that choosing a girl that resembled Summer gave them the best chance to have a child that most resembled them. Of course children and their genetic makeup was not an exact science, but for them this was the best they could do under the circumstances. They still had so many more books to go through, so they decided to look through separate books, until they found a girl with the right characteristics they were looking. When they found a person of interest, they would take a closer look at her photo, her profile, and bio. If she fit within their ideal, they would pull her photo out of the book and put it aside just as the coordinator and the doctor had instructed them to do. As they continued searching and pulling out the donors that they both agreed on, they pulled out three photos, then four, then five, and as they continued to thumb through the books, they pulled out a couple more. Finally they pulled the last book from the shelf, they had five possibilities, they had considered giving up a few books ago, but they had come this far, and they had looked at so many photos, so they decided to continue.

35

Summer was exhausted, Matt was tired of looking at all those smiling faces, but they had come so far and had only one more book to go through. They opened the final book together, turning to each other, with exasperation on their face. Matt winked at Summer, and they shared a kiss for luck. As Summer turned the pages, she wasn't sure they would find anyone who would met their needs any better than the girls they had pulled out of the books already; none of them was perfect, feeling as if their perfect donor didn't exist and coming to terms with having to settle or having to wait to find her.

Becoming more and more discouraged as she turned the pages, suddenly as she turned the next page, there, staring back at her, was the perfect girl. Matt and Summer were looking at the same photos, they looked at each other with big smiles on their face, rays of the sun highlighted the photo, as if to say, "Here she is, she is the one, she is your donor! "

Matt looked at Summer. Summer looked at Matt as she placed her finger on the photo and said, "Oh my god, this is her, this is the girl, this is our donor."

Matt pulled the photo out of the sleeve, he looked close, this girl did look just like his wife. Looking at the photo was like looking at a photo of Summer. Matt joked that Summer had put

It Takes 3

a photo of herself in the book. Matt read her bio out loud, and they checked all of her stats; this was the girl they wanted. Next question was, was she available?

"She has to be available," Summer said with excitement.

"She is perfect," Matt said. Matt and Summer had been at this for hours and hours, looking at picture after picture, reading profiles and bios. It had been a long day, and it was all very tiring. When they turned that page and saw the photo, suddenly they were wide awake and full of adrenaline; they were pumped and very excited. Matt had a huge smile on his face when he told the counselor they had a contender; well, they now had seven possible donors, but only one that they really wanted.

"There's this one girl that is perfect. Everything about her is perfect, at least on paper." The counselor followed him back to the room to see the profile they were looking at. If this was the girl they wanted, she needed the donor's client number. Then she could check the database, and retrieve her personal information and phone number; none of that information was in the donor books. It had been a long day, and as the doctor walked by the conference room, he saw the excitement and entered the room to see if they were having any luck finding a donor. He knew that this choice could be a very daunting task for perspective parents. Matt and Summer shared the seven possibilities, and they showed him which one was their first choice, the girl they really wanted; she had become their only choice. But if for some reason she was unavailable, they did have others they could reconsider. They were very excited about their choice, they read every line of her profile sheet, and they liked what they read. She had many of the same interests as Summer, she loved her family and her friends, and Matt and Summer felt for her and her reasons for wanting to be a donor.

On paper at least she seemed perfect in every way. She fit what they were looking for. As the coordinator was making the call, they talked about their next step with the doctor. Summer was changed. Did the girls really look like their photos? The doctor told them that the clinic took every photo in the books; she explained that the reason they did that was so they didn't receive retouched photos or some photo that was taken at their best. The clinic wanted current natural photos, photos that actually looked like the girls. Allowing a donor to provide photos was just too risky. The clinic was proud to provide their potential parents with photos that were real. The doctor looked at their first choice photo and profile and explained that this young lady was not one of their proven donors, she was brand-new to the facility, and if she were available, this would be her first procedure.

As he focused on Summer, he realized that the resemblance was amazing; they looked so much alike it was as if it were Summer in the photo. He read the profile: the two women were the same age, the same height, even their weight was nearly the same, and they had many of the same interests as well. The doctor commented that he didn't think they could have found a better match as far as looks and body style was concerned; this girl was exactly what they said they were looking for, and she couldn't have been more perfect for them. Matt and Summer looked at her photo again, and they reread her bio and vital statistics. Her bio was that of a real person, for she wrote about her real life, the good and bad. It had no fluff and no frills added to look good. This donor had all of the characteristics they had hoped for and more. She was creative, loving, family oriented, and of course she was beautiful and healthy, which was vital.

The wheels of change for Matt and Summer were put into motion. The clinic nurse made the phone call to find out if she was still interested in being a donor. This was always the first question, because many times after a woman gets this far, they begin to rethink their decision, and some actually back out. Throughout the screening process, donors are told that no matter what their reasons are if at anytime they decide this is not for them, they are not under any commitment to go through with this. This was a big decision, and sometimes it is more than a girl can commit to. The clinic understood and always cautioned perspective parents not to get too excited until a retrieval date is set.

The clinic told every perspective donor that no woman should ever donate if they were not completely comfortable. Prospective parents are also cautioned that at anytime during the process if a donor experiences any health issue, the donation would be stopped. The donor's health, both mental and physical, is always their first priority. As long as the donor is healthy and still committed to being a donor, they would check her availability.

As Matt and Summer waited, the coordinator made the call. The donor saw on her caller ID that the call was from the clinic, and she was surprised. It had only been a couple of days since she had been in the clinic, had her photo taken, and filled out the necessary paperwork that began the process. The nurse was calling to confirm that she was still interested in being a donor "Yes, I am." Then she went on to aks if she was available during the time frame they were looking at. "Yes, I am avalible." The nurse on the other end thanked her and told her she would get back to her, then hung up. The donor sat looking at the phone thinking *Wow, this is all happening so fast*. When she was considering this, she had talked to other girls, many of whom had never heard anything. Others actually received an e-mail stating that they had been declined. Other girls said that it took months before they were ever contacted by a clinic. But here she was, just a few days into all of this and already she was being asked about her avalibility. The nurse let the doctor and the couple know that the women they choose was indeed avavlible and willing to move forward.

"Well," the doctor asked, "should we book her?"

"Yes, book her." Matt and Summer laughed. Those words sounded so odd to them.

Summer said, "Book her, Dano." And she laughed. It was a very famous line from the old television series *Hawaii Five-0*. "Book her, we want her, book her, please."

The nurse happily returned to the phone, dialed the number again "So, are you ready to move forward?" The young lady confirmed again that she was so the nurse gave her the time frame they were working toward. The nurse went on to explain the procedure and told her that they would get the contract ready and e-mail it to her within a few days. "When you receive it, please take your time and read it thoughly, , have it looked over by an attorney of your choosing, and write any questions, comments, or changes, you'd like considered within the margins before sending it back to us". The nurse explained that if she was in agreement with the entire contract, to go ahead sign it and return it to the office via courier. When she was ready she needed to call the office and they would give her the information needed for the courier. She went on to inform the donor that the recipient couple were working directly with the legal team to draw up the contract. Both parties would have a chance to go over the final draft before signing anything. Once everyone was in agreement, the donor signs first, the recipient parents would then sign it as well, it was at this time that all the appointments would be made. Once everything was signed, they were considered "under contract,"and all the legalities were taken care of,. Once all of this was done Matt and Summer would be that much closer to becoming parents. Excitement and nervousness went through all three for very different reasons.

36

The contracts were drawn up, there were a couple of minor changes, but everything was signed by all parties. This contract was between three entities: Matt and Summer as recipient parents, the donor, and the clinic. Each party held a commitment to the other, and both the recipient and donor were told that they needed to stay in good health and to take care of themselves in order for the process to flow smoothly. Both parties were informed that they each had time to back out. If they found for any reason that they were unable to fulfill their commitment, they could still back out. Once the medications were ordered and in their hands, everything was a go—unless of course there was some medical or psychological reason, any one of them could not complete their end of the contract.

The donor would receive financial compensation for her time, commitment, and any possible discomfort that she may feel associated with the egg-donation process. The clinic's compensation ranged from about six thousand to eight thousand dollars. Any female who is considered for possible donation is required to complete a full and complete screening which includes an informational session. The physical exam that she had already received as well as a complete psychological evaluation and genetic screening. she still had to go through. All of this was for a general health assessment; it was also to screen for infectious diseases such as HIV, hepatitis, gonorrhea, chlamydia, and syphilis. The next step after that would be for both of the women to meet with the nurse or donor-egg coordinator to review the treatment cycle. This was the appointment where the donor would be educated about the entire process, and they would discuss everything about medication, test, and retrieval. This is when the coordination and synchronization of the donor's cycle to the recipient's cycle would begin. The nurse explained that the synchronization of both women's cycles could take days or possibly several weeks. In the rare instances, it could take several months, depending on the recipient and donor's natural menstrual cycle and their personal schedules. But after everything was synchronized and in place, the donor would be placed on medications for about two to three weeks to stimulate her ovaries. This was the part of the treatment that helped her to produce more than the usual number of eggs a woman ovulates each month. The nurse explained the donor's progress would be monitored frequently with vaginal ultrasounds and blood work in their office to ensure the eggs were developing appropriately. The donor would have to commit to these scheduled appointments. The doctor informed her that the first step would be the synchronization of her cycle with the recipient's cycle; he explained that this was done using birth control pills, and then after the women were in sync, she would begin giving herself injections.

"Injections? What? Needles? Really." The sound of the word *injections* made her nervous. The nurse noticed and assured her that the needles were super-, supertiny, so tiny in fact she would hardly feel them. Although nervous, if she had a problem, she knew her mom would help. The donor went through shot training and was educated on how and when to take each medication. She's shown how to prepare and give herself the shots. The donor was relieved that the needle is really tiny and didn't hurt at all. As a matter of fact, she could hardly feel it at all. It was much easier than she thought it would be, and because of this, she assured the clinic staff that she would be fine doing this. After all the training and instruction she had been given, she felt confident. She was also given a written set of instructions just in case she needed a reminder about how and what to do. She's given her injection schedule and a schedule of her all of her upcoming appointments; she's given a proposed retrieval date as well. Retrieval date is the date of the egg retrieval, this was the date if all went as planned, but if something didn't go as planned, she would be informed and whatever changes needed to be made would be made.

As she left the office, she felt excited and a little apprehensive about the entire thing, especially all that was still unknown to her. Even though the nurses and doctors explained everything in detail to her, she still had a lot of apprehension. She was glad that they gave her the written information about being a donor, but they gave her information on the entire process ahead of her, including the retrieval process. The doctors liked their donors to be well educated, and they even had some support sessions for both donors and recipients during the week. The retrieval process was also known as the egg-recovery process—same thing, just different names.

After all the medications were taken and both of their bodies were ready, the donor would get instructions from the doctor that they were ready for retrieval. Once the donor got these instructions, the doctor would give her orders to give herself one last injection. This injection was to be done exactly thirty-five hours prior to the egg retrieval; the doctor told her that the timing of this shot was absolutely crucial (so she needed to perform this one exactly on time). This particular medication would bring her eggs to final maturity. The eggs would then be retrieved using what is called sonographic egg recovery; this involves the use of an ultrasound-guided needle to gently remove the eggs from the donor's ovaries. It's a simple, painless procedure with the use of a light sedation. The retrieval process takes only about twenty minutes to complete. Donors were usually happy to hear that they would be completely "out" and more than likely she wouldn't remember a thing. The aspirated eggs are then donated to her recipient. At this point, the donor's job is done. All that was left for her to do was to take care of herself and recover. She was told that donors must have someone to drive her home because of the sedation, and a bit of discomfort she would feel. The office required information on a contact and driver prior to the retrieval; it was their way to be sure that there would be someone there for her. It was also highly suggested that she stay with someone or have someone stay with her for the first twenty-four and forty-eight hours while the sedation wore off. They instructed her to rest for the remainder of the retrieval day and to take it easy the next day or so as she resumes normal activities. The nurse told her that her period should arrive approximately two weeks after her egg retrieval. If there was anything she was worried about, or any questions, big or small, she was given a number and a nurse to call. The nurse told her to call with any question or concern, anything, even if it was information they had already covered. They didn't expect her to remember everything, and no question was too silly. Listening to all this information brought up more questions she wanted to ask others who had actually been a donor before. She needed to do more research. This was a girl who liked to know everything she could about whatever she was involved in; she needed to know what she would be experiencing before she experienced it. Her biggest fear was about how she would really feel during the stimulation phase, the injections made her nervous, but she was strong. She could do this. Retrieval day and the entire process of the insemination process intrigued her.

37

After all the physical examinations were complete, the next thing was the psychological screening; this would include a psychological test that consisted of about five hundred questions. It also included a full hour or so with the staff psychologist. The prospect of a psychiatric test sounded scary, five hundred questions was all a bit overwhelming, but it was all part of the process. She was interested to see what the outcome would be, psychology interested her, and it was a career she had even considered at one time. The appointment with the psychologist was about a week later, and the clinic needed all the results from the genetic testing before moving forward.

The office called her to let her know that the appointment was confirmed, and there was no preparation for a test of this kind, just show up and be ready for a long day. She was very interested in this test, she had a good head on her shoulders, she didn't hate her mother or anything like that, she was sure that would be one of the questions, and it was always one they asked on television.

On the day of her appointment, she sat in the waiting room in the psychologist office, She was given some paperwork to fill out, and then she was escorted to a small room with a single desk and chair. There was a tiny table against the wall that held some chilled water and some pretzel chips, if she wanted or needed a snack. The office assistant escorted her to a private room, the nurse told her to take her time, this wasn't a timed test. She was instructed to bring the entire package out and leave it on the desk when she was done and then quietly take a seat in the waiting room. The assistant explained where the restroom was as she he handed a package to her. The package felt like a book, but it was just the test.

Taking a bottle of water off of the table, she sat down at the lonely, little table and opened the package. She couldn't believe the stack of pages, 650 questions printed on one side of the paper, with spaces big enough to write a novelette in response to some of the questions. As she flipped through the pages, she was surprised at the massive amount of questions in front of her. She thought everyone had exaggerated about the amount of questions, but they didn't. She took her time as she read every single question carefully and completely, she tried to see if there were any of those trick questions, but each one sounded straightforward, needing a complete answer. She took her time and answered every one of them just as completely as they had been asked and to the best of her ability. She was amazed at some of the things they asked. They wanted to know about things she remembered at very young ages, things about her parents, grandparents, and questions about work, career, and how she felt about world politics. There were even questions about morals, religion, and where she thought her life would be in five, ten, and twenty years from now. There were some very specific questions about egg donation and her feelings about the different aspects of it. They asked how she felt if a baby was born and what about if the child somehow found her later in life. They had all kinds of scenarios in those papers, and she thought about each one, answering each one completely. The entire process was interesting, and some of the questions gave her scenarios she had never even thought of. She couldn't wait to see what the psychologist had to say to her; after she finished the entire package, she placed all the pages back into

It Takes 3

the envelope and returned it to the receptionist and took a seat in the waiting room. The receptionist told her that it would take about two hours for the doctor to go through the package, so she could go get some lunch if she wanted to, or she could come back another day; it was up to her.

She went to the cafeteria for a snack and then returned to the office to wait. This was the last part of the screening process, where they went over everything, the questions about family, morals, education, and future plans and then the questions about her reasons for wanting to be an egg donor, her feelings about the program, and the process so far. They talked about the future, hers and any possible children that may be born using her eggs. The doctor was most interested in her reasons for becoming a donor. What brought her to this moment? She explained everything in detail, how it all started with her own family, watching them go through infertility and how she desperately wanted to help but couldn't. She told him about the time she spent researching, and that's where she learned about egg donation. She couldn't help her family, but she could help someone else. The doctor asked her how she felt about there being a child somewhere in the world that she made possible. He asked her to explain her own feelings about being a donor and how she felt about the part she was playing in the entire process. So she explained to him just the way she explained it to her friends and others who asked. "Well, my best explanation is also the simplest one I could come up with. I personally feel that donating an egg to a couple who wants a child isn't really any different than giving a neighbor or a friend an egg for a cake she wants to bake." She sat back in her chair as she went on, "I've thought about this a lot, so when I explain it in these terms, it gives people a clear comparison and a way to think about it in simple terms."

The doctor was intrigued by this young lady as she continued. "If someone starts to bake a cake, they think they have all the ingredients, right? So they start dumping everything into the bowl, they need the cake, so they're short on time. Now this is happening last minute, so everything's in the bowl, but she finds that she's missing one ingredient, only one, but it's an important ingredient. Without this one ingredient, there will be no cake; this ingredient is crucial." The doctor smiles at the story that's unfolding. "Yes, she's missing the eggs, and there is no time to go to a store to get them, so she runs next door to her neighbor in desperation. She needs eggs. Now if you had eggs, what would you do?"

The doctor looked at her. "I would give her the eggs she needs."

"Exactly, so here I am, and I have plenty of eggs, so I give her the eggs. After all, you can't make a cake without eggs. Everyone knows that. I have plenty. Besides I never use all the eggs I have. Every month I throw some out. So I'm more than willing to give some to her. She's happy, I'm happy, and someone is going to have a great cake."

The doctor looked at her and nodded. "But what do you want in return?"

"Nothing, I don't want anything. As good as that cake is, I don't expect a piece. I'm just helping make something wonderful, if I can help I will."

"That's pretty clear," the doctor said.

"That's the best way I found to explain it. I tried to explain it as wanting to help others and using the terminology, but no one got it, or they thought I was all self-absorbed, thinking I'm doing this for the money or for a pat on the back, but once I started using this analogy, people got it." Her visual analogy was simple to understand, and it impressed the doctor so much that he asked if he could use it in the future; it was just so simple and easy to understand. It was obvious that this young lady had put a lot of thought into what she had decided to do. She had educated herself about the entire procedure, both hers as a donor as well as what her recipient would go through; her due diligence impressed him. This was a hardworking, street-educated young lady. She may not have a college degree, but her life had taught her more than any classroom could. Everything she had been through had been a learning experience for her. This young lady had been through a lot, and she was once a victim. She may have been crushed at one time, but she took every opportunity, every circumstance that she had lived through to learn and to grow.

As she talked, the doctor made notes in her chart. This young lady was open and honest about her life, its ups, downs, and all in between. After everything was completed, she left the office and waited for the thumbs-up or thumbs-down from them. The doctors got together to discuss their findings; she got a thumbs-up from both the psychologist and the fertility doctor. Everything's a go; it's time to move forward.

38

Summer and Matt received the news that their donor had completed all of the screening and was ready to go. They were informed that all of the tests went well, and they were ready to move forward. It's time to begin the process of their chosen fertility treatment. Summer confirmed that she was available for a quick checkup and to receive her birth-control pills. She's reminded that the pills are used to synchronize her and her donor's cycles. Summer is overjoyed; after so much waiting and so much stress, they are about to begin the next chapter of their book, the next chapter of their love story. The process has begun, and each player in this is now committed to one another, the donor and the recipients.

Summer and the donor will start taking their birth-control pills on the same day. They were both instructed that it was important to begin them as prescribed in order to get their cycles to sync. Being the recipient of donor eggs, Summer would be taking the pills to get her uterine lining ready to accept implantation of the embryo when the time came. Summer and Matt were also scheduled to meet with the psychologist to discuss their decision and how to sort through all the complicated feelings they may experience during and after the entire process. The doctor explained that the entire staff would be there if they had any

It Takes 3

questions or needed to understand more about the process and complications, if any, that could come up with her or her donor. Summer was then given all of her follow-up appointments as well as the expected retrieval date. Matt was informed that he would need to bring in a fresh sperm sample the morning of the retrieval; he explained that the sperm needed to be fresh so they could inseminate soon after retrieval. He also explained that it was best for Matt and Summer to abstain from having sex for at least forty-eight hours before the sample was collected, it wasn't mandatory, but it was considered best to provide the most optimal sample.

 As Matt and Summer took in all of the information, it seemed that things were moving forward pretty quickly now. Everything sounded good; finally they felt hope. He explained that soon after the retrieval, the eggs would be inseminated. To actually hear the words *insemination*, *embryos*, *transplantation*, and *implantation*, their excitement grew. The doctor went on to explain that after the insemination, it would take three to five days for the embryos to reach the proper stage to be transferred into Summer. Once what's called fusion occurs between the egg and the sperm, a new cell forms; this new cell is called the zygote, and as the cells continue to divide, it becomes a solid mass of cells called a morula. Once this morula reaches over one hundred cells, it becomes a blastocyte, otherwise known as an embryo. Once the sperm and the donor egg reach the embryo stage, Summer would come into the office where the transfer will take place.

 Matt and Summer smiled as the Doctor said, "Once the embryo is transferred into Summer's uterus, if all goes well, the embryo will implant itself into her endometrium, which is the lining of the uterus. And then as long as everything stays where it needs to be, that tiny embryo will continue to grow and develop into a baby, your baby." The doctor explained that the transfer is done between day 3 and 5 after the retrieval, whichever is better for the embryo, and Summer would need to be available between those days. One of those days when the embryos were ready he would have Summer return to the clinic to have the embryos transferred. Normal procedure was to implant one or two embryos, but they had chosen to have only one embryo transferred, but if she and Matt wanted, they could implant up to two embryos from this cycle.

Summer and Matt didn't know what was the right thing to do, so they needed some guidance. The doctor explained that transferring one embryo reduced their risk of twins. Implanting two embryos would of course increase their chances of multiples. At the beginning of this process, the clinic had suggested that they keep the option to freeze any high-quality embryos for possible use later on, but the donor was against that and had it removed from the contract. Freezing embryos was costly, at over $1,000 dollars for the originating process and $200 dollars plus a month, every month as a maintenance fee; that was $2,400 dollars each year, just in case, plus the original fee. It was pretty expensive. If this was something they wanted to have reconsidered, the contract could possibly be amended. As much as they were enjoying the process and all the speculation, neither one wanted to let their guard down. As much as they wanted to get excited, they were both protective about letting themselves enjoy the thought of being parents. They had been through so much, especially over the past year or so, but all the wondering about their future, about what was going to happen was finally coming to an end. The following Monday was the beginning. This was the day that they would begin the pills that would sync their cycles. In less than a week, the beginning of their beginning was going to begin; it would be the first day of a new future. The birth-control pills were going to be the easy part for both of the women, they'd both had been on birth-control pills before, and they knew what to expect, so no mystery in that. These first days were normal for the donor and pretty normal for Summer, normal for the days back when she didn't want to get pregnant.

It Takes 3

Once their cycles were in sync and regulated, Summer would take her estrogen supplements and receive regular ultrasounds to measure her uterine lining. While Summer was doing that, her donor would begin to self-administer her injectable fertility medications, for eight to eleven days. The shots would cause her egg follicles to grow at a rate much higher than normal. She would be monitored through blood tests as well as vaginal ultrasounds, during this time. Once her follicles are determined to be ready for retrieval, an HCG injection will be express-mailed to her. This is the shot that prepares her ovaries to release the eggs. The clinic will inform her of the exact time to administer this injection; this is the shot where timing is crucial. The retrieval would be scheduled thirty-six hours after the administration time of the HCG injection. Retrieval takes just fifteen to thirty minutes; a successful retrieval is marked with good quantity and quality eggs. As soon as all of this happens, Summer and Matt will be on their way to parenthood. After years of trying, frustration and pain, they were within weeks of making a long-awaited dream come true.

39

The whole shot thing still gave Stephanie the willies; although the nurses taught her the correct way to do it, the thought of sticking a needle into her own flesh made her nervous. This was the only thing that caused her anxiety, and she wondered if other donors felt as nervous about this. When she got home, she called her mom. She needed some moral support. Stephanie's mom offered to do it for her if she wanted but Stephanie assured her, "No, I think I can do this, I know I can. You know what Mom, I will do this."

Her mom and dad were completely supportive and gave her a pep talk.

"I know you can do this, honey. You're strong and you're stubborn. We're proud of you, for everything you've done. Not everyone would do something like this for someone else, family or not. You're giving that couple an amazing gift. You should be very proud of yourself!"

Stephanie felt good about what she was doing, but it was good to hear it from her mom and dad. It was good to hear it from anyone. When they hung up, Stephanie felt a sense of relief as she took a deep breath. With her parents' encouragement, she felt stronger, and she felt her courage grow with their words. Today was the day, her first shot. She took a deep breath and stuck the needle into her stomach. Feeling a little fear and apprehension, as she plunged the needle into her flesh. The needle was in her stomach. There it was, this tiny needle sticking right there in her stomach. It was so tiny she didn't even feel it. She pulled the plunger back a bit just as she was shown, then she pushed the plunger, and injected the medication. She pulled out the needle and disposed of it into the container she was given, it was done, and she had done it!

Stephanie was so excited she called her mom back, "I did it, I can't believe it, I did it, and you know what? It wasn't that bad."

"Good job, I knew you could do it!" Stephanie could hear her mom's surprise.

"See, I told you, I can do this. All I did was think about the couple I was doing this for and how excited they must be. I know that everything I go through will totally be worth it in the end."

The doctor told Stephanie that after she started the stimulation shots, she could become a bit uncomfortable. "I think I'm ready for this, all of it. Even though I might be a little uncomfortable, this is a special gift that I can give them. From what the doctor told me, this couple has tried really hard to make this happen. I guess they really want a family bad. He said they're really sweet, and her infertility came as a complete shock to them. I guess they were pretty devastated, but he says they were really excited when they saw my picture. I guess the mom looks a lot like me, she even likes a lot of the same stuff I like, that's one of the reasons they chose me. I'm so excited for them."

Stephanie continued giving herself shots through the week, everything went really well, and she felt great, until about the ninth day, and then it hit—the bloating, the uncomfortable feeling of heaviness. By the time retrieval day came, she was nearly doubled over with cramping and felt about twenty pounds heavier. Her parents took her to the clinic that morning. Her dad and mom dropped her at the front door. The clinic checked in as soon as she arrived; there was no waiting. The nurse took her to the back, but Stephanie wanted to wait to see her dad. Stephanie and her dad are very close. She couldn't think of leaving before she kissed him. Being put under made him nervous; he needed to see her before. He knew what could happen, it was rare, but still, this was his little girl. Stephanie knew how he felt, so just in case, she wanted to kiss both of her parents and tell them she loved them.

The staff at the clinic was patient. They gave her the time she needed, and after a few moments, everything and everyone was ready, including her. Stephanie's mom felt apprehensive and nervous in the waiting room. As positive as she was with her daughter, she thought this is not a necessary surgery for her to go through as every surgery carries some risk, but she didn't share her worries with anyone.

Stephanie's dad sat quietly wondering what the heck is going on back there behind those doors, the doors he watched his daughter pass through with a nurse. This entire process had been odd for her parents, but they kept their feelings to themselves, and now as they wait for it to be over, they worry. They can't help but worry about how she will feel later, not later that day, but later in life, how will she feel in the days, months, even years to come. Although she assured them that she looks at all of this as a gift, they wonder. For now all they could do was wait and be there for her.

After what felt like a lifetime, a nurse called her parents to the desk. "Stephanie's done; everything went well."

They signed her release and after-care forms. The nurse showed him where to park, but he was close to the door already and wanted to see his daughter. They were taken into the hall to wait for her. Stephanie was dressed and ready to go, but first, they informed her that everything went exactly as planned. She had produced twenty-two eggs. She was told that was really good, especially as a first-time donor.

It Takes 3

Stephanie spent some time in recovery before being released to her parents. As Stephanie was wheeled toward her parents, she looked tired. She was holding her stomach, and the nurse explained that she would feel some cramping, a little painful, like severe cramps, but with mild pain medicine, she should be fine. Steph looked pretty happy despite the pain. As she reached her parents, the nurse wheeling her handed her a beautiful gift bag.

"It's a gift from the recipient parents. They wanted to thank you. You did a great thing, you know." The nurse told her that they had dropped it off while she was in the procedure room.

"Thank you," Stephanie said as she reached into the bag to see what it was. The gift was a surprise and not something every recipient did for their donor. The nurse was also interested to see what they had left for her. Inside the bag was a lovely card and a box wrapped in beautiful sparkly tissue paper. Stephanie opened the box first. Inside the box was a beautiful willow tree statue. Willow tree statues are collectible angels, every Willow tree has a name, and this one was called Angel of Miracles. The Angel of Miracles statue depicted an angel holding a baby chick, how perfect! The envelope was beautiful, and Stephanie's name was written in beautiful artistic calligraphy. The card itself looked like a gift. You could tell that the parents took a lot of time considering both the gift and the card. It was a sweet surprise. Everyone wanted to hear what was written in the card, the statue was perfect, so the card had to be amazing. The nurse showed the statue to her coworkers; they all wondered how they found such a perfect statue. Stephanie opened the card and read it out loud:

> Dear donor
>
> Words cannot express how grateful we are to you for the gift you have given us! You have provided us with the chance to have a child, at a time when we were becoming discouraged. This past year has been difficult for us as we've faced one disappointment after another. Last July we began considering searching for a donor when we received

confirmation of my diagnoses, and we were told that egg donation was our only option if I was to carry our child myself. At first we had our doubts and uncertainties about doing this. We never thought we would find the right match. We looked through so many profiles before we finally saw yours. There were so many similarities between us. It was amazing! You were the perfect match, and we feel very lucky to have found you. We also know what a commitment it is both physically and emotionally to go through the process of injections and monitoring, and we really appreciate what you have done to help us toward our dream of having a family.

We will always remember you as the angel who helped to create our miracle.

From the bottom of our hearts, we thank you!

With much love,
Grateful and Hopeful

The card made Stephanie cry, it was such a thoughtful thing for them to do, and the message was beautiful and very personal. Stephanie knew this was a very special thank you directly from the hearts of a very grateful and hopeful couple. The words in the card made everyone tear up. You could actually feel the couple's gratefulness within the words they had written. The statue was perfect as well, a young angel kneeling, holding a baby chick; it was cute and very thoughtful.

Stephanie's mom commented, "This Mom sounds so much like you, this is something you would have done, what a lovely card." And it was.

40

In the recovery room, Stephanie had expressed an interest in knowing what happened to her eggs after the retrieval. The entire process was amazing to her, the nurses made a copy of some literature for her before she was released; it was a complete outline of what would happen to her eggs after retrival, before they were implanted into the recipient mother. It was a day-by-day synopsis:

> Day 0: This is your retrieval day. On day 0, the eggs are retrieved from the follicles that have resulted from ovarian stimulation. At this time, the retrieved eggs are counted and assessed for maturity and quality. The sperm is also prepped and readied for insemination or ICSI (intracytoplasmic sperm injection) of the retrieved eggs. Approximately four to six hours after your retrieval, the eggs will be inseminated or injected with sperm (ICSI). In normal IVF, many sperm are placed together with an egg, in hopes that one of the sperm will enter and fertilize the egg. With ICSI, once the eggs are retrieved, an embryologist will place the eggs in a special culture, and using a microscope and tiny needle, a single sperm will be injected into an egg. This will be done for each egg retrieved.

Day 1: The eggs are evaluated for fertilization; the combining of the egg and sperm should happen approximately sixteen to eighteen hours after insemination. Normal fertilization is the presence of two pronuclei, one from the egg and one from the sperm. If there are too few or too many pronuclei, that embryo is considered abnormally fertilized. All normally fertilized embryos are put into a special media that mimics the tubal fluid found in the human body.

Day 2: The embryos are briefly looked at to assess cell division. Most embryos will have between two to four cells on day 2. If the embryo has not divided by this time, that embryo is considered nonviable and is destroyed. At this time, embryology will decide if a day 3 or a day 5 transfer will occur. This is typically based on the quality of cell division of the embryos and the number of embryos available.

Day 3: Embryos at this stage usually have six to eight cells. If the recipient is having their embryo transfer, assisted zona hatching, a breech may be made in the shell of the embryo. This is also the day embryo biopsy for PGD may occur. If the embryo is not being transferred, then the embryos are placed into new media that mimics the uterine fluid of the human body.

Day 4: Your embryos continue to grow and develop into a compact ball of cells, about sixteen in all, known as a morula. If compaction does not start to occur on this day, blastocyst formation rates are decreased.

Day 5: The embryo develops into a blastocyst. At this stage, it is usually possible to grade the inner cell mass (ICM), the fetal component, and the trophectoderm cells (TE), the placental component of the embryo. Embryo transfers are often done on day 5, as well as cryopreservation of any fully expanded blastocysts. Any remaining viable embryos that are not fully developed are cultured on for possible freezing on day 6.

Day 6: Embryos on day 6 must be either transferred. If transfer was not done on day 5 or frozen. Any nonviable embryos are discarded. Day 6 is the last day that an embryo can remain in the lab without being transferred or cryopreserved.

It sounded so complicated, but it was all so interesting. As far as she knew, there had been no consideration of using the ICS procedure, but the lab would double-check everything to make sure. The plan was for the mom to be implanted on day 3 or 4. If everything went well, the doctors didn't think they would need day 5 or 6. Loaded with information, Stephanie felt pretty well informed, she knew what was happening and what was to come, and she was pretty satisfied. At this point, her part of this was done. All she could do now was hope that everything went well for the parents and that in about nine months, they would be holding their dream, made possible by donated eggs. Stephanie hoped that she would hear that the procedure had been a success; she even asked the doctor if she could be informed, and he told her that if the parents were all right with it, then yes, they would call her and let her know what happens; she hoped they would. After being so involved, she would love to hear a happy ending; they seemed like really sweet people who deserved to see their dream become reality. In the days that followed, she hoped and prayed that her couple would soon receive their dream.

41

Stephanie had read everything she could find about the procedure; she read every blog and moral opinion she could find about egg and sperm donation, as well as surrogacy. And now that her procedure was over, she thought she would go on with her life, but she needed more. During recuperation, she continued to read blogs and stories about IVF and egg donation, and some of the best information was found at: www.resolve.org. Amy Demma Esq, an attorney who has worked in this field for more than 11 years, is responsible for the writing of this and other information. Stephanie found her website at: www.eggdonationtoday.com.

There were so many myths out there, about why women donated.

Myth: It isn't your baby.

Busted!: I hear this worry from more prospective recipients of donor gametes (and donor embryo) than just about any other concern. I first address this matter in a legal context and discuss with clients that any donor (sperm, egg, embryo) should be expected to relinquish all rights to the gametes (or the embryos) as well as explicitly relinquish parental rights to children resulting from the donation. With sperm donation, this relinquishment is typically done through consents at the cryobank. With egg and embryo donation, it is recommended that relinquishment of donor rights be memorialized in a direct contract between the donor and the recipient.

Of equal concern, though, is whether or not the parent who lacks in a shared genetic connection with the child will feel a parental connection, while this should be explored with a mental health professional experienced in collaborative reproduction …the best response I have to offer is the following quote from a parent of a donor conceived child: "The child who came into my life is the most beautiful, spirited child…he is the child I was meant to have and he fills me with love every minute of the day."

Myth: It's the only option for older women.

Busted!: In addition to donor egg, donor embryo as well as adoption are family building options that many older women can consider (although there are age restrictions imposed in certain types of adoption). In some cases, donor embryo is actually a preferred option because of the lower costs and, once embryos that are available for donation are identified, this family building approach can actually be quicker than donor egg (for example, in the time it takes to go from putting a family building plan in place to actually cycling). Older prospective parents may find support and best guidance in how to achieve their dream of parenting at fertility centers but also in the offices of attorneys, mental health professionals as well as through various resources committed to providing information on alternative family formation.

Myth: Egg donors are exploited / only in it for the money.

Busted!: This is a common myth we often hear in the media. However, it is a concern that is also typically expressed early on when prospective parents are considering donor egg (sperm donors are typically offered very low compensation and donors of embryos are rarely compensated). The fact of the matter is that egg donors contend with a tremendous amount in exchange for their compensation. Their commitment of time, the often inconvenience to their daily lifestyle, the invasive medical screenings and other clinical procedures will, generally speaking, weed out from the donor applicant pool those young women who are purely financially motivated. Egg donation is simply not an easy process. Because egg (and often embryo) donors typically meet with a physician, a nurse, a mental health professional, often an attorney and perhaps other family building professionals, the uninformed applicant who may see this as a quick way to earn money or who may be lured by the promise of compensation is likely to reconsider when risks and the commitment required are explained.

Myth: "I should be worried that my donor will show up at my front door someday."

Busted!: When prospective recipients of donor gametes (egg or sperm) as well as those considering embryo donation embark on a donor search, the recipient will receive, in most cases, extensive demographic (as well as health and genetic) information about donor candidates. I remind clients who are worried about an anonymous donor searching for and finding the recipient family that the donor has received very little, if any, information on them. While anonymity is something we, as family building professionals, wonder about as technology and social media continue to evolve, the recipient family is actually at a much lower risk of being found than a donor may be. Also, should the recipient engage in a direct contract with their donor, often the contract will address the expectations of both parties with respect to future contact and/or a long-term expectation of anonymity. It is also helpful to recipients to know that donors, in fact, often express this very same concern relative to recipients searching for them. This matter, while appropriate to address in a donor contract, is one that should first be discussed with a mental health professional so that fears are addressed and a best plan (for the entire family as well as the donor) is put in place regarding future contact.

Myth: A donor conceived child is at risk for less than optimal medical care because his/her pediatrician will not know genetic information about the donor.

Busted!: In addition to the extensive medical (both personal and family) as well as genetic information made available to the recipient family, many donors will agree to be reached, in the future, should a physician treating a donor conceived child need additional medical information about the donor or the donor's family. In the many years that I have been working with donors and recipient families, I am happy to report that I have only been asked to reach out to a donor for additional medical information a few times and that in each of these cases, anonymity of both the donor and the recipient family remained intact. I encourage prospective recipients of donor egg, sperm or embryos to not only expect an extensive profile on a donor (and to ask for as much information as the donor is willing to and/or able to provide) but to also consider whether or not that donor will be available should a pediatrician want to know more about the donor or about the donor's family medical history.

This website was like a treasure chest for her; this site and the clinic she had worked with helped her separate the myths from the facts. She really liked the one about women doing this for the money, she knew that wasn't why she had done it from the beginning, but others felt that was why she had done it; it hurt even though she tried to understand that they were coming from a place of misinformation and were naive to the actual procedure. If they had any idea of the time and discomfort involved, they wouldn't think that.

Although she read about girls who had done it for that reason, she didn't see how; it was a lot to go through, and this was not an easy thing to do. In fact, the time that a donor had to commit was probably a big turnoff to many perspective donors. Then there is the injections, giving yourself injections isn't easy and finally the discomfort of producing numerous eggs. Stephanie herself felt so bloated it hurt. Then recuperation time, you cannot be alone due to potential postsurgery complications; every surgery carries with it some inherent risk, and this procedure was no different. Most of the surgical complications surrounding egg retrieval come from two basic facts about the surgery itself: first, a needle must be pushed through the vagina and into the ovary, and a number of other organs and sensitive tissues that lay nearby. The hypogastric artery (also known as the internal iliac artery) runs past the ovary, for example, as does the ureter. The surgeon often finds the ureter right next to the ovary, which puts the ureter at high risk for inadvertent damage. There doesn't seem to be very good statics on how often such complications occur. The little she did find made it seem pretty rare. Although she was pretty uncomfortable and felt a bit feverish, everything went well. But it is because of these possibilities that the clinic wanted her to have someone with her for the first forty-eight hours. Stephanie decided to stay with her parents; taking chances was not something she was willing to do. Her parents were happy to have her, and arrangements were made for her to stay with them for the entire weekend. In the hours just after the procedure, she was pretty uncomfortable, and when her fever spiked she made a call to the clinic, but other than the fever, she was doing pretty well. She was told to take ibuprophen for the fever, but if it didn't help, they asked her to call them back. The ibuprophen did its job, and Stephanie's worries were alleviated. Within a day, she began to feel better; the good thing was that Stephanie's retrieval was on a Thursday morning, so she only had to take a couple of days off of work, and by the following Monday, she was back to work and back to normal life. It felt like it had been weeks since her life or body belonged to her. With all the appointments, ultrasounds, injections, and other medications, her life and body pretty much belonged to the clinic. But they really tried to work with her schedule too, no one wanted her to miss too much work, she was doing an amazing thing for someone she didn't know, and everyone treated her as if she were. The clinic took care of her just as well as they took care of their IVF clients.

Through everything, Stephanie felt strong and confident, but she was also feeling pretty tired and ready to be done by the end. And now here she was through the entire process, and she had to admit that although the past weeks had been crazy, she was feeling pretty good about herself and everything she had accomplished. Through the entire process, Stephanie knew that the discomfort she felt would go away, but the joy she was feeling in her ability to help others in such an intimate way was overwhelming and made her feel pretty darn good.

42

Just as Stephanie was getting back into the swing of daily life, the fertility clinic called, the call wasn't completely unexpected, they had said that they would call to keep her informed. She was excited to hear from them. The fertility clinic was calling to check on how she was doing.

"I'm okay, I'm good," Stephanie told her.

"Good, if you have any questions or problems, call us, okay?" The nurse seemed genuine as she listened to Stephanie's voice.

"I will, thanks."

The call was also to inform Stephanie that they retrieved a total of twenty two eggs, they were very happy not only with the quantity but with the quality of them too . The nurse told her that they would have plenty to choose from, especially since most were considered good to excellent quality. The nurse explained that most women produce from eight to thirty-five eggs, the average is around twenty with about fourteen being usable. Stephanie's results were better than average, there were nearly twenty usable eggs, but the doctor choose eight that he considered supereggs. These were the eggs that would be inseminated with the receipients husband's sperm. From the eight, they hoped that the sperm would inseminate at least four.

It Takes 3

After three days the lab found all eight eggs were successfully inseminated and doing well; six of the eight were considered perfect embryos. The clinic made calls to both Stephanie and the recipient parents to give them the good news. They had six perfect embryos to choose from. It was all very exciting. Everything was going better than anyone could have hoped. The plan was to choose one or two of these embryos to implant into the recipient mother. There were, four girls and two boys to choose from, the sex of the embryos to be implanted would be up to the recipients, but no more than two embryos would be implanted. The choice was theirs, they could choose two girls, two boys, or one boy and one girl for implantation. It was up to them;

After so much frustration, the hopeful parents were eager to complete the procedure, but they hadn't considered the possibility of twins, but after thinking about it, they decided that it may be a good idea to give the twins thing a try; after all, who knew if they would ever be able to afford to do this again. The couple knew they wanted more than one child, but at one time? They thought about it and decided it was worth a try.

After a long conversation, they decided that they wanted to implant one boy and one girl.

The next morning, the recipient mom would be implanted with their twins. The reality of this was that not every implantation takes; there was a possibility of a miscarriage, and the possibility was even greater with twins. They had talked about this before, but it had been awhile; the doctor wanted to have the discussion again.

Because this was an implantation, the risks were higher. With twins, they could lose one or both of the embryos early on. He explained that the chance of both embryos attaching to her uterus was a long shot, but under the circumstances, he felt it was worth a try. The recipient parents chose to be implanted with one boy and one girl. If they kept both, that would be great. If for some reason only one implanted, then the baby's sex could be a surprise. Neither of them really cared if they had a girl or a boy, choosing one over the other would have been difficult, and choosing both made the choice easier. Choosing to be implanted with the two embryos meant that they could possibly have one of each as exciting as that was; it really didn't matter, they wanted a baby, and the sex didn't matter.

The night before the implantation, their excitement was so high they had a hard time sleeping. When they arrived at the clinic, they looked tired.

The girls in the clinic always thought it was cute, they were so excited, and they were receiving the greatest gift ever. The receptionist checked them in and told them to try to relax. From the moment they choose their donor, recipient parents are counseled to keep their stress levels as low as possible. The less stress the mom felt, the better her body could handle the implantation process. The clinic had everything ready, so the clients never had to sit in the waiting room more than about three minutes. This kept clients from sitting in a waiting room chair thinking and wondering about what was to come. Summer's implantation went well, the doctor told them that things looked good, but Summer was released and told to take it easy, and only time would tell if the embryos found their place and settled in now.

In the days to come, things seemed to be going well. Summer had an appointment ten days later to have a pregnancy test. The doctor told her that her HCG levels were up, and that was good. Summer and Matt were cautiously excited, and a repeat test was scheduled for two days later.

Matt and Summer returned to the doctor's office, and discovered her HCG levels had doubled.

"Well, it's official, it's confirmed, you guys are in fact pregnant. Congratulations you two!" The doctor was happy for them. Summer and Matt cried as they hugged each other.

43

After everything she had been through the months and years of trying, of hoping, of meeting doctors and specialists, test after test, the whole infertility treatment thing, the clinic visits, choosing an egg donor, Summer felt drained. But today it all seemed worth it, because finally they received their egg transfer, and things were going well.

Summer commented that she could feel changes in her body, but it had only been a couple of days. Within a week, she began to experience some cramping, but it was mild like the doctor had warned her. This morning she woke up really early. She was really nauseous, she hadn't been nauseous before, she was also cramping, but it was different, and it wasn't the same as it had been.

Summer got out of bed quietly so as not to wake Matt. She thought she might throw up so she went into the bathroom. Summer sat on the toilet and placed the waste basket in front of her. The nausea was getting worse, and she knew she was going to throw up. She thought maybe she was constipated, but she could only pee. When she wiped herself, she noticed some blood. It was a dark-red color. Just the sight of the blood made her cry, and she called for Matt. But Matt was asleep and didn't hear her soft cries. As she wiped again, she called louder as she cried harder, finally loud enough to wake him in a startle.

Matt came to her confused about what was happening, he tried to grasp what was happening, and he was half-asleep. He couldn't understand anything she was saying through her sobbing and his haze, but he saw the blood. He found the phone and dialed the clinic's emergency number. They had preprogrammed it into the phone when they gave it to him.

The number went directly to their doctor. Matt explained everything to him. The doctor reassured him that he didn't think it was anything to worry about; it was most likely the embryo implanting itself into Summer's uterus, and that was a good thing. But he could tell they were scared, really scared. He could hear it in Matt's voice and in Summer's cry, so he told them to go to the clinic as soon as they could, and he would meet them there.

Summer felt a little more at ease after Matt talked to the doctor, and she was finally able to get herself together enough to get dressed. They were both anxious as they drove to the after-hours part of the clinic.

The doctor met them there. The after-hours clinic looked like a small emergency room, there was a receptionist and a nurse waiting for them, the receptionist checked them in, and the nurse led them to the back. It was just seconds before the doctor appeared and checked on Summer as Matt and Summer held hands, afraid of what was to come. The doctor stood with them as the nurse placed that cold gel on Summer's belly for the ultrasound. They shared a look of concern with the doctor.

"It'll be all right. Let's see what we have here." His tone was reassuring.

As they both took a deep breath and held it, the nurse turned the ultrasound screen toward Matt and Summer. They let out a sigh and prayed, as they thought the nurse turning the screen toward them seemed to be a good sign.

The doctor pointed on the screen among a bunch of snow-looking stuff. "There, right there, you see that? That little sac, it looks kind of like a pea pod, that's your baby!. But it looks as if

It Takes 3

there's only one." Matt acted like he saw it but had no idea what he was looking at. Summer cried, and squeezed Matt's hand.

"One is what we wanted, one is good," Matt said.

"So what happened to the other one?" Summer asked.

"Well, all the bleeding was most likely the loss of the second one, but this baby looks great." The doctor congratulated them. "Everything looks good with this baby. It's implanted perfectly, and you, my dear, are going to be a mom. How's that feel?" As he said this, Summer cried with relief. Matt also had a tear of relief traveling down his cheek. Matt took Summer's hand and kissed her as they smiled at each other and squeezed each other's hands. The doctor performed a pelvic exam as a precaution as well, and everything looked good.

"According to the ultrasound and your measurements, you are just about four and a half weeks along, and that's exactly where you should be, congratulations! That little one is in the right place and growing just as expected, that's what we had hoped for, so just about eight months or so to go. Matt and Summer were beaming, and tears of happiness flowed as they hugged and kissed each other. They called each other Mommy and Daddy. It was an awesome sight to see couples like this, it was what kept these doctors going, and these kinds of moments touched these doctor's hearts. After the exam, Summer was cleaned up and released to go home and relax. Before they knew it, they were on their way home. Summer and Matt and baby made three. They both were feeling intoxicated with the news and the vision of that peanut or pea pod as the doctor called it on the ultrasound screen. They left the clinic with a clean bill of health and a photo of what they had seen on the screen; they got two copies and were both elated to they have the first photo of their baby in their hands, one for Matt to carry around and one for Summer. They talked nonstop all the way home, and during their conversation, they agreed that they didn't want to say anything to anyone just yet. Especially after this, they wanted to take some time to let this little one grow and for them to feel more secure. The morning had started out horribly and way too early, the fear of not knowing what was happening and the places that their imaginations took them was exhausting. They were so fearful at what could have been happening. Although they had lost one of the embryos, everything ended with good news, and they couldn't have been happier. Now, the excitement of all of this was nearly unbearable so that they decided to spend the day together, just the two of them, so they called in sick to work. Matt drove into the driveway with a big sense of relief. He helped his now-pregnant wife out of the car and up the stairs to their front door. They stood at the door for a moment and kissed each other.

Summer spoke first, "Can you believe it? We are going to raise our family here in this house."

Matt looked at her, and without a word, he swooped her in his arms, unlocked the door, and carried her over their threshold as he kissed her. He said, "This is the first day of our new life as a family."

44

A week after the scare, Summer returned to the clinic for a follow-up visit. It had been a great week, she wasn't worried about anything, she felt great, everything seemed good. The doctor was having her come in once a month, so she was to be scheduled for her next regular appointment in three weeks for her final clinic check, and as long as everything went well, she would be released to her regular OB-GYN for further care. It will be her regular OB who will take her through the rest of her pregnancy; he will be the one to actually deliver their baby. Summer had called her OB to let him know that his referral to the fertility specialist had paid off, they were pregnant, and he was excited for them. Her doctor already knew this, the clinic kept him informed, but he didn't tell her that.

Summer was ecstatic that finally she would be one of those women coming in to the office with a growing belly and complaining about getting bigger and having indigestion; she was looking forward to all of it. The fertility clinic recommended she see her doctor at least once a month throughout the pregnancy, and her doctor agreed.

During her first appointment, Summer was eight weeks along, and the checkup went well. The baby was developing just as it should, with a strong heart and a healthy mom. Summer's the perfect patient, doing everything that had been asked of her. She was feeling a little tired, so the doctor changed her prescription for a prenatal vitamin with iron. She had to have her blood drawn to check her beta-HCG levels again, just to check that they are increasing as they should. The office staff was so happy to see her, they were all very happy for her, and every staff member congratulated her and told her to give Matt a big hug from them.

Summer told them that Matt was absolutely beside himself with this, she told them that she was afraid that he wouldn't be able to keep their news quiet, and he was just too excited. Summer's doctor talked to her about everything about how having a baby will be one of the most joyous times she and Matt will ever experience. This had been a long road for them, but they were finally here. Now the real work starts, from the anticipation of bringing the baby home, to choosing a name and colors for the nursery. They will have nonstop decisions from now on. He went on to tell her that no matter how well they plan, they will not be fully prepared for what that tiny being will do to their lives, for their lives.

"You can read everything about pregnancy and what a body goes through, but you still won't be prepared for all the changes your body will go through over the next seven months, but read everything you can, because it will all help you to understand or at least accept some of these things. No matter what you read, remember that pregnancy is different for every woman. Some women glow with good health and vitality, while others feel absolutely miserable and struggle." He handed her a pamphlet that had been put together by his office. "Here is a pamphlet that lists some of the changes you might experience. It tells you what they mean and which symptoms may warrant a call to me. I hope it helps."

The pamphlet listed the following:

1. *Bleeding.* About 25 percent of pregnant women experience slight bleeding during their first trimester.
2. *Breast tenderness.* Sore breasts are one of the earliest signs of pregnancy.
3. *Constipation during pregnancy.* The muscle contractions that move food through your intestines slow down, resulting in uncomfortable constipation and gas.
4. *Discharge.* It's normal to see a thin, milky white discharge (called leukorrhea) early in your pregnancy.
5. *Fatigue.* The body is working hard to support a growing fetus, which can wear you out more easily than usual.
6. *Food cravings and aversions.* More than 60 percent of pregnant women experience food cravings, and more than half have food aversions.
7. *Frequent urination.* Your baby is still pretty small, but your uterus is growing, and it's putting pressure on your bladder. Don't hold it in.
8. *Heartburn.* You can also try raising your pillows when you sleep.
9. *Mood swings.* It's okay to cry, but if you're feeling overwhelmed, try to find an understanding ear—if not from your partner, then from a friend or family member.
10. *Morning sickness.* Nausea is one of the most universal pregnancy symptoms, affecting up to 85 percent of pregnant women.
11. *Weight gain.* Although you're carrying an extra person, don't go by the adage of "eating for two." You only need about an extra 150 calories a day during your first trimester.

Any of the following symptoms could be a sign that something is seriously wrong with your pregnancy. Don't wait for your next prenatal visit to talk about it. *Call your doctor right away if you experience* the following:

- Severe abdominal pain
- Significant bleeding
- Severe dizziness
- Rapid weight gain or too little weight gain

Summer left the doctor's office feeling as prepared as she could. She had some very helpful information and was ready for her journey. Overjoyed, she went home to give Matt the information her doctor had given her.

45

That evening Summer shared her day with Matt. She told him about her visit with the doctor and how everyone in the office sent their congratulations and hugs to him. She told him about the ultrasound they did just to be sure everything was going as planned. She shared the pamphlet with him as he read it from front to back. Matt loved taking in anything about the pregnancy. He wanted to know as much as he could about what was going through Summer's body. Summer was very excited. She was beaming, just like the pamphlet said. Matt was happy to see her back to her old self. She was healthy and happy again after the bleeding and the loss of one embryo; once again, she was walking on clouds.

Matt loved seeing his wife like this, it made him happy, he loved her smile and cherished every day with her, she was his life, his best friend, and she was everything to him. That night over dinner, Summer and Matt sat on the sofa curled up with their new tablet computer looking at baby names and nursery designs. They were having fun looking up some of the oldest names they could find. They sat laughing and enjoying thinking about their future, when they were startled by the ring of their home phone. The only people who called the home line were their parents, solicitors, or the doctors' offices. Since Summer had just seen her doctor, she didn't think it would be them, so that left some solicitor or one of their parents. They considered not getting up to answer, but thought better of it. Caller ID showed it was Matt's folks they needed to answer it. Summer was a bit of a worrier when it came to their parents. Although everyone was in fairly good health, she worried about them.

"You'll never know," she said as reached for the phone.

"You talk to her," Matt said, "'cause you know if I get on that phone, she'll know something's up."

"No, you talk to her, you'll be fine. Just remember we aren't going to tell anyone yet, not anyone." Summer reminded him she rubbed his arm and handed him the phone.

Matt answered, "Hey, Mom." As they chatted about general stuff, his mom asked if things were all right.

"Why yes, everything is fine. Why do you ask?" Matt tried to stay light and matter of fact, but his mom could hear that something in his voice. All his life, Matt's Mom could tell when something was going on in her son's life. Even now as an adult, she could still hear something in his voice. He sounded happy, but not just happy. There was a joy deep within him.

"There's something going on that you want to share?" she asked. "'Cause you sound really good. Summer okay?"

"Yes, Mom, Summer is great!" At that, she knew something was up, and Matt could feel it. When he used the word *great*, a sense of joy came over him, a joy that he couldn't stop, and he blurted it out, "She's great, she's pregnant." As fast as it came out, he wanted to put it back in as he looked at Summer. Instead of seeing a mad, angry face, he saw Summer smiling, as if she knew this would happen. Matt covered the receiver and whispered, "I'm sorry, but she was getting all worried. It just happened, sorry."

Summer smiled and said, "It's fine, don't worry about it." And she kissed him lightly. Matt heard the concern in his mom's voice, and after everything they had all endured in this quest for a child, he just couldn't keep this news to himself. His mom was always there for them, and he couldn't help himself. It was worth it too, when he told her she was so happy, she called for his dad and told him. Matt could hear the joy they shared over the phone line. It was really cute to hear them call each other grandma and grandpa, he knew his mom was crying, heck she cried at television commercials, so she had to be crying at this, Matt knew she would.

Summer could hear Matt's parents through the phone, she was sitting right next to Matt on the sofa. Hearing her in-laws excitement warmed her hear, she loved them and knew this would be a happy time for all of them. As Summer lovingly touched her belly. she thought, *What a wonderful family you have little one.* Summer had been enjoying listening to Matt talk about the months to come, she loved seeing and hearing him so excited. Finally after some trepidation and a bit of a scare, he seemed relaxed as if the ropes of dread had been cut, and he was free, free to be excited about this wonderful thing that they wanted so desperately. When he hung up, Summer looked at him with that big, amazing smile and said, "Now, you have to call my parents."

"Me? Why me, you should call your parents. Don't you think they would like to hear this from you?"

"No, you have to call them. We had a deal, neither of us was supposed to tell anyone yet. But you told, and besides, you know my dad will get a kick out of you calling, he loves talking to you.. You know how old-fashioned he is." What Matt didn't know was that Summer had already told her mom and she had probably told her father by now, but she wasn't going to tell Matt that; after all, they had an agreement and she didn't want him to know she broke that agreement first. She figured Matt had assumed that she had told her mom; after all, they were very close, he knew that she told her mom everything. After she told Matt Summer just couldn't keep this news to herself, she had call her mom right after she gave Matt the happy news.

Summer was relaxing, lying on the sofa with her legs elevated on a pillow, this was Matts idea he had read something about how this being a good position for a pregnant woman to lie in. Matt enjoyed spending time on the Internet finding information about pregnancy, and babies. Whenever he found something of interest, he shared it with Summer. Learning about things that could help make her pregnancy easier made him feel good. Summer knew from the beginning that neither of them were going be able to keep this news to themselves, but she wasn't going to let him know she cracked first, besides she knew that all this pampering wouldn't last for the entire seven months or so, so she was going to enjoy every bit of it for now. Matt knew he would continue to pamper her, but he wasn't going to argue with her; after all, she was in a delicate state. At least that's what she kept telling him.

He loved talking to her folks and couldn't believe that she really hadn't told them, but even if she had, he would love to tell them the good news, so he picked up the phone and dialed their number. Her father answered the phone, "Hi Matt, what's up?"

"Well, I wanted to talk to you about something important." Matt kept his tone steady as if he were going to ask for stock tips or gardening ideas or something. He loved messing with them. It was dinnertime, and when he heard his mother-in-law calling his father-in-law for dinner, he knew he picked the wrong time to sit on the phone chatting about nothing. After a few minutes, he heard his mother-in-law get all serious; it was time to tell them. As he began to explain the real reason for his call, he got all choked up. Once he composed himself, he let out a quick, "We're pregnant!"

"What? What did you say?" his father-in-law was a little hard of hearing. "Hold on, Matt, let me put you on speakerphone so Mom can hear you too."

They both knew what he was saying, but Summer had told them about their deal, so they weren't going to let him know that they already knew. "Okay, now what did you say?"

Matt had composed himself as he told them. "Summer and I are pregnant, and we are going to have a baby, in about six and a half months."

The next thing Matt heard on the other end of the phone was quiet, not a word, nothing, until finally he could hear a faint crying sound. It was Summer's mom crying tears of joy. Even though she knew, hearing it from Matt made her cry; he sounded so happy.

Matt handed Summer the phone and quietly said, "Here, Summer, take this. Your mom's crying. You know I can't stand it when you girls cry."

Summer took the phone from Matt. "Mom? Mom? Mom are you all right?"

"I'm fine, but hearing it from Matt just makes it all so real. I can't believe my baby's pregnant. I just can't believe it, after all this time. So is Matt just over the moon about this?"

"Yes he is, we both are." As soon as Summer got on the phone and heard her mom crying, she too broke down. Matt watched helpless as his wife and mother-in-law cried like babies; he was happy that they were tears of joy.

When they hung up, Summer's mom wanted to go right over to their house. She wanted to share this moment with the kids. Although Summer had secretly told her, this call made it all very real. She headed to get her purse and jacket, but her husband stopped her to give the kids some time alone.

"It's been a long, hard road for them. I think they need to enjoy their happiness together; they don't need the in-laws butting in. We'll have plenty of time to enjoy all of this with them," Summer's father said.

It had been some time since they had seen their daughter, and they were very excited to see them. Matt's parents felt the same way, and this was going to be very exciting for all of them. Matt and Summer's first baby and each of the parents were excited about becoming grandparents.

46

Summer's pregnancy was going very well, she was feeling great, and so far, she was loving the whole experience of being pregnant. She was enjoying every moment, every craving, and every ounce she gained; after all, it was all happening to help sustain the little life inside of her. Every day was a new experience, and she was enjoying it all. As she stopped and remembered that first time, she began feeling the butterfly flutters in her tummy, which was an odd, almost-nauseous feeling. Then there was that morning that she was getting dressed only to realize that her jeans would no longer button. She laughed to herself knowing that under any other circumstances, she would have been upset, but that morning, she ran to show Matt that she needed new pants, maybe some of those odd-looking pregnancy pants.

Summer was so excited to go shopping for maternity clothes. She enjoyed everything about being pregnant, and Matt enjoyed it all with her. But nothing compared to the day when she finally felt the first kick, it took her by surprise, she had felt some of the stretches, but that first real kick, she was overjoyed. That first one was just a slight feeling of a kick, but as the baby grew, so did the force of those kicks. It was an awesome feeling to feel her baby grow and to watch her own belly grow to accommodate their little one. The entire experience was a joy for both of them. They

It Takes 3

went to every appointment together, and Matt was right there at every moment, asking questions and learning everything he needed to know about Summer's experience and what he could do to help her be comfortable as she got bigger and bigger.

The doctor was pleased with everything, the baby was growing on schedule, and Summer was staying healthy and watching her diet. In her third trimester, Summer had begun to feel an odd sensation, a jumpy feeling at regular intervals in her tummy. The doctor told her that was the baby having hiccups. Hiccups? Really, a baby could get the hiccups while in his wife's uterus? Matt found that extremely odd. Matt really didn't believe that hiccups were possible until one evening as they watched TV, Summer felt the baby's hiccups. She showed Matt her belly, and he watched it move at regular intervals. Then Matt put his ear to Summer's belly and talked to the baby as he did this. He could hear the hiccups. Summer couldn't hear them, she couldn't put her ear to her own tummy. Matt was sure that they were loud so he turned the television off, hoping she could hear them. The sound was coming from within her tummy, the baby had the hiccups, and the entire night was hilarious. A few weeks later, they had another evening full of laughs. This was the evening when the baby's foot actually pushed out from Summer's belly to the point that you could see the entire outline of it; it was so obviously a foot that Matt had to take a photo, and it was captured. He teased Summer that it looked like she had eaten a baby, and it was trying to get out.

Summer lovingly hit Matt. "That's not funny." But despite herself, she laughed too. Summer couldn't really see what Matt was seeing, so she looked at the photo. "Oh my gosh, it is a foot." They were both amazed at the things that were happening to her body; the once peanut-size baby was becoming a full person, taking up more and more space. Whenever Summer felt the baby stretch, it was beginning to feel as if the baby was going to just break through her body, and it felt odd. Matt talked to the baby every night. Summer remembered the first time he actually felt the baby move. That night he got all emotional, it took Summer by surprise. Matt had always been good about showing emotion, but this was different. It was at that moment that she saw what a wonderful daddy he was going to be. It was also that moment that everything hit Matt, and he realized that he was actually going to be someone's daddy. Knowing you're going to have a baby and planning for it couldn't and didn't prepare them for the feelings they were experiencing. For so long the thought of being a mom and a dad seemed like a fairy tale like, they wrote the story, but it wasn't real, but this was real. The results were real, Summer's growing belly was real, it was as if suddenly Matt was hit with this incredible sense of responsibility, they were going to be someone's parent. Matt and Summer enjoyed the process of watching their baby grow, they discussed their future, they made plans.

The last couple of months of Summer's pregnancy brought with it more discomfort for Summer. Each day seemed to be longer and longer as they both worried about what was to come. What would labor feel like? When would it happen? Would they be at home? Would they be out? Would that water-breaking thing be messy? So many questions. Although they had attended prenatal classes and learned everything they could they still felt unprepared. They shopped for baby items they needed, and they had a beautiful baby shower where they received so many things for their little one. They loved the blankets and layettes that friends of theirs and their parents made for them. They received a quilt that was embroidered with their last name; they received toys, sleepers, and tons of diapers; and they had boxes and boxes of diapers. Summer and Matt had fun designing and decorating the nursery, which was done in a black-and-cream palette. It was perfect since they didn't know the sex of the baby yet. They decided not to find out the sex of the baby, they had both agreed that they wanted it to be a surprise, and they stood by their decision. Although it made things a bit more difficult and they had struggled on and off with this decision, should they? Shouldn't they? They knew everyone else wanted to know; they all kept asking. After a lot of thought, Matt and Summer decided that they wanted to wait until the baby was born, or did they? But in the end, they decided that after everything they had been through, the wait would be worth it at that moment when the doctor announced it's a...

They knew it was old-fashioned and maybe even a little silly in this day and age, but it felt like the right decision, the right way to end these past nine months. Another big decision made in their new lives, they were both surprised about all of the decisions involved in a new growing family; neither of them had any idea it would be like this. But with each decision, they felt more and more confident and somewhat ready to become parents. At Summer's seven-month checkup, the baby was looking great; besides the fact that she was getting bigger and bigger and feeling more and more tired, she was doing well. As each day moved into the next, Summer was more and more ready to see and hold this little one in her arms, instead of carrying it around in her belly. The doctor talked to them about choosing a date for a planned induction, but neither Matt nor Summer agreed with this procedure that had become common practice. Neither of them wanted to induce unless of course it was actually necessary. Necessity was one thing, but induction by choice to make thing convenient was not something they wanted to do. Both of them knew plenty of couples who did it, but to them it seemed selfish to do it for convenience's sake. They wanted their baby to stay safe as long as possible. They felt that when the time was right, the baby would know. It wasn't up to them to mess with God's plan. They both had hopes of having a completely natural labor and birth. That was what they wanted. Summer wanted to feel everything, she had worked so hard for this pregnancy, and she didn't want to miss anything; even the pain of giving birth was something she was looking forward to. Summer had always planned on having a completely natural birth. She didn't want an epidural or any other drugs. Summer was intent on not messing with Mother Nature in any way, she felt that she had already lost one fight with that lady, and she wasn't going to push her luck. So now this entire birth thing was just a waiting game.

47

At her last appointment, the doctor told them that the baby could come at any time now, and Summer would need to stay close to home and close to the hospital. Their lives were now in the baby's control, just a glimpse into their future. Summer and Matt had no power over this, and everyone knew this had to be hard for them. They were such control freaks, but not this time, and it made them laugh. The fact that something so tiny now had control of these two adults' lives was so funny. Matt and Summer found it all a rather comical turn of their lives, and even their parents and friends all laughed about it.

At her next checkup, Summer felt great, and she had more energy than she had in months. That afternoon, she felt so good she went home and got busy doing laundry, cleaning, and working on finishing some of the baby items that she had been making. Summer was really enjoying her nesting time, this was her time to get ready for her baby, but although she was enjoying this time, she was also very ready to be done with the pregnancy as well.

This night Matt and Summer enjoyed time together eating dinner in bed because after a busy day, Summer was just so swollen and uncomfortable that she needed her feet and legs elevated. The past couple of days, Summer hadn't eaten much, she just wasn't very hungry, but she stayed so busy that Matt was a little worried about her. Summer knew he was worried, but she felt great, and she joked with him that there just wasn't any room in her belly for food anymore.

That evening, they decided to curl up in the bed together to watch a romantic movie after dinner. Summer didn't eat much again, but she wanted popcorn and a chocolate bar during the movie. As she enjoyed the mixture of the salty and sweet, she was hit with a pain. It was pretty severe.

"Wow, what was that?" she said as she moved. But just as suddenly as it came, it was gone. About an hour later, it hit her again. Just like before, she didn't expect this, what was this? She wondered if it could be the beginning stages of labor. It was still a little early, but maybe they were those Braxton hicks contractions she had heard so much about. Summer needed to get up and walk around. Sitting made her feel anxious, and walking made her feel a little better, after walking around, the pain subsided, but then when she sat back down, the pain returned. This was not the signs of labor they had read about, nor was it anything they had talked about in any of the prenatal classes. But the pains were not going away, so they thought this must be labor. Matt started to keep track of the time between her contractions, the pains were still about an hour or so apart, so they knew there wasn't anything to worry about, no reason to rush off to the hospital yet. Matt had done his homework, and he studied everything he thought he needed to know so that when the time came, he would be ready. But the contractions were still so far apart, and they were still erratic. They knew they didn't need to rush off. They knew that labor, especially for first babies, could last for hours and hours. They didn't want to spend more time at the hospital then they had to. Home was much more comfortable. Matt knew all of this, but he was worried and decided to call the doctor anyway.

When Matt called the office, the answering service had the doctor call him back. When he spoke to the doctor, they were told to ride it out. This was their first baby, and the contractions could actually go away on their own, but if not, it could be Summer's body getting ready for the labor process, the earliest stages of the labor process, and that could take hours.

The doctor suggested they get some rest, to make sure they have everything ready for the hospital; he suggested a shower but to eat lightly if Summer was hungry. Once the contractions were between five to seven minutes apart for at least an hour, then they may head to the hospital. The pains came very irregular, but they were there, so they knew that neither of them was going to get much sleep if any.

Matt wanted Summer to at least rest, but that wasn't going to happen either, so she decided to take a shower; maybe the warm water would relax her. Besides, a shower would give her the opportunity to clean up, do her hair just in case they needed to go to the hospital tonight. If this was the beginning of labor, she knew that Matt was going to be a camera-happy daddy. He already was, she couldn't imagine what he would be like during the birth of their child, so she wanted to be ready, just in case. Her water hadn't broken yet, and it had been a bit since her last pain, so she thought it was better to be ready than not.

During her entire shower, she didn't have any pains at all. When she got out, she decided to try to do her hair since it had been awhile since she had any pains at all. The doctor had told Matt that if the contractions continued and reached that five- to seven-minute point or if her water broke, then they should go directly to the hospital. Their doctor told him that he was on call that evening, so if and when they got there, he would be paged immediately and would meet them in Labor and Delivery. But he didn't think he would see them, not yet anyway, and if they got through the night, he did want to see them in the office in the morning.

Summer was just over thirty-three weeks along, still a bit early to have a safe delivery. Summer knew this, and she was nervous, but she enjoyed the shower; the warm water felt good running over her body. When she emerged from the bathroom, she looked amazing, her hair was clean and full, her makeup was perfect, she had a glow about her. Summer had done all of that all by herself, but now she was tired, and she wanted to lie down. She knew she probably wouldn't sleep, but she hoped to get some rest. When Summer reached the bed as she sat on the edge of the mattress, she stood back up very quickly. She felt the warm fluid running down her leg.

She screamed, "Get a towel. Matt. Quick—get a towel" Matt stood frozen by her outburst. "Now! Get a towel, my water just broke" Matt ran to the bathroom and grabbed the towel Summer had just used, but there was already a puddle on the carpet. Summer was embarrassed; she thought that somehow she would know when this would happen. She had always thought those stories about pregnant women out in some public place when their water broke was an exaggeration. She thought that women should be able to feel this coming, but here she was, not in a public place, but she still she didn't know this was coming, and it came as a shock to her. Summer had always thought she was in tune with her body enough to know if this was going to happen, she thought she'd have some kind of warning, but she didn't. Matt gave her two towels, and he had a third trying to help her clean up. As Matt was wiping her legs down, he noticed traces of pink in the fluid. It worried him as he tried to help her to the bathroom. She felt a pressure that made her feel like she needed to urinate. As she sat on the toilet, more fluid ran out of her body, she thought it was urine, but she didn't have any control of it as she tried to stop the flow. When the fluid seemed to nearly stop, Summer wiped herself, and she noticed a little bit of pink as well. They knew that her water had broke, and she was scared. It was still to soon for the baby come. After Matt helped her get to the bathroom, he ran around the house and checked that they had all the last-minute stuff. He put things in the car, grabbed his cell phone charger, threw it in Summer's purse. He

It Takes 3

thought he might need it. He knew it was too early but this was happening, and he was nervous. He felt like he was running in circles trying to remember everything. Thank goodness Matt and Summer thought way ahead, they had packed the car with all their essentials about a week ago. They packed the things that could sit in the car, but only the things they thought they would want or need—little things like snacks for Matt, water, a spare camera just in case they forgot theirs, magazines, an iPad, spare makeup and lip gloss for Summer, and her silly stuffed animal from her childhood that would serve as her focus item. They tried to think of anything they might need or want in case the labor process was long.

Summer made herself a cute hospital gown that she wanted to wear during labor, she made it just like those hospital gowns, but hers was in a really cute baby-themed material. She made it fit her pregnant body and used Velcro so that she would be able to tailor it to her nonpregnant body after the baby was born. She made it because she wanted to be sure her bottom would be covered during the walks she had planned during labor. It was really cute as she was very proud of herself; she had never made anything like this before. She had asked the doctor if she could wear it, he and the hospital had given their permission, the doctor said they were pretty picky especially in labor and delivery, but the gown met all the specifications they insisted on. As she sat there on the toilet, fluid still leaking from her body, she noticed that the pink tinge was now a bloody liquid. It seemed to be just a little bit, so she wasn't too worried.

All of a sudden she felt a warm gush and something pass through her vaginal opening, it didn't feel like fluid, but it felt thicker. Summer felt her stomach flop as she wiped herself, she looked at the tissue, it was bright red, and there was a lot of it. Summer began to shake at the sight of it, and she screamed for Matt. Summer continued to wipe herself, to wipe the blood, frantic to make it stop, but it wasn't stopping, and Matt wasn't coming, nor was he answering her calls for help. So she tried to stand up, to go to the door to call him again, to get to the phone, something. As she stood up, there was another gush of warm, bloody fluid that puddled at her feet. Summer suddenly felt dizzy, she tried to steady herself with the wall near the toilet, she needed to get Matt. As she tried to yell for him, again she felt the room began to spin, she was afraid she was going to fall, so she lowered herself to the floor where she sat propped against the wall. Summer was scared, she hadn't felt the pains she had earlier, but the blood, there seemed to be so much blood. Once she was safe on the floor, she gathered all her strength and screamed Matt's name again.

Matt heard her, and the sound of her voice gave him chills; he came running, nearly falling on his face as he came to a skidding stop as he rounded the corner into the bathroom. He had yelled to her as he ran up the stairs, something was wrong; he heard it in her voice, but she wasn't answering him. This was not good; that was evident. But Summer didn't hear him, and she had passed out.

Matt reached for her, calling to her, "Honey, I'm here," but nothing. He began to yell at her, "Summer, Summer! Wake up, babe, oh my God." There on the floor, sitting among a pool of blood was Summer looking as white as a sheet and not responding to him. His heart stopped as he took in the sight of their bathroom and reached for his cell phone, but it was already in the car.

There was so much blood on the floor, Summer looked white as a sheet, as she came to, she sounded so weak as she spoke his name. "Matt?"

48

Matt knew he should call 9-1-1, but he didn't think he had time, he helped her to her feet, wanting to carry her, but they needed to get down the stairs, and that just didn't seem safe. He helped her down the stairs and to the car. Summer was so weak and shaking so hard that she couldn't hold herself up at all; at the bottom of the stairs, Matt lifted her in his arms and rushed to the car. He sat her gently into the passenger seat and buckled her in. He ran to the driver's side and started the car. As he drove, he dialed the hospital's Labor and Delivery phone number he had been given, he had input the direct number into his cell phone during one of their prenatal classes, and now he was glad he did. He was also grateful for their new car with its hands-free phone system. He could drive as he explained their situation to the nurse, she told him he should have called 9-1-1 as well, but he was on his way and would be there within five minutes. Summer was quiet, scared, and crying. She still had not had a contraction since before her shower. She kept apologizing for the mess she knew she was making on the seat of their new car. Matt told her it was fine, trying to sound light; after all, they had splurged for the leather seats. Matt could see the blood on Summer's legs. Summer could feel the warmth of blood escaping from her body, it didn't feel as bad as it had in the bathroom, but she could feel it. She was glad that the hospital was so close to their home, and at the speed Matt was traveling, they would be there in no time.

Summer smiled and softly said, "Just think, babe, next time we walk into our house, the two of us will be three." Then she closed her eyes, trying to rest.

Matt was afraid she had passed out. "Babe, are you all right?"

"Yea, I'm all right, I'm just so tired." Summer knew that it could be a long night; she was scared, tired, and excited all at the same time. She thought about what was to come, soon she knew they could be holding their baby, and the whole experience so far had been disappointing. Nothing was happening the way she had imagined, the way she had it planned.

Matt pulled into the emergency entrance. There was a nurse from Labor and Delivery waiting for them with a wheelchair, and she told Matt where to park and to go directly upstairs to labor and delivery. She rushed Summer directly upstairs to labor and delivery. "Come directly upstairs, you're already registered, we'll take care of everything else upstairs."

Matt and Summer had pre-registered at the hospital during their prenatal classes; Anything that could be done before hand, they did; All her paperwork was done, bags were packed, the nursery was ready, all in an effort to relieve some of the craziness that the onset of labor could bring. But here they were, rushing around and extremely frantic, the only bag they had was the heavy bag of burden and fear. Summer's contractions intensified in the elevator, the blood had soaked through her clothes and she was having difficulty staying alert. "Hang in there Summer, we're almost there" The nurse knew that Summer was in trouble. As soon as the doors opened she rushed past the labor rooms and went directly to one of the critical care units. Summer quietly she kept saying "Matt, wher'e Matt? I need Matt" but nobody was listening to her. The staff was trying to get her to settle down as they undressed her, but even in her weakened state she still fought them; they had to give her a shot to calm her down. Matt had

It Takes 3

left Summer in the hands of the nurse reluctantly, but Summer needed immediate care and someone had to move his car from the emergency entrance..

Matt parked the car and ran through the hospital's entrance, through the halls into the elevator, ignoring anyone who yelled at him to slow down. Once in the elevator, he leaned against the wall, put his hands to his head and slid to his knees as he tried to catch his breath and comprehend what was happening. Once the doors opened on the Labor and Delivery floor, he sprinted to the nurses' station. It was obvious who he was even before he said a word. Breathless he said "Summer, where is she, I'm here" Matt was frantic and for good reason, Summer was in trouble. The nurse tried to calm him down as she explained that Summer had been taken to the critical care room down the hall. Matt turned to where she was pointing but he didn't know where that was, they never showed them a critical care room on their tour; he was confused. The nurse came out from the desk and took Matt's arm "You can't go there, not right now, we need to give the doctor some time to evaluate her condition."

In the critical care room things were chaotic, as nurses rushed around getting things ready, lights, tables, instruments, whatever the doctor may need was ready. The nurse's station had already paged the Doctor, he was on his way. The nurses did their jobs with precision as they had examined Summer, placed a new pad between her legs and remained upbeat for her sake, but they knew she was in trouble, this kind of bleeding was not normal.

Within seconds, the doctor was in the room and got right to work. Everything seemed to be in a fog for Summer, she kept calling for Matt, she could tell that things were hectic, she knew the doctor was there, but all she wanted was Matt.

As Matt tried to listen to the nurse all he wanted was to be with his wife, but he couldn't; he wasn't even sure where she was.

After some time, he was taken to her. As he entered the room, he knew something was wrong. Summer looked spaced out, barely even coherent, but she knew he was there, and she held her hand out to Matt. He grabbed her hand and kissed her. "It'll be all right, babe. Soon we'll be holding our baby, this will all be worth it, I love you."

The nurses continued working on Summer and talking softly among one another. Summer was hooked up to three IVs two were some kind of medication the other one was a pint of blood, she was also hooked up to numerous machines and monitors. The nurses moved quickly and with purpose, each seemed to have a specific job, they all worked together like a well-practiced symphony. So much was happening all around them.

Another doctor came into the room to assist their doctor. He was introduced as some kind of a specialist. Matt heard them but didn't get his name or specialty. He felt a sense of relief knowing that Summer was being cared for, he felt that everything would be fine, she was getting the care she needed. As the specialist checked Summer, Matt was escorted into the hallway by Summer's OB. "Matt, Summer is hemorrhaging, we need to get her into surgery right away, we need to perform a C-section." He went on to explain that they couldn't get her bleeding under control . they suspected that her placenta may have torn from the wall of the uterus, or it may have even ruptured. "We've examined her and done an ultrasound, and the baby looked fine, for now, but that could change quickly, we need to get in there so we're taking her to the operating room."

Matt seemed hesitant, but the doctor explained "Matt, I'm sorry, but we have to do this and we have to do it now, both your wife and baby are in jeopardy."

As he listerned, Matt's mind went to Summer, to their plans and all their dreams about how they would be together during labor and how he would be there to hold her hand as their first child was born. He'd cut the cord as Summer cradled the baby

It Takes 3

in her arms, it was such a beautiful picture in his mind and in an instant it had all changed. This beautifully planned day had turned into a life-threatening emergency for both his wife and their baby. Matt stood listening to the doctor, but he couldn't think, he was scared, he needed to be with Summer and he knew that she needed him too.. The doctor had no time to consider anything other than Summer as he excused himself to return to her. A nurse escorted Matt to the waiting room, he had questions, lots of questions but the doctor was gone, as Matt followed the nurse mindlessly, he was getting more and more frustrated, scared, and angry. He was concerned for his wife as the nurse sat him down, he needed support, things were not going well but she couldn't tell him anything specific. After Matt came to grips with the fact that he was not going to be with Summer anytime soon, he took a walk outside to clear his head, to be away from the medicinal smells, and to make a much needed call to his parents. On the phone, Matt talked fast, saying a lot yet making no sense, he talked so fast he was hard to understand All they got out of the conversation was that something was wrong., he needed them. Matt sounded frantic, they needed to get to him right away. Matt said something about Summer's parents, "We'll call them, don't worry about that sweetheart, we'll all be there soon, try to relax, we're coming."

Pam immediately called Megan, she explained what little she knew and tried not to sound scared, but Megan needed to know that something was wrong. She needed to know that this trip to the hospital wasn't going to be the joyful Grandparent moment they all dreamt about. After their very quick phone call, both sets of parents got in their cars and drove quickly to the hospital. They were all worried and scared, none of them had any idea about what was happening, and they tried hard not to let their imagination run wild. All of them wondered if the baby had come, they wondered if there was something wrong with the baby? Or maybe it was Summer? Was she all right? They needed answers.

After Matt made the call, on his way back to the waiting room he saw Summer being rolled out of her room and down the hall. He ran to her bedside. She was pretty much out of it. The nurse filled him in as quickly as she could. as they continued rolling down the hall to the surgical unitt. The nurse explained that they were headed to surgery, that Matt wouldn't be allowed in the operating room, so he needed to continue to wait in the waiting room.

Matt held Summer's hand as he talked to her "Baby, I'm here, I'm here with you." All Summer could do was open her eyes and lift a finger. She was so pale. Matt saw a fear in her eyes. As they neared the doors that led to the operating room, Matt leaned down and kissed her. "I love you, sweetheart, I love you, I'm here babe, I'm here with you."

As he looked at her face, he saw her mouth the words, "coming?"

It broke his heart as he tried to sound calm and sure. "Yes, honey I'm coming, I'll be right there, I wouldn't miss it." Matt was crying, he lied to his wife, he wasn't coming, he wouldn't be there, he couldn't,they wouldn't let him. But he told her that he would; he told her that he would be there with her, for her. The nurses pushed on through the double doors, leaving Matt on the outside. He wasn't allowed to go any farther. Matt watched through the small glass window as they wheeled Summer through the doors and down the hall, until they disappeared around the corner and he could no longer see them. Matt leaned against the wall and slowly lowered to the floor with his head in his hands. He couldn't believe what was happening, and he felt sick to his stomach and stuck in some kind of a bizarre nightmare.

After a few minutes, one of the nurses who had been with Summer came through the doors, she wanted to let him know that it would be awhile before they would know anything. She explained that Summer had lost a lot of blood, and they were going to perform the C-section and deliver the baby and then

It Takes 3

they would look for the source of her bleeding. As she talked to Matt, she took his arm gently and escorted him back to the waiting room down the hall; she gave him the information she had been instructed to give and nothing more. Suddenly Matt was all alone, alone with his fear, fear for his wife and fear for his baby.

After what seemed like hours, both of their parents walked into the waiting room, they had arrived within fifteen minutes of Matt's call, but to him it felt like hours, time was moving so slowly as he pondered this situation.. Their parents had arrived about the same time and met up in the parking structure. Each was asking the other questions about what was going on, no one had any answers, they only had questions. They all went directly to Labor and Delivery, they had been in the hospital before, so they knew where to go, but when they got to the nurses' station to get Summer's room number, they were escorted down the hall to a waiting room, the room where Matt was.

As they reached the room, they saw Matt through the window, sitting with his head in his hands. Matt heard them when they entered the room and raised his head. At the sight of Matt's face, Summer's mom felt her heart sink; she knew that something was terribly wrong. She needed to know what was happening, and she needed to know *now!* Matt tried to explain the situation to them, he told them about what happened at the house, he told them what the doctor had said, but that was all he knew. Matt couldn't explain any more, he told them that Summer seemed unaware of any danger she or the baby were facing, Summer had been given medication, but he knew she heard him. He told them that Summer thought he would be in surgery with her, but he couldn't be, but he knew she heard him, and she had to have heard him. He explained that he had let her believe that he would be coming into the operating room with her, and he felt bad about misleading her. He told them that Summer mouthed, "You coming?" And he told her yes, he allowed her to think he was, and he was upset. Matt sat with his thoughts, he got lost in their plans, all those plans they had for this earlier in the day. They had been talking about all the things that they hoped labor and delivery would be, but in the blink of an eye, everything had changed. Matt kept repeating, "How could this be happening?"

49

Sitting in the waiting room, all Matt could think of was his wife lying on that gurney. He was scared for her, he was scared for their baby, he was scared for himself. He was also feeling pretty guilty for allowing his wife to believe he would be in that room holding her hand. He was alone, and she was alone, he wanted to explain why he allowed her to believe that he would be there, and why did he do that? He wanted her to know that he didn't want her to be alone, that he wanted to be there. He wanted her to know that he was there with her, he really was, every part of his being was in that room with her. Matt's heart was breaking, and not knowing what was happening to his wife was killing him. They planned on being together when their baby was born, this was a moment they planned on sharing, but what the hell happened? He had lied, and he never lied to Summer—not even a little white lie. Why had he chosen tonight to lie? All he wanted to do was hold her to tell her he loved her. Matt stared straight ahead trying to see through the solid hospital doors, he wondered what was happening, to his wife, to his baby. What the hell was happening to her, to them, and their life?

Matt felt as if he were going crazy, this had to be some kind of a nightmare, he felt helpless just sitting there, he got up and paced the room yet again. Matt's and Summer's moms could see he was distraught. He was worried and scared, and they both tried comforting him, but he just pulled away. Summer's mom needed some kind of information, he was the only one there who could give it to her, but he didn't know any more than what he had shared.

Both of the fathers paced the floor, listening to what Matt said and feeling helpless in their inability to do anything. They left the room quietly to get some coffee, hot chocolate, and water; feeling helpless was something neither of them was comfortable with. On their way to the cafeteria, the dads talked about the kids; they talked about things they had dealt with through the years. They talked about the future, things they planned to do with their grandchild; they wondered if the baby was a boy or a girl. They even shared their fears father to father about what was happening, they expressed their love for each other's kid, and they shared a tear and a hug before returning to the waiting room.

When they returned to their wives, they talked about the times throughout their lives that they thought they had no control over a situation or circumstance, but today, they truly had no control over anything that was happening, they all felt completely helpless, and in fact, they were. In between the nonstop, nervous conversations and their prayers, all you heard in the room was the ticking of the clock on the wall. If it weren't for the ticking, they would have sworn that time was standing still. Minutes ticked, feeling like hours, hours felt like days. No one came to give them any kind of an update, not about Summer or the baby. All they had were their prayers, their hopes, and each other to hold on to. Confusion, concern, and fear ran through their minds and hearts. They tried very hard to hold on to their hope and their faith. They held on so tightly that when they looked up and saw Summer's doctor standing in the doorway, they could actually hear their hope crash to the floor.

As soon as they saw his face and heard him take a deep breath, they all heard it, and they felt it. The sound of disappointment and sadness was in his breath, and he didn't have to say a word.

It Takes 3

The sound and the look on his face made Matt's heart stop, and the deep breath the doctor took, took Matt's breath away.

Matt struggled to get to his feet, but he couldn't. He also struggled to breathe and couldn't. He struggled to look at the doctor and couldn't. Matt was stuck in the moment. Each of the parents rose quickly to their feet as soon as they saw the doctor. They needed to hear something, but the doctor walked directly to Matt. He didn't even acknowledge the others in the room, he saw them, but he needed to talk to Matt.

He reached his arm out and placed his hand lightly on Matt's shoulder and sat next to him. "Matt, I'm sorry. We lost her. I'm so sorry we lost her at 9:28."

Matt nearly fell out of his chair; he felt as if someone had pulled his heart right out of his chest. Matt's body seemed to collapse on itself as he sadly repeated, "We lost, her? A girl? A daughter? Our daughter? We had a girl?" Matt's mind raced. "I never got to hold her. Can I hold her?" Matt sounded confused. "I wanted to be there, I should have been there, I should be there now, I need to be with Summer."

The doctor tried to stop him, but he went on, "How could we have had a daughter, and now you're telling me she's gone?"

"No no no," the doctor said, "Matt, the baby's fine." He stopped, took another deep breath. "Matt, it's Summer. We lost Summer." Matt looked at him with a blank stare, so the doctor repeated himself. "Matt, it's your wife, we lost her at nine twenty-eight. We just couldn't do any more."

Matt continued to stare with no reaction. The doctor went on, "You have to know that we did everything we could. She lost a lot of blood. It was just too much too fast. We just couldn't get a handle on the bleeding. She lost it as fast as we tried to replace it." The doctor looked at the parents. "I'm so sorry." He held Matt's shoulder. "I'm really very sorry, Matt."

The pain was all over Matt's face. The sound of his breath escaping from his body too fast was heart wrenching. Matt slipped from the chair and fell to his knees. He cursed the doctor, he cursed God, and he cursed himself. His body wrenched in pain as the tears began to flow. Suddenly he just stopped and calmly asked, "Can I see her?"

"Not yet," the doctor replied, "but soon. Right now they are working on your daughter, she's a little early, and there are some precautions we need to take with her. The pediatrician is with her now. It shouldn't be much longer."

Matt wanted answers; the parents wanted answers. How could this happen? What went wrong? The doctor sat next to Matt, the parents sat across from them, and he tried to explain what happened in simple terms.

When all was done, Summer's uterus had completely ruptured, and it was a miracle that they were able to save the baby. It was his opinion that her uterus had somehow torn earlier that day, and somewhere between home and surgery, it had completely ruptured. That's when the bleeding became life threatening. He continued to explain about how they had tried to pack her to help get the bleeding under control as they gave her continuous blood transfusions. He explained one team worked to control the bleeding, as another worked to get the baby out quickly and safely. After they had the baby delivered, they worked to find the source of the bleeding, but it was too late. Summer suffered three cardiac arrests before they pronounced her death at 9:28; He explained that Summer never saw their daughter; she never regained consciousness. As they listened, they were all crying, even her doctor. As they sat quietly taking in everything, the doctor regrouped. "Matt, you have a daughter, she was early, but she seems like a strong little girl." He went on, "The pediatrician seems pretty confident that there would be no long-term medical concerns."

The baby would be taken to the NICU (neonatal intensive care unit) where she would receive one-on-one care. She would stay in NICU until she was strong enough to be transferred to

It Takes 3

the regular nursery. Once she's in the regular nursery, she would stay until her pediatrician deemed her strong enough to go home.

"We're all here for you and for the baby. Anything you need, we're here, and we'll be here every step of the way. Your daughter was early, and she's pretty small. She weighed just about three pounds, she's had a pretty traumatic start, and we'll be keeping a really close eye on her for a while." The staff talked about the situation and knew that with the baby in the NICU, Matt would have time to learn everything he needed to know before taking her home.

The doctor explained, "The baby will need to be around five pounds before we consider releasing her, so you will have some time to get things ready." Matt tried to listen to the doctor, but his face looked blank. The doctor knew that not much was getting through, but the parents were listening, so he continued. The doctor tried to give them an explanation, a reason why all this happened, but there was no reason. Nothing he said and none of his words made any sense to them. Matt looked as if he were listening, but all he heard was a deafening buzz in his head. Matt looked directly at each person in the room—first, his parents, then Summer's parents, then the doctor, and finally the nurse who had entered the room at some point during all of this. There were a couple of other people in the room, people he didn't know. He knew he was looking at them, yet he really didn't see them. Suddenly Matt felt a deep sense of anger come up from deep inside. He felt his nearly comatose demeanor explode. He felt it coming, yet there was nothing he could do to stop it. Suddenly he started screaming at the doctor, but his screaming didn't make any sense.

"You're lying, you're all lying, where is my wife? Where is my baby? Why are you doing this?" Matt tried to leave the room. "Summer needs me, you're all wrong, where is she?" Matt knew Summer was fine; after all, he had promised her he'd be there; he needed to be there. "I can hear her, I told her I would be there, why are you not letting me be with her?"

Matt tried again to push his way past the doctor, he needed to get though those double doors, and he knew if he could get to her, everything would be fine. Matt could see Summer smiling, holding their daughter, cooing to her, singing to her. As Matt fought to get out of that room and through those doors, Matt's and Summer's dads helped the doctor stop him. Matt fought them hard trying to get away, to get past the doors. After a moment of fighting and being held, Matt dropped to a chair. He dropped his head to his knees and sobbed. His whole body retched in deep heart-wrenching sobs.

He knew in his heart that his beloved was gone, he knew that Summer wasn't calling him, he knew he would never see her holding their little girl. Matt was unable to process all that had happened in the past few hours, as was the rest of the family. Everyone felt his pain, but although they were all in pain, they were concerned for Matt at this moment, even the doctor felt Matt's pain.

Summer's doctor had gotten to know Matt and Summer as a couple, and he really liked them; they were a great couple. All he could think about as he left the waiting room was to thank God things like this didn't happen very often. It was as if once in a while things like this happened as a reminder that life was a gift, and a healthy birth was still a miracle. Medicine has come a long way, but it's still not an exact science. There is still so much about life, pregnancy, and birth we still don't' understand. He took a moment and thanked God for the hundreds of healthy deliveries he had experienced, but questioned times like this.

50

Matt's parents tried to console their grieving son as Summer's parents left the room with the doctor. Summer's parents needed and wanted to see their daughter and their granddaughter as well.

In the hall, away from Matt's grief, they thought that maybe the doctor could or would give them more information, they needed to talk to him, they needed something. Summer and Matt had been married for years, and although she was no longer a child, she was still their child, their only one, and they had just been told that they had lost her. The doctor explained, "In most cases of placental rupture, it's usually the baby that is most at risk, but Summer had already lost so much blood, it was just too late. Somewhere along the line with all the transfusions and Summer's inability to clot, she developed DIC. Summer's parents looked confused, so the doctor tried to break it down in very simple terms.

DIC is the acronym for "disseminated intravascular coagulation," which is a bleeding disorder that results from widespread overstimulation of the body's clotting and anticlotting mechanism; it could be illness, stress, or both. In Summer's case, it was caused by the rupture of the placenta as well as its pulling away from her uterus.

"She bled a lot before arriving at the hospital, and despite our best efforts, we still lost her." Her parents still looked a bit confused, so he went on, "DIC is an overwhelming consumption of clotting factors, which leads to unstoppable bleeding. Summer suffered a severe case of shock, which affected her other organs, such as the liver, kidney, and pituitary gland. Once the organs became involved, it became not just a serious complication, but also a fatal one."

As Summer's parents tried to listen, their thoughts kept drifting back to the last time they spent time with her, then to Summer as a child, and all her life-changing events. But when they heard the word *fatal*, it was as if he snapped his fingers and woke them. Suddenly they were back to the present, back to a present they wished they could change. What should have been one of the biggest and happiest events in her life had become the biggest life-changing event of their own lives. Today they would welcome their first grandchild, today they lost their own child, and all they wanted to do now was see their daughter. They asked and the doctor explained that he needed to talk to Matt; he would need his approval before he could allow them to see her. He thought Matt would want to be the first one to see her, but when the nurse came to tell them she was ready, Matt was still trying to process the whole thing. He wasn't ready. His parents were with him, so her parents took the opportunity to ask Matt if he would mind if they went in to see her, Matt shook his head yes, but he really didn't hear them.

Matt said yes, and Summer's mom hugged him and whispered in his ear, "We love you."

A nurse escorted them to the operating room where Summer was, and the doctor and a nurse stayed with Matt as they tried to get him to calm down.

Matt was unable to settle himself down. After his outburst, he was still shaking and sobbing uncontrollably. The doctor decided to give him a mild sedative. It would help him to calm down enough

It Takes 3

to get through the next couple of hours at least. Matt still needed to see his wife and his baby daughter. The doctor explained to Matt's parents that the next few hours were going to be really hard, but Matt needed to get through it. The medication would help him, but it was best if they stayed with him. Matt watched as Summer's parents left the room and passed through the double doors where he left Summer. He knew they led to where Summer was, those two doors he had wanted to walk through all day long, the ones that kept his wife from him. All he wanted to do was get up and go with them, he wanted to run through those doors, but his body wouldn't move. As much as he wanted to, he just couldn't move. He had so much on his mind, and he needed time to process.

As Summer's parents walked through the doors, down a long cold corridor, they began to shiver. Her mom wrapped her own arms around herself, partly because she was cold but mostly because she was really scared. Summer's dad felt his wife shaking and wrapped his arm around her as they followed the nurse, matching each other's steps. As they turned the corner, they reached a second set of double doors. This hall seemed even colder than the last, if that was possible.

As they reached the door, they saw that it said OR 3. The nurse stopped just outside the door.

"She's inside," the nurse said in a quiet voice as she held the door open for them.

They took a step inside before her father stopped. He was crying as he took a moment to hug his wife then took her hand in his as they entered the cold, sterile room hand in hand. In the room they felt a coldness that was unlike anything they had ever felt in their entire lives; it was a cold that reached deep into their bones. They saw a gurney directly in front of them, which was neatly draped with a clean, white sheet. As they entered the room further, it was obvious that there was a body under the sheet. They knew it was their daughter, they couldn't see her, but they knew that it was Summer. They could feel it. Although they believed that it wasn't really her under the sheet, it was just her body, they felt her in the room with them.

The doctor in the room gave the nurse a nod as she walked around the bed and pulled the sheet down to expose Summer from her head to her shoulders. The nurse watched Summer's parents as she folded the sheet down gently and neatly. As the sheet was brought over Summer's face, her parents caught a glimpse of their daughter's face, pale and without life. Fear and disbelief filled each of them as they grabbed each other's hands and continued to walk toward her. Their eyes were locked on their little girl's face. The smile they knew was gone, she looked so somber, not at all like Summer.

Her mom stopped in her tracks, but her dad continued to walk. He needed to get closer to his daughter. He walked with a purpose and nearly pulled his wife off her feet. Once they reached their daughter, they stood at the foot of the bed together, taking in the sight of their beautiful baby girl, a girl once full of life now lying lifeless. As her mom stood at the foot of the bed that held her daughter, she felt her knees begin to buckle. She was overwhelmed with grief and was having a hard time standing on her own. Her husband held her tightly by the hand and around her waist, helping to keep her steady. After a moment, she found the strength to walk closer to Summer, her legs feeling as if they were in a thick deep mud. It was difficult to lift each foot and move forward, but she did. She forced her body forward; she needed to be closer. Summer's mother and father let go of each other's hands, each walking to a side of the gurney that held their daughter. Each parent took one of Summer's hands in theirs. Her mom leaned down and kissed her on the forehead, like she had done so many times before. Each caressed the hand they held as quiet tears became sobs of grief.

51

After a few moments, they began to share memories with each other. She was such a special child, their one and only. They shared memories that made them smile, memories that made them laugh, and memories that made them cry. They talked about some of their favorite qualities about their daughter, they shared their favorite moments, and they suddenly realized that they were sharing their last moments with their daughter, their final memories. These were not memories they wanted. They realized there would be no new memories, no new moments. Her parents told her that they loved her; they loved being parents, her parents. They told her they were proud of her, and they told her that she was such a wonderful daughter, the best ever, and they were grateful for the time they had with her. She was their dream come true, and they enjoyed every moment they were blessed to share with her. So many memories flooded into their minds, and they wanted to share it all with her. They needed to share it with her. They had told her all this before, back when she was younger, back then she would just laugh and blush a bit. She really hated it when they would say such things in front of her friends, but they loved telling her how much they loved her. They even enjoyed embarrassing her, but everyone knew she was loved. Her parents already missed her, their hearts were broken, and they knew this feeling was only going to get worse. How could they say good-bye?

They took their time, and everyone one gave them space, but as time passed, they knew they had to say good-bye. This day was supposed to be full of happiness. It was supposed to be a blessed day, one for the memory book. This wasn't even considered as a possible outcome to this day. Today was the birth of their first grandchild. As Summer's mom thought about it, she reflected back to the day Summer was born. It was such a great day for her and her husband, and she had always wanted her daughter to someday feel what she had felt the day she had a daughter. As she relived one of Summer's favorite days, her and Matt's wedding day, she remembered it was beautiful, and Summer was so happy. She remembered the day Summer told her they were looking for an egg donor and how excited she was about finding the perfect egg girl. Then she remembered the day Summer told her she was pregnant. After so many months and so much heartache, her daughter was ecstatic. Summer was truly a gift from *God*, a gift he needed to take back. Her thoughts and memories suddenly became so much more than she could bear that she had to sit down. As she tried to sit, she couldn't let her daughter's hand go, so she continued to stand with Summer's hand in hers. The nurse saw what was happening, so she helped her by pulling the chair close enough so she could sit while still holding her daughter's hand.

As they were there with their daughter, they heard the door behind them open. Summer's dad looked up to see Matt and his parents enter the room. They kissed Summer.

"We'll always love you, baby," Matt's dad whispered. "Later, kid."

His mom leaned over and barely whispered the word *good-bye* through her tears. Summer's parents stepped away to give Matt and his parents space. Matt grabbed Summer's mom and hugged her so hard she could barely breathe. Matt's parents stood at

It Takes 3

Summer's bed, looking at the daughter-in-law that they thought of as their own; she was their daughter and they truly loved her. Matt held Summer's mom's hand as he walked to the bed with her by his side. They all stood together around the bed with their hands on Summer. Matt held her left hand. The room was quiet as Matt's dad opened up in prayer.

"Lord, we don't understand what has happened, but we know you have a plan. As you welcome Summer into your loving arms, we ask that you look after Matt and the baby as they figure out life without Summer. Give us strength as we say good-bye. Lord, Give us strength, in your son's name, we pray. Amen." Matt tried to share in the prayer, but he couldn't get any of his thoughts or feelings from his heart, every thought brought a new memory, a new tear.

Finally as he laid his head on Summer's chest, he began to talk quietly directly to her. Matt shared his love for her, he shared the pain he was feeling, he professed his undying love for her, and he told her that he would always love her. He talked about their daughter and the plans they made for her, and he promised he would carry out the ones they made together.

"Oh my God, how am I ever going to do this without you, babe? I need you." Both of their parents shared a look, and all of them quietly exited the room, leaving Matt alone to share his grief with her. Matt was in the room for a very long time. He had received a light sedative, so the nurse kept her eye on him. The hospital and staff gave Matt plenty of time to say his good-byes, no one hurried him, but when he seemed to be completely drained and finally collapsed in the chair next to his wife's bed, they knew it was time. Matt heard the door open. A second nurse entered the room, but he didn't look up. He was exhausted, and his head felt too heavy to even attempt to lift it. Suddenly he felt a presence near him, it was the nurse who had been with him the entire time, and he heard her voice, a very soft, quiet voice. "Matt, would you like to see your daughter now?" Matt felt as if an angel were speaking to him. He thought for an instant, *Is it Summer?* At the thought of it, Matt raised his head slowly, almost afraid of what he might see. As Matt worked hard to focus through his tears, looking over his wife's body, toward the door, he saw a nurse in pink scrubs with a bundle in her arms. The tiny bundle was wrapped tight in a pink-and-blue blanket. It was one of blankets that he and Summer saw around the babies in the nursery during their hospital tour. It took Matt a few seconds to realize what was happening. The nurse was holding a baby in her arms, his baby, his daughter.

As the nurse walked to his side, it all began to register, and he held out his arms. He was exhausted, but he was ready to welcome their daughter into his life. He took one look at her as the nurse laid her in his arms. Tears began to run from his eyes. She was beautiful. Matt spoke softly to her. As he just let the tears fall, they fell down his cheek and onto his little girl. He tried to compose himself as he held their baby girl up. "Look, babe, she's beautiful!" Matt even made a formal introduction to each of them. Maybe it was the sedative. He was acting as if Summer could hear and see him. The nurse was close at hand. It had been a while since he received the mild sedative, but she watched him with caution.

Matt leaned towards Summer and whispered, "Honey, we have a daughter. She's here and she's safe. Matt wheeled the baby closer to the bed, hey little one, this is your mommy. Her name is Summer Grace, she is the most amazing woman in the entire world, and you are truly her dream come true." "Babe she's beautiful, shes healthy, you did good" Matt leaned down and placed a kiss on Summers forehead. As he did this he whispered his lifetime devotion to her "Forever and always, you will be my one true love." As he kissed her Matt could still smell the slightest hint of her perfume, He lingered over her as he remembered the day he bought her the first bottle, she wore it nearly every day and now he needed to imprint her into his brain, into his soul. It was during this moment that he vowed their baby would know everything about Summer, including her scent, this scent. Matt referred to their daughter as their baby girl, and it hit him that she needed a name; she couldn't be called "their baby girl" forever.

After some thought, Matt spoke, " Samantha Grace, that's our little girls name, she will have your initials and your middle name" The name just came to him. Matt and Summer hadn't really talked about names since he and Summer had discussed it a few months ago. Matt's first impulse was to give the baby Summer's name, and he did considered it, but Samantha Grace came to him and he liked it. Summer had always loved her middle name and months ago, they agreed that if the baby was a girl, she would have Summer's middle name. After the way the day ended, the name Grace was perfect; he felt that it was only by God's grace that either one of them had made it through the day. So Grace was not only the choice, but it was also perfect for their daughter. Afttter some thought he felt that Samantha came to him because "Sam" was the only name that was on both of their name choice lists. So Samantha it was "Sam."

As Samantha laid in his arms next to her Mother's bed, Matt's heart ached as he thought, *This is how it is supposed to be.* After a moment, he picked Samantha up and held her close to Summer, the sight of Summer and Samantha together even for just that moment would forever be in his memory. He held his baby girl close as his mind snapped a picture of mother and daughter that would be forever in his heart. Matt's heart beat with sadness and despair as he held Samantha close and tight. Matt felt Samantha's little heart beating and longed for the feeling of Summer's heart beating next to his. Matt could feel life within his daughter as he held her, a life given to her by her mommy; he felt the life that was now gone from his beloved wife. He felt Summer's heart beating within their little girl. Holding Samantha made him long for the life he could no longer feel from Summer, he knew her life was gone, but his daughter's was just beginning.

52

Matt looked up with tears in his eyes and asked the nurse if their parents were still in the waiting room.

"Yes, they're still here," she told him.

"Could they come see their granddaughter?"

She explained that the baby needed to be taken to the nursery to be checked, weighed etc. "The doctor wanted to give you a few minutes with her, but it's time." She explained that the grandparents could follow her and watch as the nurses cleaned her up and such, Samantha looked good, but she would need to be in an isolette, they would monitor her pretty closely because of the circumstances of her birth. After everything was done, a nurse escorted both sets of parents to a room near the nursery. Each of the parents were overjoyed to see her, they needed to see her, they needed to know that she was all right. They all knew this was going to be a long road for her, but they were all there together, and again they prayed a prayer that was led by Matt's dad.

In the meantime, Summer had been transferred to a room just down the hall. The nurses had removed the rest of her IV tubes, cleaned her up completely, and put on her special gown, the one she made herself. The staff had heard the story about how she made it herself and how much she had wanted to wear it on this day. It was in this room that her family would share their last

It Takes 3

memories with her. This was the room where everyone would be given plenty of time to say their good-byes. The baby was good, the grandparents had a chance to see her, they watched as she was bathed, diapered, and swaddled. Samantha was beautiful, she was a blessing. A nurse escorted them to the private room where Matt sat quietly with his wife. The parents spent time talking about the baby and their commitment to her and Matt. Before leaving, Summer's mom asked the nurse about the possibility of taking a photo before they left. The thought had entered her mind, and although she struggled with it, she finally asked. She wanted to at least try to get a photo of Matt, Summer, and Samantha together. It was an odd request, she couldn't believe she was actually asking, the nurses didn't think it would be possible. But Megan went out and talked to the doctors, both Summer's and Samantha's pediatrician, this wasn't a normal request, but it wasn't unheard of either. Parents of stillborn babies did this often, but a Mom that's lost her life was much less common. Thanks to them they were able to have this moment, this picture. As odd as it sounded, photos like this had been done before. The staff understood; it was unfortunately the only chance they would ever have for a photo. Summer looked as if she were sleeping. She was very pale, so one of the nurses put some makeup on her, and it helped a lot. As odd as it was or felt, everyone agreed to do it. The doctors and nurses made it happen, and it happened very quickly. When it was done, the photos were as perfect as they could be. The first photo was of Summer, Matt, and Samantha. The second photo was of the grandparents with the kids.

The doctors had walked everyone through the process and in the end, it was something that none of them would ever forget. Although they all knew Summer was gone, the photos turned out beautiful. There was a bit of a haze that seemed to be wrapped around all of them, as if Summer's spirit was there saying, "I'm here, it's all right, I'm in a good place."

One of the doctors was an amateur photographer, it was a hobby he loved, but this was the first time he had ever done a photo like this himself. It came out beautifully, it was a sweet-looking photo, similar to the ones that most new parents took, but this one was special. Everyone there knew the actual circumstances, but anyone else looking at it would never have known that Summer was deceased and that Matt's eyes were swollen and red from all the grief and pain he felt, and that the baby was quickly swept away afterward. In the family photo, everyone was looking down, hiding their tear swollen eyes. It was a great photo even though not a single one of them were looking at the camera. Everyone was exhausted when they left the room, leaving Summer alone as they spent time together at the window where Samantha was now safe and secure. Samantha was the only one in the nursery, and she was doing well, so the window curtains were opened for the family to see her. It was late when the nurse finally closed the curtains; it was time for everyone to go home and get some rest. Matt left his car at the hospital and went home with his folks; he was going to stay with them for now. Earlier that night when he and Summer drove to the hospital, he thought he would be staying the night with his wife, but plans changed. It wasn't a good idea for him to go to his house alone, not tonight. Matt wanted desperately to stay with his daughter, but that just wasn't a possibility. Matt had spent all the time he could with Samantha, at least for now.

Summer's parents were invited to join them at their house, and they did. They all needed to be together, they needed each other, and they needed to talk about the events of the day. Each one of them still needed to talk about Summer, they needed to talk about their memories, and they needed to talk about their futures without her.

The following day Matt went to the hospital to spend time with Samantha and then he drove home, back to his house. As he pulled nto the driveway he saw flowers on his front porch. The

It Takes 3

flowers were nice, but how did anyone know? He maneuvered around them as he entered the front door, this was not how his life was supposed to be.

53

The days passed slowly, and as Matt fought to get out of bed every morning, he needed to see his daughter. He needed to plan his wife's memorial. Thankfully, he had the help of both of their parents. As much as Matt didn't want to do this, he knew he had to. Summer deserved a beautiful memorial, her parents needed it, her friends needed it, and heck, he figured maybe even he needed it. Matt didn't answer their home phone, he just couldn't bring himself to talk to anyone, the phone seemed to ring nonstop. How did people know? He hadn't told anyone, but there were a lot of messages of condolences and disbelief. Matt knew that all of these people needed a memorial to say good-bye just as much as her family needed it to say good-bye.

Three times a day, Matt would get himself together and go to the hospital where he would spend time with their daughter, his little piece of Summer. He would hold her and talk to her.

The day she was suppose to be released, things changed, something happened, some kind of an infection. Samantha had been hooked up to IVs and monitors. Matt was told that she was doing well; she was a fighter and very strong, but she had an infection so she was moved to NICU so they could keep a close eye on her.

Samantha being in the NICU turned out to be a blessing for Matt. Samantha had all the care she needed and they kept Matt

It Takes 3

informed about her condition. Matt lived for his visits with Sam. When he left the hospital and returned home he spent long, lonely hours at Summer's desk trying to write a eulogy for the love of his life. Hours upon hours he wrote, until he finally had a beautiful memorial as well as his eulogy. He didn't know if he would read it or not, but he had it written. Matt sent the memorial to the local paper, he needed to let the world know that he had lost the love of his life, he included the information for her memorial as well, so anyone who wanted to could pay their respects and share time and memories with the family. Matt did not want to make a bunch of phone calls. He was afraid if he tried to call everyone, he would forget someone important. He let the paper get the word out for him. Between visits to Samantha and making furneral arrangements, Matt didn't have the time or strength to deal with anything else. He needed to choose a photo, clothes, flowers, etc. For the memorial photo, he choose Summer's favorite snapshot of herself, he had it enlarged for the service, and he used it in the memorial for the paper as well. Summer loved that photo. He knew that she would have approved. He loved looking at all of her photos, he enjoyed seeing her smile, he loved her smile, it was a smile that lit up her entire face, as well as an entire room. When he was looking at photos to choose, he could hear her say, "No, not that one, my eyes are closed," or "Yuck, I hate that photo." He heard her critique every photo he considered. Even in death, he wanted to please her. He wanted to choose the photo that made her say, "I love that one." So he picked the one he knew she loved. He wanted to make all the right choices, from the memorial he put in the paper, to the outfit, the makeup, and the casket he chose. He wanted the memorial to be perfect. He needed to honor her the very best way he could. Every day was a day full of difficult decisions, and every day his bright spot was time spent with Samantha and their parents.

Their parents had been amazing. They were there when he needed them, but backed off when he needed time alone. Every day Matt woke up to his mother's wonderful cooking, some mornings he would eat, and some he couldn't. And she never complained. She allowed him to mourn in a way that served him. Their parents were with him for all of the difficult choices at the funeral home, and if something was unclear or to difficult for him, they picked up the pieces.

On the morning of the memorial, Matt went to the hospital to spend the morning with Sam, but this morning was a little different. This morning he prayed and thanked God that she was doing well, he was also thankful that she was still in the hospital, and although he wished she was home and stronger, he knew she was taken care of and safe there. With her in the hospital, it gave him the time he needed to get through the next few hours, without having to worry about taking care of a baby. Matt informed everyone, the doctors, the nurses, and the patient advocate who had worked with him about the memorial and that he wouldn't be around until later that night. He didn't want any of them to worry about him. He made sure everyone had the memorial information in case they wanted to attend, and he reminded them that today was the day. Matt thanked the nurses again for taking care of Samantha, for keeping her safe while he dealt with the things he needed to deal with, knowing that she was safe and well taken care of was one less thing for him to worry about. Matt couldn't wait to get his little girl out of that hospital and into their home where she belonged, but he knew she needed more time, and he needed to get through his wife's memorial first. This was one of those mornings where his emotions were all over the place. He was happy that his daughter was doing well, but he was sad for the day ahead of him. One minute he was talking and laughing, the next minute he was tearing up. One minute he was thinking about their past, and the next minute he found himself thinking about the future, a future they would never have. Matt was trying to come to terms with the fact that this was the day that he needed to say his final good-byes, just thinking about this day, saying good-bye, was overwhelming. Matt knew that he had to get through this day somehow, but just thinking about it all was nearly more than he could handle.

Matt left the hospital, got into his car, and placed his hand on the Bible that sat in the seat where Summer had last sat. The Bible held his eulogy, the one that he worked on for days. After hours and hours, he was happy with what he had written; it was perfect. Matt's words were touching, funny, and sad. It was everything he felt about his wife and their life together. He read it over and over. When it was done, he placed it in his Bible, the Bible Summer bought for him years ago; this Bible had become more important to him over the past few days. It seemed that every time he opened it, whether he felt lonely or sad, there in front of him were words of comfort and strength. Summer had written on the inside cover, "Like our Lord and Savior, I will love you forever, unconditionally and without cessation. Always know that our marriage is between us three. You, me, and *thee*! Matt, we are truly blessed we have each other, our friends and family, and our church. But best of all, we both have a love for our Lord and Savior. Always know that I love you more today than yesterday, but not as much as I will love you tomorrow. I will love you forever, in this life and beyond!"

He knew he had to take the Bible with him to the memorial. He wanted to read her words, "In this life and beyond." It was as if she knew that at some time, he would need to hear those words again. Today, he needed to hear those words.

54

Just five days ago, Matt and Summer had left for the hospital. Just five days ago, Summer felt the pains of labor. Just five days ago, they were worried about their baby. Just five days ago, Matt was still a husband with a beautiful, loving wife, but today he was a widower. Matt was now defined as a man who had lost his wife by death and has not remarried. What a definition, remarried? Really? Matt was certain that he would never remarry. Summer was his perfect mate, his soul mate. To even consider remarriage was ludicrous. The past few days Matt felt as if he was living someone else's life, this couldn't be his life, this was nothing like they planned, nothing like he thought it would ever be. This needed to be someone else's life, and they needed to take it back. Over the past few days, Matt had spent some time in their house. He needed to keep up with his bills, he needed to pick up clean clothes, he still couldn't bring himself to sleep in their bed, so he stayed with his parents. On the days he spent at the house, he would lie on Summer's pillow. It was there that he felt her; the pillow still held her scent. Their bed was still unmade, just as it was left five days ago. Being in their home was a double-edged sword for him. It was here that he felt close to Summer, here that memories flooded his mind. It was here that he remembered happy times, but it was here that he felt the pain of his loss, here where he was able to cry and feel his loss. It was here that he needed to be, but it was here that he didn't want to be. Matt spent time going through Summer's things, her jewelry box, her closet. Matt found a box labeled Matt's Memories; in the box was every card or trinket she had ever given him. Next to it was a box labeled Summer's Memories; in this box was every card he had ever given her. Summer kept every card, every note.

Matt thumbed through the contents of the box labeled Matt's Memories. It was as if she were right there next to him, as he felt her love in every card, every note, and every photo. Everywhere he looked, she was there; he felt her in every corner of their home. That night, the hours passed quickly. The night got away from him until dawn began to break through his bedroom window, turning Friday into Saturday. When Matt noticed the sun coming up, he couldn't believe that it had the nerve to rise. Matt secretly wished that the world would somehow stop before this morning. It amazed him that the world could continue to turn without Summer in it. It had been a busy night for him, it began with recording a message on their phone, he listened to it again. "Thank you for calling. This is Matt. Some of you may know that Summer and I have a beautiful baby girl. Her name is Samantha. She came into the world a little early. Unfortunately while bringing our daughter into our world, Summer was called home to be with our Lord. Our family has suffered a devastating loss. Our family would like to extend an invitation to join us at a memorial to celebrate her life and to say good-bye to this amazing woman. The service will be held this Saturday at 11:00 a.m. at God's Space Memorial Church. There's no need to leave a message. We'll see you at church. Thank you for your call."

As Matt listened, he was glad that he had voice mail and not the old-style answering machine. This way he could check the voice mail from anywhere, when and if he wanted to. He didn't have to listen to the message as it came in or see the number of calls or a light blinking. It was little things like this that he appreciated. He had turned off the ringer so he didn't have to hear it.

It was morning, and Matt needed to get ready for the funeral, but first, he needed to go to the hospital. Matt wanted to spend some time with Samantha before going to the memorial. At the funeral home, Matt's parents met him in the parking lot. Summer's parents were inside.

"Dad, I spent a lot of time on this, I need to do it, I want to do it. I was at the house last night, and I spent a lot of time going through a box of old photos, cards, and notes."

55

As Matt and his dad walked into the funeral home, Matt was suddenly less ready than he thought he would be. Despite all the hours of preparation, the writing, and the planning for this day, reality hit him. Suddenly he realized that this day was going to be harder than he thought. Just five days ago he thought he had survived the hardest day of his life, but suddenly it hit him that today was going to be equally hard.

Matt had avoided the phone all week, he only answered his cell phone for their parents, the hospital, doctors, or the funeral home, but today he couldn't avoid all the people, the questions, the looks, the tears. Today he had to face everyone, but first, he needed to face seeing the casket with his wife in it, he picked it, but to see Summer inside was something he wasn't ready for.

They all arrived about an hour early. They wanted to have some private time together just the five of them. Matt left the hospital early to go to the cemetery where Summer would be laid to rest later that day. It was a beautiful place; it was quiet and peaceful. As Matt drove to the place that would be his wife's final resting place, he saw the green drape over the area that had been set up for them. The burial site was all set up and ready, tent and all. Matt had sent a wreath to the site. It had a sash across it that said, "Beloved Wife." The wreath was made up of roses, peonies, and baby's breath—all her favorite. His wreath was the only flowers. There were no chairs set up yet, so it looked a little stark. Matt spent some time on a bench that sat near Summer's grave, and beautiful mountains surrounded him. Matt heard the birds singing and the butterflies and hummingbirds seemed numerous. Matt and Summer had been to this place years ago to say good-bye to a friend who had been very ill, and Summer had commented on its beauty. She told Matt that it was a beautiful place to spend eternity and made an off-handed comment that when she died, she would love to be buried here. Who would have thought that just a few years later, that comment would help him make this decision? That she would be laid to rest here?

After his time of reflection, Matt left for the church. The past week had been the hardest week of his life. Matt wished he were with Samantha right now and not standing in this chapel, getting ready to say good-bye to his love. His heart ached for Summer, and it showed on his face. As Matt stood at the altar in front of his wife's casket, he prayed hard to have God somehow spin the world backward and make it so that the last week had never happened. He asked God to take them back to a happy time, maybe even before all of this even began, before the egg donation. Matt didn't want Sam to go away, but if they knew this was possible, they could have taken precautions. Maybe they would have had a happy ending. He knew his wish could never happen, things can't be changed, the world cannot reverse. Matt knew that everything happened for a reason. With that clarity, he prayed for strength, understanding, and acceptance—acceptance of the all that has happened, acceptance of his wife's death and for the future that lay ahead of them. Matt prayed for his wife; he prayed for her to rest in a peace that only God could provide. Matt prayed for God to give him the ability to somehow get through this day; he needed God's help. But more importantly, he needed His help to get through day-to-day life, his future; but most importantly, he prayed for strength and to make him the best dad he could be to his little girl, their little girl.

As Matt stood there with his wife, he felt a breeze that suddenly entered the chapel; he felt a presence within the chapel. With his eyes closed, he stood there, letting himself feel the presence, hoping that when he turned around, he would wake up, hoping this was still some kind of nightmare. Matt tried to hang on to the feeling that she was somehow there with him, but his reality was, she wasn't. She wasn't there to hold his hand, to sit next to him. She wasn't there to make all of this go away. As their parents reached the front of the chapel, they stood with Matt and with Summer. They prayed and held each other. The pastor came forward to be with the family; he gave them time to be alone with the Lord and with their memories of Summer. Matt gave everyone the latest update on Samantha, he talked about how he loved feeling the life within Samantha's little body; he told them that feeling her little heartbeat somehow lightened his sadness when he was with her. Feeling her was in some small way feeling Summer. Matt talked about the time they got to do skin-to-skin bonding. He explained that in the beginning, it felt odd, but the nurses pushed him to do it, and he was glad. No one had heard about skin-to-skin bonding, except the pastor, so Matt explained it.

"It's a way to bond with the baby, for the baby especially a preemie. It gives them strength. It's proven to help stabilize their temperature and their heart rate and regulates their blood sugar. They say that because a preemie spends so much time in the incubator, on the machines, and vents, it gives us time to bond. Samantha needs me to be there for her, but the truth is I need her just as much if not more." Being skin to skin and heart to heart gave Matt's life a purpose, a purpose he needed in order to carry on with life. He told the parents that he was glad the nurses insisted on it. As Matt talked, he kept rubbing the casket and looking down at it; both of the moms saw him and stayed very close to his side. Both of them were afraid to be too far from him. They could tell that he was nervous, they knew he planned on delivering Summer's eulogy, and they knew how much he hated public speaking. This was going to be the hardest thing he would ever do, saying good-bye was hard enough, but getting up in front of so many people eulogizing your one true love would prove to be even harder than he had expected.

This morning the moms were being unusually strong, holding themselves together so well, but inside both felt as if they would die. But they needed to be strong for Matt, he was their son, and he needed them just as much as his baby girl needed him.

Each of the dads were surprised by their wife's strength and determination. As the time for the memorial got closer, friends and family began to arrive.

As more and more people arrived, Matt wanted to leave; he didn't want to be in this place anymore. Every person came up to him and told him they were sorry. He heard so many "I'm sorries", so many "I can't believe it" or "she's in a better place." He heard "God only takes the good ones" or "only the good die young." And the worse one of all was "God needed her more in heaven." When Matt heard this one, all he wanted to say was, "*No*, God doesn't need her more than us. We need her, Sam and I. She needs her mom, and I need my wife." How dare anyone say such a thing? Every time someone said this to him, it tore at his heart. Within minutes, Matt was completely tired of everything, especially all the well-meant condolences. Matt hated the words, all the "I'm sorries"; he had heard those words at least a thousand times over the last five days, and probably most of those were today. Matt hated all the hugging and the handshakes, from people he knew and people he didn't know. As he sat with his family, he had to admit that he wasn't happy to see any of these people, especially the ones he didn't know. Matt wanted everyone to go home, he wanted to go home, he wanted everyone, including their parents and the pastor, to leave him alone.

It Takes 3

As Matt sat in the front row, just beyond his wife's casket, his best friend Brian and his wife Lesley entered the chapel. They saw Matt sitting in the front pew and made their way to him. As soon as Matt saw his friend, he couldn't speak. Matt broke into tears again. Brian held his friend as they both cried. Matt and Brian hadn't seen each other in months. Both of their wives were pregnant, so it was difficult to get away. But here they were, here in a church to lay their friend to rest and to say good-bye. Both of the women were due within a month or so of each other, so visiting had been difficult, especially as the girls got bigger. They had a summer vacation planned after the babies were born, and they were all looking forward to it. When Matt saw Brian, his body just let go. He felt safe letting go with Brian there; the two of them had shared just about every life experience there was. Matt and Brian had been friends since birth; they shared everything from first birthdays, to first dates. They were best men in each other's weddings. They were like brothers, always there for each other. The day Brian told Matt he was moving because he had gotten a new job was difficult, but the day he left was harder. He was only four hours away, but they knew it would be difficult to see each other much, with jobs, families, and other commitments. But they vowed they would make time. Summer and Brian's wife, Leslie, went to school together. They had became friends because of Brian and Matt. The couples spent a lot of time together during their early years, before Brian and Leslie's move. The two women were on the phone constantly during their pregnancy, comparing everything from weight gain to baby kicks. They were at each other's baby showers. They both wanted to be at the hospital for each other too, but with the pregnancies being so close, that wasn't possible, but they both promised to talk as much as they could during labor. They never got to talk! When Matt's parents called Brian, he didn't even want to tell Lesley; she was six and a half months pregnant, she had a difficult pregnancy, and he didn't know if she could handle this kind of news, but he couldn't keep it from her either. Brian was so afraid of what would happen when he told her that he called her doctor first to get her opinion. He knew he had to tell her. So one evening as they sat on the sofa, he broke the news. Leslie was devastated. Brian told her that he wanted to be with his friend but didn't want to leave his wife, not in her condition, and he didn't think she would be able to go. Leslie told Brian that Summer was her friend too, she had to be there, she needed to be there for Matt, for Brian, for herself, but most of all, she had to be there for Summer. She had to say good-bye to her friend. Summer's death was a shock to everyone, but to die during childbirth? That was a mother-to-be's worse nightmare, something expectant parents never even consider but this was no nightmare. It was all too real for them. Lesley's due date was eight weeks away; she was very pregnant. Traveling was difficult, but not going was out of the question. She wanted—no, she needed to make the four-hour trip with Brian. Just receiving the news was difficult, but this day was emotionally draining for her. She knew this day would have been worse for her if she would have stayed home alone. Lesley and Brian were staying with her parents; Brian's parents were there as well and, Lesley was glad that their parents would be here so that she would have someone to be with while Brian was with Matt. Lesley, being as big as she was, would of course be unable to really help, except maybe to hand out the memorial cards or thank people for coming after the service. She felt huge, tired, and not very agile, but she would do what she could. As friends and family arrived, they were greeted with a beautiful photo of Summer; it was softly focused, looking as if she were in heaven looking down at Matt holding their daughter. It was a beautiful photo taken and photo shopped by a photographer friend of theirs. It was his gift to the family. He also did the memorial cards for the service.

Matt hadn't seen the cards until this morning, and when he saw them, he wept. Next to the photo was a beautiful poem written by

It Takes 3

Lesley. Matt had yet to see the poem or any of the photo. It had been set up by a friend of Summer's and the photographer when Matt was with Summer. Matt was hearing about it as the guests arrived, so just before the service began, Brian escorted him and the family to the vestibule so they could see just how beautiful everything was. The poem was a beautiful tribute to Summer and her family. Matt thought it would be lovely framed and displayed in their home. Matt knew that someday he and Samantha would cherish the poem and the photo, but today he wished it would disappear along with everyone there. This tribute was the first thing the guests saw when they entered the chapel. The photo made everyone tear up, but the poem touched every person's soul.

56

After what felt like hours and hours, Summer's memorial was finally in full swing; the pastor had some very nice words to share. From her baptism to her wedding he had been there. He shared some memories of her during her years in kids' church, youth group, and the young married group. He spoke of her performances in church and her questions about faith and God. When the pulpit was open to those who wanted to share, there was a line of people that Summer had touched in special ways. Each shared a touching story about how Summer touched or influenced their lives. After everyone spoke, it was Matt's chance to share his words, his thoughts, his love.

As he approached the podium, he looked at his parents, he looked at Summer's parents and a tear fell from his eye. Matt placed his hand at his heart as he passed Summers casket. His sister handed him a Kleenex and stood near him as he began.

"Good afternoon, For the few who don't know me, I'm Summer's husband, Matt. I wanted to take a moment to share with you some memories of my wife, my love, my friend. On behalf of our family, I also want to thank you all for coming, we appreciate you taking time out of your busy day to honor the life of Summer Grace." Matt stopped, choked up, Summer's mom handed him a bottle of water and he took a sip and began again. "I was honored

It Takes 3

to have known Summer since kindergarten, although we grew apart over the years, we reconnected in high school. We were high school sweethearts, we even spent a year in a long-distance relationship, but Summer being Summer didn't allow that for too long. Before you knew it we were College room mates." Matt stood back and took a deep breath and began again "Summer was the most amazing friend and girlfriend, she made me the happiest man in the world the day she agreed to be my wife, to spend our lives together forever" Tears streamed down Matt's face as he barely got the word forever out. "Please forgive me; I stand before you devastated and shocked by her sudden passing, our forever wasn't nearly long enough. You know I've always loved her name, it brings with it a feeling of warmth and sunshine, and that was Summer, full of life, warmth, and she is, was my ray of sunshine every day. If you were Summer's friends, you were her heart, Summer loved everyone of us, especially her parents." Matt looked at Summer's Mom and Dad and pointed to them, "She told me countless times how much she loved, admired, and respected you two, especially you John. Dad, she loved and looked up to you. You were the man that every man in her life was held up to, especially me. I know I will never quite measure up to you, but I must have come pretty close; after all, she did marry me, I have always taken that as a compliment.." Summer's Dad stood up, the two men walked towards each other and embraced. "You made her happy son, she loved you and we love you, too" John cried as he walked back to his seat. Matt went on "Summer loved her Mom too; she had told me that when she was a teenager, acting out as teenagers do, sometimes she would cry herself to sleep because she didn't think she lived up to Mom's expectations—she wanted to please her Mom, but I know that in her Moms eye, Summer was perfect, isn't that right Mom?" Summers mom shook her head yes as tears streamed down her face. "Their bond was deep and true, beautiful at times, and adversarial at other times, but it was a mother-daughter bond of pure love, respect, and inspiration. Summer often told me how proud she was of you, her mother and what a great example of strength, courage, and success you were .. In the past few months, she admitted to me that if we could be half the parents our parents were to us, our kids would be lucky." Matt stood so proud as he talked about his wife and their family. "Summer was so excited to be a mom and I was excited to see her as a mommy, she would have been amazing. If we are to make any sense out of this tragedy, it is that life is both fleeting and precious. In my last moments with Summer, I told her I loved her, I told her that I was there for her, she looked at me with her big beautiful blue eyes, and although I know she was scared, she looked confident and excited. Her eyes told me that she loved me. I kissed her, not knowing it would be our final kiss. I thought I would see her again, I thought I would kiss her again,." Matt was crying a little more, wiping his eyes and working to get the words out. "All I have now is the memory of her eyes looking excited and full of love. This is the memory I will cherish. I will always remember her excitement at being a mom, she glowed through her pregnancy, we had plans, we had dreams, and these are the things I will hold on to until the end of my life. It is also said that love is eternal. Summer and I often talked about life and death, religion, and spirituality, the mystic nature of our universe, and the powers of the mind. We spoke about our love being eternal, and I know it is." Matt turned to his wife's coffin, "Summer, I will love you more today than yesterday but not as much as tomorrow." He turned back to the guests sitting quietly with tears in their eyes, many dabbing the tears away and continued. " As someone who is strong in faith with a solid commitment to our Lord and Savior, I say with absolute confidence that Summer is not gone. I know that she is here with us today, I know she is and will be everywhere. Everywhere where there is love, light, and life, there Summer will be. She's probably wondering what all this fuss is about. I can hear her saying, 'What are you all doing here? Go home, enjoy this beautiful day, fire up the BBQ, have some burgers and a martini, but please don't cry, I'm safe, I'm here where I belong. I'll watch over you, so go enjoy the afternoon." Matt raised his bottle of water, " So with that, I ask all of you to join us at our home to share in the joy and beauty of Summer's boundless spirit as we celebrate her and her love of life. Thank you for your time." There wasn't a dry eye in the entire place. Matt and Summer's parents walked up to the pulpit where they all embraced, not wanting to let go.

Matt's friend spoke for them. "Thank you all for coming, please join us at Matt and Summer's home, if you don't know where it is, you will find directions in the vestibule.

Matt pulled away from the family he stood in front of the casket for a while before kissing his hand and placing it on top of her folded hands, he leaned over and lovingly placed a kiss on her forehead. Before they closed the casket Matt placed a bouquet of peonies inside with her. He leaned in and kissed his wife one final time. The family stood at the front of the chapel as person after person walked up with tears in their eyes to say good-bye, the family accepted the guest condolences, but Matt just wanted to be alone; he was done, and emotionally he was exhausted.

57

After the service, the family had decided to have a BBQ at Matt and Summer's home with the help of some friends in their neighborhood and their church family. The house had been set up, and the food was ready. Matt had planned on staying at the house that night after the celebration was over. Their home was special to them, and there was no better place to celebrate her life than in the home she loved so much. Matt had been out of work since Samantha's birth. He worked for a company that offered what they called NBL (New baby leave); he also had bereavement time, and he was entitled to both. Matt held on to his NBL and took his bereavement time first. Samantha was still in the hospital, so he would take that after. Matt had two weeks of bereavement, and then he would need to return to work. His parents told him to use some vacation time, but he wanted to save his time. He didn't know how long Sam would be in the hospital. Being in their house during the day was hard, but spending this first night was much harder. It was in this house that he felt closest to Summer. It was here that he felt safe to feel all his pain, and it was here that he let it out. Night after night, Matt sat with his memories. The letters, the photos, and even the bedspread on their bed reminded him of Summer. Day after day, he spent his

It Takes 3

time between the hospital and home. Regardless of how much or how little he slept, morning always came.

Matt's coworkers checked on him, his immediate boss was a pretty good guy, and he stopped by at least twice a week. But after two weeks, it was time to go back to work or extend with his NBL or vacation. Matt felt that work would give him purpose and distract him a bit; sitting at home was very difficult. He felt that having something to do would help more than hurt.

The night before going back to work, Matt tried to sleep, but all he could do was toss and turn. Whenever he closed his eyes, he would see his coworkers, laughing and chatting until he walked in. Suddenly they looked sad. Each stood and told him they were sorry for his loss as he walked by; he didn't know if he could endure that. At some point during the night, Matt finally fell asleep. He was startled by his alarm clock, he showered, ate a dry piece of toast, and drank a cup of coffee before leaving. Matt drove to the office mindlessly, trying not to remember all the times Summer came by the office. When he arrived and walked through the doors, he was relieved that he was quietly welcomed back. As he passed cubicles, he received quiet "welcome back" comments. No one knew what to say, but they had to say something. Matt reached his office and stopped. He took a deep breath as he turned the handle and stepped inside. Inside, Matt looked around. All of his photos had been removed; he looked in drawers on top of cabinets and shelves and nothing. He lost it.

He was yelling at the top of his lungs, "Where are they? Who did this? Who had the audacity to do this?" Matt stood in the doorway and looked around at every cubicle, pointing. "Did you do this? You? Who did this? Where are they?" He went back to his desk and stared at the right corner of his credenza, the corner that had been home to photos of him and Summer during their last vacation. The photo had been taken by their friend Brian when she was about four months pregnant. She wasn't really showing at all at the time, but she had stuck her belly out to look farther along than she was. They each had placed their hands on her belly forming heart, it was a beautiful photo, and he loved it. Every photo had been removed, every single one, and he was livid. Where were they? As he sat in his chair, he yelled across the office. "Where the hell are my photos!" Every person in the office, probably in the entire building, heard him.

Hearing him, his boss came running. "Matt, calm down, calm down. I have them. I thought it would be better for you when you came back if they weren't staring at you. I'm sorry. But first, calm down."

"You took them?" Hearing this, Matt began to let go. His tears flowed as they sat and talked. They talked for a long time, until it was lunchtime. Matt wanted to go home, he didn't want to stay, but his boss had other plans. Matt had been out for two weeks, and his boss needed him back. Lunch was long, the two men talked about everything, and Matt understood that it was time for him to work and to get back to as normal as possible for now. Matt would need to catch up and get his assistant ready for his NBL before he left. Matt would be taking a maximum of six weeks off when Samantha was ready to come home. Matt had a wonderful assistant. Everyone in his life, everyone at work had been wonderful during the worst time of his life, and they had vowed to continue their support. Matt was grateful for each and every person in his life; many of them had stopped by from time to time bringing a meal, a snack, or a dessert. It was during this time that Matt realized just how wonderful the people in his life were; he was very grateful for each and every one of them. He was grateful for each and every one of his friends, but his boss was the one that had been honest with him; he was the one who knocked him back into reality. He was the one that told him he had other obligations. He was the one that didn't sugarcoat anything.

At lunch, his boss told him that he needed to be back. He needed to get everyone caught up on his files so that when he did take his leave to be with Sam, they would know what to do. They talked about how working full-time was going to be difficult, easier when she came home. Having her in the hospital would give him some time to get back in the swing of daily life. She was safe, and he could go before and after work. His boss agreed to give him a longer lunch so he could go to the hospital then too. Matt agreed, and as the days went by, Matt got up, went to the hospital, then to work. He spent every lunch with her and then back after work. The nurses always offered to get him dinner, but being at the hospital was his time with Sam. he would get a quick bite on his way home, or he would eat when he got home. There was always food left for him there. Matt took no time to socialize with friends, and his free time was spent with his parents or his in-laws, either at the hospital or at their homes. Matt's life revolved around four places: the hospital, work, his parents, or Summer's parents.

As each day passed, he was amazed at the changes in Samantha. It seemed that every day, she was getting stronger and bigger; even within hours he could see a difference. The days turned into weeks. Finally the pediatrician told Matt that Samantha would probably be going home around her original due date. There were certain milestones she needed to meet beforehand. These milestones had been explained to Matt throughout Samantha's stay. Matt had been given a card that listed some of the important milestone:

1. *Stay warm.* A baby cannot go home in an incubator, so before a preemie can go home from the NICU, he or she needs to be able to stay warm in an open crib.
2. *Take all feedings by mouth.* Although occasionally babies are sent home from the NICU with a feeding tube, most babies must be able to take all feedings by mouth before NICU discharge.
3. *Breathe without oxygen.* Babies must be able to breathe well without oxygen before they are sent home from the NICU. The exception is babies who were born very early

or who had severe respiratory problems in the NICU. Those babies may go home with a nasal cannula on very low oxygen settings.
4. *Outgrow As and Bs*. Apnea and bradycardia are hallmarks of prematurity, and most babies outgrow them before they go home from the NICU. If babies have met all other milestones for NICU discharge, though, and are having only mild apnea and bradycardia, then they may go home with a portable heart and breathing monitor.

About three weeks later, Sam was strong enough to be taken off the oxygen. Two days later, her feeding tubes were removed. Sam was maintaining her temperature and had grown to just over four and a half pounds. The day for her homecoming was fast approaching. Each of Samantha's milestones was celebrated; the cafeteria cashier always brought over a cupcake with a candle in it to celebrate each and every one. Matt could now go into the NICU and hold his daughter without a nurse helping with all the tubes and monitors. Each of the grandparents could visit her on their own. The pediatricians encouraged them to come in as often as possible; the cuddles and love were the best medicines for Sam. The day they received the news that they were going to move her into a step-down unit on the other side of the NICU was a happy day. Matt and the parents had been given a tour of the unit when Samantha was born. When Samantha began to do well, they took them on a second tour. The first tour had been when they were handling a lot of stress. The step-down nursery is quieter and a lot calmer than the NICU. There are fewer machines because the babies no longer require the type of intensive care the NICU provides. Babies need fewer tests now too, but they still need a lot of care and rest to continue to grow and recover. The transition to the step-down unit serves as a rehearsal of sorts. It brings a family to the point of being ready to take the baby home. Once Samantha was moved into the unit, Matt took on a bigger role in her daily care. He commented that he was beginning to feel like a real daddy. He became more and more confident with the changing and feeding of his tiny baby girl. He spent as much time as he could with her, as did the parents. In this unit, the grandparents had the ability to care for their granddaughter as well, and each of them was there with her as often as possible. Matt was learning all of Samantha's sounds and what they meant. She had a high-pitched, squeaky sound that seemed to mean she had a wet diaper, and a deeper *wah* sound that seemed to coincide with her being hungry and ready to eat. Matt's mom loved watching her son with his daughter. Everyone could see the love he had for his little girl, she was indeed the apple of his eye. Summer's parents were very impressed by Matt. Throughout everything, he stayed strong and focused. Their daughter would have been very proud of him. Day after day, Matt's schedule was the same: hospital, work, lunch at the hospital, back to work, a quick hospital visit, dinner, then back to the hospital until he was kicked out. His days were always the same, and he had settled into his routine nicely. Most nights he slept pretty well, knowing that Sam had all the care she needed, but there were still many sleepless nights as well, nights full of the nightmare that had become his life. The closer the time came for Sam to come home, the more anxiety he had begun to experience. Matt began to worry about being alone with this tiny, little being. He began to have nightmares about not hearing her cry or forgetting her somewhere; his nightmares had changed from the past and his wife, to these strange new parent nightmares. Suddenly everything was becoming so real, he knew that soon he would have a little one in his home, she would be his life, Samantha would be there depending on him.

58

Although Matt felt very confident in the hospital caring for and feeding his little girl, the thought of being alone at home with her made him nervous; thinking about it made him feel less and less confident. Matt expressed his fears to Samantha's pediatrician, he also spoke to the parents about it, Summer's Mom spoke, "Matt, we're all her for you, you won't be alone, not ever." The pediatrician told him to keep a list of questions or concerns. The nurses assured Matt that he was not going to be left alone once he took her home; no matter what time of day or night it was, they were there to help and willing to do anything he needed: babysit, shop, whatever.

Summer's memorial was only a few weeks ago, but to him it felt like a lifetime had passed. All the visitors that had come were settled back in their own homes, living their own lives. Some of their close friends had called, and a few stopped by the hospital from time to time, but Matt wasn't ready to spend much time with anyone other than Samantha. While Matt tried to put the pieces of his life back together in their lonely, dark house all alone, he tried to put the finishing touches on Samantha's nursery. This morning he got up, got ready, but instead of leaving, he just sat in his chair, he sat there thinking about the past months, losing track of time and losing himself as he daydreamed about spinning the

It Takes 3

earth in reverse, turning back time, like in the movie *Superman*—if only that were possible. As Matt considered the possibility, the house phone rang, the sound was deafening as it broke the silence in the house, and it also broke his concentration, bringing him back to reality and the earth spinning in the same direction as it had over the past months. Whenever the house line rang, it was important. Matt picked up the receiver and looked at the called ID; it was the hospital. Matt answered it, holding his breath as he hesitated, but as soon as he heard the upbeat voice on the other end, he relaxed and exhaled.

"Hi, Matt, this is Cindy. I'm calling to let you know that Samatha's doing great, the doctors say she'll be ready to come in a day or two, are you ready?"

"Really?" Matt was so excited.

"Yep, it's time to make any arrangements you need to make." She told him that the doctor had just left new orders for her and baring any change, Samantha would be going home. When Matt hung up, for the first time in months he felt a true sense of happiness and excitement; he felt hope that the house would become a home again. He wanted the house to be a happy place again; he longed to hear laughter, to have friends and family over for BBQs again.

Matt made calls to the grandparents to tell them the good news, and everyone wanted to be there for Samantha's homecoming. Matt was grateful for their offers to help, but he wanted to bring Samantha from the hospital; he wanted her homecoming to be theirs alone. As happy as this day was going to be, he knew that he would have to deal with his sadness at what the day was supposed to have been. As much as both parents felt they needed and wanted to be there, they understood and respected his decision, they agreed to give him this time, but they wanted him to know they were there if he needed them.

Matt's mom voiced her concern about him doing this alone, but she quickly backed down when Matt sternly told her, "Mom,

I love you, and I appreciate you wanting to help, I understand your concern, but this is what my life is now. I have to figure it out on my own, I can handle it, I will handle it, and the sooner I do this, the better. But I promise if I need anything, I will call you, okay?" He saw the disappointment on his mom's face as she said okay. Matt meant what he said, she didn't have a choice.

But she went on, "I understand, I know you will be fine, but you call if you need anything. Okay, anything?"

Matt smiled. "Okay, Mom, I will."

Matt had a very similar conversation with Summer's mom as well, but he was a lot gentler with her, explaining how he felt and not just telling her how it was going to be. He asked that she give him this time with his daughter, this first night especially.

He went on, "We would love for you and Dad to come over the next day, maybe in the afternoon?"

"We would love that; maybe we could bring over some lunch?" she sounded excited.

"That would be great; we'll see you then." Matt was sweet with his mother-in-law. When he realized that he had extended an invitation to his mother-in-law, he knew he needed to do the same for his mom, so he called her back and invited her to come over in the morning around 9:00 a.m. and to bring some bagels and cream cheese. He knew he couldn't invite one of the moms over and not the other. Matt had been at the hospital every day since his daughter was born; they received many cards, notes, stuffed animals, flowers, and baby blankets. Matt brought things home to his parents on a regular basis. The evening before Sam was to be discharged, he checked everything at home. The crib was ready, the sheets were washed, the swing was set up and waiting, he had plenty of diapers and tons of formula. The car seat was in the car all strapped in and checked by the local police station. Summer had insisted that they have the installation checked. "You can never be too safe," she would say. Everything was ready for Samantha's homecoming, everything that was except him.

It Takes 3

Suddenly he was a nervous wreck, pacing the house, checking and rechecking everything. He considered calling his parents and having his mom stay with him for a few days. No, he could do this, he knew what to do, he spent enough nights at the hospital, he had been taught by the best!

Finally while sitting Sam's nursery, in the chair Summer had chosen for herself, specifically for nursing and rocking their daughter in, Matt fell asleep. When he woke, he felt a sense of calmness, the night was full of memories of the day they bought the chair and most everything else for the nursery, it was a happy time for them, and it made him relax as he felt Summer's joy and the fun they had.

Matt woke up excited as he showered, grabbed a quick bite, and left for the hospital. When he arrived and walked into the step-down unit where Sam had spent the last days of her stay; the entire Labor and Delivery and NICU staff was waiting for him. Every one of them had been wonderful. They had Samantha all bathed and ready to go home, they even dressed her in the outfit that Summer wanted to bring the baby home in. They went over everything Matt needed to know—Sam's feeding schedule, the brand of formula she had been on, and her sleeping schedule. They went over everything one last time. Matt had been caring for Samantha as much as he could, but it had been under the watchful eyes of the nurses, he had gotten very confident over the past weeks at just about everything. Matt took in all their suggestions as he gathered the last of Sam's things, strapped her snugly into her car-seat carrier, and was ready to take her home. Matt had his diaper bag packed with all the necessities, the nurses loved the manly diaper bag.

"Where did you ever find such a masculine diaper bag?"

Matt explained that Summer had bought it for him as his first Father's Day present, back when she was pregnant. She was so proud of herself for finding it; none of the staff had any idea there was such a bag out there.

Matt took a beautiful handmade blanket out of the bag as he told the nurses, "This was my blanket my grandmother made it, she passed away just after we found out we were pregnant. She had started a blanket for Sam but never got to finish it. I wanted to wrap Sam in the love my grandma had for her, even though she never got to meet her great-granddaughter."

Matt told everyone about his grandma and wished she were there to meet the next generation, but his wishes were just that, wishes; he explained that his grandmother passed away suddenly, but she knew there was a new generation coming. He explained that he had kept the blanket with the hope that someday he would be able to wrap his own children in it, and today he was able to do just that. The nurses enjoyed their time with Matt, he was always grateful to them even after losing so much and now he had a new baby to care for all on his own. It was a lot to deal with, but he was handling it all with grace. The nurses were human, they knew what he had been through, but he was a very handsome man, built like a finely chiseled statue; he had a strong physique, and although he had lost a few too many pounds through all of this, he still looked good. When he first came into the NICU, he was just a bit heavy, but on this day, he looked a bit thin; a few good meals would do the trick. One nurse found herself with a huge crush on him, she worked hard at not flirting with him, it would have been inappropriate on so many levels. But he was sweet guy, it was hard not to.

She found herself thinking, *If only we met at another place, another time.* Sam had been the only baby in the step-down unit, and it looked like a party room, full of balloons, banners. The staff decided to give them a going-away party, complete with an adorable little cake. It was sweet, and all the gifts were thoughtful and very useful—bibs, hand covers, numerous receiving blankets and handmade blankets, a tummy time exerciser, a bouncy seat, some musical toys, a night light, and boxes upon boxes of diapers in all sizes. Matt was surprised and grateful, even Sam's grandparents

It Takes 3

were there, the nurses had invited them, it was a very nice party, and even nurses from the night shift had come in during their time off. Doctors, x-ray, respiratory and administration staff stopped in as well. It was nice and completely unexpected. There was so much stuff that it took a full entourage to get everything to his car. Stuff filled his trunk, and more stuff filled his passenger seat. There was so much stuff that it was a good thing the parents were there with their vehicles, because they had stuff too.

The entire staff was happy to see Sam with her daddy, she was doing so well and had a great prognosis, although she came too early, she was meeting all of her milestones and doing really well. Everyone said their good-byes, they asked Matt to bring Samantha in once in a while so they could see her grow, he was given the date of their annual celebration the hospital threw for their NICU patients. Matt was told that it was a day of celebration they all enjoyed, they had NICU graduates from one-year-year-olds to adults who came to celebrate life. Matt was given a few important phone numbers, even some private numbers, but each was given to him for purely professional reasons. But he knew there was a nurse or two who gave him the numbers for ulterior motives, they tried not to show it, Matt could tell. The crushes were flattering, but he was nowhere near considering any kind of female companionship let alone dating. It was much too soon. But he knew he might need some advice or help in the coming days, so he took each number with gratitude. Matt locked Samantha's carrier into its base, checked all the straps, closed the door and climbed behind the steering wheel, put the key in the ignition, started the motor, and put the car in drive. Matt slowly pulled away into a world unfamiliar and scary, with his baby girl safely in the backseat.

59

Matt drove off to his new life as a dad, a single dad, although scared and a bit apprehensive, he felt ready—well, as ready as he could be. The drive home was uneventful. As a matter of fact, Sam slept the whole way, not a peep out of her.

When Matt pulled into the driveway, he turned to look at her and said, "Well, little one, here we are. This is our house, our home." Matt unlocked her seat from its base and carried her to the house. When he reached the front door, he stopped and stood at the entrance with his new baby, their new baby. Matt remembered the day he and Summer celebrated their baby in her belly; he remembered picking her up and carrying her over the threshold. Today he was standing in the same place with that very same baby, but without Summer. Matt thought that the three of them would cross the threshold together. Instead it was just the two of them. Matt got Sam settled in her swing and sat down next to her. Suddenly he felt exhausted. Sam looked comfortable and content in her pretty pink-white-and-green swing.

It was too early for bed, but as Matt sat in the chair, he fell asleep until a tiny whimper woke him. The sound was cute and so light, it made him smile when he realized that it was coming from his baby girl, the new little lady in his life. Their first day went by quickly. By nightfall, he was completely ready for bed.

It Takes 3

His life revolved around four-hour feedings, according to the schedule he was given, the one she had been on in the hospital. But that evening after Sam's 6:00 pm feeding, Matt laid her in the bassinet next to his bed. He lay across his bed where he just stared at his little girl, and within minutes, he too was out like a light. A few hours later, Matt woke to a soft cry. In his dream state, he almost wasn't sure it was real, but as he woke up, the sound began to get louder and a little louder; this was real all right. Matt lay on the bed and just listened for another moment. He was enjoying the sound, and he was told to let her cry a bit; it helped to strengthen her lungs. Suddenly the silence of the house was broken, it was alive again, Matt lay on the bed and took it all in. Moments later, he got up, changed her, and then fed her one of the premade bottles the hospital had given him. Matt fed Sam as he thought to himself, *This is easy. There's nothing to this baby thing. Everything is ready for her. I don't understand what all the fuss is about. Baby sleeps, wets and eats. I feed her, change her, and clean her. What's so hard about that?*

That evening as Matt sat on the sofa with Sam, he decided to warm up one of the meals that had been dropped off for him. So far it had been an easy few hours. All of a sudden Sam let out a scream that made Matt jump. Immediately he picked her up, she didn't stop, so he stood up with Sam still screaming. He tried bouncing her, nothing. He changed her, fed her, burped her, and changed her again, but nothing helped. Matt had never heard her scream like this, and no matter what he did, she wasn't calming down, and he was getting frustrated and worried, so he called his mom. She could hear Sam screaming.

She asked, "Did you feed her?"

"Yes, of course"

"Did you change her?"

"Yes, Mother, I changed her."

"Did you burp her?"

"Yes, yes, I did all that, but she's screaming. Nothing I do is helping."

"Did you try the swing?"

Sam had been in the swing before, so while talking to his mom, he placed Sam in the swing. It's worth a try. In seconds, Sam was quiet. "Thanks, Mom, I just couldn't think with all the screaming."

"You're welcome, we'll see you tomorrow."

Matt belted Sam in. *Better to be safe than sorry.* He heard Summer's voice in his head.

Look, honey, I'm being safe, he thought as he turned the music on, and Sam looked around with her big blue eyes. She stopped panning the room when she spotted the mobile hanging just above her seat. Matt remembered the day he and Summer set the swing up. Summer insisted on this particular mobile. It was all pink and frilly and played her favorite songs. Matt had watched as Summer sat and stared with tears in her eyes at the mobile. Now tears came to his eyes as he sat and stared at the it, remembering that evening. He sat and listened to the sound of Henry Mancini's "Brian's Song" playing from the mobile. As he listened to the sounds, he tried to remember if there were words to this beautiful arraingement of music.

Matt saw Summer sitting next to the swing on the floor, her head moving gently from side to side, humming the tune as it played. Matt remembered Summer sitting near the swing listening to the song smiling that happy contented smile of hers. He looked at Sam, swinging back and forth to the sound of the music, and he could see that same smile on her little face. He knew if he told anyone Sam was smiling, they would say it was just gas, but he knew it was a smile. Sam was just a baby, but he saw the beauty Sam shared with her mom; then suddenly he remembered that Sam didn't actually share Summer's DNA. Sam shared DNA with another women, a donor, but to him she looked just like Summer. Matt wondered if it were possible she could have somehow received some of Summer's traits or DNA because she carried her.

It doesn't matter, he thought as he watched Sam enjoying the swinging movement. As hard as it was to have these visions and memories of Summer—they flooded his mind often—he was glad he had them, as they kept Summer close to him. Within moments, Sam fell into a deep, contented sleep. Matt relaxed as he felt Summer's presences, he knew that she was somehow sharing this moment.

As Matt sat quietly, he remembered Summer's journals, she loved to write. Matt went to her desk, opened her drawer, and there in front of him was her last journal, the one she kept during her pregnancy. He started to read it, but couldn't, so he put it back in the drawer; he just wasn't ready yet. He opened the large file drawer, and there sitting on the bottom of the drawer were four empty books; he took one and began writing. He started writing to help him remember special moments, special things she said, and special times they shared. He wanted to capture the past couple of months, before he forgot important details. He needed to write about their loss. Matt caught up to where Summer had left off, this meant that he had to relive the past few months, the rush to the hospital and that dreadful night he lost the love of his life. Once he started writing, the words began to spill from his mind to his fingers, through the pen and on to the page. Whenever he decided to stop, he couldn't; the words just kept coming, so he kept writing. It all came out, the fear, the pain, the excitement, and the joy; everything was there on the paper. He went through all those emotions again, he relived all that fear and all the pain, it just out of his mind, through his fingers to the page. The memories just poured out of him, and he knew it was good that he was doing this while it was all so fresh. When he finally stopped the sun was rising, beaming into the window and onto the page he had just finished. It was morning. Suddenly he realized that he hadn't heard a peep out of Sam all night. He went to her bed, and she was lying there completely content and asleep. Matt considered going to bed to get a little sleep before she woke up, but instead of going to bed, he found himself back at the desk and continued to write. He wanted to share all of the events of the past months, he needed to keep it simple, there were a lot of big medical words he wanted to keep as simple as possible so that his daughter could understand it when she read it someday.

After getting all caught up with the events of the past month or so, Matt committed to find time every night after Sam went to bed to write about their life and their growing up together. He found that writing helped and he knew that someday these memories would be priceless to both of them. Matt was so afraid that he would forget to share something important with her, and this was a way for him to remember it; he knew his journaling would be good for both of them. He wrote in two journals, one that he wrote all about Summer, from her infertility to their pregnancy; he wrote about their lives together, from the very beginning to the end. He wrote about everything from her silly little fears to the biggest hopes and dreams for her life, their life.

60

Being home every day—as enjoyable as it was—had begun to take a toll on Matt. After four weeks, he wanted to go back to work, to get back to life. With his parents' support and willingness to help with the baby, he returned to work two weeks early. After just a couple of months, Matt missed seeing Sam during the day, and he wanted to put her in the day care at his office. Having her at the office day care would give him more opportunities to spend time with her, but he also knew that both Summer's mom and his needed and wanted more time with their granddaughter. After some thought, Matt decided that he would be willing to compromise. Sam could go to day care three days a week and spend one day a week with each of the grandparents; they all agreed.

Over the past weeks, food from friends and local church had slowed down, leaving Matt to fend for himself more often. Once in a while, someone would drop off some food and baby items, but it wasn't as often as it had been. Matt was grateful for all the help he received through the hardest days, but he needed to start doing more of these kinds of things for himself; he always knew that the help wouldn't last forever, and he appreciated every bit of it. Summer's best friend and neighbor still came over once a week to do laundry and clean the house, but she had her own family. It was time for him to consider hiring a service to handle the household; he had a gardener already. Everyone had been wonderful, but he needed to get on with his life, and he needed to take control of their daily life. Matt was offered a new position at work, one that involved working from home. He had been sitting on his decision; he just wasn't sure he could do it.

This was the morning the company needed his decision, there was a board meeting scheduled, and he needed to be ready. As he sat at the table, he could hear Summer's voice in his mind, *Babe, take the job, you can do this, you can't sit around feeling sorry for yourself forever. This is what we dreamed of, you need to do this, it will be good for you and for Sam!*

Her words were gentle within his mind. Summer's words pushed Matt toward the door; as he opened it, he felt a chill, a breeze that pushed him and seemed to say, "Now get going. Matt remembered a moment so long ago when he stood at the same door, when he and Summer were in loving embrace, when he kissed her, and today he could feel that kiss. As he grabbed the doorknob and turned it, he heard Summer's words in his mind. He saw her face. *You can do it. The world is waiting for you.* Those words repeated themselves over and over again. Matt looked up as if Summer were standing beside him, and he heard his own voice, "I can do this. I will do this."

At the office, management talked about the job, the pay scale, and what was expected of him. They offered him free day care for Samantha and a nice vacation package. The one stipulation they required when he worked from home was that during scheduled conference calls, Samantha needed to be in day care or otherwise taken care of so the clients wouldn't hear a crying baby. The money was exceptional, and with the loss of Summer's salary, it was perfect. Matt took the offer, he felt good about his decision, and he met his parents for lunch to tell them about the promotion.

That night Matt went home and contemplated everything the day had been to him, from his conversations in his mind with

It Takes 3

Summer, to the meeting, to lunch with their parents; it had been a good day. As Matt sat in his living room with his daughter swinging by his side, he was lost in feelings of optimism, and even a bit of happiness; he knew Summer would be proud of him, and he enjoyed the feeling. Matt had made his decision based on having this beautiful little girl he had to care for. He knew that from now on, his world would revolve around her. His choices would be made for her and because of her, the days of Matt doing what Matt wanted to do had been over sometime ago, but now not only did he have someone else's feelings and thoughts to consider, but he also actually had someone else's life to consider. Every choice he made affected Samantha in the most profound way, and this was the moment that Matt vowed to be the best daddy he could. He knew Summer would be looking out for them; she was still his biggest cheerleader, always had been.

Matt looked up toward the sun and said, "Small steps, honey, this is such a different life from the one we dreamed of, but I'm doing it. I can't believe I'm doing this without you. God, I miss you." Matt's statement was true; this was indeed a completely different life, a completely new life, one without his life's love. That evening he spent time with Sam, reading to her from Summer's journal; this one was among her belongings he brought home from the hospital. It was the journal that she had started the day she found out she was pregnant. Actually it included the day before; she had written about the drugstore test she took and how she felt while she was waiting for the results. It was a daily journal with entries every day for the thirty-three weeks before her admittance to the hospital. Matt enjoyed reading her words, reliving her excitement, reliving their excitement; he had vowed to write every day, but this just solidified his commitment. After reading, he knew that someday Sam would enjoy reading about all of this too.

His other journals were for him and Samantha, their lives together, their growing and learning about each other. Matt even labeled his first journal "Matt and Samantha, the Early Days without Summer." He thought of using *mom*, but Sam never knew her as mom. It was something he fought himself about because Summer was her mom. She carried her for those months, so he put *Mom* next to Summer in parenthesis. This was his book, the one he would write in, the one that he wrote his own memories from the past few months.

After putting Sam to bed, Matt would write about their day; after getting so much joy from Summer's journal, he was committed to do this every day. It was his time to write all about his feelings, Sam's accomplishments, his hopes, and fears. Matt found so much joy in what he was doing that he told both grandparents about it; he even asked Summer's parents if they would write about Summer's childhood and their favorite memories of her through the years. Matt's parents wanted to write about their own memories of their daughter-in-law, memories they wanted to share with their Samantha, so all of them began their journals. Each added favorite photos or report cards, notes or other mementos to the journals. Matt's parents wrote about when they first met Summer; his mom even wrote about kindergarten, and her memories from those early years. They wrote about some of the things Matt would say about her, even before they started dating, like she was "the coolest girl ever," she's like one of the guys," "she was easygoing and so much fun." Then there was the story about when he talked to them about wanting to ask Summer to marry him; they enjoyed writing about her and how much they liked her from the very beginning. They wrote about how quickly they grew to love her. They wrote how she was and always would be their daughter, and they wrote that she had always been more than a daughter-in-law to them. Each one of them found solace in their own writings, their own memories. Reliving all of it was hard for them, but as hard as it was, they each enjoyed reliving the memories of a woman they each loved very much.

It Takes 3

Matt's return to work had been a very dark day for him, leaving his daughter and walking into a place where everyone knew Summer so well, a place she coaxed him to go, a place she loved to share lunch with him. They had been together over ten years, through those ten years, Matt had worked his way up the corporate ladder with the support and encouragement of his wife. Matt was successful in everything he did, he knew what he had to do, and he knew how to do it. But now he felt lost; he had to admit that he didn't know what to do, or how to do it, without Summer.

61

It took some time, but Matt was finally beginning to settle into his new routine, working at home, dropping Sam off to one of the grandparents or day care; spending dinner with them and talking about his day, was good. But his favorite time of the day was always after he and Sam got home, this was his time with Samantha, and it was a relaxing time for him, time to play and read with his favorite girl in their favorite chair. Every night he would get Sam ready for bed, they would say a prayer and ask her angel mommy to look after them. Matt enjoyed watching Sam grow, except when it was time to retire something that Summer had bought for her; letting go of these things was like letting a piece of Summer go.

Samantha grew a noticeable amount while he was away at work and even more between bedtime and morning. One night he put her to bed in a cute little sleeper, now the sleeper just fit her, but it wasn't tight. By morning, her little toes and legs were scrunched inside the sleeper; it was amazing. Both sets of parents adored her and were great with her, but after nearly a year of them watching her, Matt decided he wanted her in his office day care on a full-time basis. Samantha was getting bigger and more of a handful, and he wanted the parents to be grandparents, not sitters. They all understood, and as much as they loved having

It Takes 3

her, they were ready. Samantha was getting bigger and heavier. She was crawling around now and required more attention. They would always be there if Matt or Sam needed them for anything.

A night out or just a little time away, they were there. Matt promised that he would see them for dinner or just for a visit at least once a week. It would be a time they could enjoy Sam, with no work involved. Matt loved having Sam in the day care at the office, she was so close that he spent his lunchtime with her, and he could do this every day if he had time. He knew many parents who did this, especially when their kids were toddlers. Matt enjoyed watching other parents, especially the dads with their daughters. The three- and four-year-olds always made him smile, watching the girls turn their big, tough dads into daddy princess, drinking ice tea from tiny plastic teacups, pinkies up of course. These dads sat and chatted endlessly with their daughters; other dads sat with their sons, talking sports or trucks. There were two couples that he worked with that ate with their children every day. Whenever he watched them, he felt a twinge of pain as he thought about Summer; he remembered the days Summer would come to the company cafeteria for lunch, and they'd watch families share lunch. He ached to have lunch with his girls. Matt tried to ignore them, but every so often, they caught each other's eye, and he smiled as he thought, *They have no idea how lucky they are.*

Samantha went to day care every day. Matt rarely worked from home; he actually enjoyed being at the office and spending lunchtime with her. All too quickly their lunches went from bottles, to baby talk and mashed food, to peanut-butter-and-jelly sandwiches, and tea in tiny cups, pinkies up. Samantha was growing so fast it was nearly inconceivable. Their conversations went from baby talk to decisions on what to wear and what park to go after school. Matt prided himself on being one of the "Daddy princess." Samantha crowned him the "Best Daddy Princess, Ever!" Samantha had no idea what a job was; she told her grandparents that her daddy went to school in a different room because he was bigger.

Sam's innocence always made Matt smile; she had started day care in their infant program, then she was moved to the toddler program, and now she was in the prekindergarten program.

Sam spent four years in the same building as her daddy, and for four years they were able to spend lunchtime together. Sam was a sweet, easygoing child, everyone liked spending time with her, and she was a little people magnet, just like her mother. Sam seemed to excel at most everything she did; she loved arts and crafts, music, and learning to write. Sam had been an early walker, early talker, and she was potty trained by two. She loved to learn, she knew her ABCs and colors by two, and by four, she was more than ready for kindergarten.

Matt worked with the school to provide challenging things for Sam. Summer's parents found a program for young gifted children. They told Matt that it was an afternoon program designed for children between the ages of four through eight. The kids work computers and open them to different languages and cultures, different forms of art, and hand crafts. They also have a reading program. It sounded wonderful, so with Matt's approval, they enrolled Sam.

The program had all kinds of special events for parents to participate in on the weekends. Summer's mom thought it would be good for Matt. The weekends would be a time for him to get out and meet some new people. Maybe some single moms? Matt was in it for Samantha and for no other reason. Samantha enjoyed the class, and her favorite thing was the hand crafts; she was learning to crochet, knit, and do embroidery. It was good for hand-eye coordination, but she liked making things. Samantha also enjoyed being with the older kids. She was learning to read and play big-kid board games like Memory and Trouble. She learned quickly and was soon beating the older kids.

It Takes 3

One weekend a month, the school held a showcase, when the kids got to show off their crafts, paintings, or other skills. The showcase was done just like a big important gala. Over the years, it had become so popular that they held a silent auction. Each of the children chose an item for the auction. Most of the parents bid on their own kid's work, but the money went to a good cause, and the kids loved it. Matt was glad Summer's mom found this program; it kept him and Sam busy and gave them something to look forward to at the end of the month.

Between day care and the after-school program, Samantha was always receiving invitations to birthday parties, dinner parties, holiday parties, BBQs, and pool parties. Matt declined most of them, except the occasional birthday party of a friend of Sam's. Matt received personal invitations as well but declined most of them. Most of the invitations were obvious setups. A few of the single moms had their eye on him or had a friend they wanted to introduce him to. Matt received invitations all the time—women from work, day care, and the after-school program. Some were nice, but many of them were annoying. Matt received daily invitations to get a drink after work or to dinner at some woman's home, but he wasn't ready. He enjoyed his friendships but wanted nothing more.

Matt decided that this summer, the summer before Sam started kindergarten, would be different. This summer he would have fun; they would have fun. Matt had been so sheltered that he hadn't had much fun, but this year would be different. Sam would be going to a regular school, and that meant changes for both of them. That meant no more lunches spent together, no more daddy princess time no more pinkies up. Matt's heart already ached for the time he would miss with her. Samantha would be going to a new school, most of her friends at day care would be going to other schools, and the kids and parents they knew could be gone. Matt decided to make it a point to accept more play dates, birthdays, and BBQs. He wanted to connect with parents and children who would be going to the same elementary school as Sam. He wanted to connect with the ones who would be going to different schools to keep the friendships they had. Matt had put a lot of thought into this. The final summer at the day care was the summer that Sam would turn five. She had never had a birthday party. Matt had never felt up to throwing a party. Besides, he and Summer never saw a reason to have a party for a child who was too young to enjoy it. The day care always made her day special, but a party was just out of Matt's comfort zone. He never wanted to share her or the day with other people, not even little people. Samantha's birthday carried the grief and heartache of his greatest loss, and that was never going to change.

Matt decided that this day needed to belong to Samantha, it needed to be a happy day, and their grief needed to find a new day to live in. He vowed that from this year on, from this day on, this was Sam's birthday—a day to celebrate and enjoy, not a day to be sad and somber. Since Sam's first birthday, it had been a day spent with family, a day they shared together. For the past four years, Sam's birthday was a day full of memories of the past. It was a day complete with cake, ice cream, and presents, but it was never the happy day; it should have been. Matt vowed that from now on, Sam's birthday would be all about Sam. Yes, it was the day they lost Summer, but it was also the day that Samantha came into their lives, and they needed to celebrate that. Every year, Sam's Grandmother Megan gave Sam a special gift; it was never anything new, but it was always something very special. They were things that Summer loved when she was a child, special little things that Summer's mom had saved all these years. They always read, "I'll always be with you, happy birthday, baby!"

Samantha was still too young to know or understand the meaning of it all, but they all knew how special those gifts would be to her someday. Matt always felt sad when Sam opened the gifts, he wondered if he should let them continue, he decided

It Takes 3

that they could, he wanted her to know about her mom, but the details could wait until she was much older.

Summer's mom wanted Sam to have Summer's things, the toys, the books, even the jewelry Summer had. She hoped to give it all to Sam when she was old enough. After a long conversation with Matt, they decided that she would just give her things. They decided that she would no longer wrap them for special occasions. Samantha was getting older, and Matt was afraid she would begin to ask questions. Matt didn't want her to know that her mom died while giving birth to her, not yet. It wasn't time. He wondered if there ever be a time to tell her. How do you tell someone that?

62

The past five years had gone by so fast. It seemed so long ago that Matt lost Summer, yet it also seemed like just yesterday. Matt knew he wanted to throw Sam a big party when she turned five. It was something he and Summer had talked about when she was pregnant. Five was what Summer called a milestone birthday, she shared her memories from her own fifth birthday party. To her, it was the year that she became a big girl, ready to go to the big school.

This year would be a new beginning for him as well. Matt felt he had come a long way, he had come through the grief and although his heart still hurt, this year he was beginning to enjoy his own life again. Matt was looking forward to having a party, it was a huge step for him, but how does a dad plan a little girl's fifth birthday party?

Sam loved playing princess especially with him, she was always the princess, and he was always the prince; she loved tea party lunches and her plastic crown and scepter. Sam loved to dress up in some of her mom's old gowns and heels that Matt had kept.

She would always ask, "Am I a pretty, pretty princess, Daddy?"

Matt would respond with, "You are the prettiest of the pretty, pretty princess, Your Highness."

It Takes 3

When Matt asked her what kind of a party she wanted, she had told him that she wanted a princess party. Matt wanted her party to be special for both of them; it was kind of his coming-out party as well. There hadn't been a party in their home since Summer's baby shower, which was over five years ago. It was time. Matt wanted to plan the party, but he was lost, especially when it came to a little girl's party.

Matt's neighbor and friend Amber had come by to check in, he told her what he wanted to do, and she offered to help. Amber was Jennifer's mom, and Jennifer was Samantha's friend. The girls were the same age, the parents were in parenting class together, and they lived right next door, so they had a lot in common. The girls' birthdays were just a few days apart, and Amber was the party master. She and her husband celebrated everything, and she could plan and decorate a full event in just a few hours. Matt was grateful for her offer, and he accepted right away.

Amber had been there for Matt through the years. She was a good friend of Summer's and felt her loss deeply. Jennifer and Sam had become best friends. They had been in the same day care and would be going to the same elementary school.

Jeff, Jennifer's dad, and Matt had become good friends, and they spent time shooting pool or darts while BBQ-ing. It was Amber that Matt confided in. She was who he went to when he had questions about girls. Over the past year or so, Amber tried to get Matt to start dating. She had a few friends come to their dinners or BBQs. She hoped that one of them would catch Matt's attention, but Matt wanted nothing to do with dating. He had told Amber that he wasn't interested in a relationship and that he had the best of the best and didn't think he would ever love another woman. Besides that, it wouldn't be fair to ask someone to be in Summer's shadow. This month Matt was concentrating on the birthday party, he wanted it to be the best party ever, but first, they had two other parties to attend, so they needed to go shopping to buy a gift for each of the children.

Matt took Samantha and Jennifer with him to the toy store to buy a present for each of their friends. Matt had never been in a toy store, and this store had everything—not just toys, but this also had clothes, computers, video games, and baby stuff.

Sam headed straight for the clothes, Matt smiled, she was her mother's daughter. Summer loved clothes. Samantha inherited Summer's love for clothing, and within seconds, she had found the cutest princess dress ever and wanted to buy it, but she didn't want to buy just one. She wanted to buy two, one for Jennifer and one for herself.

"Look, Daddy, we could be princess twins. Can we get them, Daddy? Please?"

Princess twins? Those two words gave Matt an idea. Since the girls' birthdays were so close, and they had many of the same friends, maybe they could have a double party?

As the girls looked at the clothes, Matt called Amber. "Hey, Amber, I just had an idea. What do you think about the girls sharing their birthday party?"

"What made you think of that?" Amber asked.

"Well, the girls were looking at dresses. They want to get twin dresses, so it got me thinking, why not do a party together. There are so many parties over the summer. Maybe it would be fun if the girls have theirs together? What do you think?"

The phone was quiet, and then he heard, "I bet the parents would thank us for that. You're right, there are a ton of parities coming up."

Amber listened as Matt told her about Sam wanting a princess party. "That's what Jennifer wanted too. This would be perfect." Amber started talking about what they could do, and he loved her ideas. Amber offered to do all the planning. Jeff loved the idea as well. After all, the girls were always together, and their party would be no different. Matt was already at the toy store, so he bought anything and everything for a princess birthday party. With the girls' help, he picked out princess napkins, princess

It Takes 3

plates, princess goody bags, tiaras for ten other princesses who would be their guests, and of course they bought the presents for their upcoming parties. It was a good day; the girls had a blast and loved that they were going to have their party together.

63

The first party of the summer was for a little girl named Sarah. She was shy, and she invited Sam, Jennifer, and two boys from school to her party. She had cousins and neighborhood kids there too. Her party theme was "The Sea." Everything was mermaids, pirates, and fish. There was a treasure chest full of party toys and a pool complete with a mermaid swimming around. Really, there was a mermaid, a young lady dressed in a mermaid costume, swimming around the pool. There were a few kids in the pool with her. Her parents even had lifeguards sitting in tower chairs, just to be safe. There was a huge pirate ship bouncy house in the yard, the kids wore hats that they decorated, most of the boys made pirate hats, and the girls decorated sun visors with starfish and shells.

Sarah had on a cute pirate bandana and large fake earrings with a black patch on her eye; she had her nails painted black, red, and white and the cutest painting on her face. Sam loved the mermaid and fish that seemed to cover Sarah's right cheek and neck. Matt noticed a young lady on the large patio painting the kids' faces. She had a nice spot under the shaded patio.

When Sam saw Sarah's face, she ran over to her to get her face painted too. Sam choose a scene from *The Little Mermaid*. It was the one with all the treasure and the thingymabob. It was sparkly,

It Takes 3

and Sam loved it. Later Sam returned to get her nails done. They too were all sparkly in gold and turquoise. Sam sat with the face painter for a long time, she needed to let her nails dry, the two talked until another partygoer came over. Sam played with Sarah for a little while, then returned to get a painting on her arm. Sam was spending a lot of time with the face-painting lady. Before the party ended, she had her face painted, her arm painted, her hand painted, her fingernails done twice, and they were working on her toes when Matt asked if she was being a nuisance.

"No, not at all, she's fine. We take turns when the other kids come over. I tried to get her to go to the bounce house, but she says the kids are too rough." Sam showed her dad all her "tattoos" and showed him all the pictures of others that she could get. She tried to talk him into getting one, but he declined. Sam walked around and showed Matt the different paints and the nail polishes, gems, and stickers. Suddenly she was a little chatterbox. Matt had never seen her like this. Sam was usually the shy one, and she rarely spoke to anyone, let alone a stranger.

After walking around, Matt reached out his hand. "Hi, I'm Matt, and this little chatterbox is my daughter, Sam, Samantha. At least she looks like my daughter. Hey, little girl are you my daughter?"

"Daddy, you know I am," she whined at him as she rolled her eyes.

"Yep, that's my daughter all right. I'd know those rolling eyes anywhere."

"Hi, I'm Stephanie" Stephanie held out her hand, Matt took it in his and gently gave it a bit of a squeeze "Well, your chatterbox is absolutely adorable. She loves glitter paint and nail polish, she's a little girl after my own heart." Stephanie held Samantha's hands, checking her art work "I think I've found myself a new best friend. I hope you like what we did." She leaned in and whispered "It washes off. Pretty easily"

Matt smiled as he admired the art work "I love it. You're really good. Did you do all that freehand?"

"I did, and thank you. I can paint an anchor on your arm if you'd like."

Matt considered it for a moment. "Maybe later, we need to get some lunch. Are you hungry?"

"Thank you, but kids are very unpredictable, so I don't eat suntil I close up. I'm here to provide a service so I stay available just in case one of them wants to have something done. Besides, if I ate at every party, I'd be as big as a house."

"Well, let me know if you need a drink or anything. I'd be glad to get it for you."

As Matt walked away, he found himself wanting to know more about this woman, so he stopped, turned around, and asked, "So, you do this kind of thing often?"

"Not too often, but lately I've had at least one party every other weekend or so. I love doing it. I enjoy the kids' faces when they see their face or nails."

"You do this as a business?" Matt asked.

"No, not really. I mostly do it as a gift for my friends' kids. But at every party, I have other parents that hire me, so I probably could do it as a business. But since most of my clients are friends, or friends of friends, I'm more of a guest, so I get to enjoy the parties as well." Matt didn't even think about the food he was going for as he sat in the chair reserved for her little clients. "After the kids get their fill, I become just another guest. I get to mingle with the other guests. But this keeps me busy and the tips are nice too, I always leave with a few extra dollars, even when I do this as a gift to the kids, it's a fun way to make a little extra money and have a social life at the same time."

Just then a little girl ran over crying, holding out her hands. "I messed up my pretty nails."

It Takes 3

"Oh, it's okay, don't cry. Let's fix that right up, and they will be even prettier. How about a crown with some pretty diamonds?"

"Really?"

"You bet."

Matt got out of the chair, when he saw and heard the child in crisis. The little girl was so excited that she was getting some diamonds that she stopped crying and climbed into the chair, sat up straight, and placed her hands on the table in front of her. She knew what she was doing.

"Excuse me," Stephanie said, "but we have an emergency."

Matt smiled and said, "I understand."

Matt walked away to join Samantha, Jennifer, Amber, and Jeff for some lunch. Amber noticed the time Matt spent with Stephanie, and it brought a smile to her face as Matt walked toward her. He noticed her childish grin.

"What is that smile for?" he asked as his face turned a bright red. He felt it, but he ignored it.

"Well, I saw you and Steph over there in the corner. You two looked pretty cozy. Does Matt have a little crush?"

"Don't be silly, I don't even know her. It's just that Sam has been over there for so often I was afraid she was being a nuisance. Stephanie's so patient with all these kids, and she does beautiful work. Is she a friend of yours?"

"Yes, she is, she's both a friend and talented. You've seen Jennifer's room?"

"Yeah, I have."

"Well, Stephanie is the one that painted it. She did that before Jennifer was born, and five years later, Jennifer still loves it."

Matt looked intrigued. "So you've known her for a while then?"

"Yes, we've been friends for years." Amber smiled at the thought that Matt may actually be interested in her friend. "Are you interested?" Amber asked with a tease.

Matt shook his finger at her. "Not like you're thinking." Matt noticed that Stephanie's ring finger was empty, so he assumed she wasn't married, but to be sure, he asked Amber.

"Wow, you noticed. You're very observant, my friend. I'd say that's a step in the right direction. No, she's not married, she's not involved with anyone either, just in case you're wondering."

Matt suddenly felt self-conscious. He didn't want Amber to think he was trying to pick up on her friend at a kid's party. After his conversation with Amber, he made a conscious effort to stay away from Stephanie during the remainder of the party. Samantha was with Stephanie yet again, getting another painting on her ankle this time, and Sam was with Stephanie as the party ended.

Matt heard Sam ask when she was going to see her again as he walked up to retrieve her. He heard Stephanie reply, "Soon, I hope, I have a lot of parties coming up, and I bet I'll see you at least one of them."

Matt stood back and called Sam's name, as other children came to say good-bye to Stephanie. Stephanie saw Matt and wanted to say good-bye to him, but he kept his distance. He didn't want any more teasing from Amber.

At home, Stephanie was all Sam could talk about. She didn't talk about the kids, the party, or the mermaid in the pool.

"Can she come to my party, Daddy, *please?*"

Matt wasn't thinking. "Who can come to your party?"

"Stephanie, the lady you talked to. Can she come? Please?"

"Oh, Sam, I don't know. Sarah just had her at her party. You don't want to do the same thing Sarah did, do you?"

"Yes, I liked her, look at my pretty nails. She's really nice too,. *Please*, Daddy, can Stephanie come?"

It had been years since he felt anything like this, but at the sound of her name and his daughter's desire to have her at the party, Matt found that his heart was beating faster and his palms were a little sweaty. Matt didn't remember ever feeling like this, except maybe

It Takes 3

in High School. As he remembered that day so many years ago, Summer's face came to mind. This young lady reminded him of her. Maybe it was just the blonde hair? Whatever it was, he didn't feel he was ready to feel like this but here he was feeling like a school boy again.

64

Matt and Amber worked together planning the girls' party. It was going to be a great party. Not only was it going be a birthday party, but it was also going to be an end-of-summer party. The girls were going to be starting kindergarten soon.

Amber had already taken the girls shopping for school stuff, while Matt worked. Having Amber helped Matt and made things easier for him. Kindergarten was a big deal, the girls had been in "school," but this was a transition for all of them. Matt remembered shopping for new school clothes with his mom, and he was more than happy to relinquish that to Amber. The girls had a blast as they tried on clothes and shoes, picking out whatever they liked. Amber was good at steering them to the proper choices, but she enjoyed telling Matt about the wild clothes and the outfits the girls tried to con her into, but she was a strong mom and only allowed them to buy acceptable items. She told him that it was a challenge at times, but she stayed strong, like a warrior in the midst of battle at times. Amber's synopsis of the day made Matt laugh and feel a huge sense of gratitude that he was not on that battlefield with two strong-willed girls. Matt knew he would have lost, and his five-year-old would have probably started school looking more like a streetwalker than a little girl.

It Takes 3

Matt insisted that the party be at his house, he explained his reasons to both Amber and Jeff, and they thought it was a great idea as well. This was going to be their first party since they lost Summer, and he was very anxious about it. Sam was superexcited. She wanted to decorate everything with balloons and sparkles. Sam kept asking about Stephanie and if she can come and do her face and nail painting. Every other sentence out of Sam's mouth was something about Stephanie. After the millionth time, she was becoming annoying.

Stephanie had intrigued Matt, and he wanted to have her come to the party, to have a face and nail painting thing, but he felt strange about it, especially after Amber's comments. Just the sound of her name brought feelings deep in his being, and he wasn't sure what he should do about it. The first time he met her, he wanted to spend time with her, he wanted to get her phone number, but he never did.

After his conversation with Amber, knowing they were friends, he knew that if he needed it, he could probably get it. Matt was having thoughts and feelings about a woman he didn't even know, and these feelings scared him. He didn't want to do anything that would be disrespectful to his wife or her memory anyway. He wondered how long was long enough. It had been five years, he knew it was time, but could he move forward, could he ever be with another woman? Just thinking about her made him feel like he was cheating on Summer, and if he felt like this just thinking about it, how could he ever go on a date?

Matt felt something drawing him to this particular woman, he had met many women over the past five years, but he had never had this kind of a feeling, this kind of a magnetic draw. This particular woman intrigued him. Not only was he drawn to her, but his daughter seemed drawn as well. Matt saw that there was some kind of an unspeakable connection between Sam and Stephanie. Matt never did ask for Stephanie's number, he was afraid, but Sam wanted her at the party, and so did he.

The party was upon them, and it was too late. Matt, Jeff, Amber, and the girls worked all morning to get ready, and by the time the first guest arrived, everyone and everything were ready. There seemed to be a new life in their home, it no longer felt like a sad little house, but it felt like a happy home again. Everything looked beautiful and very regal with its princess theme. The front of the house looked like a castle, and as guests arrived in their princess attire, Matt's dad took photos. The invitation called for the girls to dress up like their favorite princess. Matt smiled at one of the little girls who came dressed in a beautiful party dress complete with a tiara and a banner.

"What princess are you?" Matt asked.

"I'm not a princess. I'm a queen," she said in a little smug voice. Her mother explained that she had just been in a beauty pageant and won queen of her division, so she wanted to be a queen, not a princess. She wanted to wear her dress, banner, and tiara. "I hope you don't mind, sorry for the little attitude, but she's a little full of herself right now. It's the first time she won one of these things."

"Oh, I see. No, we don't mind, she's adorable, and every princess party needs a queen," Matt answered.

Jennifer had chosen to be Cinderella, and Sam was Belle. They both had the complete outfits, gauntlets, heels, and all. Each girl was invited to come as their favorite princess, they came as everything from Snow White to the Ariel of *The Little Mermaid*. Matt and the grandparents had kept Samantha and Jennifer busy. The decorations in the backyard were a surprise as well as the cake.

Amber took care of everyone outside while Matt gathered the two birthday girls for their royal entrance. The back slider opened, and the royal march began to play. Matt had gotten each girl a bouquet of flowers, he made a red carpet that led directly to their castle cake, the whole thing seemed really silly to Matt, but he was loving the girls' reaction to it all.

It Takes 3

The smile on those girls' faces and the giggles they shared were priceless. As the girls reached the cake, something caught Sam's eye. As Matt walked behind them, he looked to see what it was that had his daughter's attention. Amber noticed Sam's eyes lit up like fireworks as she took off at full speed toward a tree in their yard. Matt looked toward where Sam was running, and there under his favorite shade tree was Stephanie. He couldn't believe his eyes, all her stuff laid out and ready for the kids. Matt watched as his daughter bolted right to her. Sam was holding out her arms.

"Stephanie, you're here!"

Stephanie saw this little blur heading right for her with a huge smile, arms outstretched. She knelt down and let Samantha jump into her arms and hug her so hard she couldn't breathe. Stephanie smiled when she saw Sam and her excitement. She was very happy to have been invited.

Amber and Jeff were like family to her, they had been friends forever, but on this day, she felt especially drawn to Samantha. When Matt saw her he knew Amber must have invited her and he was really happy to see her. Stephanie walked Sam back to the cake where everyone sang "Happy Birthday" as the girls blew out their candles. There were five candles for each girl on each side of the cake. After blowing out the candles, the girls were allowed to play with their friends. There were games set up, and they could get their nails done or jump in the castle bounce house.

As soon as the candles were out, Samantha ran to Stephanie's table. She wanted pretty, sparkly nails with diamonds on them. Samantha told Stephanie that she asked her daddy if she could come to the party, and here she was.

Stephanie was invited by Amber, she hoped Matt would talk today, when she met Matt, she felt something, and she had hoped he would call her, but he never asked for her number. Stephanie talked to Amber about it, and Amber thought she saw something between them as well, but Matt hadn't said anything since Amber mentioned a crush. Stephanie didn't know about that conversation, she just thought that maybe her feelings were wrong, and maybe he wasn't interested. She asked Amber about him over the past few weeks. Amber told Stephanie about Matt and Summer. It was a beautiful story with a tragic ending. Amber told Stephanie about Matt's difficulty moving on, and she told Stephanie that she saw a light in Matt's eyes whenever he talked about her. There was some kind of a connection between them that took Matt by surprise. Amber told Stephanie that Samantha's being drawn to her was the biggest surprise to her. She explained that Samantha had never connected to anyone like that, not even with her after all these years. Sam seemed comfortable with Stephanie in a matter of minutes. Amber told her that it was sweet to see, and if it took her by surprise, she was thinking about Matt's feeling about it.

Stephanie told Amber that she felt drawn to both Sam and Matt. It was weird, but she couldn't stop thinking about either one of them. Stephanie had never been a girl to peruse a guy, but when he didn't call, she called Amber to offer her services at the girls' party, for the girls, but she admitted that it was also a chance for her to see Matt again, and hopefully make a connection.

Everything was perfect, and everyone seemed to enjoy themselves. The kids played games, ate, laughed, and giggled like only girls can.

Stephanie stayed busy with the kids for about the first hour or so. After that, she was free to enjoy the party. Stephanie knew most of the party guests, so she mingled and chatted comfortably. She caught herself watching Sam and Matt. Sam had her daddy doing all kinds of silly girly things, and Matt did it all, smiling the entire time. Watching Matt interact with his daughter warmed Stephanie's heart; he was wonderful with her.

The girls opened their presents, they got all kinds of stuff, but when they opened Stephanie's, Sam danced around as she held up her dress.

It Takes 3

"Look, Daddy, it's my favorite color! My most favorite color! Can I put it on, can I?" Sam wanted to put it on right then, but she had to wait until after she opened her other gifts.

Matt told her that she couldn't be rude, but after she could go up to her room and put it on. Samantha opened every gift, thanked everyone, and then ran off to her room with her dress. When she returned, she had the dress on and looked adorable. The dress was a very light coral color, an unusual color to be a five-year-old's favorite, that was for sure. Stephanie had chosen it because she loved the color, ever since she saw it in the movie *Dirty Dancing*. Coral was a hard color to find, but it seemed to be popular this year, and when she saw it, she bought it. Sam's coloring was nearly the same as hers, so she knew the color would look beautiful on her.

Jennifer's dress was a sunny summer yellow. It would look beautiful with her auburn hair. The girls were like night and day. Sam was so thrilled with her dress, while Jennifer opened hers and set it aside, moving on to the toys and other fun stuff. But Sam had been intent on changing her clothes as soon as she opened the dress, and nothing—not even her favorite toy—would sway her.

Sam ran directly to Stephanie, and the sight of Sam laughing and smiling with this woman stole his heart. As he watched his daughter interact with Stephanie, he missed Summer more than he had in a long time. His heart hurt, and he wished she were here with her today.

Sam was becoming such a girly girl, he wondered if he were up to the journey, he thought about the past five years, and so far it had been pretty easy. Sam had been easy from the moment he brought her home. He fed her, changed her, played with her, loved her, while she slept all night and usually woke up in a pretty good mood. They had some rough moments, but all in all, she was pretty easy. She was no longer a baby, and there in front of him was his future. His little girl growing into a big girl, he saw what a woman could give his daughter that he couldn't, what she was missing. Something about this woman, the woman with his daughter, something about the two of them was special; he could see it in his daughter's face. There was some kind of an unspoken connection. Was it just that they were both female? Or was there something more?

65

During the party, Matt found the courage to talk to Stephanie. They spent most of the day talking and hanging out with each other. They spent time playing with the girls, laughing with each other, with the girls and with friends. Amber sat back and watched Matt and Stephanie together. She watched them with Samantha and thought they fit together well, like a cute little family, as if Stephanie was the missing piece of Matt and Sam's puzzle. She found herself hoping this day would lead to something. After the party, everyone helped clean up, every little princess gave a helping hand, and they whistled while they worked.

Sam's grandparents gave kisses and hugs to both of the girls and left after making sure all the dishes had been washed and put away. Soon all the girls were gone except Jennifer and Samantha, who played with their new toys, leaving the adults Jeff, Amber, Matt, and Stephanie outside. Jeff was ready to go home, he was tired, but before he could get his family together, Stephanie said her good-byes. She wasn't ready to be alone with Matt, not yet. Amber had told her all about his past and his pain, so she knew this was a difficult day for him, but he seemed happy, and although she wanted to stay, she wanted him to be the one to ask her. Before she left, she gave Matt her card. She hoped he would call her and not for another party.

Amber saw what she did and smiled. Amber couldn't wait to talk to Matt, but Jeff wanted to leave. Amber gave him a beer and a half of a sandwich, and they all sat on the sofa, exhausted from the day. They were enjoying the quiet. The girls were busy playing with their new toys, they were full of energy, both were on a sugar high, but no one cared. It was their birthday, and they were having fun. Their parents were having a good time as well, so why cut it short.

Jeff told Matt that he noticed he and Stephanie together. "So, my friend, what do you think of her?"

Matt looked surprised by the question. "She's sweet. We had a good time together. Sam sure seems to like her. That's a good sign, right? Kids and dogs? If kids and dogs like someone, they're good people, right?"

Jeff laughed. "Yeah something like that, but what do you think about her?"

"Well, I think, I need to think about it." Matt was skirting the question.

Amber chimed in about her observations of the day. She told him that there was obviously something between them, some kind of interest, connection—something. She thought Matt owed it to himself to at least give Stephanie a chance. "I think you need to pursue this, see what this is. I was watching you guys together, and it was as if there was a completeness there." Amber shared her feelings. "Matt, you deserve to have someone in your life, she's perfect, I think you need to spend some time with her, and I'll watch Sam for you. I say go for it, not just for yourself but for Sam too. I'm telling you there's something there."

Jeff chimed in, "Yeah, I saw Sam with her. She seems to really like her. I've never seen her like that before, not even with us, and we've known her forever. There's something between those two."

Matt felt embarrassed when Amber picked up the card Stephanie gave him and tossed it at him. "Call her, Matt. She left this for you, make a date. It can't hurt, see where it goes. There's definitely something there." Jeff agreed with his wife; it was time. They gathered Jennifer's things, congratulated each other on a wonderful party, and said their good-byes. "Matt, use that card, call her—tonight."

Matt was holding the card in his hand, turning it over and over in his hand. Should he, shouldn't he? Could he?

After everyone was gone, all Matt could think of was Stephanie. His mind was preoccupied with thoughts of her, visions of her, and even her scent haunted him. He and Sam got fast food for dinner, she loved Taco Bell, and since it was still her birthday, they ate there. It was a day full of junk food, so why not complete it with Taco Bell?

On the way home, Samantha fell asleep in the car. While he carried her up to bed, he realized how heavy she was getting and thought that he wouldn't be carrying her much longer. Matt changed his sleeping daughter and tucked her into bed, thinking, *When did my baby get so big?* He watched her sleep for a bit before going to his office to download the photos from the day.

As he went through them, he found himself looking for Stephanie, he wondered if his first thoughts about her looking like Summer were more than just the blonde hair. But with each photo he looked at he only saw Stepanie, yes she had blonde hair, but anything more than that, he didn't notice. Samantha had talked about Stephanie all throughout dinner and she was still wearing the dress Stephanie gave her. After she fell asleep, Matt took the dress off his daughter and laid it neatly on her chair. Matt walked to the living room, sat on the sofa, pulled the card Stephanie gave him out of his pocket and picked up the phone. He wanted to call her, but he couldn't push the buttons.

Too soon, he thought as he placed the receiver back on its charger.

The next few days went by. Sam wouldn't wear anything but the dress Stephanie gave her. She talked about Stephanie consistently. Every woman looked like Stephanie to Matt, she was everywhere, yet she wasn't with him.

After a week of torture and denial, he picked up the card, and this time he pushed the numbers and dialed. His hand was sweaty, his throat was tight, his heart was nearly pounding out of his chest, he felt nerves, he didn't even know he had. A huge relief flowed through his body when her voice mail picked up. Matt did leave a message:

"Hey, Stephanie, this is Matt. I'm sure you remember me, or at least you will remember my little chatterbox. I'm calling to ask you to dinner, without the little chatterbox. You can call me back at 555-579-7777. Hope to talk to you soon."

When Matt hung up, he felt relief; this was in her hands now. Within minutes, his phone rang. It was Stephanie, and he loved caller ID. When he saw her name and the number, his heart felt as if it stopped for just a second. Before picking up, he laughed, and he felt like a high school kid, nervous about getting a call from a girl. Matt quickly picked up his phone. "Hey, Stephanie!"

"Hey, stranger, how's the little five-year-old chatterbox?"

"She's good, I swear she's grown since turning five."

Stephanie made small talk. "She is a little sweetheart, and yes, I would love to go to dinner with you. When were you thinking?"

Matt smiled. "When would you be available?"

Stephanie wanted to make it easy for Matt. "I think you should choose since you have Samantha, make it easy on yourself, I'll make it work."

"Well, how about Saturday? Her grandparents will have her this weekend."

Stephanie teased as she took her time. "Well, let me check my schedule—dinner Saturday. Well, I could move Jeff to Sunday, Brian to brunch, and Jack to breakfast." She started laughing. "Yes, that sounds good. What time?"

Matt laughed; he liked her playfulness. "Well, you sound pretty busy. Maybe we should do it another time?" They both laughed as Matt asked in a serious tone, "Would you be available around noon? I was thinking about going to the harbor for lunch, then a stroll along the beach, or maybe a harbor cruise. What do you think?"

Stephanie laughed. "You know what's funny, I have been busy every single weekend, but this weekend, I'm actually completely free. So, yes, that will work. It sounds like fun."

"Okay then, shall I pick you up, or would you prefer to meet me there?"

Amber told Matt about Stephanie's first-date rule: "She's smart. She always drives herself to the place—just in case she always wants a way out if she needs it."

But this time, it was different; this guy was different. "You can pick me up. What time?"

Matt gave her a time. She gave him her address and directions to her condo. When they hung up, he realized that he had just scheduled his first date with another woman in over fifteen years. They were going to be together, just the two of them in a couple of days, he felt anxious and maybe even a little guilty, but he was looking forward to their date.

Stephanie was excited, there was definitely something special about this man. Matt didn't tell anyone about his date, he felt odd calling it a date, but he was very excited to see Stephanie.

The day worked out perfect. Sam's grandparents would have her for the entire weekend, so there was no need to say anything about his plans. Matt talked to Summer's photo, he felt a peace wash over him, the sun washed the room in a soft glow, rays of sun highlighted the photo, and Summer was smiling. He had a photo of Stephanie laying next to Summer's frame, he printed it out the other day. The photos were both taken outside and had similar backgrounds, It was at this moment that he noticed some real resemblance between Summer and Stephanie. He had thought about it before, but dismissed it as their hair color. But here with these photos in front of him he wondered Was it a coincidence, the pictures were very similar, or was it real? He wondered if he was attracted to her because she looked like Summer? He never even realized that they looked alike, until now. After more consideration, he came to the conclusion that he was attracted to blondes, always had been, so being attracted to Stephanie was not unusual. This was the first time he noticed the resemblance, he never thought of Summer when he looked at Stephanie, and knowing this made Matt relax. After a busy workweek, Friday night came, and Sam's grandparents met Matt and Samantha for dinner. Afterward they took Sam home with them.

Samantha loved being with her grandparents. She had her own room at their place, her own toys, and she had Grandpa wrapped around her finger. Matt never worried about Sam at Summer's parents; he knew that she was well taken care of and very much loved. She was their pride and joy, Matt was usually the one who was lonely, but this time when she left, he was excited. He spent the evening planning his date, from what to wear, to where to eat. He printed a couple of cute photos from the party to give her. Matt went to bed by 11:00 p.m. and got up early with a new excitement. He took the entire morning getting ready for his "date." Matt packed a bathing suit, a blanket, an umbrella just in case as well as a change of clothes. He packed some towels, snacks, and a bottle of wine. He was ready for anything that could possibly come up.

On the way to Stephanie's, he stopped at a florist to buy a bouquet of flowers. Mom had taught him to never to show up at a lady's home without flowers. As he was driving to her house, he ran through other dating 101 tips he had learned so many years ago. He wondered if things were different today. Did men still open doors for ladies? What about pulling a chair out? As he drove, he got nervous, and once he was in front of her house, he looked towards her address and noticed the curtains move. He smiled, evidently she was nervous too. Matt walked to the door with his armful of flowers, rang the doorbell, and waited patiently.

Stephanie didn't want to seem too anxious, so she took her time, he could tell she was making him wait, and he saw the curtains move again. When the door opened, a ray of sun fell onto Stephanie's face, as if it were kissing her ever so gently. Matt felt it was Summer giving her blessing yet again. Stephanie was even more beautiful than he had remembered, she was wearing a beautiful summer dress and comfortable sandals, and her hair was long and down, framing her face perfectly. Matt noticed that the dress she had on looked similar, maybe even the same as the dress she gave Sam for her birthday. Matt noticed the color first. When he said something to Stephanie, she was surprised he noticed.

He explained, "I have seen that dress nearly every day since you gave it to her. She won't wear anything else."

Stephanie smiled. "I guess we'll have to get her another one then."

Matt didn't know if it was proper or not, but he opened the car door for her. He was raised a gentleman and still was. Right or wrong, this was him. Stephanie seemed to like the gentleman behavior. He smiled at her as he walked around the front of the car to his door. He got in the car and started the engine.

"I thought we could start with lunch, you hungry?"

"Yes, actually I am." Stephanie hadn't eaten a thing all morning; she was just too nervous.

On the way to lunch, they both felt comfortable and at ease with each other. They talked and laughed all the way to the harbor.

Lunch was at a casual restaurant, outside looking over the harbor. They both enjoyed their lunch and of course the company, they both felt relaxed and talked about everything, and it was if they had known each other forever. The conversation was light, yet personal, they talked about their work, their families, and about their friends Amber and Jeff.

After lunch, they decided to continue with a nice walk around the harbor, going into some of the unique harbor shops. The day went by very fast and ended with an ice cream from the local creamery. Matt drove Stephanie home even though he didn't want the day to end. It was a great day.

66

Matt was quiet as he drove, he wanted to ask for a second date, but he didn't want to scare her. Matt walked her to her door, and he wanted to kiss her as the two stood staring at each other without a word. Finally Matt asked if he could kiss her.

Stephanie pointed shyly to her cheek. "This is our first date, and I make it a rule not to kiss on the first date."

Matt felt silly for asking and was a little embarrassed. This was one rule he had never heard of. "The cheek is as far as I'll go."

"The cheek?" Matt laughed as he looked around to Stephanie's backside.

"Not that cheek," she said as she gave him a little swat. "This cheek," she said as she leaned forward and kissed Matt's left cheek. Matt felt her soft, warm lips on his cheek, and he wanted to grab her and lock lips with her, he wanted her lips on his, but he didn't want to scare her away. This was a girl with morals and standards, and he liked that.

Matt asked, "So when is it appropriate to share a kiss?"

"Well, that all depends," she said.

"On?"

"Well, I'm not really sure, but know that a real kiss could come later." And she laughed. "If there's a later?"

It Takes 3

Matt smiled at her. "I would love for there to be a later. How about tomorrow? Is that later enough? I don't pick Sam up until dinner, but we could do lunch and maybe that harbor cruise?" Matt had thought of asking her to do the dinner cruise this evening, but he didn't want to bore her by being greedy with her time.

"Lunch and then a harbor cruise, that sounds great. You know I've have never been on the harbor cruise."

"It is really nice, very relaxing, and they serve a pretty good buffet too. It's nice to see the area from the water. As Matt reached out to kiss her cheek, he said, "Tomorrow then, I'll pick you up at ten. We could get a cup of coffee after we get our tickets, no rush."

Stephanie was happy she would get to spend more time with him, she enjoyed his company, and he enjoyed hers.

That evening Matt couldn't help himself. Before calling it a night, he dialed Stephanie's number; he wanted to talk to her, to thank her for such a great first date.

Stephanie had been thinking of him as well. When her phone rang, it made her smile when she saw his photo on her phone. They each had taken pictures of each other throughout the day; each picked a favorite to use in their phones. They talked for hours about their day and other things they wanted to share with each other. Stephanie thanked Matt for the wonderful day, and Matt told Stephanie it had been one of his best days in a very long time, and she felt the same way. They talked about dating, how it had been a long time for him, and her colorful dating past, including her attempt at online dating. She told him that it didn't go well.

Stephanie asked Matt if he had seen the movie *50 First Dates*.

"Yes, it was funny."

"Well," Stephanie said, "I took the whole on line dating thing to a new level. I must have been on at least 75 dates, It was an experience that I blogged about."

"Serious, you blogged about all those guys?" Matt looked surprised.

"Yes, I did, but I never used their names. I used code names. It's pretty funny, when I read it back. You can read it if you want." She gave him the web address.

Matt asked, "Are you going to write about our dates?"

Stephanie started to say no; then she realized that he said *dates*, not *date*. "Well, I don't know. Should I?"

"Well, if you do, I hope it's all good."

"Well, so far, so good" Stephanie said. "But, no, I don't have any blogging plans, that was a long time ago, but I must say looking back on it, not one of them were memorable for the right reasons."

"Weren't you afraid to meet total strangers?" Matt looked concerned.

"Maybe a little at first, but I always met them in a public place, and I let my family or a friend know where I was and the name of the person I was with. My parents hated the entire thing, but it was an interesting experience." Stephanie had no reservations about anything, she felt comfortable with him. Matt felt the same way with Stephanie, and he told her about one of the moms at Sam's school coming over to help with some of household chores, dressed in a sexy maid's outfit.

Stephanie laughed when Matt told her that he was so shocked, he had asked her to leave, and Sam was only about two at the time.

"Being a widower was like having a sign on my back. I felt like a piece of meat. Actually I felt like a pastry in a bakery case, surrounded by a bunch of weight watchers, drooling over something they couldn't have."

"Cake, why cake?" Stephanie asked.

"Because I'm so sweet of course. This started right after Summer died; women offered to do anything and everything for me." Stephanie laughed so hard she snorted, which made Matt laugh. "I don't mean that like it sounds, but being a widower with a baby brought out a bunch of crazy women. I got all kinds of food along with all kinds of proposals, and some were downright nasty." As Matt talked about this kind of stuff, it brought the conversation to a very real level. He had brought Summer's name up so Stephanie took the opportunity to ask about her.

"Amber told me a little about her." Matt was someone she was very interested in, and she had some questions. "How long has it been since you lost her?"

"Well, Sam just turned, so five years? Its been a long time."

"It is, have you dated much?"

"No, not at all, it's taken me awhile to get there, but it's time, I'm moving forward. I know there's a future for me and for Sam. To be honest, I never thought I would even survive the whole thing, especially in the beginning, but I have. I know Summer wouldn't want us to be alone, she'd want me to fall in love again, I hope I will. What about you?"

Stephanie thought for a moment; he had been so honest with her, she had no other option then to be honest with him. "I would love to find that person I'm meant to love forever. Did Amber tell you that I was married once, a very long time ago."

Matt was surprised; he hadn't heard about that. "No, she didn't? What happened?"

"Well, I was young and fell in love. Looking back on it, it was quite the whirlwind. We knew each other from work. Once we started dating, six weeks later, he asked me to marry him. I knew it was crazy fast, but I was twenty and in love. I said yes, we told my parents who were shocked of course, but they couldn't stop us and they knew it. My parents—God bless them—sat for hours talking to us about how fast we were moving, but we were stubborn, and we were doing this. Within three months, we made it happen, my parents helped, and we got married in their backyard, a simple family wedding. After two years, one night at dinner with our folks, he dropped to one knee and asked me to marry him again, he gave me the engagement ring we couldn't afford two years earlier, and he even had our minister at the restaurant to perform the renewal. It was a scene right out of a movie, I was in love, and I thought he was too, until I started getting baby fever. He knew I wanted kids, and we agreed to wait a couple of years. Well, two years went by, then three, then we're into our fourth year. I tried to bring the subject up, but all he talked about was traveling, new cars, computers. If the word *baby* came up, he changed the subject. Whenever I tried to talk about it, it became an argument, so it was avoided. Until one day, out of the blue, just after our fifth anniversary, he told me that he didn't want kids, no kids, ever. He felt he needed to do as much traveling as he could, while he could, and he didn't want some kid in his way. I was devastated. We had a terrible fight. I couldn't believe what he was saying. Now we'd been living with my parents for nearly a year to save for a house, we'd even found a place we loved, and this all happened when we were in the offer stage. We had no money; he had two tickets to Europe complete with hotels and tours already booked. He wanted me to go, he figured living with my parents was the perfect time to go. I exploded, 'Are you—— kidding me?' I screamed, I cried, I wasn't going, so he wanted a divorce. I asked him why he married me then, he knew what I wanted, and travel was never in the plans, not like that. Do you know he had the nerve to tell me that he married me because I was hot, and I looked good on his arm. Of course I went to my folks, told them what had happened, and I thought my dad's head was going to explode. My mom was like a mother lion about to eat her young. By the way, don't ever piss my Mom off."

Matt listened and couldn't believe that a guy could hurt someone he loved like this. Stephanie continued, "Anyway he left my parents' house that night, and he never looked back. He called me when the divorce papers were ready, I signed them, he didn't have anything, and I didn't want anything from him. I just wanted to move on, to put him in my past. It was the worst time in my life, and I didn't handle it well. I don't usually tell people this."

It Takes 3

Stephanie hesitated as if she were waiting for a signal that it was safe to continue, safe to share a very personal experience. Matt took the silence to assure her, "go on, you can tell me." "Well, I ended up in the psychiatric hospital, my mom took me there, it was for my own safety, I was pretty messed up." She stopped, she was crying, Matt heard her, "it's OK" he said.

"Sorry, I'm always afraid that people will look at me differently if they know I spent time in a psychiatric hospital."

Matt knew all too well what she'd been through. "No, not at all, I get it, I totally understand how something like that can affect us. I'm surprised I wasn't committed, but I had Samantha to think about, she was my strength, my reason for getting through the days. A broken heart can be devastating, you had all your hopes and dreams wrapped in this guy, I know a divorce isn't a death, but when you're the one hurt, it's pretty close, I would guess. It's taken me five years to even consider a different future for myself, but I'm here, and you're here. It's time to choose our paths, going forward. I didn't spend time in a psychiatric hospital, but if it weren't for that new baby needing me, I think I could have." Matt was so understanding.

Stephanie felt comfortable with her feelings. "But what happened to you is so unthinkable. It makes my divorce seem minimal. Matt, you lost your wife. Sam lost her mom."

Matt hesitated and then said, "And you lost your hope and dreams."

"I know, and it's really hard to trust now, I've dated, but every one I chose just wanted to have fun. No one wants a real commitment. I've always wanted to settle down, marry a nice guy, have a family, but finding the guy that wants the same thing seems impossible. I would love to be a stay-at-home mom, but I'm fine with working too. My friends think I'm old-fashioned. They can't imagine being a stay-at-home mom—cooking, cleaning, and raising the kids."

Matt smiled and said, "Well, that does sound like one of those *Nick at Nite* shows, but I like it. Would you wear pearls and a dress to vacuum?" Matt laughed at the vision in his own mind. He continued, "Most of today's women want someone else to raise their children, clean their house, and cook their meals, so you are pretty rare, you know." Matt yawned, he was tired, and he heard Stephanie yawn too. "Well, I guess we should get some sleep, leave something to talk about during our date tomorrow. I'll pick you up at ten, okay?" He looked at the clock. "That's seven hours from now. You okay with that?"

"I'll be fine. I'll see you in seven hours." Stephanie was excited to see him.

Matt smiled through his yawn. "See you tomorrow, sweet dreams."

Stephanie looked at her receiver. "Goodnight, Matt." With that, they hung up.

67

Date number two was followed by date number three, then four, and so on. Matt and Stephanie saw each other as often as possible; they enjoyed lunches, dinners, and the movies. They were getting to know each other, and they really liked each other. Their dates never included Samantha; they agreed to keep her out of their new friendship, at least for now. Sam got to see Stephanie at friends' birthday parties or BBQs with Amber and Jeff's family. Every time Sam saw Stephanie, she ran to give her a big hug, and she always spent as much time with her as possible.

Sam continued to get her to come over for dinner. She begged her dad, "Please, Daddy."

But Matt held his own ground; it wasn't time yet for that. Matt hated keeping Stephanie from his daughter and his daughter from Stephanie, he knew they cared about each other, but it was too soon, and Stephanie agreed. Matt was falling for this girl. He remembered back when he vowed that he would never love another woman, and here he was. Matt knew Stephanie was special, she could be that someone special in his and his daughter's life, but he didn't want to rush anything. It was already happening faster than he was comfortable with, but at the same time he couldn't help himself. He wanted to be with her, and he wanted to spend every moment he could with her. Although Sam and Stephanie had known each other for months now, he wasn't ready to bring Stephanie into his life with Samantha, at least not yet. After six weeks of serious courting, Matt had flowers sent to Stephanie's office. Stephanine was an occupational therapist, she worked with some amazing people, so when the flowers arrived they all wanted to know who they were from. Stephanie blushed as she read the card that accompanied the flowers.["Well, it's been six weeks and although this isn't a proposal, would love it if you would join *us* for a day at the zoo? Pick you up on Saturday at ten?"

In small letters at the bottom, he wrote, "Let's see where the next six weeks lead.us" The word us was in bold capitalized letters, so she knew he was including Samantha in this date, a big step for them. His words brought tears to her eyes and a smile to her face. Stephanie was surprised, they were going to the zoo all three of them, she was very excited as she dialed Matt to accept his offer. Matt saw her name on his phone and answered right away. Stephanie didn't even say hello. All she said was, "I would love to go to the zoo with you. But one question, I don't have to wear white, do I"? They both laughed. It felt good to find the humor in such a painful memory. Both Matt and Stephanie had a lot of pain in their past, and they had only shared some of it with each other. Matt really liked Stephanie, he liked her honesty and her imperfections, and the more he was with her, the more he liked her.

After about four months, he told his parents about her, he shared with them how they met, and they could tell that he was very taken by this woman. As he opened up, he even told them that he thought he might be falling in love with her. The words escaped out of his mouth before he processed the thought, and the words even surprised him. Matt's mom smiled, it had been a long time, he deserved to be happy, and his dad wanted to know more. Matt told them that he was worried about how and when he was going to tell Summer's parents.

It Takes 3

"How do I tell them that I'm falling in love with someone else? That I'm moving on? If I don't understand how I could fall in love again, how can they? How can I do this? Summer and I had such a love. If Summer was really the love of his life, how can this happen? How can I even think of falling in love with someone else?"

He had so many questions of his own; how could he defend his decisions to them? Matt really thought that the love he had for Summer was a once-in-a-lifetime kind of love, and if that were true, how could he fall in love with someone else? Matt was confused and concerned, he wanted to love Stephanie with the same abandonment that he loved Summer, but was that possible? Matt's mom told him to just let things happen and not to ever compare the two—a first love is always a first love, good or bad. She explained that this new love is their love, and it will be special. Stephanie sounded special, and of course Matt was special. She told Matt that God has a plan for him; He always has. As they talked, he knew that he would have to tell Summer's parents, and probably sooner than later. He asked her about when she thought was the right time to tell them. Should he tell them they're dating? Dating? They weren't just dating; he was falling in love. Should he tell them now, or should he wait? Matt knew he wanted to be with Stephanie, and he felt she was his second chance at a forever. Because of the way he felt, he didn't want to wait, but he didn't want to hurt them either.

Matt loved Summer's parents. No matter what happened in his life, he didn't want to jeopardize their relationship. His mom and dad offered to talk to them, the four parents were friends, and they were comfortable talking to them. This was a subject that came up from time to time, parent to parent over the years. Summer's parents felt Matt deserved to have someone special in his life, they had told him to date, but this was real.

Matt's parents were thrilled to see and hear the happiness in Matt. Although they had met Stephanie at Sam's party, they wanted to get to know the girl who brought all this happiness back into their son's heart. Sam was always talking about Stephanie, she had captured their granddaughter's heart sometime ago, so she must be pretty special. His parents couldn't explain it, but even at Sam's birthday, there seemed to be some kind of a connection with them, a connection that seemed almost magical. Matt thanked his mom for her support and willingness to approach what he felt was going to be a very difficult situation. Little did he know the parents had talked about Matt finding someone through the past few years. The parents met, they talked about Sam and Matt, then suddenly, Stephanie's name came up. It seemed that Sam had been talking about her constantly. Summer's mom asked if she was someone Matt was seeing. Her question caught Matt's mom off guard.

"Would that be a problem?" his mom asked. "No, of course not, we'd love to see him find a nice girl. He's been alone for way to long." She continued, "We met Stephanie at Sam's birthday party, she seemed wonderful, Sam sure seems to like her. So, is Matt seeing her?"

With that clear, concise question, the entire table was quiet. Matt's mom had to reconsider her approach to the subject. So she began by explaining what Matt had told her. "Yes, Matt and Stephanie are dating." She told her that Matt was feeling like he was falling in love; she shared his concerns about loving another woman and their feelings about it. Summer's parents were fine with everything.

Summer's dad chimed in, "Well, she is a beauty, you know. She was so nice to us when we met her, she even offered to give me one of those tattoo thingies of hers. She made me laugh, she reminds me of our Summer, she looks a bit like her too. Didn't you think so?" Everyone ignored his comment, but each one of them thought about it for a moment.

It Takes 3

"Well, she seems really sweet, and Samantha is really drawn to her. He deserves to be happy. He's had enough heartache for a lifetime." Summer's Mom told them to give Matt their blessings.

That night, Matt's mom called him to let him know that lunch went well, and he had everyone's blessing, especially with his choice of woman. "By the way, Summer's dad said it was about time!"

Later that evening, he called Stephanie and told her that everyone was happy that they were dating. Now that the parents knew it was time to let their friend Amber in on their romance. The next evening they had an early dinner, then stopped by Amber and Jeff's, rang the doorbell, and stood together arm and arm. When Amber opened the door, she was surprised to see the two of them, together.

"Yes, we have been dating, thanks to you."

When Amber heard the word *dating*, she jumped up and down, hugging them so hard she nearly knocked them off the porch. Amber invited them in, they talked and laughed, they waited for Jeff to come home. Amber began to hit them with the questions, "When did you guys start dating? How long have you been dating? Does Sam know? Do your parents know? Why haven't you told me?" The questions just kept coming.

Matt explained everything, and it all made sense, but she gave them a hard time anyway. Amber couldn't believe that they waited so long to tell her, she had been trying and wanting to get them together, they were perfect for each other. How could they have kept this from her? How did she not know? After listening to them, she understood and regardless of how long they had kept this secret from her, she was thrilled for them. The next Saturday, Stephanie and Matt were having a BBQ at Matt's house, and they wanted Amber, Jeff, and Jennifer to join them. They invited Matt's and Summer's parents as well. It was kind of a get-to-know-each-other day. Amber teased Stephanie about staying at Matt's the night before, but that was something they weren't ready for: they still hadn't told Samantha that they were dating.

On Saturday, Stephanie arrived at Matt and Samantha's, rang the doorbell, and waited. Matt was in the kitchen, he knew it would be Stephanie, so he decided to have Sam answer the door.

"Sam, honey, could you get the door for Daddy?"

"But, Daddy!" Sam was never allowed to open the door herself. She always had to have an adult with her.

"It's okay, I'm right here, but never answer the door unless I tell you to, okay?"

"Okay, Daddy."

"Go ahead, now don't keep our guest waiting."

Samantha went to the door and opened it; she felt like a big girl. As soon as it opened, Sam screamed, "*Stephanie!* You're here, you came!" Sam was so excited. She grabbed Stephanie's hand and led her to the kitchen. "Look, Daddy, look who's here!"

Matt looked busy at the sink. "Who is it? Who's here?"

"It's Stephanie, she came, she really came." Sam was so excited. She was talking a million miles an hour.

Matt and Stephanie shared a smile. "I see, well, welcome to our home. Sam, offer our guest something to drink." Sam looked confused.

So Matt asked, "May I offer you a cup of tea, m'lady? Some water? Anything?"

"Thank you, kind sir, I would love a glass of water," she said.

Matt held out his hand toward the chair at the counter. "Sit, please, relax, make yourself at home."

"No." Sam said as she grabbed Stephanie's hand and pulled her to her feet. "Come see my room, I even made my bed all by myself, it's really pretty. Daddy painted it, I picked the color, but Daddy painted it. I got to help; I always get to help." Sam couldn't stop talking; she was so excited to have her friend in her house. She had so much to show her,

68

Sam led Stephanie up the stairs to her room; at the top of the stairs, they turned left. Samantha's room was right in front of them. Her room was one of the prettiest princess rooms Stephanie had ever seen. The room was done in pinks, purples, and whites. It was one of those rooms that little girls dream of. It was the room that Stephanie dreamed of when she was a kid, complete with a beautiful bay window with a window seat. There were pillows placed perfectly on the window seat and toys neatly on the shelves; she even had a toy chest with her name on the front. Sam had a large closet full of clothes, all neatly hung color coordinated. Sam's furniture was also perfect, a four-poster bed and coordinated furniture. It wasn't all matchy-matchy; it was perfect. Sam's side table held a single, pink sparkly frame. The sun was coming through the window, which made the frame sparkle. A bright-light spot caught Stephanie's eye. Stephanie spotted the photo from across the room. For a split second, she thought it was a photo of her, so she took a second look. Was it? She walked over to the photo. Her eyes were glued on it, trying to figure out who it was a photo of. At first glance, it looked like her, but upon a closer look, she saw it wasn't. She walked over to the bedside table and picked up the frame for a closer look. Sam saw Stephanie looking at the photo. "That's my mommy. She's an angel in heaven. Do you know my mommy?"

"No, honey, but she's very beautiful, just like you." As she said it, she reached for Sam and picked her up, hugging her for just a quick moment. Stephanie's heart went out to Sam. This was the first time that she'd seen Summer, and seeing her made her real. Stephanie couldn't imagine life without her mom. Sam never had her mom in her life. Sam had a lot to say about her Angel Mommy shes pretty and super nice. Daddy says she loves me very much; I love her. Sam talked about her moms life in heaven and how she helped keep her and her daddy safe every day. Samanth had no real life memories of the woman she called angel mommy, but she had a picture, Matt had done a good job letting his daughter know about the women that gave her life, he worked hard to provide his daughter with a connection to the face in the photo.

Stephanie held the photo up next to Sam's face. "You know" she said in a very sweet voice, "you, look just like her!"

"I do? Sam asked "Really?" her eyes lit up.

Stephanie smiled at the little girl's excitement "Yes, you do, you're a very pretty girl just like your angel mommy" Stephanie looked at her, then whispered "you know what?"

"What" Sam asked full of curiosity.

"I think maybe you're going to be even prettier when you're all grown up"

Sam took in a deep breath, "Really? Wow I'm going to be pretty.

Sam looked at Stephanie as she took the frame into her own hands and held it up to Stephanies face. "You're pretty too, you look just like my angel mommy too."

Stephanie teared up thinking about her own mom and how much she would miss her if she weren't around, but Samantha had no chance to know her mom at all.

It Takes 3

All of a sudden a sense of overwhelming gratefulness flooded Stephanie, gratefulness for everything she and her mom were able to share through the years, the good and the bad. This little girl had no memories of her mom and never would; she had nothing, not a single moment she could cherish, all she had was a photo. Stephanie was impressed at everything Matt had done to make sure she knew just how much her mommy loved her. He had placed that photo next to Samantha's bed the day he brought her home from the hospital, and it had remained there all these years. Every night when he tucked his baby girl in, he sent up messages to Summer. This was the same photo they used for her memorial. It was a beautiful photo of a beautiful women. As Stephanie placed the frame back on the table Matt walked in the room. He hesitated at the door when he saw his daughter sitting on Stephanie's lap and heard them talking about Angel Mommy. As he listened, he heard Stephanie sharing her thoughts about Angel Mommy and how special Sam was to have her own special angel in heaven; he smiled at the sight and the sound of Stephanie loving his little girl and his wife smiling at them from within the frame. It was quite a sight. As he stood enjoying the moment, seeing the three faces of the the ones that he loved, warmed his heart; the sight gave him a calmness deep within his soul. It was this sight, that made him realize that he not only enjoyed Stephanie's company, but he loved her, he had fallen in love with her somewhere between that first birthday party and this moment.

Matt walked into the room and sat on the bed next to Stephanie and Summer. He wanted to tell Sam that he and Stephanie were dating but wasn't sure how to start that kind of a conversation with a five-year-old. He knew he needed to keep it simple but wasn't sure she would understand. "Hey, Sam, you know how Stephanie is your friend?"

"Yes, Daddy."

"Well, do you know that she's my friend too." Matt stopped, trying to figure out what to say next.

"Of course I know that, I'm not a baby, I have eyes" Sam sounded so grown up and a bit snarky. Then in her cute sweet voice, wiggling her pointer finger. "Are you two day-ting?"

Matt was surprised at the words. "What do you know about dating?"

"I know about dating. It's when a boy and a girl like each other, they play together, hold hands, and some kiss, stuff like that."

"Well, yes, that's true." Matt was surprised at Sam's knowledge.

"Do you guys do that?" she asked with a wink in her eye.

"Well, if we did how would you feel about that?" Matt asked Sam.

First thing out of her mouth was, "Daddy and Stephanie sitting in a tree, K.I.S.S.I.N.G," she went on to finsh her song, complete with a little dance. When she finished she put her hands on her hips and asked. "Are you gonna get married? People who date get married you know. That's what James's mommy did. She dated James's daddy, and then they got married and had a baby."

Both Matt and Stephanie laughed. "No, we're not getting married." But Matt quickly followed with, "Not yet."

Sam looked sad as she said, "But maybe?"

"Well, maybe, someday," Matt said.

"Maybe" Stephanie added with a smile.

Sam smiled and chimed, "Well, I think you should! Can I be in the wedding? I wanna be a flower girl. Can I be a flower girl?"

Matt was embarrassed at the innocence of his daughter, he turned red as he held her shoulders and led her out of the bedroom. "Enough you, come on let's go have a BBQ."

Sam grabbed her daddy's hand and then Stephanie's hand. She took their hands and placed one into the other. "There," she said. "Boyfriends and girlfriends hold hands."

When Samanthas friend Jennifer walked into the backyard for the BBQ with her parents, all Samantha could talk about

It Takes 3

was Matt and Stephanie being boyfriend and girlfriend. The girls sang, "Matt and Stephanie sittin' in a tree k.i.s.s.i.n.g. First comes love, then comes marriage, then comes baby in a baby carriage."

After about the twentieth verse, Jennifer asked Stephanie, "Are you gonna have a baby?"

Amber laughed, she didn't know that this relationship had come so far, so she responded "Yeah, are there any more secrets you need to tell?"

Stephanie laughed, "No, I think everyone is pretty much up to speed now."

The day was nice. Everyone enjoyed the BBQ and got to know each other a little better.

69

Matt and Stephanie spent time together with Samantha as often as possible, hanging out at the house, going places, doing things all together. Spending time together was always nice, but both, Matt and Stephanie enjoyed their private nights whenever they could get them. The parents were all wonderful about taking Sam, it was nice to have three sets of parents willing to have Sam so Matt and Stephanie could be alone, building their relationship as a couple without the inquisitive eyes of a five-year-old. They spent time with family and friends as a couple and also as a threesome, Stephanie held the words family at bay, because to her they were not a family, not yet at least.

One evening Matt took Stephanie out for a beautiful romantic dinner, just the two of them. Afterward, he drove down to the harbor where they had their very first date. They watched as the sun set over the ocean, Matt held Stephanie under the moonlight; he looked at her, held her face in his hand, and kissed her gently. It was a kiss like she had never felt in her entire life. It was a deep passionate yet soft and gentle kiss. It was a kiss that came from deep within his heart, it certainly wasn't a kiss just from his lips. As she kissed him back, she melted into him. He felt her passion, it was a kiss that came with more than passion, she kissed him

It Takes 3

like he had never been kissed before. It was the longest kiss either of them had ever experienced.

When they finally came up for air, he looked deep into her eyes. "Stephanie, I love you." He heard the words come out of his mouth, he didn't plan it, they just came out, and it made him blush. He took a moment and thought about what he said. "Yes, I love you. I really, really love you."

Stephanie stepped back and looked at him. "Really?"

"Yes, really," he said.

Stephanie smiled as she held his face in her warm hands. "Well, guess what?" she said. "I *love you too*! I love you, and I love Samantha."

Matt took her into his arms and hugged her as he swung her around. "I love you. How about we go back to the house, just you and me? I'll call my parents and make sure Sam's okay. They're keeping her for the night, but I like to check on her. "We'll pick up something for dessert, and go back to my place.."

Then Matt thought about what he had just asked. "So? What do you think?"

Stephanie paused for a moment, more for effect than to really think, she was in love with Matt and ready for the next step "I think that would be lovely, let's go" She grabbed Matts hand and led him back to the car. Being in love scared Stephanie, too often it ended in pain for her, but from the very beginning this felt different; Matt was different. She was ready to explore this relationship, ready to commit to it and to Matt in every way. It had been a long time for Matt, and he was nervous, but this woman was special. He knew it, he felt it. Samantha loved her, and she loved Samantha; things were going well. They were both ready to move forward.

Matt and Stephanie had yet to spend an entire night together; tonight he didn't want her to go home. When Matt opened the front door he felt like a kid sneaking his girlfriend into his room, instead of a man inviting his love to stay over, it was silly but that's how he felt. After they talked to Sam and told her good night, Matt lit the fire while Stephanie poured them a glass of wine. Matt put on some soft, mellow music and they cuddled on the sofa. They talked about the evening. In each other's arms, they both felt comfortable, and any nerves that they felt quickly disappeared. They made love right there in the living room, starting on the sofa, falling to the floor, giggling, and laughing like first-time lovers do. Everything happened much too quickly for Matt, he wanted so desperately to take his time with her, but it had been a really long time, he felt bad for Stephanie. He was surprised, nothing like this had ever happened to him, at least not since high school, he tried to apologize, but Stephanie wouldn't let him. She was fine, and he was loving and gentle.

"You can make it up to me later." She loved him and it had been a long time for her too.

"I don't know about you, but I'm hungry, pizza?" Matt was hungry, it had been hours since they ate at that fancy restaurant..

"Sounds good." Stephanie grabbed her phone and ordered a large pizza. Before the pizza arrived, they made love again or tried to. Their attempt failed again, but this time they were cut short by the doorbell. They had been lost in each other and it startled them back to reality.

Stephanie laughed, "Pizza's here!"

Matt quickly threw his pants on, like a kid whose parents had just pulled into the driveway. Stephanie sat in the floor in front of the fire, laughing. "I could get it, you know." She was naked right there in his living room, lying on the floor like a Greek goddess.

"God, you're beautiful," Matt said as he threw her a blanket from the sofa. "But I don't share."

Matt paid for the pizza and gave the delivery guy a big tip because he didn't want to wait for change; after all, he had a goddess to get back to. Matt set the pizza on the table and returned to his lady; he needed to finish what they started. After a long successful love making session, he was hungry, the pizza

It Takes 3

was cold, but they were hot. Stephanie warmed the pizza, and they enjoyed the fire, talking about their future, their hopes and their dreams. After a couple of slices of pizza and a beer, Matt invited Stephanie to share the night with him. Matt had recently redecorated his bedroom, he bought a new bedroom set, painted the room, and even remodeled the bathroom. It was an entirely different room than the one he shared with Summer. Matt started the project sometime ago, he took a break, but after he met Stephanie and spending time with her, he decided he needed to finish the project, and he did. This was their first night together, and it was beautiful; it was also the first of many beautiful nights.

Matt met her entire family, including her brother, who seemed a bit distant, but his daughter was adorable. She took to Matt and Samantha right away. Months later after Stephanie moved in, Matt decided to have a family dinner, with everyone. The dinner would include about twelve guests, so he decided to have it catered by their favorite restaurant; he wanted the evening to be as easy as possible, having it catered seemed like a good idea. Everyone arrived on time, Stephanie's parents, Summer's parents, Matt's parents, Stephanie's brother, his wife and daughter, Amber, Jeff, and Jennifer too. It was going to be a great night. Matt offered drinks to everyone, Jennifer and Sam helped hand them out, Matt had set out some appetizers, and everyone chatted easily. Dinner was set up and served by the restaurant staff. Matt had everyone sit at the table, everyone chatted, so he used a knife on the side of a glass to get everyone's attention.

"Before dinner is served, I wanted to thank each of you for taking time to be here with us tonight. I thank God you're all here, I thank you for your support. Each one here is important to us, and everything you've done or will do for us is greatly appreciated. We wanted to take a moment to thank you and to thank God. May He continue to bless each of us as we continue to move forward. Now, let's eat."

Dinner was great, everyone was relaxed, and the table was full of love, laughter, and terrible jokes. Matt and Stephanie smiled at each other as they cherished the evening. The restaurant's staff did a great job. They cleared the table, served coffee and tea, and asked Matt if he was ready.

"Yes, bring it in." Matt used his remote to change the song on the stereo, he'd made a special playlist with special song just for Stephanie, just for this moment. As it played, a young man carried out a beautiful cake. No one but Matt knew what was happening. Stephanie heard the song and commented how beautiful it was.

"It's just for you," Matt told her.

As the cake was placed on the table, instead of setting it in the middle of the table, they set it directly in front of Stephanie.

"Is it your birthday?" Sam asked.

"No, it's not."

Matt stood up, walked over to Stephanie, took to top off the cake, then, knelt on the floor, on one knee "Stephanie, Will you marry me?"

There on the cake were the words "Will you marry me?" In Matt's hand was a beautiful ring box with a light shining on the most beautiful ring she had ever seen. Stephanie's mouth dropped, and the tears began to roll; she put her hands over her wide-open mouth. Tears flowed from her eyes, and she shook her head. She tried to speak, but the words wouldn't come; she mouthed the word *yes* and a squeaky *yes* came out. She grabbed Matt, kissed him, and buried herself in his shoulder. The family cheered, tears flowed.

"What happened?" Sam asked; she didn't understand. she and Jennifer had been fooling around when Matt asked Stephanie to marry him.

Matt heard her. "Come here, Sam." He got on one knee in front of his daughter, and he held her hand. "Samantha Grace, would you take me and Stephanie as your parents? Would you be our little girl forever and ever?"

Sam asked, "Does that mean we get to be a family? I get to have a daddy and a mommy, like Jennifer?"

"It sure does, sweetheart."

"Okay, I want that." She danced around. "Will I still have my angel mommy too?"

Stephanie knelt down with them. "Honey, you will always have your angel mommy. She will always be there for you, forever and ever."

Sam smiled. "Do I get to be the flower girl?"

"Better, you get to be my junior maid of honor. What do you think about that?"

"I want to be the flower girl." There was more laughter at the innocence of this little girl.

"Okay, you can be the flower girl." And the wedding planning began.

70

Matt and Stephanie were officially engaged. It was time to share everything about their past, about Summer, and how Samantha came to be; everything from childhood to babies came up. Matt and Stephanie were asked about children; they both wanted more. It was the baby talk that brought up Sam's story, the way she was conceived, all the difficulty and heartache Matt and Summer went through before finally choosing to use an egg donor. Stephanie's brother shared their own experience with infertility, but it was nothing like what Summer and Matt experienced. Summer's parents talked about Summer and the joy she felt when they found her perfect egg donor and then when she became pregnant.

Stephanie listened, she hadn't told anyone about her experience as an egg donor; she hadn't even told Matt about it yet, it never seemed important. But suddenly it did; she had to tell Matt. She needed to share her experience with him, first. Summer's parents shared the story of Sam's egg donation; egg donation wasn't something many people were familiar with. Stephanie was surprised that Samantha was a product of egg donation; she looked so much like her mom. Stephanie's mind reeled; she really hadn't given much thought to the final product of the procedure she endured. But here it was right in front of her. It was hard to

It Takes 3

fathom, that a two-week span of a woman's personal time could result in a child, a beautiful child like Sam. When she finally talked to Matt about her experience, he could see how personal this was. The fact that it all started from the love she had for her brother, she wasn't upset, but she was a little sad. She told him that what made her sad was that going through all of this didn't bring her and her brother any closer, and that hurt. She began her journey because of him and his wife; she thought it would bring them closer. Stephanie didn't have children of her own, but her brother did now, he and his wife Beckie had a beautiful little girl. She thought that after the birth of their daughter, maybe then they would realize what a gift Stephanie offered. But nothing changed. Over the years, whatever caused the distance only got worse. Her brother felt she had done this donation thing for selfish reasons; he had no clue what it took. Stephanie found it even more amazing that the short period of time a woman spent being an egg donor could result in a gift like Samantha. A gift that touched so many lives, Stephanie was one of the lucky few who got to see how being a donor, giving this gift, touched not just the recipient parents and the donor's life, but how it also touched grandparents, aunts, uncles, cousins, and friends lives. Suddenly Stephanie realized just how huge this was. Stephanie thought about what to say and how to say it, so she told Matt, "There's something you don't know. I was an egg donor."

Matt looked at her. "Really?"

She told him about her brother and sister-in-law, how she wanted to help them. She told him that she couldn't help them, so she decided to help another infertile couple, she told him how she signed up with an agency. "I did a lot of research, and I felt good about it, but I never realized just what a gift it was, until now." When Matt told her about Sam's beginning, it warmed her heart. When Stephanie told Matt she had been a donor, it warmed his heart as well and endeared her to him even more. Stephanie explained her feeling about being a donor. Matt was taken by her words, he could feel the pride she felt, and how proud she was that she was able to help a couple become a family. Matt knew that feeling, he lived it, and he had Samantha because of a women just like her.

Stephanie listened all about his and Summer's experience, the trouble they, had and the gift they received. He told her that even though he lost Summer, as painful as that was, he had Sam. Sam was Summer's greatest desire in life, Summer enjoyed her pregnancy: everything about it—the cravings, the weight gain everything. She never felt fat or sick; she felt beautiful and healthy throughout the entire seven months. Matt told Stephanie everything. She saw the joy he felt from the gift they received as well as the sadness of his loss.

After everything, Stephanie asked him about the clinic. When he told her, she was surprised. It was the same clinic where she had been a donor. They talked about the time frame and realized they were clients of the same clinic at about the same time. Matt told her about choosing their donor and the criteria they wanted. "Summer wanted a young lady that was as much like her as possible, same build, same blue eyes, same hair color, and we found her."

Matt's words rang in her ears; she thought about the doctor on the phone, telling her why her recipient parents choose her. Stephanie thought of the photo next to Sam's bed, the comments people made about Sam looking like her. Even Summer's dad commented how she resembled Summer. She just figured that they were both blond haired, blue eyed, but now she wondered. Her mind flashed to all the little things that were said. Could it be possible? She asked Matt about the actual dates he and Summer were at the clinic. The dates were within the time that she had been a donor. Her head swirled with the possibility. She told Matt what was going through her head. Same clinic, same time frame, the fact that she and Summer looked so much alike, and then there was what the doctor said to her. Could it

It Takes 3

be a coincidence? They had a wedding to plan, so they put their wonders aside, neither of them thought it was possible, but they had to admit that they wondered. They met with both sets of parents regarding the wedding, but now there was something else to talk about.

Matt and Stephanie invited their parents to dinner at a nice restaurant, the reason for the dinner was to go over some important wedding details, but this subject had taken precedence. It seemed too important to keep from them. Stephanie brought up their suspicions first. She told Matt's parents all about her experience as an egg donor and why she decided to do it, just to bring them up to speed.

Then she spoke to both parents. "The reason we're telling you this is because Matt and Summer were going through their medical procedures at the very same clinic. Now we don't know any of this for a fact, but there seems to be quite a few things that have us wondering. We're wondering if it's possible that Matt and Summer were the recipients of my egg donation."

All four parents gasped at the same time. Could this be possible? Matt listened. Stephanie did a great job of explaining all this as simply as possible. It sounded like something an author with an amazingly romantic mind made up. But this was their life she was talking about; they were living it. Matt had lived through the greatest pain, only to receive the most precious gift he had ever received, all made possible by a compassionate, caring women, brave enough to donate a precious part of herself. And now they were wondering if this woman was about to become his wife; they were wondering if this donor was about to be Sam's mom. Was this companionate, caring woman their donor? Did they choose the woman, or was there a higher power involved? Did they find each other? Or was this their destiny? It was almost too much to comprehend, too much to take in all at once. Their parents seemed to be doing just fine, taking in all the information, digesting everything they were being told.

Matt's mom spoke up first. "Is something like this even possible?" She also wondered if this could be why Sam seemed to have such a natural draw to Stephanie from the moment they met; they did seem to share some unknown bond. After listening, they all wondered if Sam and Stephanie were linked by genetics. Was there really some kind of an unexplained connection between genetic parents and children? They all had so many questions. If Stephanie was the egg donor, all Sam really had was some of her genetic makeup, she had Matt's DNA as well, and how much of Summer did she have? After all, Summer carried her for seven months? But truth is, without Stephanie or whoever the egg donor was, there would be no Samantha.

After a long night, they all agreed that they wanted to find out but debated on telling Summer's parents. But by the end of the night, Matt called them and invited them to come over. He and Stephanie needed to talk to them about Sam and the wedding. Matt knew they would be fine. After all, they knew everything so far. It wasn't as if they kept the details of how Sam was conceived from them; they had always known.

When they arrived, it was an evening to remember. They talked about the past, about Matt and Summer's experience with the clinic, then they talked about Stephanie's experience with the clinic, and by the end of the night, they knew everything. They were more convinced than anyone that this was indeed a possibility. Each of them saw Stephanie like they had never seen her before.

Summer's mom cried as she looked into Stephanie's face and said, "Oh my, you really do resemble our Summer. I remember her telling us she wanted a donor that looked just like her, and you do. I bet this is true. It has to be. I can't believe I hadn't seen it before. I remember her telling us about the girl they chose. She was so excited to find someone so much like her. I'm sure you were her angel. When she found out she was pregnant, she called her donor, her angel. Wouldn't that be something if that angel is you? Regardless she would have loved you, you know. By the way, whatever happened with your brother?"

"He and his wife had an adorable little girl, all on their own. Once they stopped worrying about it, they seemed to get pregnant. Matt and Beckie have Cassidy and Olivia now. They're good."

Nothing about this possible connection was fact, just speculation, but then Matt remembered something. "Hey, I just remembered. Summer wrote a thank-you note and bought a figurine for our donor. We left it at the clinic the day we dropped off my specimen for insemination. It was in a pretty floral gift bag. We left it at the desk."

Stephanie looked at him with a look that took everyone's breath away. Quietly, she asked, "Was the figurine by any chance an angel kneeling with a little chick in her hands? A willow tree figurine?"

Summer's mom began to cry. "Oh my god, yes, yes, it was. I was with her when she picked it out. Oh my God, you were her angel."

Matt looked at her with a look of love. "It has to be. You have to be the one that gave us the greatest gift in the world."

Summer's mom spoke, "And now God is blessing you for your caring and compassion for others by giving her back to you."

"It fits perfectly," Matt said, "but we need a DNA test to be sure. We can all believe it, and the pieces all seem to fit, but shouldn't we know for sure?"

Summer's mom and dad were concerned. "If Stephanie is Sam's genetic mom, where does that leave us in her life?" It was a question that tugged hard at everyone's heart, not just theirs, they needed to know. "If the DNA comes back as we believe it will, will we still be Sam's grandparents?"

"Oh my," Stephanie said, "of course you will. That will never change—no matter what. Summer carried her, she gave birth to her, she loved her, she is and always will be your granddaughter no matter what the results are."

Matt spoke, "Mom, Dad, we both want you to be in Sam's life forever, and we want Sam to know all about Summer. After all, she was, is, and always will be her mommy, her angel mommy."

The night was very emotional, and it went very late. Everyone was tired, the wedding was getting closer by the minute. They weren't going to get any real answers wondering, so Matt wanted to get the test started as soon as he could; he knew DNA testing was a long process, and he hoped that they would get the results in time for the wedding. Matt and Stephanie included Sam in just about everything regarding the wedding plans and their new lives together, everything except this night; the subject matter was just too grown up and confusing.

71

The evening ended with every one of them curious to know if this could be possible, if Samantha could actually be the genetic child of Matt and Stephanie. Could it be that a gift given by Stephanie, an anonymous egg donor years ago be a gift she herself would receive? Just the thought of the possibility of something like this happening was more than any of them could wrap their heads around. Stephanie and Matt talked about the past, they talked about Samantha, they wondered. Could it be possible that this beautiful little girl, the product of an anonymous donation, a gift Stephanie gave to a stranger, be the same anonymous gift Matt and Summer received, the gift Summer gave her life for?

Matt and Stephanie called the clinic and made an appointment to see if this were possible. Their days were busy, with work, Samantha, and the wedding, but they made time for this. It was important; this was something they needed to know.

The following week, Matt and Stephanie met with the doctor at the clinic, they had questions, and they knew that he could help them. It had been nearly seven years since either Matt or Stephanie had been in the clinic, the chance of anyone remembering them was slim, but they should have their files. They should be able to tell from the file if in fact Stephanie was the donor for Matt and Summer. After seven years, the clinic had changed. It had been redecorated, and it looked beautiful. Stephanie looked around to see if she recognized anyone, but all the girls were young. Her coordinator was about the same age as her mom seven years ago, so she would have been in her sixties by now, probably retired, Stephanie thought.

Matt didn't recognize anyone, but his time at the clinic had been pretty limited. If he were to recognize anyone, it would probably be the doctor. Matt and Stephanie signed in and waited. They were going to the doctor's office, not to a room. This was a consultation only. When they were called back, even the back office girl was younger. They hoped that the doctor would be the same, but he wasn't. This doctor was much younger too. Stephanie and Matt explained why they were there and asked if something like this was possible.

The doctor looked perplexed. "Well, possible? Yes, it would be possible, but highly unlikely. We have so many donors that the chance of a donor and recipient even meeting is nearly impossible. I say nearly, because nothing is impossible, and since both of you live in the area, there is a slight chance. But when did this take place?"

Matt gave him the dates he and Summer were clients and the date of their embryo transfer. Stephanie gave him the dates that she went through her procedure and the date of her egg retrieval. The doctor was shocked, the dated of the retrieval and the insemination made it a very big possibility, but again the doctor said it was still highly unlikely. The doctor took all the information and asked that they give him a couple of days to see if they still had the files. He explained that about five years ago there had been a terrible fire in the office next to theirs, and they lost a lot of the old files. Since then they keep old client records off site. Any client they hadn't seen in over twelve months went to their off-site storage. He told them that the entire office had to be redone, it had been a long time, but if the files were there, it would be easy to know if in fact Stephanie was Matt's donor.

It Takes 3

If they were not able to retrieve the files, then the only option would be to perform DNA testing. The doctor explained that DNA testing would take weeks; if the files were not available, he was happy to perform the test for them. Matt and Stephanie explained to the doctor that they were getting married in a few weeks and would love to have the answer before then.

"I'll get on it. We'll do our best," the doctor assured them.

Matt and Stephanie left the office with high hopes that they would find the records and have an answer by the following week.

The days passed slowly as Matt and Stephanie waited for the clinic to call; all the waiting brought back memories of the last time they were clients at the clinic. After a week, Matt called the office, and the receptionist took his number and told him the doctor would have to return his call when he returned from vacation. Another week went by.

It had been over two weeks since Matt and Stephanie were in the office when the phone rang. Matt grabbed the phone and saw the clinic's number; their hearts stopped. Stephanie took Samantha upstairs to get ready for bed, she wanted to hear what was happening, but they didn't want Samantha to hear. Sam was old enough to ask questions, and they weren't ready to explain all of this to her, not yet. Stephanie could hear Matt on the phone, but she couldn't make out what was happening. He wasn't on the phone for very long before she heard him say, "Well, thank you for trying. Yes, that would be fine." And he hung up.

When Matt went to Stephanie, she could tell things didn't go well, but with Samantha up, it wasn't time to talk about it, so they put on their happy faces and spent the evening with her. It was a Friday night, Stephanie made some popcorn, they watched a silly movie, and Sam fell asleep on the sofa between them. Matt carried Sam to her room, she was fast asleep, and Matt was anxious to get to Stephanie. Stephanie knew the news wasn't good, so when Matt sat down, she leaned over and gave him a big hug.

"Well, he said, it seems that the our records were some of the ones destroyed in that fire; there's nothing left—nothing. It's as if we were never there. But he said we can come in tomorrow for the DNA test."

But time was not their friend, the DNA test was not a matter of life or death, and no matter what, they were going to be Samantha's parents. They were curious, but it wasn't something they needed to cancel appointments for or take Sam out of school for. The wedding was in two weeks, it didn't matter to Matt, but Stephanie wanted to know. When Stephanie decided to be a donor, nothing like this was ever brought up or even considered, what were the odds? But here she was today, wondering if this child could be hers. Stephanie struggled with the two feelings. The one being that Sam's genetic relationship wouldn't and shouldn't matter. The second feeling she struggled with was why then did it seem so important to know? If she had never met Sam, would she be thinking of her, wondering about her? Or would her life just move on, not even considering it? What if she knew there was a child? Would she feel a connection or a need to know about it? No matter what, she needed to know, so they made an appointment.

On the day of their appointment all three of them went to the lab with all the necessary paperwork, and all three of them had their cheeks swabbed. Matt and Stephanie told Samantha that it was something they needed to do for the wedding, and that wasn't a complete lie, but it wasn't really the truth either. So once it was done, it was just a matter of time. The wedding was a week and two days away.

Early the following Monday they received a call from the lab. It was too soon for the results, Matt answered the phone, and a very nice guy explained, "It seems Stephanie's sample was misplaced or lost, I'm so sorry. We have Samantha's and yours, Matt, but without Stephanie's, we can't provide you with the results you are looking for. I'm sorry for the inconvenience, but we need Stephanie to come back into the office for a new swab."

Matt told Stephanie what had happened.

"Are you kidding me?" Stephanie was angry. "The wedding is in six days, I have my last fitting is today, I can't change it. Tomorrow we have the final menu changes, Wednesday I have my hair and makeup trial, I can't do this now." Stephanie was crying.

"Honey, we don't have to do this now. We can do it after the wedding."

"No, I need to know. Don't you need to know?"

"No, I don't really care. We know what we know, and does it really matter? Would you feel any differently about her?"

"No, it won't change how I feel, but I need to know, I can't explain it, but I do."

"Well then, what about Thursday? If we wait till Thursday, they said it was best for all of us to provide a fresh sample. What do you think?"

Stephanie checked her schedule. "Yes, Thursday works, but not until after three." "Good, that works, we can go after work, and after school, they're open till six. Maybe, we can pay to have the results expedited."

On Thursday, they all went to the lab to have their swabs redone. The lab was expediting the test for them. Hopefully they would be able to get preliminary results before the wedding. The lab was very straightforward and made no promises, but they said, "We'll do our best, but it's going to be close."

72

It was the night before the wedding and no call from the lab in spite of the expedited request.

The entire family had a nice dinner together. Stephanie and Sam were spending the night with Stephanie's parents. Stephanie asked Matt sometime ago if Sam could stay with her, she wanted to be sure he approved before asking Sam. Stephanie thought that maybe Matt would want her to be with him, but he thought a girls' night was a wonderful idea. When Stephanie asked Sam, she was superexcited, making all kinds of plans for the night. It was all she talked about for days. "I'm going to spend a night with my new mommy at my new grandparents' house."

This was going to be a great memory for all of them, a happy memory. Stephanie took Friday off, so the girls could spend the whole day together with Amber and Jennifer, they had manicures and pedicures, and the girls were feeling all grown up. The lady doing their pedicure began to work on the girls, and they both giggled and squirmed so much that Stephanie and Amber felt sorry for them. The ladies working on their kids were so patient Stephanie knew they had to tip them well, the moms were having fun watching the girls.

Stephanie's mom had set everything up for an all-girls evening, before meeting at the restaurant. They all had a nice dinner before

It Takes 3

calling it a night and settling in. Matt's parents went to Matt's house with him. Matt had invited Summer's parents as well; He wanted Summer's parents to be involved as much as they felt comfortable, after all they were his parents too. They were pleased to be invited. Having Summer's parents and his parents with him gave the five of them time to reminisce, it was a happy time in all of their lives, but it was sad too. Moving forward, they would all be family; this was a time to just be together, to look forward to the future, a future full of love and happiness. After so many years of pain and sadness, they finally found happiness. During dinner, as Matt's Dad said the blessing, they each thanked the Lord for this happy event, this was a day that none of them expected or thought would happen, and they were all very grateful for it. The evening ended early for Matt, not because he was tired, but because he wanted to read and relax before he went to sleep. He wanted to give the parents some time alone, he knew this was hard for them, especially for Summer's mom and dad.

Matt had'nt thought about the DNA test. It could wait until after the wedding.

The house was quiet, and everyone had gone to bed. Matt was still awake. It was only around 11:00 pm, so he called Stephanie. The girls had just finished their second movie, and they were getting ready for bed. Matt had a chance to talk to Sam before Stephanie tucked her in for the night. Samantha told her daddy all about their day, she was sleeping in the big bed with Stephanie, and that they were getting picked up in a big limousine in the morning. Matt laughed at her, told her that he loved her, and would see her in the morning.

Stephanie took the phone and tucked Sam in, kissed her, and talked to Matt. Stephanie wanted to ask if he had heard anything, but she knew he would have told her if he had. Matt didn't, and she didn't ask. He was right. It really didn't matter. Tomorrow she would be Sam's mom regardless, but she was curious. They talked for a little while, and then it was off to bed. Stephanie looked at her dress hanging in the entryway, it hung perfectly from the chandelier, her dad had to use a ladder to hang it there, it was a beautiful dress, and she couldn't wait for Matt to see her in it.

Stephanie crawled in bed next to Samantha, looking at her beautiful angelic face and promising to be the best mom she could. Stephanie said a little prayer, "Lord, thank you for giving me this gift. Summer, thank you for taking care of Sam for those months. I know you can see just how amazing this little one is, thank you." As Stephanie drifted off to sleep, she thought about Samantha being in the world because of three very special people. It made her cry, she cried for Samantha and Matt's loss, she cried for the joy she felt, the promising future they had, she cried at the possibility of Sam being her biological daughter, she cried for the family they were going to be and for the their future.

Stephanie fell asleep, exhausted. Matt was at home unable to sleep, he tossed and turned, and then decided to get up and check everything. The next morning was his wedding day; he was worried he might forget something. Matt was wearing a tux, he never cared for tuxes, but Stephanie insisted. She wanted a traditional wedding, and a suit just wouldn't be the same. Matt agreed, he had a pair of cuff links that Summer gave him on their wedding day, and he wanted to wear them. Stephanie agreed they were important to him and she wanted him to wear them; she was comfortable with his memories as well as his love of Summer. Stephanie knew that Summer would always be a part of their lives. She accepted that a long time ago. He checked to make sure that everything was ready for the morning, including something special for Sam. Satisfied that everything was ready, it was time to get some sleep, but he just tossed and turned. Matt lay in bed, watched some television, tried to read, but he was wide awake. Matt decided that maybe a snack would help, so he quietly walked downstairs. Once downstairs, he checked the front door to be sure everything was locked up. Going to the kitchen, he passed the entryway table. Something on it caught

It Takes 3

his eye. It was a note written by his father. Why had his father left a note? He saw his dad before they went to bed. Did he get up and write this? Matt picked it up. The name of the DNA lab was written with a phone number. Under it was just one word, *results*. Matt felt his stomach do a flip. Results? There was no way they could have the results already .It was to soon, or was it? Matt dialed the number. There was no answer, just a recording he listened. They had Saturday hours. They opened at 7:00 a.m. It was already 2:00 a.m., so in five hours, someone would be there to talk to. Matt's mind reeled; all he could do was wonder what this was about. He got a snack, a couple of Mom's cookies and some milk, and headed back to his room. He turned on the television again. Somewhere between 3:00 and 4:00 a.m., Matt fell asleep. His alarm was set for 6:30 a.m. so he could get up before anyone else, shower, and make that call.

The alarm was prompt as usual. Matt was afraid he would be tired, but he was wide awake as he jumped in the shower and smiled at the day that was in front of him. The warmth of the water felt good on his body. He shaved, brushed his teeth, and put on Stephanie's favorite cologne. He dressed in comfortable jeans and a T-shirt. Matt was dressing at the church so he wouldn't wrinkle his tux.

At exactly 7:00 a.m., Matt picked up the phone in his room. With shaky hands, he pushed the numbers on the paper. Someone on the other end picked up.

"Thank you for calling Dynamic DNA. How may I help you?"

Matt's heart skipped a beat. His first thought was Stephanie; he wished she were standing with him as he explained who he was. Matt was put on hold. Then one of the lab technicians came on the line. "I know that you and your fiancée are getting married today and were hoping to receive your results." Matt held his breath as the technician asked about the wedding while he pulled up the results.

13

Matt was thinking about everything that had led up to this day, about how the three of them fit together, and he wondered if they really needed these results. They wanted to have the answer, but did they really need to know? Did Stephanie really need to know? If it didn't really matter who Sam belonged to genetically, then what was the big deal? But if Sam was genetically Stephanie's, what a gift it would be for her. As Matt listened to the technician read the results one at a time, he made notes. He took his time and asked for clarification when needed. Afterward, Matt read back what he had been told, the tech confirmed, Matt wrote everything down so he could share it with Stephanie, but when? When should he give her the results? Later today? Before the wedding? Or maybe on their honeymoon? When?

Matt couldn't sit still. Everyone was asleep. At about 8:00 a.m., the phone rang. Matt picked it up on the first ring, he thought it was the lab calling back, but it was Samantha. "Good morning, Daddy."

"Good morning, sweetheart. Are you ready to get married?"

"Yes, I am, I'm gonna be good."

She went on and on, she was adorable, Matt didn't want to cut her short, but he still had things to do. He needed to get her off

It Takes 3

the phone and do what he needed to do, but Stephanie wanted to talk to him. "Good morning, husband-to-be."

"Good morning, beautiful. It'll be husband in a few hours." Although Matt needed to get off the phone, he was glad that they had a moment to talk. Stephanie told him her hair was still in rollers, and the hairstylist was there, so she had to go.

As he hung up the phone, everyone was up, and he announced that he was going out for doughnuts. He woke up with a terrible sweet tooth and wanted doughnuts. Matt knew that CVS opened at 7:00 a.m., and he needed to get a card for his bride. He meant to get it days ago, but Stephanie had been with him every time he thought of it. He didn't want her to see him buying it.

When he returned, he had everything. He went to his room, signed the card, and placed it all in the envelope, sealed it, and took a deep breath. He was ready. Matt came downstairs and commented about the smell and how hungry he was; he knew the nerves would be a good excuse not to eat too much. Matt humored his mom and saw how happy it made her. He also noticed that the waterworks had already started, but instead of being annoyed or thinking she was silly, her tears made him tear up too. Another memory for their memory bank.

After all, how often does your mom make your favorite breakfast when you're thirty something on your wedding day? Matt hugged his mom, excused himself, and went upstairs to finish packing up his things before heading to the church. Stephanie was feeling more and more like Sam's mommy. Sam kept calling her mommy all night. At first, she was being silly, doing it on purpose, but by the end of the night, it seemed normal and comfortable.

Sam loved Stephanie, and Stephanie loved Sam, they really were amazing together, they enjoyed spending time together.

Amber, Jeff, and Jennifer were in the sanctuary when Matt arrived. This gave Matt a chance to talk to Amber about his plan. He told her what he wanted to do and gave her the card with very explicit instruction. "Give her this card just before you walk down the isle, tell her not to open it until Sam is almost to me, OK?" Amber smiled at him, "OK, yea, I can do that" Matt hugged her "seriously, it's imperative that she open it then and not a minute sooner." he explained that he wanted what was in that card to be the very last thing she read before becoming his wife. Amber assured him that she would do exactly as he asked. He had done everything he wanted and needed to do. He was completely and totally ready. The only thing left for him to do now was to get dressed and wait, wait for his new life to begin. As the minutes ticked by, he became more and more anxious. Matt was ready to get the show on the road. He watched as guests began to arrive, Matt and the groomsmen were reminiscing in a private area until it was time for the guys to take their place at the front of the church, and for Matt and his folks to take their place. All of the planning had brought them to this moment. It was time to make this dream a reality. The ushers closed the doors so the girls could line up in the vestibule without the guests or Matt seeing them. Stephanie watched as Sam practiced, pretending to place the rose petals on the ground; she was adorable in her little gown.

As the music began Matt entered the church with his parents through a side door in the back. When they reached the altar, Matt hugged each of them as his mom whispered something in his ear, something that brought a tear to his eye as she turned to take her seat front and center.

Matt and Stephanie had her parents sit on the groom's side, and his on the bride's side, for two reasons: one was to signify the joining of the two families, and the other was because at every wedding, they noticed that the parents never got to see their kids' faces, especially during the vows, the most important moment in their children's lives. That never made sense to them; this was their chance to do something about that. They sat their parents where they would get the best view of their own child's face as they commit their lives to one another. It made sense to them.

It Takes 3

At exactly 10:00 a.m., the wedding music signified the beginning of the ceremony. After a few bars, the doors opened and the bridesmaids began to walk slowly down the aisle to a traditional wedding march. Everything about this wedding was traditional, from the music to the vows and every person in attendance were people who were important in their lives, friends who had agreed to be witnesses to this beautiful promise of a forever love, a love between two people, a love between Matt and Stephanie. Matt never considered this could have been possible seven years ago. Stephanie had all but given up on her dream of a happily ever after, but here she was. Tears had been flowing all morning, everyone was there, and everything was in place. Even through the tears, everyone was smiling. This day was a labor of love, and it was turning out to be perfect.

As Amber took her place, she kissed Stephanie on the cheek and said, "I'm so glad you and Matt found each other. I love you, sweetie." Amber and Stephanie had become best friends; they were so much alike, and they loved spending time together, with the guys and the girls too. Stephanie had chosen Amber to be her maid of honor, and she was perfect. As she prepared to walk down the aisle, she handed Stephanie the envelope. She explained per Matt's instructions, she was not to open it until Samantha reached the middle of the aisle and not a moment sooner. Amber made Stephanie promise just as Matt made her promise to do exactly as he asked. Stephanie took the envelope; Matt had written, To my WIFE in bold letters; it made her smile.

Amber stepped to the middle of the doors, stood there for a count of ten, then began to walk. As she took her first steps, memories began to flow, she missed her friend Summer, but at this moment, she thanked God for Stephanie; she thanked him for bringing such a wonderful woman into Matt's and Sam's life, into her life. Stephanie was perfect. Amber's mind relived so many memories. The day Summer and Matt moved next door, the BBQs they had together, the day they told her they were expecting—all of it flowed as did the tears. She relived the day that Matt and Stephanie told her they were dating. As she reached the front of the church, she gave Matt a look, a wink, and a nod of her head signifying that she had done exactly what he asked her to do. Stephanie was curious. What was in that card? What was Matt up to? After Amber entered the church, the vestibule doors closed quietly behind her. When Amber was settled into her place of honor, the music changed.

As the doors opened again, everyone saw her, standing there in the middle of the massive doors—a tiny figure dressed in a beautiful white dress and huge smile on her face. The smile grew bigger and bigger as the doors opened wider and wider. When Matt saw her, he stood a bit taller, felt a pride well up inside; this little beauty belonged to him. She had a smile so bright and so big that it made everyone in the church smile, especially him. Matt had never seen his little girl look happier, and it filled him with love. She looked like a miniature bride, smiling right at her daddy. As Samantha began to take her first step down the aisle, she hesitated, and she looked to her right. Stephanie's hands were making a forward, moving motion to her. Suddenly Sam looked scared as she looked around the church and saw all the people.

A slight voice could be heard lovingly coaxing her, you could hear her, "Go ahead, honey. See Daddy?"

Sam shook her head yes.

"Just walk to Daddy. It'll be all right. I'll be right behind you."

Samantha took one foot off the ground and moved it forward. It was a step she took with great care. Sam's smile turned to a look of concern, but as she began to walk, looking at her daddy, her smile came back. Sam had been practicing consistently since rehearsal; she was so cute and so confident. Where was that little girl? Matt smiled at her, and she smiled back, looking more and more comfortable. He thought that at any minute, she may break into her princess wave or maybe dance. The thought of it made him laugh out loud. Jeff heard Matt's slight laugh, and he smiled

It Takes 3

as if he knew exactly what Matt was thinking. As Samantha walked slowly toward the front of the church, she carefully laid red rose petals down the center of the white runner. She took her time and laid each and every petal with great care. Samantha was meticulous, she was the flower girl, and it was an important job. She did it perfectly. Sam took her time and walked directly to her daddy, just as she rehearsed. When Sam reached Matt, he leaned down, picked her up, and gently hugged and kissed her. This small gesture touched everyone's hearts. As he placed Sam back on the ground, something caught his left eye, something very bright and very white. The sun was shinning through the lovely stained glass windows, and he thought he was seeing a vision. It was just a second, but it was a bright-white light that caught his eye. He took a deep breath before actually focusing on the brightness itself. The light was so bright, and it took him a moment to refocus, but when he did, he looked up, and standing between those massive vestibule doors stood a vision, his vision, a beauty among beauties.

It was the most beautiful vision Matt had ever seen. Standing with her dad, tears streaming down her face. Stephanie was holding her dad's arm tightly with a bright smile on her face amid the tears. She was dabbing her tears with her grandmother's handkerchief. Her father also had tears in his eyes; they were the perfect vision of a father and daughter on her wedding day. The two of them looked like a picture, like two actors in a movie, well rehearsed and waiting for their cue. In Stephanie's left hand, she held a beautiful bouquet. Her right arm was wrapped around her father's left arm. In her right hand, Matt saw the envelope that held the card he had left for her. Stephanie held the card up, ever so slightly, just enough for Matt to see. He could tell by her face that she had read it. Samantha stood with Matt as Stephanie took her first step toward them, toward their life together.

Matt squeezed Sam's hand. Tears flowed freely down his cheek. Stephanie stepped into the church, thinking about her new life, a new life as a wife, Mom, and a family.

At the altar, Matt and Stephanie turned toward each other, card still in hand. They each took one of Samantha's hands in theirs. This wasn't rehearsed, it just happened, it was meant to be; all three of them center stage at the altar, committing theirselves to each other.

As the minister began the ceremony, Amber took Samantha and placed her to the side, this was their moment; the part of the ceremony when they pledged their love and lives to each other. This moment, these vows needed to be between just them; this was their commitment to each other. As they recited their vows, committing their lives to each other, rays of sunshine fell on them like a warm hug. After Matt and Stephanie exchanged vows and rings, the two of them placed a beautiful necklace around Sam's neck. Sam laughed as she asked Stephanie to kneel down, she and Matt placed a similar necklace on Stephanie. The necklaces were something that Matt had designed it looked like a heart, but it was a sideway "3" designating the three of them and the fact that sometimes life takes three to make dreams come true. As the minister announced them Husband and Wife and family of 3 (for now). Family and Friends laughed, cheered and clapped as Stephanie held the card "to her heart." The message Matt wrote in the card card simply read, "Congratulations, Mommy! I love you!"

Questions

Discussion Questions

- Is this book believable?

- Was there a particular scene that stood out for you?

- Was the story well developed or were there loopholes that made the book lose its interest?

- Did the author present the story in a realistic way?

- Were the characters lives and struggles addressed in a believable way? Site examples

- If you could meet any of the characters in the book and ask them one question, who would it be and what would you ask? Explain why.

- Would this novel make a good movie? Why or why not, who should be cast as the main characters?

- What is the significance of the title? Why do you thin the author chose this title? Would you have given it a different title? Explain.

- What surprised you most about the book?

- Were there any moments that you disagreed with the choices of any of the characters? What would you have done differently?

- Did you think the ending was appropriate? How would you have liked to see the ending?

- Have your views about the subject matter changed after reading this book? How?

- Would you consider being or using an egg donor?

- Are there any other books that would compare to this book? If so how does this book hold up?

- What did you learn, take away or get from this book?

- Would you recommend this book to a friend?